MW00528737

"Fasten your seatbelt! Parker Hu[...] in rapid action sequences that f[...] [...]ould [...]e[...] [...]ings really happen? Are they happening now? And he weaves into the stories the power of faith in the midst of the chaos. I could not put it down."

Shan Gastineau

"Once again Parker Hudson has hit the mark. Powerful characters with a hint of sensitivity and you feel like you are there. It's as if he sees into the future. I recommend this read to everyone! I look forward to the movie."

Wilma Hall

"Parker Hudson has crafted a thriller that delves into the dark side of our high tech culture with its temptations of money and power, while at the same time espousing courage and integrity. The result: a page turner you will not be able to put down!"

Susan and John Yates

"*Enemy in the Room* is full of realistic characters responding to life with choices that are sometimes regrettable, occasionally laudable, but always engaging. Faith is woven into their lives in a way that is genuine and believable – a far cry from the religious caricatures that are so often found in modern entertainment. What an enjoyable and inspiring read!"

Becky Hoover

"Parker Hudson's *Enemy In The Room* is a great read at a great pace."

Bryant Wright

"A page turner with substance and passion. A thriller with a message which is proving to be prophetic for our time. *Enemy In The Room* describes an enemy impacting our country, our homes, our children, and our very lives. Parker writes with wisdom, concern, and hope. His characters are flesh and blood, and his many subplots coalesce into an exciting ending and a great read."

Caroline and John Dean

"*Enemy In The Room* is truly entertaining and insightful. I was eagerly turning pages. And not just entertained—I actually found myself having a better understanding of the world around me. Parker Hudson is a great author and teacher. He puts on paper things that I have been deeply troubled by but have not had the words to express.

"I think Hudson has given Joel Rosenberg a run for his money with this one."

"I could relate to every element of the story. I loved the conversations. Hudson had to have had help with the female relationships. The interactions are so believable and actually "spot on" to conversations I have had with women when developing personal friendships with them. I don't ever remember reading a male author who had the ability to keep female relationships authentic.

"The book gets five stars. The ending is exciting. I recommend the book to everyone, young men and women, and to anyone struggling (which is everyone). I think this book could break the ice and open up conversations between moms and daughters, friends and neighbors, fathers and sons. Let's just say that I loved the book."

Kathy Paparelli

"Parker Hudson is one of my favorite American novelists, and *Enemy in the Room* is his best so far. As an Iranian-American who has lived in the US for the past 35 years, I was drawn to this novel. Not only because its plot involves Iranian-Americans, but because it is written as a warning. It shows what could happen to the West because of a small percentage of Muslims who have decided to follow the violent side of Islam and promote terrorism. My hope is that *Enemy In The Room* will further open the eyes of Americans who continue to believe in politically correct 'tolerance', and refuse to face the reality of the greatest threat of our time."

Iraj Ghanouni

"Having read Parker's previous books this one did not disappoint. What a story!

"Or is it? As you read *Enemy In The Room*, you will have to remind yourself that this is a work of fiction. The storyline takes current day events and situations and weaves a path towards what could be, so you find yourself praying for yourself, your family, and our nation.

"The plots and characters leave you in suspense. In addition, the ills of humanity that manifest themselves through our behavior are captured all too well. But you are not left there. The book's story of redemption, captured through love and grace, leads the reader to a place of redemption and peace. You must read!"

Carla and Roy Smith

"*Enemy In The Room* is a masterpiece of intrigue, suspense, the grit of life, redemption and forgiveness. It delves into who we are and where we live. Family, business, career, money, entertainment and the forces governing them all. The story is so real you'll feel like you are living it.

"This is fiction at its best. Well written, researched and carrying an eternal lesson. You get to know the characters so well you'll want to invite them to the house for dinner or hope you never see them again. The dialogue just flows and the story flies. Entertaining and enthralling."

Charles Paparelli

ENEMY
IN THE
ROOM

PARKER HUDSON

ENEMY IN THE ROOM

Copyright 2013 Parker Hudson

Published in Atlanta, Georgia by Edge Press, LLC

Edited by Danelle McCafferty

Cover design by Marshall Hudson

Printed in the United States of America

International Standard Book Number 13: 978-0-9666614-3-9

International Standard Book Number 10: 0-9666614-3-5

Library of Congress Control Number: 2013948904

All rights reserved.

For information:

www.parkerhudson.com

Dedicated to the memory of Dietrich Bonhoeffer and the many Germans of goodwill who, though they did not agree on every issue, recognized their true enemy and did all that they could to try to stop the horrific catastrophe that followed.

1

Because it was chilly that morning, no one noticed Ahmad's oversized sweater as he paused to let a family enter the church in front of him. Greeters smiled and shook the college student's hand, just as they had the previous three weeks, only this time they added, "Happy Easter." He smiled and nodded. "Yes, Happy Easter."

They filed into the huge building, a mega-church it was called. *It is large,* Ahmad thought, *about the same as our Mursi Abul Abbas mosque in Alexandria.* He walked quietly down the center aisle toward the large stage with the crucifix hanging above it. From all sides rose the cacophony of chatting women and bleating children. *How can this be a house of worship?*

He took a seat near the front and began flipping through the service program. A family with three children moved in next to him, all dressed in their Easter finest. The oldest child, a blonde girl of not more than eight, sat next to him in a white dress. She looked up at him and smiled. He nodded and smiled back, then returned to the program, although he wasn't reading.

My cousin Karim was the third martyr to hit a Jerusalem bus. It was all my father talked about for weeks. What will he say about me, today, in America? In this place?

He smiled as the congregation stood and began singing about Jesus Christ being risen today. *What blasphemy! Allah has no son.* For the third time that morning, he put his hand in his pocket and ran his finger along the smooth metal of the trigger which was connected to the explosives, nails and metal filings wrapped around his upper body.

Thirty minutes later, as the sermon wound down about God's love and sacrifice—*as if Allah the All Powerful would imagine to sacrifice himself for people!*—his heart started beating faster. One more hymn, some prayers, and he knew the communion would begin.

As the ushers moved up the aisles to indicate each row's time to go up front, he said a prayer to the only real Allah, and stood up. He walked to the center of the serving area, where he would be in the middle of the greatest number of people. The little girl wound up on his right. As he fished in his pocket for the trigger, she smiled up at him again.

The priests—a man and a woman—were coming around with the bread and wine. *Allah, you cannot be blasphemed as a wafer! The imams are right—these people are beyond saving.*

The priest held out a wafer to him. Instead of taking it, he turned around and shouted, "There is no god but Allah. Muhammad is the messenger of Allah!" Then he screamed and pulled the trigger.

From two blocks away a short message was sent via a handheld. Within five minutes Trevor Knox had read it.

That evening David Sawyer was sitting alone at the large mahogany desk in his study, once a spare bedroom on the first floor of their home. A Persian rug accented the hardwood floor, and an antique grandfather clock stood by the door. He looked up from his papers. Almost ten. *All those people killed and maimed in that church today. How could anyone do that?*

His wife Elizabeth took two steps into the room with a book in her hand. "David, won't it keep until tomorrow? They've just confirmed the bomber wasn't Iranian. He was Egyptian. His father was beaming on USNet, saying how proud he is. Let's watch the news in bed. You've done enough tonight."

He caught her reflection in the oval mirror between the curtained windows and nodded to her. "Mom called, worried that it might be an Iranian student this time, particularly during the Persian New Year. If my father were alive today, he'd reenlist. So much has changed since they came here. Not sure I want to go to the Hafezis' tomorrow night to celebrate the Persian New Year after all those people were killed."

She walked around the desk, stood her book on its edge, and gently shook her still mostly blond hair. "You know we have to. It's March. They were your parents' closest friends in Tehran, and they'll be offended if we don't go."

He sighed and looked around his desk, then back at Elizabeth. "So even more reason why I have to finish this stuff tonight. We've got a big meeting with Trevor on Tuesday. Lots riding on it. Kristen's been in New York all week. I have to report on six site acquisitions. Paul needs my input for the real estate part of the budget, and I want to focus Trevor on Capital Tower before someone else buys it. The money we'll save there should earn a nice bonus for the Sawyers this year, which we certainly need. So I see a long night. How about you? Do you have to go in tomorrow?"

"It's tax season. Gotta be in the office to help the walk-ins."

"Good luck to them, and to you!" He smiled. The clock chimed. "Hey, let's call Callie. Isn't it still early in California?"

"I was just thinking the same thing." He picked up the phone and pushed a preset number. Elizabeth came close and put her book on his stack of papers. He held out the handset.

Elizabeth listened to the rings, then frowned. After the beep, she said, "Callie, hey. It's Mom and Dad. How are you? We wanted to say hello. How are your courses going? When will you know if you got the part in that play? Call us tomorrow. Don't forget to call and wish your aunts and uncles a Happy New Year. We love you very much."

She shrugged and returned the handset to the cradle. "She almost never answers."

"Maybe she sees it's us."

Elizabeth nodded. "Maybe. Or maybe it's her new boyfriend. I'm glad you have a lot of family in L.A. to keep an eye on her."

"At the university? But at least they're there if she needs them."

She shook her head. "I can't believe she'll graduate in just over two years."

"Are we getting old?"

Elizabeth came around behind him and began to rub his shoulders. "No way. Not us. We just started early. And Rob will keep us young. He's been playing that virtual game in his room for hours."

"He's fifteen and a boy. He'll be a human being again in about six years, if we're lucky."

She smiled. "Were you like that?"

"No, I was perfect."

While she kneaded, he looked at the pile of papers. *I need to hand off more. But who's ready?*

After five minutes she bent down and kissed a gray spot on the side of his head. "Come to bed when you can."

He swiveled in the chair, stood up and hugged her. "Thanks. As soon as I can."

"I love you, too, even if you are Iranian."

"American," he smiled. "Born and bred here—as American as you. Just with Iranian parents. You inherited all those wonderful folks when you married me."

She put her head on his chest and wrapped her arms around him. "I know. A Southern girl marrying a Persian from California. What were we thinking?"

"I think it's been pretty wonderful."

She paused, her head on his shoulder. "Yes. But I worry about your family over there. Have you heard from Omid?"

"No. It's gotten crazier and crazier. Omid sent a text two weeks ago that he and Goli were OK, but nothing since. I'm waiting to hear whether the phones that we sent through his Turkish friend arrived safely."

"And with no one arrested. What does your cousin say?"

"I'm sure she wishes that her son and new daughter-in-law would stay away from politics, but Omid seems to be intent on trying to help fix what's wrong. Anyway, I can't help us or any of them if I'm unemployed, and that may happen if I don't finish this stuff." He gently pushed her away and motioned to the desk.

She smiled. "Trevor Knox will never fire you. Where else would he get someone to work so hard for so little pay?"

"There are plenty of people who would gladly run real estate for USNet."

"But none would be as tall, handsome or smart as you."

"OK. You better go to bed now before I follow you and really don't finish this stuff."

She smiled. "All right. But just remember it was your choice."

"I know. I know. Not fun. We could always skip the Hafezis' tomorrow."

She picked up her book. "No way. We have to do that. It's the Persian New Year, and you are your mother's son. Good-night. Don't stay up late. I love you."

"Good-night. I love you, too." As she walked down the hall to their bedroom, he sat, looked at the stack, and picked up the top paper.

Early the next afternoon David paused from reading a report and glanced across his desk on the thirty-third floor of Midtown Tower. The afternoon sun played off the impressive assembly of office towers downtown, only a few miles to the south. Beautiful. And most of them built while he'd been in the game—the past twenty-five years or so. It certainly wasn't Manhattan, but pretty respectable for a city that had hardly been on the map when he started.

Those were good people back then. He eyed the overflow of papers and reports that needed his attention. He now led fifteen people in the real estate group at USNet. *Fifteen.* Several years ago—when they were still called Knox Communications—there had been thirty-five, before downsizing and outsourcing.

The team today is sharp, too. Kristen, Todd, Cheryl, Chris. And they're great with technology. But you still have to write.

He reopened a document on his computer and sighed. *I'll have to finish the Capital Tower report for tomorrow.* He bent forward and twisted his wedding band under the desk. *Elizabeth won't be pleased if I have to work after tonight's party.*

Two floors above Sawyer in the penthouse of Midtown Tower, his boss, USNet's CEO, Trevor Knox sat alone at the large desk in his paneled office. After pushing a button with his gold pen and hearing the lock click on the office door, Knox swiveled to a single monitor embedded in the desk's surface. He typed a special code memorized as a nursery rhyme seventy years earlier in his native Egypt.

The founder of one of the world's largest communications, television, movie and technology companies had long since become bored with the view from the top of Midtown Tower, even though there were windows on three sides. At least twice a day, and usually more often, he took time to review his Real Time Intercepts, or "RTI" as it was referred to by the few who knew of its existence.

As he read the afternoon's summary in silence, he typed questions for further study by his two RTI lieutenants concerning intercepts from a cabinet member in Syria and a NATO commander in Germany.

Twenty minutes later he closed the RTI program and, using a code name and encryption that made these communications untraceable, he emailed one of several stock brokers whom they used in Singapore, where the markets were just opening. Knox placed two large buy orders, and one sell order through a chain of dummy companies maintained for that purpose. Simon North, a retired British Air Force general with his own consulting company in London, received an email with only a previously authenticated code for the sender, instructing him to contact a specific person at NovySvet Aerospace in Moscow. Finally Trevor folded up three reminders and placed them in his coat—two for tomorrow's meeting with Paul Burke, head of USNet's U.S. operations, and one for David Sawyer in real estate.

He rose and unlocked a small closet, then took out his prayer rug, spread it on the inlaid parquet floor, and removed his shoes and socks. He turned to the sink in the same closet, washed his hands and feet three times, then his face. After passing a hand over the whole of his head, wetting his still dark hair, he knelt and prayed out loud in Arabic, *La ilaha illa Allah. Muhammad rasul Allah* ("There is no god but Allah. Muhammad is the messenger of Allah."). He recited the first surah of the Qur'an from memory and went through his ritual prayer. Then he gave Allah thanks for the church bombing the day before, which was being covered extensively by all the media, An obscure RTI-funded foundation paid the salary of the campus imam who befriended the student a year ago, and another even more secret source would soon send a large payment to his family. Trevor ended his prayers by giving thanks for the last few hours' intercepts, which would bring more opportunities.

When finished, he returned the rug, straightened his shirt, and put on his shoes and socks. He unlocked the office door and glanced around his desk to be sure that all the devices were set on standby, the drawers locked, and the security light on.

Phyllis Jordan, Knox's personal assistant, entered from the reception area in response to a small light on her desk. They had been together for many years, starting when Knox had arrived in America at age twenty and was little more than an assistant at the radio station owned by his Egyptian immigrant uncle, whose son Ellis had created a vision for telephones and computers.

Gray haired and dwarfed by her tall boss, Jordan was a totally loyal gatekeeper. "It's time to leave—you've got the Cinema Group meeting tomorrow morning in Los Angeles."

Coming around his desk toward the one wall in his office with no windows, covered instead with awards and pictures of himself with important people from the past four decades, he touched a button beneath the chair rail. A door opened to a paneled hallway leading through an exercise area to his apartment.

"Yes. My workout clothes are in the hamper. Tell them to power up the helicopter. I'll get my coat and head to the roof. Do you have the university awards packed?"

"In your briefcase."

"Good. I'll call early from L.A. We'll do the Operations and Real Estate updates by video conference, right after lunch here. Let Paul and David know in the morning."

"Yes, sir. Have a safe trip." She smiled and turned.

"Thanks. We'll talk tomorrow."

Omid, the son of David's cousin in Iran, and his wife, Golnaz, or Goli as he and the family called her, owned a small translation business in Tehran. Omid had learned English at home and studied engineering at university, while Goli had a gift for languages in general; they enjoyed a steady business. With a loan from his family, Omid had opened an office two years earlier on Mirdamad Avenue in Tehran, above a woman's boutique and a jewelry store. At the moment they employed three other translators, who, like them, were only a few years out of school. Married just a year, they were contemplating whether to start a family in the turbulence that surrounded them in Iran.

After closing their office early because of New Year's celebrations planned later with their family, Omid and Goli walked three blocks to the Shalizar Coffee House; she wore the traditional veil outdoors, both because of her nominal faith and to avoid any hassles from the Basij, who patrolled the streets in unmarked cars. There had been such hope only a few years earlier, when the regime that had rigged the elections was replaced by the ruling mullahs. But quickly that hope turned bitter, as the new regime adopted all the policies and tactics of the previous ones. It was as if the actors were wearing different masks, but it was still the same tragedy.

Inside, the coffee house was packed and noisy. As their eyes adjusted they caught sight of Morad and two other friends, saving seats for them in the far back corner. They smiled and waved.

The men shook hands while Golnaz watched, and then they settled in and ordered. Omid had known Morad all his life. He had a good job with an oil company, but like so many others, wanted his country to change and to open up. Still single, Morad had become the unofficial leader of their group, which had stayed in touch since graduation. The other two men had been their university classmates, seemingly also dedicated to changing the course of their country. Ramin and Kamy had been close friends of the others for six years, and although one never knew who might be working for the Savama, or secret police, the five friends spoke and planned freely together.

Before the coffee arrived, they caught up on their families and the celebration of New Years. A few minutes later, Morad, stirring more sugar into his cup, lowered his voice and leaned forward. "The demonstration will be at Vali Asr Square at four next Friday afternoon, in ten days. This will be the first in almost a year, and we hope that a good crowd will assemble before the Basij arrive."

"When will the first tweets start?" Goli asked.

"At three," Ramin replied.

Shaking his head, Omid said, "The Basij will be ruthless."

They fell silent. Finally Morad said, "It will be what it will be. We have to put pressure on the regime again if there is ever going to be change. Now that the mullahs have the bomb, they are unafraid. With the world watching, we must not be silent."

Omid nodded and squeezed Goli's hand under the table. He then brought his other hand to his face and rubbed his mustache to cover his mouth, in case anyone was trying to read lips. "As promised, we have New Years presents for each of you."

Goli opened her bag and passed three small boxes to Morad under the table.

Omid continued. "Clean phones from the outside, along with a list of our numbers. The Savama cannot have tagged them or know who owns them. Please continue to use your other phones for regular calls—and to show to Savama if necessary—and use these only to call within our group. Also to text and take videos on Friday."

Ramin smiled. "How did you get these?"

"Let's just say that Allah has provided. We have five more."

They paused, then put the new phones in their pockets. The second university friend, Kamy, looked around and spoke softly across the table to Omid, as he reached for something in his bag on the floor. "Omid, I have a full list of all the students who have been arrested over the past three years, and what happened to them." He leaned toward the center, offering the package under the table.

"What? How did you get it?" Omid asked, taking the large envelope and bringing it to his lap.

"A friend of a friend. Can you get it posted?"

Omid's closest friends knew that either he hosted an antigovernment website overseas, or he knew the people who did. Either way, if you gave information to Omid, it usually wound up on the internet in a few days.

"I—I'm not sure," Omid said, darting his eyes around to see who might be listening or who might have observed the exchange. He had to consider the risk of leaving the coffee house with this potentially explosive information.

"The list is real. And official."

"That's what I'm worried about," Omid said, smiling and looking at Goli, whose countenance had not changed.

"It's important that it gets out. Families want to know what has happened. And so do relatives in the West."

"I know. I know. Here, keep it tonight, and give it to Morad in the next day or two in private. Morad, please read it over, and if you think it's genuine, bring it to the office along with one of your oil company's contracts to translate. Then we'll deal with it. OK?"

The other young men nodded. "OK."

An hour later, as they left for the trip home to their flat in the Elahiyeh part of northern Tehran, Goli said to Omid, "Thank you for being careful."

Putting his arm around her, Omid said, "If Morad vouches for it, then it needs to be published. But I want to live to see our children's children!"

She smiled back at him. "As do I," she said softly.

At that same moment in a working class London neighborhood, Jamal, a young man who had emigrated with his family from Iran when he was a child, entered a small warehouse not far from his local mosque. He was greeted by his imam and several close friends, who shook his hand and hugged him.

After donning a robe made especially for the occasion, he sat on a stool in front of a blue blanket. Lights came on, and the imam started the video camera.

Over the next few minutes Jamal only had to glance at his notes twice, as he explained why he hated the West and was proud to be Allah's next suicide bomber.

2

As David rode up the elevator that Tuesday morning, checking his handheld, he felt the dull ache and scratchy eyes from too little sleep. *Elizabeth was right; I couldn't turn it off.* He had to finish a few things after the big New Year's celebration with the older Persian couple's family, and he hadn't fallen asleep until two. The festivities had begun on a somber note for the misguided student who had bombed the church on Sunday, but soon the families moved on to celebrate the millennia of good things about Iran, rather than the fanaticism of the last decades.

Now it was 7:45. Despite the headache, he felt ready for anything that Trevor Knox or Paul Burke might ask.

The double doors into the real estate group were open and the lights were on, but the receptionist would not be in for thirty minutes. Their offices wrapped around a corner of the floor, with the reception area directly off the elevator lobby. The décor was cream colored walls, dark green carpeting, and light brown trim. Behind the reception area was a spacious conference room with a view of the city.

David walked the silent hallway to his large corner office, noticing a few lights beyond the break room. He dropped his files on a conference table to the left of his door, took his briefcase over to the desk, and plugged in his laptop. The first new message from Phyllis Jordan informed him that the meeting with Knox had been moved from that morning to just after lunch. He took a deep breath. *So I'll get a cup of coffee and ask Julie to rearrange my day. Actually, it's better.*

"Hi." It was Kristen Holloway. She smiled as he looked up from his computer, and he motioned her to come in. A tall, striking woman in a dark blue suit, Kristen's auburn hair was pinned up, giving her a very businesslike appearance.

"How was New York?" he asked.

She walked over to his desk, a mug of coffee in each hand and a folder under one arm. "Your early morning sounds are unmistakable. I brought you a wake-up present." She put one of the mugs on his desk.

Reaching for it, he faked a grimace. "Thanks. Not much sleep last night."

"Sorry. How much longer does the Persian New Year's celebration go on, anyway?"

"Thirteen days in total. We've got five more. But I'm cutting back after last night, "

She raised an eyebrow and smiled. Kristen's soft demeanor, freckles, and the unnerving twinkle in her eyes belied the first impression of a no-nonsense businesswoman, and these qualities were so obviously genuine that they threw even the most hardened negotiators off balance, particularly those of the male gender. David had recognized these disarming traits when she first interviewed two years earlier. She had arrived with a broad residential real estate background; David had helped hone her knowledge on the commercial side, and now she could handle just about any assignment.

He continued, "And no one says it exactly, but the memorial service for the church bombing, all of the coverage on the Middle East, and the President's address coming later this week don't lend themselves to festivities."

Kristen nodded. She thought of the terrible carnage portrayed on the 24/7 news cycle, and paused. Finally she said, "We finished the office lease. The crew should be there today starting the fit-out of our new space."

David smiled. "Good. Did we have to give much?"

"Just the usual sorts of things." She shrugged. "It's nice to be wanted. I've been on the other side, negotiating with a lot less than USNet's credit rating behind me."

He nodded as he took a sip of the coffee. "Glad to hear it went well. Do you know if Todd's in?"

"I saw his car in the parking deck."

He called Todd Phelps's extension.

"Hey," Todd raised a cup of coffee to Kristen a moment later as he walked in, a pad in the other hand. The younger man was about Kristen's height and obviously in good physical shape. Todd's older brother—by about ten years—had been in David's high school class, and the boys and their families had been close. When the older brother was killed in a car crash their senior year, David had done his best to fill in for him with Todd. Many years later, when Todd was finishing business school, he approached David about a job. David enthusiastically encouraged him and over the past year had acted as both employer and mentor.

Todd smiled at David. "You look terrible. What happened?"

"New Year's in March, on a Monday. An old Persian tradition, as you may remember from years ago with my parents. Anyway, I need to talk with both of you," David began, motioning them to chairs around his conference table.

"Kristen, Hong Kong shouldn't take much longer. So I'd like you to work with me on buying Capital Tower. Todd, that will free you up to focus on Minneapolis and Moscow. OK?"

"I'll give Kristen the Capital Tower acquisition file," Todd responded.

"Bill Porter is the broker. You know him, don't you, Kristen?"

"Yes. He also represents lots of tenants downtown. No matter whom he's representing, he always seems to get what's best for Bill."

David nodded and leaned forward in his chair. "I want to buy Capital Tower before anyone realizes what a steal it is—below replacement cost. Assuming we can build a sky bridge, it will work well with the Grand. It's a great opportunity to create a signature USNet headquarters at a very visible location."

The two younger members of the team exchanged glances. "I hadn't thought of that," Todd admitted. "A great use of the Grand's extra parking. And we'd save a ton on rent."

Kristen smiled. "Did you think of this all by yourself, great leader?"

He accepted her compliment by leaning back. "I got the idea from reading numbers and looking out the window. It's what they pay me to do. Let's hope it works. It would be nice for our team to make a big impact on the bottom line. Good for *all* of us." He smiled. "But let's have a quick catch up on your other projects before everyone else arrives."

A few hours later in Long Beach, just south of Los Angeles, David's daughter Callie swiped the alarm clock and grimaced at the sunlight that cut between the curtains in her bedroom. "It's late," she finally said.

"Umm," Alex Spalding, her boyfriend, offered from beneath a pillow.

"Last night was late, too."

Emerging slowly, Alex reached for her. "But good."

She moved his hand and nodded. "Not now. I gotta study for a test in two hours."

"You'll do fine," he said, replacing his hand.

Smiling, she put his hand behind his back. "And what if I don't do well? My parents will kill me."

"But you're so beautiful and it's so early."

Moving to the edge of the bed, she looked at him. "Maybe, but I've still got the test. And since you're an aspiring actor with no job and no money, I don't want to flunk a course and have Dad think about lowering my allowance."

"When your Dad called the other night, maybe I should have answered and told him that we're in love and to send more money."

She stood up. "No way. I don't think telling him that you've moved in would mix well with his Iranian background."

"Is that why you're so beautiful? My beautiful Arab girlfriend!"

"I am *not* an Arab! My Dad's family is *Persian*. Trust me—Muslim Iranians and Muslim Arabs get along about as well as French Catholics and English Protestants did. They *fought* all the time." She hit him with a pillow.

"Ow!" he laughed. "It's too early for history."

"Do I look like history?"

"No, definitely not."

"Anyway, I called Mom yesterday, and they're cool. But Dad's working too hard, as usual."

"Yeah, that's the thing about work."

Running her hand through her jet black hair, she moved toward the bathroom. "How would you know?"

Sitting up, he grimaced. "Hey, you know I'm trying."

"Well, maybe you should try harder, and earlier. And maybe lighten up on the recreational hits a little, 'til you get a job or get back in school. We can't afford them."

As she half-closed the door, he threw the pillow her way. "You're no fun in the morning."

She looked out, putting toothpaste on a brush. "But I don't recall you saying that last night."

At that same time Callie's father was walking up the curved, carpeted staircase to the office of Paul Burke, the U.S. Chief Operating Officer of USNet.

"Hey," David said, depositing his files and sitting at Burke's polished mahogany conference table.

On the corporate organizational chart they were unequal equals. The two men were about the same age and enjoyed working out in the corporate gym and playing golf together. Paul Burke, almost bald, was head of U.S. Operations, which made him de facto #2 in the company. But he had counterparts in Europe and Asia. David Sawyer, on the other hand, ran real estate operations worldwide, interacting with all three managers, and, like Burke, reported directly to Knox. The result left David and Paul as near-equals in the U.S., and they helped each other whenever they could.

As David took out copies of his real estate summary they heard a noise coming from the video screen on the wall, and Knox slid into his chair facing them, live from Los Angeles.

"Gentlemen." He smiled and nodded, his eyes darting to the agenda in front of him. As was customary for all of the company's executives, Knox wore a straight collar white shirt, dark suit and conservative tie. "It's beautiful out here. We've had a full morning, and at lunch we'll give five million dollars in university prizes from our USNet Free Speech Foundation. And I've asked the foundation board to consider a large grant to the church that was bombed on Sunday."

"That would be very good," Burke said.

"Yes." He took out his gold pen and lightly tapped it on the table as he ticked off their agenda. "Let's see. Paul and I need to talk about the U.S. numbers, the purchase of E-News and several other possible acquisitions. But there's also a lot of real estate, so, David, please begin."

Sawyer started through his list, but before he could mention Kristen's nearly completed negotiations for their new office space, Knox interrupted.

"I've decided not to expand in Hong Kong, David. I'd rather divide the operation between Singapore and Seoul. In fact, cut back in Hong Kong to a minimal presence and instead expand in Beijing so that we can better influence the Chinese government."

David felt his hands tightening around the thick report on their new Hong Kong office, but he replied in an even voice, "You suggested that we expand in Hong Kong last fall. We've already hired people there."

"I understand." The pen made a single tap. "But for now I want to pull back from Hong Kong and focus on other Asian cities. And since we're behind in securing space, please hurry to find suitable locations."

David nodded. "All right." He swallowed. "The next item on our agenda should save some money." He summarized his plan to purchase Capital Tower, add it to the Grand, and create a new headquarters for USNet, all of which he demonstrated would substantially reduce their operating budget. "What do you think?"

Knox considered for a moment and then nodded. "Sounds good."

He knew that Knox's informal OK was all he needed to take the project to the next decision point. He made a note on his pad.

David moved through the rest of the agenda. As he finished the last item, he pushed his papers together and turned to Paul Burke.

But Knox interrupted. "David, I've got one more thing. Our movie production here in Los Angeles is exploding. We need to expand and vertically integrate the process, from hiring the actors to shooting the movies to distribution. Paul has had a team working secretly on the acquisition of ten companies. We're close, but we need you to assess the real estate. Paul will give you a confidential list of the companies, and we need your input, without anyone knowing why you're looking. Can you do that?"

"How quickly?"

"Two weeks."

David looked down at his papers and pursed his lips. He turned his wedding band beneath the table. "Isn't President Harper going after the kinds of movies we make? I mean, I like them as much as the next guy." He smiled. *Particularly the site visits.* "But aren't she and Congress about to kill the industry?"

Knox sat up. "Harper can try, but we have the votes in Congress to prevent her from hurting us. She's playing to her political base, trying to dictate what Americans watch. What we give them doesn't hurt anyone." He smiled. "The good news is that all the talk from the White House has people in the adult movie industry nervous, so now is the time to buy. That's why we need your input quickly."

Sawyer glanced once at his colleague, then back to Knox on the screen. "All right. We'll get it done. When can I have the list of the firms and facilities?"

Burke moved a folder on the table in front of him. "It's ready for you."

David picked up the folder and flipped through the first few pages. "We'll start today, and we'll be discreet."

"Good, David," came the reply from the screen. "Now, if that's all the real estate, Paul and I will finish up the budgets."

David rose, the expanded pile of papers in his hand. "I'll be back to you as soon as I can."

A few hours later Callie Sawyer and her brother Rob were exchanging text messages.

Calliente: What's up?

RobSaw: About to start SW 2100. How was ur test?

Calliente: OK. But no time to study.

RobSaw: Same. History tomorrow.

Calliente: I remember Ms. Gillstrap.

RobSaw: She's tough.

Calliente: You play videos a lot.
RobSaw: I'm good. You act a lot.
Calliente: I'm good. ☺
RobSaw: Hope so. When's ur first movie?
Calliente: Not sure. Five years?
RobSaw: Sooner. U R good.
Calliente: Thanks bro. How are m&d?
RobSaw: The same. Work and worry.
Calliente: OK. Gotta go. Good luck in the street war.
RobSaw: Thanks.

Late that afternoon Paul Burke knocked on the open door to David's office. "About what happened in Knox's office," Burke began as he walked in and took a seat. "the only thing I knew about was the Cinema Group acquisitions in Los Angeles. The first I heard about dumping Hong Kong was when you did."

David shook his head. "The good news and the bad news are that we work for Trevor Knox. Do you think he knows how much we've already invested in Hong Kong?"

"It doesn't seem to matter. Can you make the change?"

"Probably, but we're pretty thin. I'll have to take up the slack. Kristen will get Capital Tower kicked off here, then she'll head to Seoul and Singapore. I gave Moscow to Todd this morning, but now I'll take it. I was just writing an email to the broker who helped us last year.

"I obviously can't ask Kristen or Cheryl to work on Los Angeles. Kristen gets upset about the Platinum Club. What would she say about our movie sets?" He paused. It was an occasional discussion point among the company's senior executives that Knox travelled to Los Angeles more often than business issues required; he seemed to take a personal interest in this particular USNet product. "Aren't our films about one hundred percent porn now? I don't remember them being that way when we started."

Burke cleared his throat. "Adult films," he corrected, "and the profit is incredible. It's a market that's exploding for us, and these acquisitions should be even more profitable. We're just going where our customers take us. The only competition is the free stuff being posted on share sites. So now we're funding two of those as well, and sharing the income with the people who provide the material. A regular cottage industry on the internet."

"I'm so proud. Well, anyway, I'll get the ball rolling on the movie companies in Los Angeles and then go to Moscow. So, how are your budgets?"

Burke leaned back. "They're fine. Quarterly earnings will be up again. If we were a public company the Wall Street guys would love us. But, tell me, do you need more staff?"

David looked at his friend for a long moment. "Paul, we need at least twice as many. You don't just read a book and do a multi-million-dollar lease the next day. Todd and Chris are good examples. They're not as far along as Kristen, but they're starting to be productive. What we talked about upstairs should take a much larger team several months to finish."

Burke thought for a moment. "Lay out the new real estate group space in Capital Tower for twice as many people. How does that sound?"

He smiled. "I just hope we live to see it."

"You're home early," Elizabeth said, as David opened the door from the garage. She was slicing potatoes at the kitchen's central island; he walked over and kissed her cheek. A pile of clothes spread onto the ceramic tile floor from the laundry area behind the kitchen, the dryer whirred, and roasting beef sizzled in the oven.

"I just felt like coming home on time."

She stopped and turned to him. "Are you OK?"

"Yeah...sure. I'm just a little tired after last night, and felt like coming home at six."

"Well, we like that." She smiled and picked up another potato. "Dinner's going to be a little late. My last client hadn't filed her taxes for years. After you change, go check on Rob. I think he could use some help with a big history test tomorrow."

"OK," he said, heading toward their bedroom and trying to remember what era Rob was studying.

Ten minutes later he had changed into khaki pants and was standing outside their son's bedroom on the second floor. He thought he could hear Rob talking. He knocked, but there was no response. He knocked louder. Then he tried the door. Locked.

Inside the room, Rob was standing on a special virtual reality floor plate. He wore a helmet and vest, and carried a plastic gun simulator; all three were connected wirelessly to his computer, and then to the Internet. Almost as tall as his father, Rob's helmet and vest made him immense; he carried his machine gun with practiced ease. From inside his helmet he peered around the corner of a virtual brick building in a burned out portion of the central business district

The street he looked down was wide and deserted, with only a few nearly destroyed cars littering the way. The late afternoon sun created shadows on the left side and bursts of light on the right, reflecting off the few still unbroken windows. One car was smoldering from an earlier fire. Rob looked across the street to his right and nodded to his best friend and partner, Justin Napier, also fifteen. Justin had taken cover behind a building on the opposite corner. Crouched behind each of them were the two newest members of their team. Rob and Justin edged out into the street on opposite sidewalks, their machine guns at the ready on their shoulders, training them back and forth across the cars and the open windows of the adjoining buildings. Without looking, Rob heard the new team members taking up covering positions behind them.

"I saw one of them run this way," Rob said into the microphone in his helmet.

"Yeah, a little guy with a pistol," Justin replied.

"There are probably more." Rob made it to the first car, which had apparently crashed into a light pole when its driver was hit. No one was inside. Justin continued down the street, while Rob paused, using the car as cover. Rob began to train his machine gun over Justin's head when out of the corner of his eye he saw a flicker of light in a second story window on his side.

"Upper left!" Rob yelled, and quickly turned his machine gun toward the window, arcing out a spray of bullets.

But he was not fast enough. The gun barrel in the window flashed. Justin went down as the fiery tracers hit all around him.

"Aagh! I'm hit," Justin screamed.

"I'm coming," Rob yelled, running to his right and continuing to fire into the window, while their comrades came up and added firepower to the melee.

"Watch our backs!" He made it to Justin and began dragging him into an open doorway. As he did so, a grenade floated across the street and landed on the sidewalk next to them. Without a moment's hesitation, Rob scooped it up and threw it back toward the window where he had seen the barrel. Grabbing Justin, he rolled into the doorway as the grenade exploded a foot from the window, sending shrapnel up and down the street.

"Come on," Rob said, as he dragged his friend inside. Justin was holding his upper leg. Blood gushed out around his fingers. Rob pulled out his first-aid kit and applied pressure to the wound. "I'll get you out of here," he said. "You're going to be all right."

A new team member—Rob couldn't remember his name—ran up, took one look at Justin, and quickly turned away.

"I'll cover the door," he said.

The door. Someone was knocking. What?

David knocked again, even louder. The door finally opened, and his son stood before him—baggy shorts, shirt tail out, a virtual reality helmet on his head, the visor up. "Oh," came the greeting, as Rob turned and walked back to his entertainment center.

"Hey, how was school?" David asked his son's back.

"Huh? Oh," he turned to his father, putting on his virtual reality gun, toggling the connect switch, and moving toward the USNet Virtual Reality floor plate. "Good."

"How are you doing?"

Rob smiled from inside the helmet. "It's awesome. There are, like, about ten thousand of us all linked together and we're fighting Street War 2100. I'm on the blue team. When you knocked I was helping Justin. He's wounded. I gotta get back. You ought to see this gun I've got." Rob picked up a three-foot plastic wand and plugged it into the connection point on his belt. "This baby fires both hollow point shells and grenades. You ought to see it splatter 'em."

David knew about the games that USNet sponsored online, twenty-four hours a day. Virtual reality groups came together from all over the world to fight epic battles, street brawls, aerial dogfights—anything the USNet programmers could imagine. There were now over a hundred such battles going on continuously. Individuals logged in and out, keeping their characters and roles intact as the battle progressed. Besides charging well for participation in these virtual battles, USNet had chat rooms, strategy sessions, and cyber magazines dealing with each one; and twice a week outstanding individual efforts were noted and the videos of their exploits replayed for the other participants. Rob played Street War 2100 almost daily.

"I'm sure it's awesome," David replied. "How you been doing?"

"I've been online since school, 'til I had to pause when you knocked, and I've only been, like, wounded once. And"—he flipped his visor down to review the battle summary up to that point—"I've killed five and wounded twenty."

David spoke to the opaque visor covering his son's eyes. "What about school? Mom says you have a history test tomorrow." He glanced over at the books lying on the bed.

"Yeah. Sure. I'll look at my notes after supper. No sweat." He turned back to his terminal.

"Well, you need to study, but I'm glad you're enjoying this stuff."

Rob pushed Enter and then stepped onto the VR floor plate, looking over at his father. "It's awesome. Like, wait a minute." He swiveled the helmet's microphone in front of his mouth. "Yeah. I'll be there in a second. Hold on." He placed his free hand over the mike. "Dad, I gotta go. They, like, need me. Let me know when dinner's ready." He started to turn away.

"OK."

"Blue Nine is back. Where are you, Blue Ten?"

Rob faced away, and David watched him for a few moments on the VR floor plate, ducking and firing his "gun" at the enemies he was seeing in his visor. David turned, held the door as if he were going to say something else, then closed it and went downstairs.

"He's having fun," he said to Elizabeth as he entered the kitchen, "and it's a good way to learn that you have to take your lumps, get up, and keep fighting." He walked to the refrigerator for some iced tea.

"But what about his history test?" Elizabeth asked from the breakfast area, as she set the table.

David shrugged. "I'm sure he'll do fine. It's just a break after school, before he has to study. He'll be OK."

"I'm not sure. He's a different person this year."

David smiled. "He's a teenage boy. He'll be different every day."

"No, I mean really different,' she said, shaking her head. "And isn't that game that he plays from USNet?"

He stirred some sweetener into the tea and then put down the spoon. "Yes." He nodded without looking up. "And all of the equipment we bought him is very expensive." He turned to face her. "I don't want it to go to waste. It's just a game, made possible by technology that our company provides to the world. I think we should let Rob use it, and not bug him over one test. He'll be fine."

"But I think we should..."

He raised a hand. "He'll be fine. Trust me. I was his age once."

She started to say more, but David picked up his iced tea and headed for the den. She shook her head and put down another knife.

That evening around a conference table in a private school's boardroom in Detroit, twelve men were reviewing spreadsheets that showed their foundation's progress for the year. The meeting was led by Rahim Tahymouri and Amir Ali, the co-chairs of the charitable organization.

Rahim guided the men's eyes across the report. "As you will see, moving from left to right across the headings, we have figures for the total number of cities where we have Community Organizers, Candidates, Elections Within a Year, Elected Officials, Community Centers, and Schools. And the change in each category since last month."

The men nodded and spoke among themselves.

Amir continued. "The results are better than we expected. Allah is to be praised, and you are to be congratulated. Our budgets for campaign spending and teachers have tripled in the past year, but for good reasons. So far every candidate we have supported has won. Within an average of two years after each election, we have had a Community Center or School up and running, with dedicated teachers in place, spreading Allah's truth and starting the cycle again."

One of the men asked, "Will we have the funds to pay for this growth?"

Rahim answered. "Of course our local collections are important to insure the community's involvement, but our special sources have assured us that there are unlimited funds available—it is up to us to create the opportunities."

"And so, gentlemen," Amir added, "please turn the page to the list of cities where we hope to plant a new mosque by the end of the year."

3

Sunday evening Kristen Holloway was in blue jeans and a white shirt, alone in the breakfast room of her high rise apartment. There were windows on two sides. The container from her low carb dinner was perched on one corner of the table; Tchaikovsky's *Serenade* played quietly from the living room, where the off white walls contrasted with the many potted plants and several original impressionist paintings. "Better to own a few good things than a lot of junk," her mom had always said.

With a pencil behind one ear and a calculator nearby, she was working on her taxes. When the phone rang, her Caller ID displayed a number that she hadn't seen for a long time.

"Kristen. Hi. It's Richard Sullivan."

"Hey. How are you?" She turned in her chair to look at the sunset.

"We're fine. Susan is out of college and both she and Tommy are doing well. People in general are still occasionally unhappy with each other, so my legal business is busy. Janet is seeing some results in the legislation they're passing, so she's certainly happy."

"I think her class in Congress has done a great job."

Janet Sullivan's background had been in television, but several years earlier she had run for and been elected to Congress as part of former President Harrison's call for a return to traditional values and conservative economics. Those same values were the basis for President Susan Harper's victory and Janet's re-election the previous fall. Janet commuted to Washington while Richard remained a partner in his law firm.

"Well, it's all thanks to our last two presidents. They haven't been afraid to take a stand. But how are you?"

"I'm fine. USNet keeps expanding, so there's lots of work for us real estate types. I'm going to Asia next week."

"Sounds glamorous for a cowgirl from Texas."

She smiled. "It just *sounds* that way. On about the second fourteen-hour plane trip, it turns into a job."

There was a moment of silence. Then Richard spoke. "Kristen, the reason I'm calling is that Janet and I have been dealing with a phone call I got this afternoon. I have no idea who it was. He said he knew about our relationship and that I should persuade Janet to vote against Harper's media reform bill."

"Richard, what information could he have? That was years ago."

"I'm not sure. Somehow he knew details that only you or I could have known. It was pretty graphic."

Kristen's voice rose, and she pointed with the pencil. "Richard, I haven't told anyone about our affair. Ever. Except Janet, with you."

"I know. I'm not sure how he got the information. But I had to call you in case you get a call. too."

"No one has called me. What are you going to do?"

"Nothing. He may think that he can blackmail me. But he apparently doesn't know that you, Janet and I met years ago, that she forgave us, and that we've all moved on. And that I want the media bill to pass as much as Janet."

After a pause, he continued, "But they may make what we did public just to try to discredit Janet for her values, and by association, the President. So we may all get a lot of unpleasant attention."

Kristen put down the pencil and rested her forehead in her hand, "Whoa. I thought this was over long ago."

"Me, too. But somehow it's not."

She sighed. "However unpleasant it may be for me, I know it will be much worse for you and Janet. And the kids. I'm sorry."

"He said that they have tapes of us talking on the phone."

"Tapes? From years ago?"

"Yes. I don't know how or when."

"I hope it's not true."

There was a silence. Then Richard said, "It's another reason to be glad, after God intervened in our lives, that we met and asked for Janet's forgiveness. She is an amazing woman. I truly believe that she never thinks about it. I guess we'll just have to trust and see what happens."

"Yes."

"Call me if you hear anything, and I'll do the same."

Late that same evening USNet's CEO, Trevor Knox, was back in his penthouse apartment after finishing a dinner with a European banker. Walking the short distance to his office, he said a silent prayer and unlocked the special computer embedded in his desk.

He noted that Simon North had already set a meeting with NovySvet Aerospace outside Moscow. And there were three stocks to buy in bulk, plus two recommended to sell.

When he finished the summary, he typed an encoded email to Akbar Kamali and Victor Mustafin, the leaders of his RTI team.

Kamali and Mustafin were the only individuals in the U.S. who knew that Trevor was a key leader in the worldwide force to impose the rule of Islam across the globe. This goal was the ultimate use for RTI's information and income. And only the three of them worked on RTI's most secure Special Operations projects.

Akbar Kamali, an Iranian, had been a veteran with the Shah's secret police, the Savak, before finding true faith at the time of Khomeini's revolution in 1979. Trevor had asked an old friend from their early university days in London, Saeed Zeini, a rising star in Khomeni's radical ruling circle, to make sure of Kamali's conversion. Given his English skills, Kamali was a natural choice to bring to the United States once Trevor had gained control of USNet.

The following year Trevor recruited Victor Mustafin, a Kazakh, whom he knew through mutual contacts in the Muslim Brotherhood. During Soviet times future leaders in Kazakhstan were trained in Moscow and therefore spoke fluent Russian. Victor's father had provided that opportunity, but his mother made certain that his first love was always her native country and their one true faith.

Together, given their complementary skills and contacts, Kamali and Mustafin, a Shi'a and a Sunni, made a formidable team to utilize the unique information gathered through RTI's intercepts, both in the U.S. and abroad.

Trevor finished his messages, sat back, and smiled. *Allah is great! Thank you for all the French cities now governed de facto by Sharia Law. Thank you that there are more of us in English mosques than there are Anglicans in English churches.*

Thank you for these dithering Americans, their constant political bickering, and their indecision. Now that our brothers in Iran have the nuclear bomb, we can apply pressure in ways that were impossible only a year ago. Who will dare stand up to us? A church bombing one week, an election win the next, a mosque zoning victory, and yet we are always portrayed as victims of discrimination, at least on USNet. Trevor smiled. *Now is the time to create chaos in their governments and to put Brothers in power at every possible level. Our ultimate victory may be a few decades away, but it is coming, and now is the time to make a great advance. Our own people don't understand what we are doing—but one day they will find themselves in power— because of us.*

He glanced up at the city's lights, shining for miles. *And RTI provides the information and the funds to make it even easier.* He remembered his first small office at Knox Communications, where he worked for his uncle after arriving in America from London, over forty years before. There had not been a single window. And then the day, years later, when he had fallen out with his cousin, Ellis.

Trevor recalled that the split had actually been on the same day, over twenty years ago, that he had hired David Sawyer, an American with Iranian parents and a nominal Muslim background, to run their small real estate group. He had been impressed with Sawyer's experience in negotiating cell tower sites, and felt comfortable with his family's heritage.

After walking Sawyer to the reception area, Trevor had climbed the stairs back to his office, which was once a corner bedroom in the old Victorian house that Knox Communications had occupied for years. From there he and his cousin Ellis had operated the radio stations that they inherited from Ellis's father.

Through the open door of his own office, he saw Ellis standing over his neatly organized desk, looking through several stacks of daily reports. Before Trevor could speak, his cousin started toward him, waving a handful of papers.

"Trevor, I told you to stop doing this!"

His face turning red, Trevor closed the door and met Ellis in the middle of the room. "Why? No one ever said the phones are secure. They're open! We learn some incredible stuff." He nodded at the reports and transcripts in his cousin's hand.

Ellis, slightly taller and three years older, held out the papers. "But our customers *think* they're having private conversations, and they don't expect to be listened to, recorded and written up."

"Tough."

"You've got to stop. My father would not condone what you—we—are doing. What if someone finds out? Our license as the independent cell phone provider is an incredible opportunity. We can't blow it because you like to listen to people's conversations."

Grabbing the papers from his cousin's hand, Trevor shot back, "First, no one will find out. They are our phones, our system, and we use only a small group of trusted people to listen and record. Second, I don't do this because I "like" to listen to other people's phone calls. I do it because whatever we will earn from charging for cell phones use is nothing to what we can earn from knowing all this information. The government just handed us the license to do it, with no strings attached. Don't you see how amazing this is?"

"And how wrong."

The younger cousin walked to his desk, put down the papers, and sat in his chair. He swiveled slightly to glance at the foliage in the afternoon sun, then turned again. "Ellis, you understand all this technology—the phone business was your idea, starting with radio phones and now these cell phones. But people I understand. We can make a *lot* of money from what we'll hear every day."

The older cousin stood across the desk. "But I've told you that I won't permit us to steal information from unsuspecting customers."

Trevor rose again to face Ellis. "Won't permit? Look, you may know computers and phones, but I raised the money and put together the license application that won this gold mine. Don't talk about 'permitting'. Like it or not, we're partners, and I say that knowing all this information—new every day—is the best part of what we have."

"No. The phones themselves are more than enough."

"We're talking about the chance to know almost every new idea, make investments, and even influence events."

"Including blackmail?"

The younger man smiled. "For now, let's just collect information and see where it leads. Think what it could mean for our people to have this information."

"*Our people*? I've lived in the U.S. almost all my life. This nation has been wonderful to us. Look at this opportunity that we have, the son and nephew of an Egyptian immigrant. *These* are our people."

"Never! I accepted your father's Anglicized name to join his business, but I've never given up my identity. These people oppose Islam. Qutb, an early member of the Muslim Brotherhood, saw it all here decades ago: filth, materialism, greed, democracy. Only Islam will bring people back to pure life, merging faith, government and everyday life. It is the only way. And the West opposes all of this. They killed our people, including my father, your uncle. We must revenge his death. All their deaths! Revenge is a sacred requirement that Allah will honor with His blessing."

Ellis turned, walked to a window, then retraced his steps while Trevor watched. He came close to the desk. "Trevor, it was terrible that your father died in prison, along with so many others in the Muslim Brotherhood. But it was Gamal Nassar, a socialist and Egyptian nationalist, who had your father killed. Hardly a Western democrat. And he wanted a modern country, not a throwback to mistreating women and burning books that the Muslim Brotherhood is always espousing."

"What do you know about the Brothers?"

"Enough to know that they would be a disaster for any country they tried to rule."

"Are you crazy? They are the world's only hope! Look at what they do in Iran. Even though they are Persian Shi'a, they are a true Islamic state, with religious leaders in charge. It's incredible! We hope for the same thing in Egypt, and in all the other countries with governments pandering to their Western masters."

Ellis took a deep breath. "Look, Trevor, we've been through this before, and we're not going to solve the world's problems. Let's come back to our phones. You know how badly I feel about your father's death; I'm sure it's why my father gave you half of everything, for which I'm glad, because we built this business together. But this cheating is wrong. Knox Communications is not going to do it, no matter what you think. You don't have kids. I can't tell my two boys to play fair if I'm going to steal information and use it to outbid or outmaneuver others. If necessary, when I get back from Charlotte tomorrow, I'll call a meeting of our investors and tell them what you've been doing and ask them to confirm that we must stop."

Trevor sat down, his arms folded tightly. "You always think you know best." He spoke in Arabic, which Ellis did not understand. He looked intently at his cousin. Then he said in English, "I won't let your personal sense of right and wrong kill this sweet deal."

"And how will you stop me? I know the investors. They won't like what you're doing any more than I do."

Trevor was silent, his lips pursed and he shook his head slightly from side to side.

Ellis turned to leave. At the door he looked back. "I'm taking the King Air. In the morning I'm going over the proposed cell tower sites around Charlotte. When I get back we'll try one last time. Maybe one of us will have to go. It's not what I want, but I can't be in business with someone, even my cousin, who doesn't see the difference between right and wrong."

When there was no response from Trevor, Ellis left, closing the door behind him.

Trevor sat almost motionless for several minutes. He looked at the disheveled stacks of paper—of *information*—now in a mess on his desk. He pulled out his gold pen and rotated it, tapping the desktop with each turn. Finally he picked up the phone and dialed a number he had memorized a month before.

"Yes?" said a man's voice on the other end.

"He's on the way. The King Air."

"OK." The line went dead.

Turning from the memory of the following day's corporate plane crash, Trevor closed his eyes for a moment. *All those years ago. Why couldn't Ellis see the power in this gift from Allah?* Trevor had made sure that his cousin's wife and sons were well taken care of after the plane crash, but he almost never thought of them as family. They were just like all the other Americans. Blasphemers. Enemies of God. *Allah be praised that my eyes are not blinded by this country, and that we can do so much with what He has given us. The problem now is that there is almost too much information.*

He swiveled back in the direction of the keyboard, turned his gold pen nervously a few times, and then typed instructions on several RTI issues that required his lieutenants' special skills He ended with, "President Harper's media and entertainment legislation must not pass Congress. The legislation must fail."

At noon the next day the elevator doors opened in the chrome and glass lobby of Capital Tower, and Kristen Holloway exited, concluding her walk-through with the property's listing broker, Bill Porter.

Putting her notebook in her large purse, she turned to face him. "Tell me again the asking price."

"Eighty-five million."

She grimaced.

He shrugged. "Downtown is hot again, and we'll just have to see if anyone wants it."

"If we're interested, what would it take to stop the process? Would an offer close to full price do it?"

He looked away, and then returned her gaze. Finally he said, "I'll ask the owners whether they want to negotiate with USNet alone, or let the process run for three weeks."

"Please do, Bill. And I'll report to David. We'd like to get the ball rolling."

Porter nodded. "I'll check with the owners and let you know."

Sitting at his desk that afternoon, Todd Phelps, David's most experienced direct report after Kristen, was running through his email while talking on the phone with an old business school friend, Mike Campbell.

"Have you seen the new Audi roadster?" Mike asked. "It's incredible."

"That it is. I'll never afford one on my salary."

"I picked one up on Saturday."

Todd looked up from his screen. "No way."

"Yeah. Metallic blue."

Todd paused. "No way for me, with a wife and two kids."

"I'll show it to you when you're here. Right after we negotiate the lease."

Todd shifted. "Yeah. Good. Listen, the lease is important to us, too. That's why we're coming up on Wednesday. We need space in Minneapolis for next year's expansion of the publishing group, but the rental rate has to be right."

"We can deliver space to you in nineteen months, max. It'll be the best space in suburban Minneapolis, at the best rental rate. USNet's lease will let us fund our construction loan and get started on the project, so I promise you that the rental rate is going to knock your socks off."

Todd finished an email note and pushed Send. "Uh, great. But the folks across the street say the same. And they're a couple of months ahead of you."

"Fine. But you need to check their permit situation. We hear they have problems, and you should compare the offers. I'm sure we'll be less expensive."

"I hope so. David Sawyer is really focused. He wants to visit our Chicago projects on Wednesday morning, shoot up to Minneapolis that afternoon, and have dinner with you and Gillespie. We'll spend the night and see the other project in the morning. How does that sound?"

"Except for imagining you in that other project, it should be fine."

"Can you meet us at the airport on Wednesday afternoon?"

"Sure. And listen, Todd, while you're here, we'll talk about how to simplify this decision."

Todd swiveled around to the window. "What do you mean?"

"We'll discuss it when you're here on Wednesday."

"OK. See you then."

"Can't wait."

4

WEDNESDAY, APRIL 6TH

Two days later, well before dawn on Wednesday, David finished his second cup of coffee, wrote a note on their kitchen pad, and left it by the percolator.

Hope you have a great couple of days. Let's go to dinner when I get back tomorrow night.
I may be going to LA soon. Will try to see Callie.
I love you.
D

A few hours later, as he and Todd Phelps walked past baggage claim at O'Hare airport, David checked his handheld and noticed that there was an urgent message to call Kristen.

He and Todd shook hands with their two Chicago hosts for the morning, and then he apologized that he had to call the office. As they walked toward the car David speed-dialed Kristen's number.

"David, hey. Our online news this morning is reporting that the Chinese government has just instituted sweeping changes in Hong Kong."

"Like what?" David asked, cradling the mobile phone on his left shoulder.

"Like a declaration that Hong Kong is now to be integrated completely into the mainland economy, that the 'great experiment' is over. Private ownership is to be phased out in the province."

"You're kidding."

"I wish. It's all still sketchy, but one of the first bullet points is confiscation of all large land parcels and major buildings, and a tripling of real estate taxes."

"Not good, to say the least."

"But, David, do you realize that if Knox hadn't changed his mind last week, as of yesterday we would have been locked into a long-term lease for a ton of space in a nationalized building?"

Sawyer paused, shifting the phone as he changed hands with his bag. Todd and their hosts, who were deep in conversation about their Chicago visit, walked ahead.

"Sometimes the man is uncanny."

"I guess. Anyway, hopefully we have a leg up on moving to Seoul and Singapore. I imagine that a lot of companies will be bailing out of Hong Kong, too."

"Yes. When do you plan to go out?"

"Next week, once you tell me how high I can go on Capital Tower with Porter, so we can nail down a Letter of Intent."

"We need that building. Offer full price, and we'll agree to a thirty-day due diligence period. That ought to get it for us."

"Will do. I'll call Porter this morning and give him our standard letter at the asking price. Good luck in Chicago and Minneapolis."

"OK. Say hello to Porter for me."

He hung up, turning his attention once again to Todd and their Chicago hosts.

Later that night in Minneapolis, the two USNet real estate executives walked out of a French restaurant with Mike Campbell and Frank Gillespie, the developers of Brookglen. They had toured the site that afternoon. Over a superb dinner they had discussed rental rates and delivery dates. Because the two USNet visitors were going to see a competing project in the morning, nothing was settled, but the discussion was productive. And David made it clear that going forward, Todd Phelps would be the point man for USNet's decision-making process.

As they walked toward the two hosts' cars, Frank Gillespie said to David, "I'll drive you to your hotel. Let's let these two young guys relive their business school days."

"Fine by me," David acknowledged. Turning to Todd and smiling, he said, "Just remember we're starting early, so be bright eyed and bushy tailed in the morning."

"Of course," Todd agreed, as he and his friend opened the doors to Campbell's new Audi.

As Todd admired the interior, Campbell backed out and headed for Cabaret, a late-night watering hole for the single and affluent. Even though Todd had a wife and two young children, he looked forward to a few hours with his friend, and to checking out the local ladies. He had been unfaithful to his wife on three occasions, although he had never planned any of the events. They just "happened" while he was traveling. And everyone else did it, Todd imagined. It occurred to him that maybe tonight something unplanned might happen again, and he smiled.

As they drove downtown, they talked about where their friends from graduate school had landed. Mike seemed to keep up with everyone. It sounded to Todd as if most of his former classmates were making a lot more money, which he decided to file away and mention to Sawyer.

After recounting the high incomes of several of their friends on Wall Street, Mike said, "We have a plan that could help you in that department, Todd."

"What do you mean?"

"I mean, we've allocated a significant sum in our Brookglen development budget for financing fees. Since securing the USNet lease will reduce our loan interest, that's worth a lot of money. We'd reward anyone who helped us with our financing."

"I'm still not sure what you have in mind."

Mike glanced over at his friend and then back to the road. "I mean, Todd, that we've budgeted $250,000 for you if we can enter into the USNet lease in the next sixty days."

"For me?"

"Yes. Cash, check or money order. Where and how you want. I recommend a suitcase full of cash or a deposit in a Channel Islands bank. And of course neither USNet nor the IRS ever needs to know, so you can keep it all."

There was silence for a moment as Mike's proposal sank in. They exited the interstate and stopped at a red light. Mike added, "And it's not like you're doing anything wrong. Ours really is the best development on the west side of Minneapolis. We're just facilitating a decision that you would make anyway. It truly is a well-earned financing fee."

"And no one will know?"

"No one, my friend. It's all yours."

"When?"

"Half next week and half when we sign the lease."

They drove into the Cabaret parking lot. Todd smiled and looked at Campbell as they pulled in next to two other expensive drives. "I'll definitely think about it and let you know." *This may be my double lucky night.*

David went back to his hotel room and, after catching up with Elizabeth on Rob and her day, plugged in his laptop to review two documents that he needed for the next morning.

There was an email from a former employee whom he'd fired a year earlier for spending too much time on the internet, even after several warnings. The parting had not been pleasant.

I wonder what he wants?

Wednesday 20:15
To: David Sawyer
From: TonyB
Subj: Amateur Mid-East Bombshell Does It All

David,

I only met your daughter a couple of times at company outings, but for your sake, family man, I hope this isn't her!

Your friend,

Tony

There was a link to a website run by USNet for amateur adult video postings, and David was aware of the content. He clicked.

In a few seconds the title came up and the video started. It was a half-lit bedroom, a boy and girl in bed. The girl looked just like Callie. *What are they doing?* Then she spoke to her lover and turned toward the camera. It *was* Callie, or her twin.

He stood in disbelief. *What is she doing? Who is that guy? I can't believe it!*

He watched for a minute and was repulsed. He reached for his cell phone and called her, but it went to voice mail. *No, not the phone. We need to talk face to face. What will Elizabeth think? Should I tell her? What if someone else recognizes her? I can't believe this. Maybe it's not really her.*

That Friday afternoon Omid and Goli left their apartment at two and walked in the general direction of Vali Asr Square. They carried a shopping bag and looked like any other couple on the way to the market. After stopping at several shops, they arrived across the street from the east side of the square at three forty-five, next to the door of an apartment building.

Omid stood close to Goli, but they did not touch. "I'll be back in an hour," he whispered.

"Do you have to join them today?"

They both knew that security cameras mounted all over the city were watching and recording. "Yes. I must be there. And you must do your part. But please stay back from the parapet wall so that you can't be seen from the street. If it gets bad, just hold the camera up, but stay behind the wall yourself."

She looked up at him. He smiled. Then he reached into the shopping bag and quickly moved a green scarf into his pants pocket. He turned and rang the bell for the top floor apartment.

When the speaker answered, he said, "It's Omid."

The buzzer sounded and he opened the door for his wife, who went inside and started up the stairs. After a few steps she turned and nodded. "May Allah go with you," she mouthed.

Several hours later on a viral website there were over thirty minutes of video, apparently taken from a roof overlooking Vali Asr Square in Tehran. One minute the park was almost empty, but the next there were thousands of demonstrators, seemingly of all ages and both genders. Many were wearing green scarves across their faces, and a large number had the same facemasks used by the Occupy protestors in the West. They had signs denouncing the regime and calling for free and fair elections. As they chanted, uniformed police gathered on the south end. But the plain-clothed Basij started attacking the group with whips and sticks from all sides. The video clearly showed demonstrators on the fringes being singled out, beaten to the ground, and dragged off.

Then the police moved in as a group, swinging clubs and throwing tear gas canisters. Near the end, the first shots were fired. It was not clear from where, but demonstrators screamed and ran as several in the crowd went down. The camera caught the scene of one young woman, clearly wounded and bleeding badly from her upper body. Her friends were helping her, but the Basijis descended on them and beat the men who were trying to help her. As they went down, a Basiji grabbed the woman by the hair and dragged her in the opposite direction. Then the screen went blank.

5

WEDNESDAY, APRIL 13TH

Several days later, Todd Phelps was stuck in the morning traffic. As the cars inched forward, he fidgeted with his cell phone, bouncing it gently on the leather of the passenger seat. Finally he dialed a number in Minneapolis. "Mike? Hey. It's Todd. I know it's early. Are you up?...Good. Listen, I've been thinking about our conversation. In fact I haven't thought about much else...No, not even her, and she was beautiful. See how you messed me up? Anyway, if we do this, are you sure we can keep it just between us?...Well, it has to. And you're right that you've probably got the best project. I've been studying your package again. Your lease cost does turn out to be lower, at least in the early years, which are the most important...OK, good. Look, I mean, if we're going to pick you anyway, why not earn a fee, right?...Yeah. And no one knows, right?...How do I set it up?...OK, email me the address at my home computer and I'll send whatever he needs. He can do it in a few days and then I'll have an account, right?...Awesome. Well, I'll call you when it's set up and you can wire the fee on down...Yeah, sounds great. I can sure use it. Give Mary and me some breathing space. And no harm done, 'cause yours is the best project anyway...Yeah, well, hey, me too. I really appreciate it, man. This means a lot...Yeah, for both of us. I'll call you when it's ready. Have a good one."

Todd pushed the End button and smiled. He put the cell phone on the passenger seat and slid in a CD, the route he was taking that morning no longer seeming quite so difficult.

David sat at his desk just before noon, swiveled to look downtown, and briefly reflected on the past few days.

Since returning from Minneapolis, his plate had been filled to overflowing, but his mind had been on Callie. And on Omid and Goli, after the demonstration in Tehran on Friday. That morning he'd finally received a short call from someone in Europe asking him to call his cousin Omid in Tehran later that day—the usual way that Omid let David know that he needed to talk.

As soon as he had arrived on Monday he met Kristen, usually calm and unflappable, who had angrily recounted that Capital Tower was headed for a bid despite their full price offer. Since she was departing for Singapore, she would coordinate their final offer from there by email before the deadline set by Bill Porter.

David had received similar status reports from the other members of his team. Todd seemed to have Minneapolis under control. He had worked on organizing his own trip to L.A. later that week, and then to Moscow.

But at the moment his thoughts were closer to home. *Was that really Callie? It couldn't be.*

He picked up the phone and dialed her number. Again, the answering machine.

"Hey, it's Dad. I'm coming out to L.A. on Friday for business. I won't be there long, so I don't want to see the whole family, but I'd love to see you. How about if I take you and your roommate—and maybe even the new boyfriend Mom told me about—to dinner that night? We can all meet at your place and go from there. About seven? Call or email, and I'll see you then. I love you."

> To: Bill Porter
> Cc: David Sawyer
> From: Kristen Holloway, Singapore
> Subject: Capital Tower
> Dear Bill,
> David Sawyer has authorized me to increase our cash offer on Capital Tower to $92 million, almost ten percent more than the asking price. All other provisions of our previous offer remain unchanged. My assistant is sending the original copy of our revised offer to you by courier so that it arrives before the deadline.
> I want to reiterate that USNet will move to a binding contract to purchase Capital Tower along with a $1 million deposit immediately upon acceptance by the owners of our Letter of Intent.
> We look forward to hearing from you as soon as you have the opportunity to review our offer with the owners. I will be back in my office next Monday. If you have any questions or need additional input, please contact me by cell phone or email. Thank you.
> Kristen

Trevor Knox welcomed his two RTI lieutenants, Akbar Kamali and Victor Mustafin, the latter by videoconference, to their regular monthly meeting in his office. He motioned Kamali to sit at the smaller of his two conference tables, with Mustafin on a screen next to it. Kamali had a cover job as senior IT/Security manager for USNet, but Mustafin remained "outside" and therefore had more operational freedom. Together they ran the clandestine RTI intercept network that had mushroomed out of Knox's early listening to cell phone calls. Now most of the work was done by computers, trained to find, analyze and catalog valuable texts, using voice and email key words. None of the RTI operation was electronically traceable to USNet or to the three men. To further insure their security, Kamali never physically visited any RTI facility, and Mustafin never came to USNet.

Knox greeted them in Farsi and in Russian. Mustafin would be the RTI duty officer that night, a task rotated around the clock by only twenty trusted men on a staggered schedule. Any matter considered to be of moderate or higher importance was routed to the duty officer, who could then also relay it to Mustafin when he was not on duty himself. If he was unavailable, the inquiry went automatically to Kamali, but the sender thought he was communicating with Mustafin. Knox only acted through these two trusted Muslim brothers, or via encrypted email showing an authentication code and no sender. They spent a lot of money for the best IT systems and hackers; they believed that their RTI intercepts and actions were invisible.

As a matter of routine Knox checked the control panel at his desk which tested for bugs and insured that electronic white noise would foil any attempt to record their conversation. He removed his coat and joined Kamali at the table with a pad and his gold pen. He nodded to the Iranian.

"We're in reasonably good shape on the equipment side," Kamali said, looking down at his notes. "David Sawyer's team just purchased telecom bunkers in three cities. He and everyone think that USNet is opening co-location facilities for website hosting. At our current rate of information growth, they should last until about the end of the year, when we'll have to buy, build or lease more space, and buy more servers."

In virtually perfect English, Mustafin added, "On the analysis side, we're already pushing the limits. It's easier to add fifty computers than ten competent analysts. Our computers are matching connections and key words a thousand times faster than just two years ago. Who could have foreseen all of the handhelds, and all of the wireless hotspots? We're literally being flooded with unencrypted emails with every kind of business and personal detail imaginable, which senders can't imagine we're reading. And we've barely touched all the information in uploaded videos and social media."

Knox nodded, then made a note on his pad. Mustafin continued, "The change in Hong Kong was easy to track because several emails indicated it was about to happen. But catching a single phone call or email with crucial information is getting harder."

Knox agreed. "Having enough qualified people is going to be more challenging, particularly since we don't want them to know what they're doing."

"Exactly," added Kamali. "The good news is that the analysts don't have to be sitting in the U.S. We're hiring in Asia, South America, and Africa. And we're using their local conflicts to recruit bright people into what they think is their cause's intelligence effort. We just want you to know that despite everything, the system is not perfect. And soon we'll have to expand or reorganize the duty officer slot. There's so much information coming in that it's difficult for one person to digest and act on it all."

"OK. But we obviously have to be careful with duty officers. We must know and trust them completely—or have them on a short leash. And that's just to handle the regular business intercepts—they can never work on or know about our Special Operations. Even on the business side we have to give them a vivid picture of what will happen if they betray us. Hopefully your share of our RTI profits will continue to motivate you to use caution." They both nodded. "Then let's get on to the most recent projects."

Kamali began, "We now have eight major automobile manufacturers around the world paying us a million dollars a month for our reports on their competitors. Of course none of them knows that our sources are their competitors' emails and phone calls. Ditto in aircraft, weapons manufacture, banking and pharmaceuticals. Next month we'll begin the same in oil and gas—software, computer, and securities firms are slated by the end of the summer. Our total business-related gross is now about $150 million per month and climbing.

"In the past thirty days we made almost $40 million from people and firms who pay us to remain silent about what we know about them. And the big number, as usual, was the $825 million we netted on third-party stock purchases and sales. Our portfolio of non-USNet related stocks is now well over $50 billion."

Mustafin glanced at his notes and continued. "As for our other work, through our foundations and charities, Allah be praised, we are now supporting the campaigns of 215 local and regional Muslim officials in Europe, and 73 here in the US. In every major mosque in America we have at least two members of the Brotherhood, funded by us, who are insuring that pure Islam is taught and preached. Through the foundation in Detroit, we're secretly funding the Brotherhood as community organizers in twenty American cities, and we expect to add ten more this year."

"How about buying the churches?" Knox asked.

Mustafin smiled. "It's working well. So far our 'Foundation of Faith' has purchased—let's see—368 churches and leased the buildings back to their congregations. They need the cash for renovations, and the rent we charge them is very low. Taxes are up, giving is down, and our foundation's cash is very attractive to a strapped congregation. Many at each church won't be alive in twenty years when their lease is not renewed and their house of blasphemy becomes a house of worship for Allah. At the current rate, we should purchase over a thousand churches in most US cities and suburbs, complete with all the required zoning and parking, within the next three years. Then, starting in about ten years, overnight we will have mosques everywhere."

Knox and Kamali glanced at each other and nodded as Mustafin continued.

"Simon North reports from Moscow that by this Friday we should close on the controlling interest in NovySvet and their new missile targeting system. No one has anything like it, and, once the capability is fully developed, we should be able to use it against our enemies with great results. Of course Simon doesn't know who he is working for, and we'll keep him as the bridge until we figure out what to do with it."

"But we need a long range missile delivery system equal to this new technology," Knox injected.

"Yes. And we have the RTI filters set to look for anything that could lead to buying or securing one by any means," Kamali replied.

Mustafin continued. "On Special Operations, of course our greatest project is the Ramadan Gifts planned for this fall. Salim's hard work in the Army for these many years is about to create great results. We have one martyr for New York, and one for Los Angeles. The destruction and confusion will be immense. Salim has five Stinger missiles hidden in El Paso around Fort Bliss. Everything appears to be on track."

"Finally, we have a lot of Special Operation political action in progress, as you know. Our trial run with this initiative is to stop President Harper's bill to regulate movies and the internet. We're well into it, and we should see results over the next few days."

"Good. The sooner the better," Knox replied. "We're about to acquire even more assets in southern California, and we need to squash any chance that censorship will come back. These people want all of the thrills that their money can buy from us. And, as long as they buy it, we might as well enjoy producing it." He gave them a look. They knew of his habit of "interviewing" their youngest adult movie stars well into the night whenever he visited the west coast.

"And as we've discussed, using Special Operations for this political purpose is just a warm up. Now that Iran and Pakistan both have the bomb, we can bring more leverage to bear on the politicians to vote our way, and the information we have through RTI gives us huge leverage." He smiled. "When we bring this pressure to bear, there will be unexpected votes from county councils to Congress that no one will believe. So use it well. Is that it?"

"Yes, I think so," said Kamali, looking at his colleague, who nodded.

Rising to signal the end of their meeting, Knox said, "We're in the middle of a lot of profitable projects, and, Allah willing, about to create a great defeat for this female Crusader President. As the Prophet instructed, we will either defeat her or destroy her. Keep up the good work, gentlemen, and keep me informed."

It would be late in Tehran, but David knew that Omid didn't mind. So as he drove home he used his cell phone to call the number that his IT people had helped him set up in Estonia, which then dialed Omid's new, clean cell phone. Omid always worried that someone could be listening, but the USNet IT team assured David that the system was secure, particularly with the new phones that David had sent to Turkey, where one of Omid's friends had picked them up on a business trip and returned with them to Iran. Nevertheless, Omid was rarely more specific than he had to be with his news or his requests, and so David responded in kind.

"Hello," the familiar but groggy voice said in Farsi.

"Omid. Good morning, it's David." He could hear the relief as the young man switched to English.

"David! So good to hear you. Thanks for calling."

"Of course. Are you OK?"

"Yes, yes we are fine. Thank you."

"Allah be praised."

"And thank you for the New Year's presents."

"They arrived OK?"

"Yes, and they are most helpful."

"I wish I could do more to help. Please tell me how we can."

"You are already a great help. Thank you. And I do have one request."

David and Elizabeth had visited Tehran once, many years earlier, and Omid's emailed pictures and calls kept them up to date on family and friends with whom they felt close. David had never met Goli, Omid's new wife, but he hoped to help them come to the U.S., at least for a visit, since Omid seemed determined to stay and bring change to Iran.

"Cousin"—as Omid always called him—"I've uploaded a list of recipes that my uncle has used in his restaurant. It's created some friction with him— he thinks they are family secrets. So I would like to understand better how to create a new website in an obscure location. Can you help us?"

David looked out at the suburbs through which he drove and thought for the hundredth time about the risk that Omid was taking.

"Of course. Shall I have Abigail call you tomorrow? Shall she use the next number on the list?"

"Yes, my uncle is really upset with what we've done."

"OK. We'll do it. And I'll fund whatever you and Abigail agree to."

"Thank you, Cousin."

"It's not much, and it's the least I can do, given what you and Goli do every day."

They then traded news about their families.

As Omid was finishing the call, he said, "A friend was approached by some of the younger mullahs, who said that they're tired of the same old dinners and want new recipes, like we're offering."

"Be very careful, Omid."

"Yes. We're checking. Thank you, Cousin."

"I'll give Elizabeth, Callie and Rob your news."

"I hope to meet your children some day."

"Yes. Here, at our home. And soon."

"As Allah wills."

"Stay safe, Omid."

"I will, Cousin."

6

FRIDAY, APRIL 15TH

Two mornings later Jamal was perspiring heavily as he drove his office supplies delivery truck under the arch at the entrance to the New Brighton School in northwest London. He had made this same run for three years, and the security guard at the gate waved him straight through. Before him was a large grass quadrangle, full of running and jumping elementary school students from England, the U.S. and most countries of the world, surrounded on all four sides by the two-story stone edifice of the historic institution.

As he glanced at the children, he knew that some of them were the sons and daughters of Muslims, but he recalled his imam's instruction that since they were at this international school, side by side with infidels, they were not real Muslims.

Normally he drove halfway up on the left side of the playing field, then turned under an arch between the buildings and went around to a loading area in the back. But today, using a schedule supplied by other Brothers working as staff at the school, he timed his arrival to coincide with chapel for the older students in the building to his immediate left.

So he drove part of the way to the arch, then stopped the truck and got out. His hands were sweating, but he thought again of the large sum of money that would arrive at his home just two days hence—money that his parents, brothers and sisters desperately needed. From under the seat he pulled an AK-47 assault rifle with an extra large clip, and felt in his coat for the extra clips and the wireless trigger.

Jamal walked around the front of the truck; the children on the playing field were in plain sight. He flipped the selector to full automatic, raised the gun, and began shooting the children and the few teachers who were monitoring their play. After the first few shots, as children fell in bloody pools, others screamed and ran away. He calmly took down the ones on the far side of the field, ejected the spent clip, reloaded another, and kept firing.

He and his imam had calculated that twenty seconds should be the right amount of time to bring the maximum number of faces to the glass windows surrounding the quadrangle. That was about two long clips. So as the second clip emptied, Jamal screamed, "There is no god but Allah. Muhammad is the messenger of Allah!" and pushed the trigger on the radio in his pocket.

The truck was loaded to the top with explosives, surrounded by ball bearings and nails. The carnage at the school killed fifty-five students and injured two hundred.

From down the street a short message was sent via a handheld. Within five minutes Trevor Knox had read it.

Two hours later David had deplaned in Los Angeles but had then stopped with several others a few feet from the gate in front of a television screen, viewing the latest update on the mass murder of children in suburban London, including a clip from the statement of condolence to all of the families expressed by President Harper to the British Prime Minister, on behalf of all American citizens.

How incredibly senseless. What if Callie or Rob were at that school?

Standing next to him was a well dressed couple in their fifties who had been across the aisle from him on the plane. They had exchanged pleasantries during the flight. The husband now said to his wife, "Damn Muslims. Why are they always doing this? We should send them back to the desert."

David continued to face the screen but heard himself say, "That McVeigh guy in Oklahoma City wasn't a Muslim, and he killed hundreds."

The man turned and looked at David, seeming to notice for the first time his slightly dark complexion. After a pause, he said, "Uh, you're right. It's not just Muslims. Lots of people are crazy. But you have to admit that the Muslims seem to revel in it, and you never hear about any Muslim trying to stop it."

David turned his head slightly, not wanting to appear confrontational. "You're right that you almost never hear. But there *are* Muslims trying to stop it. They just have to be very brave to stand up to suicidal thugs with guns. Like a German trying to stand up the Nazis." He nodded and moved down the concourse, pulling out his handheld to read his messages. One of them concerned their new space in Moscow.

Friday 18:35
To: David Sawyer
From: Andrei Selivanov
Subj: Moscow Office Space
Dear Mr. Sawyer,

As you requested, we have done a preliminary study of available space. In general, the market is rebounding, rates are starting to firm, but there are still ample choices of both first and second generation space.

I understand from your assistant that you are out of town until next week. In the interim, we have created a site for you with summary information, exterior pictures, and internal videos of the six most likely properties. Please go to http.207.438.229 and log in as DSawyer, password Exec to view the presentation. Let us know if any of these appear to be particularly feasible, or for some reason are not suitable. We look forward to seeing you soon in Moscow. Call or email with your input.

Andrei

Late that afternoon David parked his rental car in an empty space about twenty yards from the townhouse in Long Beach that he rented for Callie and her roommate. It was in a residential area of two- and three-story homes and apartments. Despite a long day of looking at adult movie properties, he was not tired. Like everyone else in America, he had been following the awful events at the school outside London, and USNet had just identified the terrorist as an English deliveryman from an Iranian family. Most world governments condemned the killings, but so far the Iranian government had been silent.

He thought again of the conversation in the airport. *Has everyone gone mad, killing children in the name of God, or Allah, or Whomever? Surely, if there is a God, he will punish these people, not send them to heaven. You can't do such things and not be punished!*

He took a deep breath, rubbed his forehead, and opened the car door. He smelled outdoor grilling and heard children playing. From the backseat he took a bag with bread and cheeses, locked the car and walked up the sidewalk.

The townhouse had a small front yard and a covered doorstop. He crossed the yard, took another deep breath, and knocked.

He heard the latch move and the door opened. "Hi, Dad."

He smiled. "Callie."

She was dressed in a long blue skirt and white top with half sleeves. They hugged, then she stood aside.

He entered the living room. A breakfast room and kitchen were toward the back. Stairs on the right led to bedrooms. It was a typical rental unit with furnishings from a mid-range furniture store.

"Dad, this is Alex Spalding."

The young man was dressed in gray slacks and a striped shirt. "Hello, Mr. Sawyer."

David recognized the boy from the video; they shook hands.

"Hello, Alex." He turned quickly. "Callie, here, I brought some hors d'oeuvres."

"Great." She took the bag, looked inside and smiled. "Let's have some before we go out." A dog barked next door. "Have a seat. Would you like some water or tea?"

"Water is fine." He moved to a cushioned armchair across from the sofa. Callie went into the kitchen and began filling glasses.

Alex sat on the sofa and asked, "Did you have a good trip out?"

"Yes. Uneventful. And then a busy day."

Callie returned with a glass for each of them. "And what have you been doing?"

"Uh, looking at properties. The usual real estate stuff."

She smiled. "Good." In the kitchen she put the hors d'oeuvres on a plate and then placed it on the coffee table, joining Alex on the sofa, her hands on her knees.

"Where's Jane?" David asked.

"She's visiting a sick uncle this weekend—he's not expected to live long. She told me to tell you hello."

"Thanks. So, I haven't seen you since Christmas break. How are you?"

"Great. Studying hard. Exams will be in a little over a month. I'm rehearsing for the year-end musical. Maybe you and Mom can come out. How was the Persian New Year?"

He smiled. "It almost killed me. The rest of America doesn't know about our national tradition, and so it turns out to be many late nights followed by many early mornings."

As Alex sliced cheese, Sawyer asked, "And, Alex, where do you live?"

The young man turned quickly to Callie. "About two miles away. It's not far. But not as nice as this." He smiled at the older man.

The visual from the video rebooted in David's mind.

The three sampled the cheese and chatted about Callie's fine arts program, work, the Sawyers' extended family, and Alex's aspirations.

"I want to go into marketing after college."

"Where are you in school?"

"I'm taking a semester off to work."

"Where are you working?"

Alex glanced at Callie. "I've got a couple of offers that I'm considering now."

There was a pause, and when David spoke, his hands were so wet that he had to wipe them on a napkin. "With our reservation I think it's about time we go, but first I have to ask a question. Has either of you ever heard of a video called *Amateur Mid-East Bombshell Does It All?*

Alex's eyes widened. Callie looked confused. She shrugged her shoulders and shook her head. "No. Why?"

Alex shifted on the sofa and looked down at his hands.

Sawyer leaned forward. "What about you, Alex?"

"I, uh. Since I guess you've seen it, I obviously can't pretend that I don't know about it."

"About what?" Callie asked, turning to him.

He continued to look at his hands. "I guess about ten days ago when we were, uh, you know, together, I put my video camera on the shelf and recorded us."

David watched Alex's explanation register on his daughter's face.

"You mean"—lowering her head to see his eyes—"upstairs? Together?"

He finally looked up and nodded. "Yes."

"And you put it on the internet?"

He nodded.

"On my company's video share site."

Callie looked at her father. "Your company has a share site for videos?"

"I'm not proud of it, but, yes."

She turned again to Alex. "And you put us on the internet for everyone, including my father, to see?"

"I had no idea that he would see it."

"Do you check the site often, Dad?"

"No. Never. A former colleague saw it and sent me the link."

Now Callie looked down. "So my boyfriend put us on a website run by my father for the world to see. And I guess it will be there forever. Maybe our grandchildren will watch. What were you thinking?"

There was silence.

"The point is," David said, talking faster and tapping his finger on the table, "I don't decide what my company does. But you can decide what you do. Callie, how do you think your mother would feel, if she knew? What do you have to say?"

"Mr. Sawyer—" Alex started.

"I'm not talking to you." David paused. "For all I care, you can go. In fact, you should probably leave."

Callie held out both hands. "No. Wait." She turned to Alex. "I can't believe that you did that without telling me." He lowered his head. Then she took a deep breath and faced her father. "I'm not a little girl any more—I guess that's obvious. I didn't know about the video, and I'm sorry that Alex did it and that you saw it. But, yes, I'm the one who participated. That was my choice. I love Alex, and he loves me. We plan to get married after school. So don't talk to him like that."

"What?"

She straightened. "Yes, we love each other." She took Alex's hand.

"He hasn't got a job, he puts you on the internet for kicks, and you want to *marry* him? In my parents' day you would both be dead. Or worse."

She moved closer to Alex, who was still focused on the floor, and said, "Well, it's not your parents' day, and we're not in Iran. How would your parents feel about your great website?"

Sawyer lowered his voice. "Alex, I think you'd better leave. I want to talk with Callie alone."

She squeezed his hand. "No. Alex lives here. He can stay."

"He *lives* here?"

"Yes, with me."

Alex started "Callie, I think I should—"

"You're staying. Anything Dad wants to say to me, he can say to both of us."

Silence. Alex looked at Callie, who was returning her father's stare.

Finally David asked, "Callie, what are you doing?"

"Nothing. I love you and mom. But I've grown up."

"This isn't growing up. This is making bad decisions." Silence again. "Do you think I should continue to send money so that you can keep this piece of crap in your bedroom?"

Now Callie leaned forward. "Alex is a good man. He was an A student. He's very talented. It was my decision for him to live here. He's just had some bad luck."

"Looks to me like he's fallen into some very good luck. Alex, are you proud of this?"

"I..."

When Alex didn't answer, David took a deep breath. "That's what I thought. Well, I tell you what. Since you two are so in love, I think that you should figure out how to support each other with that love. Callie, either Alex leaves now and never comes back, or I'm not going to send another dime to pay for anything. No school, apartment, or anything. You can't live like a married couple when you're not married, on me."

"So I have to choose between my father and my fiancé?"

"Fiancé?" Sawyer laughed. "When's the wedding? Usually the father of the bride is let in on the details."

Callie turned to Alex. "I know we can do it, somehow. I'll work this summer, and I can probably graduate in three semesters. You can get a job, and then I'll help you finish."

He nodded.

Sawyer felt as if a hole were growing in his chest. "So you're going to pick Alex and poverty over remaining our daughter?"

"It's not my idea. It's yours. I don't want to choose." He noticed a tear in the corner of her eye, but her back was straight.

"I can't have our daughter living unmarried with a man, a man who has no money and no common sense. And you want me to support you?"

"That's enough about Alex, Dad. You don't know him."

Sawyer rose. "I know enough. And I guess I know enough about all of this. Callie, we live by the consequences of our choices. You seem to be making yours. I can't imagine what I'm going to tell your mother. Or your grandmother." He shook his head and looked down as the two young people on the sofa stared back.

Then he turned and left.

Five minutes later he was still sitting in the car just down from Callie's townhouse replaying everything that had just happened. Twice he almost went back inside to plead with Callie, the love of his life after Elizabeth. But he wasn't going to beg. Clearly she was in the wrong. Then the couple came out and turned the other way, walking down the sidewalk hand in hand. He started the car and turned toward the hotel. Even though tomorrow was Saturday, he had a full day of visits scheduled to review several adult movie properties for USNet.

This is insane. My company has helped make our daughter into an amateur porn star, and now she's left us..

7

SATURDAY, APRIL 16TH

Knox spent the weekend at his private compound, built into the side of a wooded hill on a lake far outside the city. Divorced for three decades with no children, Knox's female companionship had consisted of a string of mistresses, the latest of whom he now kept in seclusion at his large home. And his company's constantly revolving talent in California.

But he was pursuing a different passion this Saturday morning.

Concealed in one wing of the home, partially extending into the rock of the hill itself, was a prayer room. Only he had the key and the code to enter. He had spent an hour alone on his face, praying to Allah. Thus cleansed, he rose and walked through a doorway, swinging a heavy metal door shut behind him. The rustic wood paneling hid the lead lining that made this the most secure of all the places from which he could contact the rest of the world.

There were chairs for three people, and all of the usual USNet monitors and equipment. He slid into the chair in front of a unique video conference console. At the appointed time he typed in the numbers and letters from the next one-time code on the pad that he and his fellow believers had exchanged in Paris all those years ago. They had assembled in France at a secret summit called to write The Project, the blueprint for much of what had since occurred. And the code pads which they had exchanged were virtually unbreakable, since each page was used for only one transmission, and then discarded. A moment after accepting the code the screen came to life, and there, in Saudi Arabia, was Saeed Zeini.

Knox smiled and greeted his old friend in Arabic. "You don't look a day older. Only broader."

"May Allah be kind to you as well, Tarik," Saeed replied.

Trevor had not heard his real name spoken by anyone in several years. "He is. He certainly is. How are you?"

"Well. We continue to use the information you send us to amass great wealth and advantage for his purpose. And to 'encourage' others to work with us." He smiled. "Other than to see your face and hear your voice, for what purpose did you wish to speak today?"

Turning serious, Tarik—Trevor—said to his friend, "In line with our strategy in The Project, I think our imams, mullahs and politicians should adopt a conciliatory tone toward the West for several months. I hate these infidels more than you can imagine—I have to live here—and the Easter attack on the church and yesterday's work at the English school were perfect in their messages. So now, as we agreed, we should reduce the violence for a while, and use other means to advance our cause. We will, of course, return to violence again when the opportunities are right. And we are working here to create such an opportunity later this year."

"I understand, but occasionally we also have to remind our own people who the enemy is. And how we will defeat our enemies—even those 'intellectuals' who live among us. Like the ones we crushed a week ago in Iran."

"Yes, but not so powerfully that we provoke the enemy to act against us. Look at France. Sharia Law is now ruling in many areas, and the authorities are afraid to question us. In England there are more mosques than churches. In America we are using 'one man-one vote' to elect our believers in all the large cities. Soon we will have whole towns and several cities' districts where we are the majority of those who vote. And their own educators and media are using 'separation of church and state' to rewrite their history and question their own beliefs. I tell you, Saeed, in just a few years we will control Europe, challenge the Church of England, and rewrite the laws in at least five states to Allah's principles. Just using their own weaknesses against them. I'm here; I know. We will control Europe in one generation, and America in two. Then we can eliminate anyone who disagrees with Allah's truth, wherever they live."

"These are indeed great advances, Tarik, and the funds that Allah and you provide have helped in many ways to accomplish them. Right in line with The Project's goals. But we must keep our own people aware, especially the young. The seduction of the West is powerful. Look at Egypt, Libya, and Iraq. We must whip up hate against the Great Satan to keep them from straying. And continued attacks in America and Europe remind them of the consequences they face if they oppose us."

"Yes. But right now we should pull back for a short time. Some here are starting to realize that Islam is on the rise, as if that were not Allah's plan. They are moving to put Jewish and Christian precepts back into education and even their laws. We have made such progress, and so many non-believers are doing our work for us that I don't want too much violence to awaken our enemy. Next week we have the special election in Tampa, which we've been supporting, for example."

"I understand. I will speak with the others."

"Thank you. Tell them to reduce the attacks for only a few months, and then we will strike again. In fact, I think it is time to rid the world of this female Crusader President. We will talk more about that soon. But for now Allah is delivering our enemies into our hands while they sleep and watch videos."

"I will do as you say"

"Allah is great," Trevor concluded.

That Monday the USNet real estate team was assembled at the home office. After arriving from the West Coast at 5:45 am with three hours sleep, David had driven home, showered, said hello to Elizabeth and Rob, gulped a quick breakfast, and then headed to the office. He made no mention of his meeting with Callie.

"Hey," Kristen said from his office doorway at 8:45, her computer bag over her shoulder.

He smiled. "Hey yourself. I guess I shouldn't feel so bad. I only came from L.A."

"Tell me about it. I actually made it to the ballgame yesterday. Good thing it was a blow-out. I took Terrell Myers from Glenn and Ashworth, and I kept nodding off in the sun and apologizing for falling asleep on his shoulder."

"Sounds exciting."

"Strictly business. Anything to further USNet's relationship with our lead lawyers."

"Your sacrifice is noted."

"See you at ten."

Kristen walked to her office, deposited her bag on the chair, and headed for coffee. After catching up with her colleagues, she returned to her desk and checked her inbox. Full. She quickly went through it, looking for the rare important or personal letter in the midst of all the junk.

She was reviewing the week's to-do list, which she had created on her handheld during the long flight east, when her phone rang.

"Ms. Holloway, hey, this is Davis from USNet News downstairs. There's a piece that just came in on the wire from New York. Some group called Truth in Politics. Never heard of 'em, actually. But, like, hey, anyway, this piece says that Janet Sullivan—you know, the Congresswoman—like, that her husband had an affair a few years ago. And, anyway, I'm calling because it says they have recordings of calls between her husband and this other woman, and it's someone named Kristen Holloway. Isn't that weird? I'm just calling to give you a head's up that you may get some crazy calls today."

"Thanks, Davis. Thank you very much."

"No sweat. Be interesting to know who the real Kristen Holloway is."

"Yes. Yes, it will. Thank you." She hung up.

As soon as she did, the phone rang again. She almost didn't answer, but she noted the area code on the digital read-out and picked it up.

A familiar voice. "Kristen?"

"Yes, Richard."

"I'm glad I caught you. You've been traveling, and I wanted you to know that guy called again. I told him that my wife already knew about the issue, so there was no one to blackmail. He didn't seem to care. I don't know if these people will really do anything, but I wanted you to know."

"They've already done it."

"What?"

"They've just issued a press release in New York. The news desk downstairs just called to warn me about someone with my name in the story. It shouldn't take long for your phone to start ringing, or for them to figure out that I'm the other woman."

"I'm sorry."

Kristen closed her eyes. "Richard, surely, given that there can be no blackmail, this will blow over."

"I hope so. Janet may have to issue a press release...just a minute." There was a long silence, then he came back. "Kristen, I'm sorry. The phones have lit up here at the office, and my assistant needs help."

"It's hard to believe this is happening. Call me when you know more."

"Thanks, Kristen."

She hung up, then whispered a prayer for wisdom and strength.

On the other side of the real estate group, Todd Phelps was going through the same boot-up process in his somewhat smaller office. While waiting for his email to appear, he quietly closed his door and pulled out his cell phone, dialing a number on the Isle of Man that he had been given the previous Thursday, along with his initial account information and passwords.

"Mr. Blevin, good afternoon. It's Todd Phelps."

"Oh, hello Mr. Phelps," came a cheerful reply with a British accent.

After an exchange of pleasantries, Phelps gave the required passwords in the proper sequence for that day of the month. Satisfied, Mr. Blevin said, "The delivery that you expected has been satisfactorily received."

$125,000. Thank you, Mike. No strings. No taxes. And only the first half.

"Thank you, Mr. Blevin. I'll be back in touch in a few weeks with additional instructions."

"Very well, sir. Have a fine week."

"I certainly will. Thank you." He smiled.

A new day is starting for us. Mary is going to be very happy.

As he walked to their conference room, David nodded into the offices of several members of his group as they finished up early Monday phone calls. They gathered and took places in no particular order, except that David sat at the head of the long mahogany table nearest the credenza on which were the coffee service and two boxes of bagels and doughnuts. The latter were a tradition from David's earliest days in the industry. The men were in shirt-sleeves. Everyone had notepads. The view, as usual in good weather, was filled with real estate.

"Good morning. We're obviously handling a lot of projects right now, so let's help each other—brainstorming and questions are, as usual, more than welcome. But we've also got to move along or we'll be here until lunch. Kristen, would you like to start?"

Kristen reported on her trip to Singapore and Seoul, where she found reasonable replacement space for their aborted Hong Kong office. Then she turned to Capital Tower. "I spoke with Bill Porter as I was leaving Singapore, and he said we can expect the owners' decision this week. As you know, we bid significantly more than the asking price, so we certainly should get it."

Kristen then went on to her other projects, and she was followed by her colleagues. When it was Todd Phelps's turn, he described their progress on the successful sale of a surplus warehouse in south Texas, and on an industrial lease in New Jersey.

"In Minneapolis, our evaluation of the proposals offered by Brookglen and Overlook is almost complete. While they are close, it looks like Brookglen is offering us a better product and a better rate. We'll be making the decision next week."

"Just watch out for those guys," offered Chris Grable.

"What do you mean?"

"Well, I heard they promised Data Plus the moon on some suburban Chicago product, but they came in over budget and four months late. It was a disaster."

"That's news to me. Mike Campbell and I went to B-School together. He's assured me that they'll finish on time."

"I'm just letting you know."

"And," Sawyer added, looking at Phelps, "please be sure that you really compare apples to apples, whether Mike's a friend or not. That requirement is date sensitive since we have to move out of other space. So choose Brookglen if they're the best, but don't let your friendship cloud your judgment."

"Absolutely not, David. We'll only choose the best."

"All right, then if that's all from you guys, here are a few words on my deals. In Los Angeles I reviewed properties with brokers and then strategized with our L.A. team over the weekend. We're planning to sell the excess office space but retain the studios and production facilities for long-term capacity. We can expand as our operation grows." He stopped, thinking of Callie. The others were looking at him, waiting for him to finish

"On Moscow, I'm going over next week. Andrei Selivanov has created a website with virtual tours of several spaces. Hopefully, based on his work, I can arrive, choose a space, start the lease process, and get out in four days."

"What is the take on their new President Temirov?" asked Cheryl Miller.

"So far, it seems favorable. Committed to democracy and reform. He apparently spends a lot of time talking about moral rejuvenation, just like President Harper."

"When I was over there last year, " added Todd, "before the election, the people we met with seemed to like him. He says he'll try to reduce taxes and make it easier for people to buy homes and apartments. The Russians have enormous untapped wealth tied up in their apartments."

"Hey, Todd, maybe you should be the Russian President's real estate advisor," chimed in Tom Meadows.

Sawyer smiled with the rest and said, "Well, Temirov was only elected a month ago and already he's announced that he wants to have a summit with Harper this summer. He wants to talk about reviving morality and ethics in both of our countries. Seems like quite a task. How would you even measure reviving morality?" He shook his head.

"There would probably be ways," volunteered Kristen. There was a pause as all eyes turned to her. She smiled. "I don't know. Maybe by measuring divorce, teenage pregnancy, alcoholism, abortions, crime, STDs, the number of new porn movies, strip clubs, even SAT scores and tax audit results. I've never thought about it, but actually there ought to be lots of ways to measure the positive effects of emphasizing basic right and wrong. And with everything going on in Europe, China, the Middle East and Iran, keeping the Russians as friends might be a good idea."

There was silence as they skated out onto the thin ice of values, morality, beliefs—generally taboo subjects in business. Most of them looked down at their hands, not wanting to move out any further on the ice. Finally Sawyer broke the silence.

"Yes, I guess you're right. I hadn't thought about it in that way, either. It's funny that Russia seems always to be under a cloud, yet other countries get away with the same or worse, and no one says anything. So, anyway, those improvements seem to be what Temirov is after, and I guess in President Harper he has a potential ally. Maybe they *will* make some difference, but I wouldn't bet on it. For now, we're there because they have great software people. Anyway, I think that covers my two major projects. Anything else?"

As they rose to go and most of the men headed for seconds at the credenza, Kristen said to David, "Can I see you?"

"Sure."

Five minutes later they were seated at Sawyer's small conference table near the window. Kristen had closed the door. David rubbed his temple. "Do you want some more coffee?"

"I'm fine, thanks. Or at least as good as I'll be for a day or two."

"Yeah. Hey, one good thing about getting older is that jet lag doesn't affect you as much. If you don't sleep anyway, then not sleeping on a plane is about the same as not sleeping at home."

She smiled. "Great. I'll reapply for international work in twenty years. By the way, are there any more details about the school killings in London?"

"Only that the killer was born in England to a family that was originally from Iran." David paused and looked at Kristen, who knew his background. "Does it seem to the rest of the world that everyone with my background—or actually anyone connected in any way to Islam—is capable of such outrageous carnage?"

She shook her head. "Of course not," she answered. "Only a few terrible crazies. I would only add that some groups within Islam do seem to provide a cover under which those few terrible people are able to work. Sort of like what used to happen in the Protestant and Catholic communities in Northern

Ireland until they abandoned revenge—but the Jihadists operate on a much larger and more deadly scale."

He nodded. "I wonder why that is."

"Of course I'm not sure, but it seems like Islam is more than what we normally think of as a religion. It's so much about every aspect of life, like an ideology, that I can understand why some people go overboard."

"But isn't your faith—Christianity—also about every aspect of life?"

"Yes, but I would say more on a personal basis. Not specifically about government and rules on almost everything you can do or think. And not about killing someone if he or she decides to think differently!"

He looked away. "Yes, I guess you're right. I just hate to be even partially painted with that brush because of my family. I don't think of myself as a Muslim or a Christian or anything. I just try to do the right thing."

She smiled. "I know. I need to talk with you about that."

He raised a hand. "You've certainly told me about your faith. I think I understand what you believe. I'm glad it works for you."

She paused, thinking. "I guess Islam has never had anything equivalent to the Reformation. It's as if the old Roman Catholic Church of a thousand years ago were still all powerful, issuing edicts to governments and expecting total submission. In my personal opinion, excesses like that happen whenever the focus shifts from personal faith to 'religion.'"

"I guess I can see that. Hopefully someone or something will help make that shift in Islam. But, anyway, you asked to meet, and I know it wasn't for a comparative religion class. Sorry. But I do appreciate your perspective." He looked at her, as if to give her the floor. *I should talk to Kristen about Callie. They met a few times before Callie went to school. She can probably help me understand what to do next.*

"In five minutes you may want to rethink that, but thank you. David, I'm...I guess I need your help, and I need to tell you something. I suspect it's going to affect my work, at least for a few days or a week."

"What is it, Kristen?"

"You've heard of Congresswoman Janet Sullivan?"

"Yes. One of Harper's strongest supporters. Very smart. Used to work in television, I think. What about her? She's not even from this state."

"Right, on all counts. Well, several years ago..." She looked up at her boss. "I had an affair with her husband, Richard, who is an attorney."

There was silence for a few moments. He leaned forward and wrapped his hands around his mug. "You? Kristen, I never would have imagined."

"I know." She clasped her hands. "I know. Look, it was several years ago. I'm a different person now. The experience changed me. And Richard, too. Neither of us is the same. I almost never talk to him. But..."

She took a deep breath.

"I was a young residential real estate agent on the way up. He was an older attorney with a little gray hair, two teenage children, and a marriage that seemed to be breaking up. I know now that I encouraged him to leave Janet. Thank God he didn't. I was terrible. Richard and I both did terrible things. But that's all behind us. Has been for years. As I said, God changed us, and we're different people from those days, but I don't imagine that the press will understand that."

Sawyer couldn't help thinking of Callie. Finally, he asked, "What do you mean, 'the press'?"

Kristen moved in her chair and brushed back her auburn hair with her hand. "Someone telephoned Richard just before my trip and threatened to expose our affair unless he persuaded his wife to vote against Harper's media bill. The one that would restrict adult movies, like we make." She paused. "Richard called to warn me. He couldn't be blackmailed, because he and I met with Janet a year after the affair, confessed what we had done, and asked for her forgiveness. But now, today, I guess to try to discredit anyone associated with the President and this proposal, they've put out a press release through some group in New York. So, I guess this is their follow-through on the threat. It might turn into a media circus. He's already getting calls. I expect that I will. David, I'm sorry. I guess it might get a little crazy for the next few days, so I thought you ought to know."

"It's just so hard to imagine you, Kristen. You're so...so..."

"I know. Think how I feel. Everything I now know to be true about life and my faith is instantly trashed by my past. This may hurt a lot of people, starting of course with Janet, their kids, my friends, our department, President Harper, maybe even the bill she's trying to pass." She looked down, her shoulders slumping. "It's hard to realize all the repercussions we cause others by what we do."

"What would you like me to do?"

She looked up. "I'm not sure, David. I've never been here before. I'm embarrassed. I'm going to get phone calls that I don't want. You may get some. So I don't know. Maybe just some understanding and some slack for now to help me get through this. I love what we do, and with so much on our plate right now, I've even managed to let *you* down. "

David remained silent when she finished. *My daughter. Now my best exec.* Finally he spoke. "Kristen, of course. Take as much time as you need."

She broke into a small smile, her hands together in front of her on the table. "Thank you."

There was a knock at the door and David's assistant opened it, taking a step inside.

"Your voice mailbox is full, and Mr. Burke says that he needs to talk with you about a personnel matter. And, Kristen, Trish tells me that you have a lot of phone calls as well." She waited.

"OK," David said, rising. "I'll call Paul. Kristen we'll just do our best to get through the next few days."

She stood and pushed her chair back under the table. "Thanks. I'll stay on top of Porter and the other deals." She nodded to his assistant on her way out, hearing the phone ring in her office as soon as she was in the hallway.

At Zhukovo Airport on the east of Moscow, where NovySvet maintained a large facility, Simon North had completed the acquisition of the company the previous afternoon. Retired General Yevgany Beleborodov, the director of NovySvet, was now, thanks to North, a rich man. Today the two former generals from opposing cold war forces had flown together an hour further east, where they stood on a high bluff overlooking a wide, almost treeless valley in which the snow had melted but no plants yet bloomed. Each wore a heavy coat against the late afternoon chill.

They were actually on a covered platform built on the edge of the bluff, and ringing the platform were monitors and communication devices, manned by several NovySvet employees. They could simultaneously view whatever was happening in the valley through binoculars or watch close-up on the monitors.

As they stood looking out over the valley, Beleborodov spoke. "As you know, the key breakthroughs in this technology will be the use of multiple satellites, both stationary and low earth orbit, to illuminate the target. We have the one in orbit now, launched by the Russian government for a fee that we paid. They think it is a communication satellite—which it is—but they don't know about its other capability. This satellite has our encrypted sequencing, which makes detection almost impossible, even as the target moves. You have seen the videos, but now you will see it in action." He pointed to the valley and nodded to the men behind the monitors.

With their binoculars they could see a soldier on a dirt road in the valley, carrying what appeared to be a pistol connected by a cable to his backpack.

Around him were both vehicles and the charred remains of past targets on what was clearly a large firing range.

"In rapid sequence our soldier will illuminate the brick wall you see to his left and the unmanned automobile to his right. In this monitor you can see what he sees on the ground."

"The soldier assigns a unique ascending identifier to each target just before he illuminates it. His backpack transmits the encoded identifier at the same instant the pistol illuminates the target. Every time the pistol 'fires,' the specific light frequency transmitted to the closest satellite is slightly different."

The soldier dropped to one knee and fired the laser. Although there was no visible light or noise, a number instantly appeared in the upper right corner of the screen. "The wall has been assigned that discreet targeting number."

As the soldier repeated his firing sequence for the auto, Beloborodov turned to North, gesturing upward with his right hand, speaking in clear but accented English. "Just as we instantly receive the target identifier here, so does the satellite. It uses GPS to fix the position, and the target is locked on."

At that moment the automobile started to move, guided by remote control.

"A target is identified only once. It is thereafter illuminated continuously by a random sequence of low power laser shots from the satellite. With your funding, once we have more satellites in place, the illumination will sequence between them in a random pattern set by that hour's encryption key, and we will be able to track faster moving targets, like airplanes. And it will be almost impossible for a defender to lock onto the source of the illumination. The result"—he gestured for North to use his binoculars—"is almost continuous illumination, as the target moves its position is constantly updated."

They watched as the auto began driving up the valley on a dirt road, and the soldier was no longer visible.

"In a weapons-free environment," continued General Beleborodov, "the unique target numbers can be assigned automatically to the best offensive assets. They could be cruise or ballistic missiles launched from hundreds or thousands of kilometers away. Today we will simulate that environment with two short range, shoulder launched missiles from over that hill. Each one has now been assigned one of the target numbers. We should see results any moment now." He smiled again as he raised his binoculars.

North followed, choosing to focus on the auto. He watched for a few moments as the vehicle propelled itself up the dirt road, undulating with the terrain. There was a sudden orange flash in his binoculars as the auto disappeared. He looked out and saw a simultaneous flash destroy the wall. Only after the flashes did they hear the sound of the incoming missiles.

Now it was North's turn to smile. "Impressive, general, very impressive. Tell me, is there any time limit for when an attack has to be launched, once a target is designated?"

"Theoretically, no. So long as there are satellites orbiting overhead with our illuminators onboard, logged into our system—which should be possible in two years with your help—one could theoretically illuminate a target one day and not actually fire on it for several days."

"Can a target tell that it is being illuminated?"

"Eventually of course there will be countermeasures. We're working on them ourselves. But for now only the initial illumination from the first source carries enough power to be detected. By interfacing through GPS, the ongoing illuminations are aimed, knowing within a few meters exactly where to look. This only requires relatively low power. For that reason, and the changing frequencies, illumination is hard to detect."

"Excellent. So, one could 'tag' a moving target in one place and then, as long as a suitable missile was in range, fire on it much later, in a completely different location?"

"Yes. Impressive, isn't it, sir?"

"Indeed. I think we have made a wise investment in NovySvet. My congratulations to you and your staff, General Beleborodov."

"Thank you, Mr. North. Now, if you don't mind, I hope that you will join me and our officers for a small party at our base *banya* before your trip back to London. I think you will find the experience to be quite invigorating and healthful." He winked.

"It will be difficult to be more invigorating than the last thirty minutes, general," replied North, "but I've always wanted to try a real Russian *banya*, and I can't think of a better time or place."

"Excellent, excellent. Let us return to our car for the short drive. And once we are there, I have some ideas on how to improve beyond what you have seen today. We will discuss them while we relax."

"And there is some new German laser-splitting technology developed by A.G. Thelkein that we just found out about, and we want to share it with you."

"Really? I've heard rumors. How did you find out about it?"

North smiled. In fact, he did not know the answer any more than he knew for whom he had just purchased NovySvet. All his engagements with this client were done with untraceable messages and codes. But the money was always good. "That doesn't matter. The main thing is that we know the results from their latest tests, along with the compounds they have used, and we will give them to you."

Opening the door to the Mercedes for his new boss, General Beleborodov said, "This will be very good, our working together."

"Yes, exactly," North agreed.

Two hours later Kristen sat alone in her office, her door closed. She had spent much of the morning responding to her colleagues as each of them heard some portion of the news and came to see her. Todd, Cheryl, Chris...each in turn. She imagined what they were saying in the real estate group—indeed, throughout USNet—as she finished her report on office space in the Far East, left Bill Porter a voicemail, and shuffled the paperwork on several other projects.

She had declined any comment to Sam Bartholomew, one of USNet's on-the-air reporters, who had interviewed a Ms. Amanda Martin-Davis of the group Truth In Politics. The interview, slotted for the second segment of the Noon News, was just beginning, and Kristen was watching on her computer.

"As you know," Ms. Martin-Davis began on screen, "Truth In Politics, as a public service, searches out untruths and hypocrisy in the public square. Over the weekend one of our supporters sent us tape recordings captured from several cell phone conversations between Janet Sullivan's husband, Richard, and another woman, which clearly shows that they were having an affair. This from the husband of a woman who pushes 'family values'"—Martin-Davis made quotation marks with her fingers—"and wants the rest of us to live by her own narrow definition of morality."

The camera came back to Sam Bartholomew. "We have a portion of one cell phone conversation." Kristen felt her stomach tighten. As the audio played, the transcribed words were simultaneously printed on the screen over a still picture of Richard Sullivan appearing to be leaving a church with his wife, a Bible in his hand.

"Richard, how did you like lunch today?"

In her office, Kristen gasped at the sound of her own voice, all those years ago.

"It was awesome." He laughed.

"What about the new sheets?"

"All the better for the main course."

She laughed. "Do you have to go back to the office?"

"Hey, I just left your parking deck. Give a guy some time to regroup."

"All right. But what about Thursday? And when are you going to tell Janet that you're through?"

"Thursday is definite. You know the other is more difficult. We'll talk about it then."

"All right. But I hate sharing you."

As she listened to the tape, tears flowed down Kristen's cheeks. She blotted them with her handkerchief, trying not to smear her make-up.

"OK. We'll talk. So, go sell some real estate, and I'll see you in two days."

"Bye. I love you."

"See you then."

The camera came back to Ms. Martin-Davis. "As you can hear, we think it is ridiculous for Janet Sullivan, or anyone else in Congress for that matter, to be telling the American people how they ought to live their lives."

"Ms. Martin-Davis," said Sam from a small insert superimposed next to her, "how exactly did you come by this tape? Is it recent?"

"Our supporter is a technical person who has apparently been scanning cell channels for years and only recently realized what he had. And, no, it's from several years ago. But that doesn't make any difference since Sullivan, President Harper and others are trying to tell us that there are 'eternal truths' on how to behave."

"USNet has, by the way," said the reporter, "matched the voice print to be that of Richard Sullivan, a well-known attorney, and we've tried today to contact him and Congresswoman Sullivan. Neither has yet responded to our calls. We should also say that the woman on this and other tapes released today by Truth In Politics is Ms. Kristen Holloway, who, ironically, now works in the real estate group here at USNet. Thank you Ms. Martin-Davis."

As the news program cut to a commercial, Kristen moved the mouse on her desk and closed her computer. She sat alone for several minutes. *Everyone in the department and everyone I know will have seen that report, or its repeats during the afternoon. And my dad. I've tried to do everything so differently since those days.* She closed her eyes, the tears coming again. She wanted to talk with Richard but knew that she should not initiate the call. She prayed for strength and wisdom.

Todd Phelps had just finished watching the same interview in his office when his phone rang.

"Hey, Todd, it's Mike. What's up?"

Todd smiled. "Not much."

"Say, do you know this Kristen Holloway woman, the one that's been sleeping with the Congresswoman's husband?"

"Well, yeah. Sure. She's right here in our department."

"Really? Hey, what's she like? Have you been getting any?"

Todd shook his head. "No. No. She's good looking, even hot. But I mean, you would *never* have imagined if you knew her. Never."

"Really? Well, bring her up to Minneapolis on your next inspection, and we'll see about it. Don't hide assets like that from your friends!"

He smiled again. "OK. But, I promise, Kristen is not what you'd think from that story. It might be nice if she were."

"Well, listen, did you get the package we sent to the islands?"

"Yes, thank you. It arrived in good shape."

"Everything all right?"

"Yes, as far as I can tell. But, listen, what about the overruns in Chicago on that project you did for Data Plus?"

"Not our fault. The city issued the drainage permits and then revoked them for three months to study the site again. In the end they didn't change a thing. Insane. We couldn't help it."

"Well, just be sure this one goes OK."

"It will. No sweat. Hey, we'll see you soon. And give that Kristen a squeeze from all of us."

Kristen checked her face in the compact a final time, then opened the door of her office. Her assistant, Trish, looked up from her work station and smiled. She stood and hugged her boss. Kristen whispered, "Thank you." As she backed away, Trish handed her a fistful of message slips.

"I figure you need something to do." Trish smiled.

Kristen felt that everyone in the office was looking at her, but she took a deep breath, nodded to Trish, and started toward David's office. As she walked, she leafed through the stack in her hand and noticed a message from Bill Porter.

She knocked on David's open door. He looked up. "Can I buy you a sandwich?" she asked.

"How about a drink?" he replied. They both smiled. "Actually, I have to meet a broker at Foster's with a possible tenant for our Channing Green space. But thanks. I saw the interview. I'm sorry, particularly for the tape and all of that personal stuff. It was tough."

She looked down. "Yes, it was. I saw it, too. But, like I said, we don't often think through what we're doing, especially when we're told that if it feels good we should do it. They leave out the consequences part."

"Kristen, you're one of the best people and best real estate executives I've ever known. I'm sure this will blow over."

She nodded. "Thanks. I feel like I've let everyone down."

"We'll make it." He paused. "I've got a phone slip from Bill Porter. I hope it's about Capital Tower and not this mess. Shall we call him?"

"Yes." He moved the phone. Standing in front of the desk, Kristen pushed the button for the speaker and dialed the number.

Porter came on the line and, after some pleasantries with Sawyer, Porter said, "David, I don't enjoy telling you this, but your offer was not the highest. It was beaten by another buyer."

Kristen had been silent while the two men talked, but now her eyes narrowed, and she slowly shook her head. "Bill, this is Kristen. Listening to you, it just doesn't make sense. Do you or your firm have any connection to the winning bid?"

"The money is foreign."

"Fine. But do you or your firm have any connection to the buyer?"

"Kristen, I can't tell you who the buyer is. I signed a non-disclosure agreement."

"I'm not asking you to tell us who the buyer is. We just want you to confirm who the buyer isn't."

"I can't say."

"Sure you can. Just confirm that it's not you. If you don't, then we must assume that you *are* either the buyer or part of the buying group."

"Assume what you want. We have several subsidiaries under our umbrella here. One is in development. I just can't say."

Rising from his seat and leaning over the speaker phone, David injected, "But, Bill, you are the *marketing* agent. You saw all the offers, including ours. You could simply bid more. That is clearly unethical."

"Even if what you say were true, my job is to get the best price for the seller."

Kristen added, "But not by misrepresenting your role as both an agent and principal."

"Think what you want, Kristen. I'm not saying anything more until after the due diligence period."

"Bill, if this is true, we will be *really* upset. And I'm sure it's illegal, too."

"Hey, looking at this morning's news, you're in no position to judge anyone."

Kristen turned in her chair and looked out the window.

David spoke. "That has nothing to do with this. Bill, one last time, are you the buyer or part of the buying group?"

"No comment."

"Then we'll have to alert our attorney."

"Go ahead, Sawyer. I've got nothing to hide. I did the best possible for my client. Sue me if that's what you want."

"It's not what I want. But I also want to know that the broker with whom I'm negotiating all the details of my offer is not also a competitor."

"Get a life. This is business."

"Thanks, Bill. You've clearly been a great help."

"Go to hell, Sawyer. Sorry, Kristen. Good luck to both of you." The line went dead.

Kristen, still facing away, said in a whisper, "It's been a great morning." She turned to him. "I've always said that Bill doesn't miss any chance to look out for Bill. I hate to be cheated out of that building."

"I'll call Terrell at Glenn and Ashworth and tell him what we think has happened. Hopefully he can propose a solution."

"That combination is so perfect for our headquarters. It was a great idea, David. I'm sorry if I botched it."

"You didn't botch it, Kristen. As you said, it looks like Porter literally stole it from us by bidding more than we did, once he knew our offer."

"Well, on that note I'll have a sandwich with Todd and some of the guys"

"I'll find out what we can do about Porter. Now I've got to update Knox and Burke on all of this."

"Thanks, David."

Pavel Sivyakov had been sitting at the kitchen table in their one bedroom apartment in Arzamas 23, a "closed city" 500 km southwest of Moscow, for almost thirty minutes. His wife and baby daughter were asleep. He nervously strummed the table and sipped his beer. The caller was late.

When his cell phone rang, he jumped. The caller did not introduce himself, but said, "I understand that you have a special product for sale."

Pavel started to speak, turned the phone away, cleared his voice, and began again. "Yes. Three GoFor prototypes. They are copies of the American

Tomahawk Block IV cruise missile. Plus one mobile ground launcher which carries all of them."

"What is the range?"

"1,800 kilometers."

"How did you acquire them?"

"I work at the factory where we make them, and these were declared 'defective' by my friend and supervisor, Dmitri. We were supposed to destroy them, and the paperwork says that we did."

"But they are operational?"

"They are perfect."

"How much?"

"Five million dollars, including the launcher. Cash"

"We'll take them."

Pavel smiled for the first time. "How shall we do it?"

"Where are they?"

"In the launcher. In a warehouse. We have welded sides to the launcher to disguise it as a long-haul lorry. It looks just like a thousand other trucks."

"OK. I will call you back at the same time tomorrow."

"Good."

The line went dead. Pavel took a pull on his beer, then opened the refrigerator to get another.

Less than a minute later, their conversation came up on an RTI screen.

Callie unlocked their apartment door and was surprised to see it as she had left it that morning. She put her book bag and laptop on the breakfast room table and went upstairs to their bedroom. Alex was still in bed.

"You had an interview this morning," she said in a loud voice, shaking his foot.

"What? Oh." He pulled the pillow from over his head and rolled over. "I must have gone back to sleep."

"Great. How are we going to make it if you don't get a job?"

He propped up on one elbow, looked at the clock, and rubbed his face. "I'm sorry. I'll call'em."

She sat on the bed, looking out the window. "I was coming home to tell you that my Uncle Reza said that I could work ten hours a week in his real estate office. He's always seemed kind of stern and mean, actually, but if he'll give me a job, I'll take it. They'll pay me to do filing and help organize stuff on their system. His son, Yusef—we used to call him Joseph, but he changed it—

is a few years older than me. He's been back from the Army a couple of years, and doing pretty well in the business. My uncle said that I can shadow Yusef one day a week and learn all about residential real estate." She turned to him. "I figure in California, that's a good business to be in."

"Yeah. That's great."

"But I can't go to school full time and work at my uncle's office while you do nothing. Since you're not in school now, Alex, you've got to get a job."

"I know. I will. I'll call them in a few minutes."

"And we really don't have the money to buy booze and pills."

"They're not much, and they make us feel good." He picked up a pill bottle from the table and shook it, moving towards her. "You like them as much as I do."

She smiled but moved away. "Not now. Maybe on the weekends. But first we have to pay the rent."

"We will. Don't worry. We will. And I've got a plan to get some money."

"What is it?"

"Give me a couple of days."

She turned her head slightly. "It better be legal."

He nodded. "It is. Trust me. A couple of days."

After lunch David had finished his report on the Los Angeles studios and gave Paul Burke an impromptu briefing on the project, as well as on Kristen's situation and Bill Porter's seeming theft of their purchase. Burke concurred that they should seek legal advice.

Other than a gulped breakfast that morning, David had not seen Elizabeth or Rob since the previous Tuesday, before his trip to Los Angeles, so he was glad to pack his laptop at five o'clock and head home early.

"Hi, again." He smiled as he came in the kitchen door.

Elizabeth put the day's mail on the center island and returned his smile. "Hi yourself. Do you live here?"

He stepped over and hugged her tightly. "I think so. At least I have some vague recollection. This time, though, I hope to spend a little more time. Maybe even chew my food."

"Good, because we're having steak on the grill. You're cooking."

He leaned back. "Sounds superb. Where's Rob?"

She glanced upstairs and frowned. "Where else?"

"Did I ever tell you that you're beautiful?"

"Only after long trips."

'Come on." He smiled. "You know I'm better than that. You're *always* beautiful." He walked to the refrigerator. "How did Rob do on his European history test?"

"He barely passed. Don't you think we should...?"

David raised his hand. "Yes, but later. Let me change clothes and start the grill. Then we can talk. OK?"

She smiled. "Sure." Then her expression changed. "What is all this news about Kristen Holloway and some Congresswoman's husband?"

"Soon," he said, as he walked toward their bedroom.

Twenty minutes later they were seated next to each other on their outdoor patio, the spring evening inviting them outside with the fragrances of dogwood and azaleas, and a hint of warmer days to come. David had changed into khaki pants and a knit shirt.

"I had no idea when I left this morning that we would spend much of the day on Kristen's affair with Richard Sullivan."

David told Elizabeth as much as he knew about Kristen's history. "How would you react to the news if you were Janet Sullivan?" he asked her.

"I'd probably kill Kristen. And of course my husband. Can wives get away with that in Iran today? Or would the next woman just move in as a younger wife, sort of a relief pitcher for the husband's later innings?" Elizabeth smiled, and he grimaced.

"Maybe we should move over there and take up baseball. Sounds interesting."

"No thanks. Team building has its limits, and I draw the line at the front door. Anyway," she went on, turning serious, "it was those *tapes* they're playing every hour on the news. It would be bad enough to find out that your husband had been having an affair, even years ago. But when I heard those taped conversations today, it was like 'now', you know? The two of them sounded so happy. That would *really* hurt." She took a sip from her glass and set it down on the armrest of her chair. "Especially after all the things Janet Sullivan has said about morality and the family."

David turned to his wife. "Kristen says that all three of them have changed. And that Janet forgave them several years ago."

Elizabeth paused then said more slowly. "Is that possible? Do you think that people can really change?"

"I didn't know her then, but she seems completely different from the voice on those tapes."

"How does someone change that much?"

He shrugged. "I don't know. In Kristen's case, I think it's her faith."

"Hmm. We don't do much in that area, do we?"

David was silent.

"Sally Schofield at work invited me to a Bible study at her home next week," she continued, "and I thought I might go. Just to get back in touch. I like some of the other women. What do you think?"

David took a sip of his drink and looked out across the backyard. "That would be fine. Why not?" He took a deep breath. "Now, I have some news closer to home that's not good." He told her about his meeting with Callie and Alex, and about their living arrangement. He did not mention their internet posting. As Elizabeth's face registered her dismay, he ended with "Did you have any idea that they were living together?"

"No. I knew she was excited about him and wanted us to meet him, but not that they were living together."

"Well, they are. And I told her that we could not support her if that is her choice."

"You mean, cut her off financially?"

"Yes, and in every other way."

"Wait. She's our daughter. We shouldn't just abandon her."

"She has abandoned us. It's clear. She has chosen Alex over us."

Elizabeth was silent for a moment. "David, this isn't the Middle East."

He turned to her. "I was waiting for that. Elizabeth, I grew up in a nominally Muslim home, but today I'm about as Muslim as you are Christian. This isn't about geography, politics or religion. It's about family and the consequences of bad choices. Plenty of American Christians and Jews would do the same thing. I'm not going to have her stoned. I do love her and want her back. But not with that creep. And, by the way, she runs a good chance of dishonoring our family. What if someone told my mother? *Callie* has chosen this course, not us."

"But it sounds like you made it a choice between him and us."

"How can we send money, when we're also trying so hard to pay off our debt, to support this outrageous behavior?"

Elizabeth paused again. "I hate what you've told me. But it's not fair to mix Callie's education and the bad investments we made."

He started to speak, but she raised a hand. "Let's not talk about our debt right now, David. It will be there, but Callie may not be. And think about it. Doesn't similar outrageous behavior help support us?"

"What do you mean?"

"Didn't you say that you were just out looking at adult movie studios, and isn't USNet into video sites, X-rated television, internet gambling—all that?"

"That's business. Callie is our family."

"Yes. But we, in essence, live off other people's less than perfect behavior. Maybe we should try to understand Callie and keep talking."

"What other people may do is not our business. But Callie and Rob are. And I'm glad to keep talking—but she has to dump Alex. That's the choice she has."

"Parents or boyfriend."

"Yes. And please don't call her."

"What?"

"I've given her a choice, and I want her to understand it. Things are not the same. We can't give in."

"I can't talk to Callie?"

"Not for a while. She has to feel the difference, and we have to be united on this."

"You didn't ask me."

"You weren't there. It just came out of the conversation. But now we have to stick by it."

"Or what?"

"Or she'll continue to use us to support a boy and a life-style that go against everything I believe in."

"I understand your anger, but where did the 'belief' suddenly come from?"

He paused. "I'm not sure. But you know what I mean. Basic right and wrong. Growing up in a church in the South someone must have told you that it's wrong for unmarried people to live together. And I think it says somewhere that you're supposed to honor your father and your mother, not take their money and live with your boyfriend."

"I don't think living together was a major topic then. But they did mention the back seats of cars." She was silent for a while. "OK, I get it. I'll go along for a while, but I'm not agreeing to cut Callie off forever. She means too much to me—to us. At some point I'm going to call her and talk about all this. She needs us."

The sound of children playing outside two houses away punctuated the silence.

He turned to her. "You know I don't want there to be problems. Rob is just going through a phase. Hopefully Callie will figure it out soon about Alex. I just want you and them to be happy."

"Hmm. I'm pretty happy, or I was until this conversation. I'll give Callie a week to think about what you said, but then I'm going to call her. She's our daughter."

"If you have to."

"I do."

"Hey, the grill should be hot enough now for the steaks. How are the potatoes doing?"

"Wait about ten minutes. I almost hate to ask, but did anything else happen today?"

"Yes, as usual, given all our projects. But one thing just blows my mind." He gave her a summary of the Capital Tower situation with Bill Porter.

When he finished, she asked, "What will Trevor Knox think? I bet he'll be angry."

"He's due back from Mexico tomorrow. I've briefed Paul, and tomorrow we'll have a real estate meeting with Trevor. He doesn't like to lose, particularly to a rigged deal. He will *not* be pleased."

There was a loud crash upstairs. The first time it had happened, months earlier, they had rushed to find the problem; now it happened frequently enough that they were no longer concerned. Rob became so involved in his virtual reality games that he would contort himself into difficult positions to "fire" around virtual rocks or to hide in difficult spots. So occasionally he simply slipped and fell on his virtual reality floor plate, usually with a crash because he protected his equipment.

"He's going to break a bone," Elizabeth muttered, looking up at his window. David shook his head and took another sip. She continued, "Actually, I think he's already broken something, but not a bone. David, Rob is 'off' somewhere. I mean really, and I mean almost all the time. No, listen, it's not just a 'stage'. Even when he's unplugged from that stuff, you can tell that he's thinking about it. He can't wait to get back to it. It's taken over his life. Look at his grades. Look at us. We never see him except when he passes through and occasionally eats. David, it's not right. We need to unplug that equipment and get rid of it!"

"Elizabeth, I'm concerned, too. But we've got cutting edge equipment that cost a lot of money. There must be another way. Maybe we can limit his hours."

"Fine," she said with an edge to her voice. "Do it. I don't see how we'll enforce it. But we've got to do something. If Callie is going to have to live with consequences for her bad choices, then Rob needs them, too. We're losing Rob to all that 'stuff'. I'm *very* serious. We have no idea what else he sees or does on the internet. It scares me."

"OK. I'll think about a solution."

She touched the armrest with her index finger. "David, I..."

He raised his hand. "Really. I understand."

She stopped and looked at him. "All right. But, this is not good. I want you to talk to him."

"I will. I promise."

8

TUESDAY, APRIL 19TH

Trevor Knox was at the console at the front of the cabin in his corporate jet as he re-crossed the Atlantic from a USNet Europe meeting early the next Tuesday morning. He had read through his RTI messages via encrypted satellite link. Using a headset to reduce the airplane noise, he was talking on the secure radio/video link to Akbar Kamali.

"Akbar, the demonstration of the NovySvet technology as reported by Simon North exceeded my expectation. They have the nucleus of an incredible weapons system which in a year or two can be deployed against targets anywhere in the world. "

Kamali nodded on the screen. "And we may have a lead on a cruise missile in Russia."

"Yes, I saw that in the messages. How good that would be, with NovySvet right there."

"We will figure out who is involved."

Knox continued, "Also, we should move to purchase the controlling interest in Ezon Communications. Send an email to Cleve Danforth to set up a meeting with them tomorrow to explore our purchase. Of course Cleve won't know what we know about their problems, but eventually we'll offer to cover the undisclosed 'accounting irregularities' in their CFO's emails."

Kamali smiled. "Cleve must be happy with his success each time he gets an email from his special anonymous client that sends him to negotiate with a company that's not even for sale, and he walks away controlling the board. He probably thinks he's an incredible negotiator."

"He is. But our extra information certainly gets him to the right targets." Knox put down one note, picked up another and tapped the desk with his gold pen. "Let me ask you about our campaign against President Harper. It looks like Senator Pritchard is ready to take a fall with those gambling payoffs. And you have ten other congressmen and senators on Harper's team ready for surprises this week. But what about this Sullivan situation? How could you have missed that the woman her husband was seeing now works for us?"

Knox could see Kamali grimace. "There is no good explanation, other than we just missed it. We were focused on Richard Sullivan and the affair he had several years ago, not on the other woman."

"But a simple check would have told you." The plane banked slightly to the left.

"I know. Sometimes we just have too much information to sort through. We have the ability to check virtually everything about everyone for the past fifteen years. The problem is, where do we stop? In this case, we knew we had them on the old cell phone intercepts, and we knew it would embarrass the Congresswoman, so we stopped there and moved on to others."

"Well, it's embarrassing to have USNet even tangentially in a story like this, since we work so hard to keep RTI separated. You should search all of these upcoming revelations for any connections to us."

"Yes. The woman, Kristen Holloway, is in real estate. We'll focus the media through our usual sources on the Sullivans, and away from the Holloway woman."

"Good. I think that's it. And you're probably right that we need to expand the number of duty officers. There *is* a lot of information flowing through our system now, and we don't want to miss anything important. You and Victor should start putting together a list of people with the motivations we need as duty officers. I'll take a look when you're ready. And now I'll try to get a little rest before we land."

"Yes. Good night, sir."

Knox turned off and locked the console, then swiveled in his chair and pushed buttons that turned it into a comfortable recliner. He noted the time and thought through his meetings scheduled for Tuesday, then dropped off to sleep.

That Tuesday morning David was behind his desk preparing the real estate briefing for Trevor Knox and Paul Burke, scheduled for right after lunch.

As he finished reviewing the agenda for their meeting, David glanced over to his credenza at the picture of Elizabeth and their children taken two years earlier. He placed the agenda in his outbox and took out a legal pad. At the top of two pages he wrote, "Callie", then "Rob". Below each name, as appropriate, he wrote "Alex, Money, Porn, Drugs, Sex, Internet, Bad grades and Other?"

On each page he wrote "Solutions and Action Steps." He looked at the pages on his desk, pen in hand, ready to create a plan of action to help each child, just as he did with business issues. He was still staring at them when the phone rang. "Mr. Sawyer, it's Phyllis Jordan. Mr. Knox has had to change his schedule and wonders if you can do the real estate briefing at twelve instead of two?"

"Sure, Phyllis. We're almost ready."

"Thank you."

He pushed the pages together and started to throw them away. But instead he opened a desk drawer and put them in a file marked "Personal." He closed the drawer and turned his attention back to their meeting.

An hour later he and Paul Burke took seats at Knox's conference table.

"Thanks for changing the time, gentlemen. I find that I have to leave for Brazil this afternoon. David, I know we have a lot going on, but can you keep it to fifteen minutes today? Hopefully we'll have more time next week."

"Sure. I'll hit the high points." He passed copies of the agenda to the two men and began working his way down the list.

Ten minutes later he was on the next to last subject, Capital Tower. He explained that it appeared that the listing agent bettered their offer by a small percent after reviewing all of the other bids.

"Who is the marketing agent?" Knox asked, pulling out his pen.

"Bill Porter."

"Give me a sense of the magnitude of what he is doing to us, assuming this is true."

"If we could borrow virtually all of the purchase price, which is below replacement cost, at today's low rates, and values continue to increase downtown as they have for the past two years, the difference to us over a typical ten year hold could exceed fifty million."

"You mean this guy is going to steal the building and fifty million from us, and we're just going to let him do it?" Knox asked, his voice rising, the pen pointing.

"No, not at all," Sawyer replied. "I'm meeting at four today with our attorneys, and we'll figure out a course of action."

"Fine. But keep me informed. Send me an email after your meeting. I hate losing, and particularly to a thief."

"I will. Now, our last subject is Los Angeles. Here is a separate report I prepared after touring the target facilities with local agents. Paul, it gives you an idea of the values that we assign to the real estate in each company, and whether we recommend to use or sell each facility."

Knox and Burke looked at the package Sawyer handed them. It contained a summary by company, with pictures and maps of each facility and its probable value.

"This looks quite comprehensive, David. Thank you. I'll read it on the way to Brazil and get back to you. Paul, this should be a big help with your financial analysis."

The agenda had been covered, and the meeting was coming to an end. David's stomach turned, and, thinking of Callie, he said, "Trevor, about Los Angeles. The company's strategy for XXXtra Cinema. Is it to grow that operation?"

Knox, who had been making a neat stack of his papers, stopped, looked puzzled, and asked, "Why wouldn't we, David? It's enormously profitable."

"I know. But, well, I'm just not sure that these movies are the best use of our money and our people."

Knox smiled. "David, as you've just seen, the people at XXXtra Cinema are a group unto themselves. Other than the kind of planning you're doing with them right now, they stand alone. If most of them weren't doing that stuff with us, they'd be doing it with someone else. That's the kind of people they are." Knox smiled, but Sawyer did not respond.

"And as for our money, what else has both the current returns we're seeing there and the opportunity for almost unlimited growth? What those folks do is a *very* common language." He and Burke chuckled, and David nodded. "So what's the problem?"

David was silent as he stood and finally shrugged a bit. "I don't know. You and I are both from traditional Muslim backgrounds, and while I understand our legal rights, I'm just not sure that pornographic movies are the image that's best for USNet."

"David, this is America. Americans want these movies, and making money is a *great* image for USNet. And most people don't link us to our movie subsidiary. Anyway, American law says that they're not pornography. They're *adult movies*. They're art. Protected by the Constitution. Surely you haven't been listening to the lies that our esteemed President makes up about our industry. Trust me, David, these movies are great for America."

Picking up his papers, David retreated. "OK. I just thought I'd ask. Have a good trip to Brazil, and I'll email you about Porter later this afternoon."

After his meeting with their attorneys on the Porter situation, David was still playing catch-up from his trip to L.A. Somehow he had to get it all done, *and* prepare for Moscow. Meanwhile, it would be another "dinner is in the oven" evening for him, and dark when he got home. He had left a voicemail for Elizabeth, letting her know that he would be home late. *Callie and Rob* had been jumping into his mind all afternoon, and he pushed deeper into his work in order to block out thoughts of them.

As he finished a review of the space they were about to lease in London, his phone rang. Kristen's cell phone.

"David. Hi. I'm meeting a cabinet installer at my apartment this afternoon. Any word on Porter?"

"I'm about to write an email to Knox and Burke, whom I briefed earlier, and I'll copy you. Other than having Terrell call and generally threaten Porter with legal action, there doesn't appear to be much we can do."

"Not what we hoped. Well, OK. I'll see you tomorrow."

"Have a good evening."

FOR IMMEDIATE RELEASE

Tampa, FL (USNet). April 19. In a stunning upset, Hassan Farrahi won Tuesday's special election and becomes the first practicing Muslim to win a seat on Tampa's City Council as the new representative for District 8.

"This election proves that the American Dream is alive and well for everyone," Farrahi said tonight in his acceptance speech. "We must all come together as Americans, whatever our backgrounds or faiths. I will serve my district, but I will also serve all of the people of this great city, and of this great country."

Farrahi, born in Iran, has lived in Tampa since childhood and was an honors graduate of the University of Central Florida. For the past ten years Farrahi has been a community organizer in the growing, predominantly Muslim sections of Tampa. Known for his work to improve the school system, Farrahi narrowly defeated Frazier Morris, a businessman who campaigned primarily for fiscal responsibility.

Farrahi will be sworn in at next week's city council meeting.

9

David received an email that morning from an unknown sender. It simply read, "Call your cousin."

So just before leaving his office for lunch, he picked up his cell phone and dialed a new number in Estonia, and a moment later he heard Omid's phone ringing in Tehran.

"Omid, hey. It's David."

"Hello, Cousin!" came the joyful reply. "How are you?"

"We're fine, thanks. How's the family?"

"Goli and I are well. We just got back to our apartment after work. A lot of new orders for translations, I'm glad to say."

"Good. How about our business?"

"That's why I wanted you to call, so I can thank you. The new sites are working well, and they seem to be secure. We can tell that my uncle has been pinging, trying to hack in and close us down. But Abigail has given us some strong defenses."

"Great. How about the gifts we sent?"

"Excellent. Can you send us more cards to go in them?"

"Of course. How many?"

"We can use as many as you can send, to stay ahead. My other cousin will be in the same place again in a month, if you can send them there."

"I'll do it this week."

"Thanks."

"OK. How's everything else?"

"There seems to be a group of mullahs—and now not just young ones— who also want to try different recipes. We have an Iraqi friend talking with them and encouraging them to look into a new menu. They say that they want to change."

"That would be great. But isn't that what others said, until they owned the restaurant?"

"Yes. But now they've seen the result of the wrong manager."

"I hope you're right. Keep talking, but please be careful."

"I will, Cousin, I promise."

David put down his cell phone and picked up his USNet landline phone, then dialed an intercom number.

"Abigail? Hi. It's David. Can you get me twenty more SIM cards, please?"

Claudia Coleman of *Journal* magazine was at her desk later that morning, hoping for a call-back from Congresswoman Janet Sullivan, or someone on her staff, to discuss the information released by Truth in Politics. Instead of a call, she received an email with an advance copy of a press release that would go out that afternoon.

> Washington, D.C. April 20. Congresswomen Janet Sullivan has the following three point response to yesterday's "revelation" by Truth in Politics.
>
> 1. For the past several weeks my husband, Richard--and by extension myself and Kristen Holloway—have been threatened by unnamed people who thought that they could blackmail him into convincing me not to vote for President Harper's media bill. This threat was explicitly stated, and the consequence for his failure to cooperate was to be the release of this information. So yesterday's news was not the spontaneous act of a curious individual, but in fact a precisely timed political move to discredit me, and by inference, President Harper.
>
> 2. The reason they released it is because they could not blackmail my husband. He and Ms. Holloway disclosed this situation to me years ago. They asked for my forgiveness. Because I knew that their remorse was real, and that God had changed them—and me—on the inside, I freely forgave them. So there is no story here about anger, mistrust, or revenge. Instead, the story is one of thanksgiving, trust and joy. Richard is a wonderful husband and father, not to mention attorney and partner. I trust him completely. People can be changed. We three are all living proof of that.
>
> 3. Whoever was behind the blackmail must be worried, because I remind you that President Harper's media bill only asks for three things:
>
> First, that *all* transmissions into our homes—TV, cable, satellite, internet—be "G" rated by default, unless the owner of the account specifically asks for something different. We're not trying to censor

anyone or anything, just put the burden to receive it on those who want it, not on the rest of us who constantly have to check, monitor, worry and guard our children against it.

Second, that for anyone to view anything other than PG on the internet, he or she must have proof of being twenty-one, or consent from a parent. There are new tools in advanced development which will allow for positive identification of the person actually logged on, like a cyber driver's license.

Third, that everyone associated with the 'adult' movie industry, meaning crews, actors, distributors, sales people, etc., must also be at least twenty-one. We do not let our children drive cars at fourteen or drink at eighteen. Some parts of the internet and certainly pornography are just as dangerous and powerful as drinking or driving, and we want to be sure that children are not involved.

Those changes, all of which only protect children and families, are the reasons that unknown people are trying to blackmail me and other members of Congress. We suspect that those who oppose us are not concerned about free speech so much as about money—being able to hook young, unsuspecting people at an early age—like tobacco successfully did.

The Congresswoman will be available to answer any additional questions at her regularly scheduled press briefing on Thursday afternoon at 1:30.

Claudia read the information twice, then called her assistant. "Please find a number for Kristen Holloway at USNet. I think she works in their real estate department."

Victor Mustafin was by himself at his computer, several printed phone transcripts arranged on his office desk beside him. He was piecing together the information in the calls which they had intercepted before and after Pavel Sivyakov's offer of the cruise missiles in Arzamas-23. And they then broadened the search to include calls to others made by each party to that fist call. None of the callers used encryption, or seemed the least bit concerned about interception.

It was clear that young Sivyakov and his four friends had concocted quite a plan to steal three GoFor missiles from the factory where they worked. And, a month after the paperwork on the destruction was submitted, they seemed to have pulled it off. The missles' launcher on paper was on a trip to the factory in the Ural Mountains for refurbishment, while in reality it was hidden several kilometers out of the city in a small warehouse which they had rented to do work on their autos. But their late night metalwork was really disguising the launcher as a common lorry.

The missiles had been smuggled out in key pieces and then reassembled by the five experts, and reunited with the launcher.

Mustafin was impressed with their ingenuity. And he understood that phone encryption would not have made sense to their group. But he could not understand the laziness of those trying to buy the missiles, because they were clearly the Russian national police, either working on a sting operation, or hoping to grab the product and then sell it themselves.

Claudia Coleman was lucky. Late that afternoon, Kristen answered her own phone at USNet.

After Claudia introduced herself, Kristen said, "Well, I saw it was a 202 area code and thought that it might be Janet Sullivan. I don't think I have anything to add to the press release that she put out earlier today."

"I understand. I just wanted to confirm that you agree with everything in that release."

"Yes, Janet let me proof it before it went out."

"So you are on a first name basis?"

Kristen paused, then explained and reinforced that she had asked for and received the Congresswoman's forgiveness, and the three of them had moved on. Kristen had changed cities and begun working for USNet.

"That brings up an interesting irony here," injected Ms. Coleman. "Trevor Knox, the CEO of USNet, is certainly an outspoken critic of the President's proposed legislation. This episode has had a potentially negative impact on both the President's legislation and on an employee of USNet. Do you share Mr. Knox's views on the issues Mrs. Sullivan has enumerated?"

Kristen paused then said, "I work in USNet's Real Estate Group, Ms. Coleman, not in corporate policy. I think I'm reasonably good at what I do, but, no, personally I don't share Mr. Knox's views on these subjects. If he asked me, which he hasn't, I would take USNet out of adult movies all together. I'm sort of embarrassed that we own those studios. What good can they possibly do anyone? And to the extent that they encourage promiscuity, surely they hurt our society on many levels. But, again, Mr. Knox is his own man, and he has certainly been successful at everything he has done. I just wish we didn't do adult movies."

"Thank you.   And my last question. Do you think there could be a 'conspiracy' to blackmail members of Congress on this bill? Isn't that a bit farfetched?"

"All I can tell you is that it happened to us. It's not easy to live with. I guess you should check with others."

The next morning Knox was again airborne, on the way back from Brazil. He had concluded a secret agreement to control more than seventy percent of that nation's telecommunications assets through various interlocking companies, allowing him to begin raising prices.

As his Falcon jet sped north, he logged on to Real Time Intercepts through his console and was soon face to face with Victor Mustafin. "Victor, I have a potential Special Operations mission. There's a real estate man who is trying to steal fifty million dollars from us, and he needs to be persuaded that this would be unhealthy business for him to pursue." Knox gave him the details for the mission. "I'll follow up with an email tomorrow once I've gathered all the facts from David Sawyer."

"Yes, sir. I understand. There's more news, not good. We intercepted an uplink of an article that will be in tomorrow's edition of *Journal* magazine. A reporter called the Holloway woman in USNet's Real Estate Group. I think you ought to see it. But you won't like it. I'm sending it now."

When he finished reading it, Knox sat with arms crossed in his expensive swivel seat, glaring at Mustafin.

"I can't believe this. I *told* you to check *everyone* involved in these plans, to be sure that there were no links to us. Now we've got the press looking for a blackmail plot and a USNet employee criticizing one of the most profitable parts of our business!"

"Mr. Knox, I'm sorry. We're doing that from now on, to the third level of possible connections, even though we're overloaded. Meanwhile, no one will ever be able to trace the various threats to one source. They were all made in different ways, some general and others specific."

"The Holloway woman has got to go. We can't have her at USNet. Criticizing our adult movies. After that interview, every reporter, especially the few who are friendly to President Harper, will feel free to call and ask her opinion about anything we do. I'll tell Sawyer to fire her."

"With all respect, sir, you might want to hold off a week or two on that. You don't want to link all this too closely and make her a martyr for expressing her views."

Knox was silent for a moment. "You may be right. But the result must be the same. We'll need a reason, like the debacle on this Capital Tower project. I'll tell Sawyer to look for a good reason to get rid of her."

"Mr. Knox, on a more positive note, we have a list of eight possible new RTI duty officers that we've assembled from personal knowledge and intercepts— all mid-level employees who have handled large responsibilities, but right now can be motivated by personal problems or their need for income."

Knox nodded.

Mustafin continued. "Akbar and I would like you to review the summaries of why we believe these people will be motivated to participate. If you'd like, I can email them to you now."

"Yes, I'll take a look. Thanks. Maybe with more people watching the data flow we won't have these lapses."

"I'm sure you're right, sir."

10

FRIDAY, APRIL 22ND

David sat alone at his desk two days later, on Friday afternoon, a stack of property reports, lease abstracts, budget drafts, and space requests piled next to his inbox. He had been working on them since four, and an hour and a half later, he realized that over the upcoming weekend he would have to handle all the issues that needed his input before he could depart for Moscow.

And then there were those pages in his personal drawer. He opened it and pulled them out. *Elizabeth won't let me leave without doing something about Rob. And I'm sure she wants to call Callie.*

He had always believed in goal setting and planning. His father had told him that Allah rewards hard work and good plans. Although David did not believe in Allah the way his father did, he did believe that planning produced results. And that God, if he existed, rewarded those who did right. Every quarter his team put together a Master Goal List, then broke down each complex goal into a series of action steps. For twenty years much of his success had been the result of organizing and achieving goals through action steps.

Now he faced an unfamiliar list of goals. *Bring Rob back to the real world. Rescue Callie from a jerk, sex and probably drugs.*

He was determined to write *something* on the paper. *These are problems just like business problems. I can solve them. I've just got to think them through, maybe ask for some advice, and write out the solutions. Then implement the plans. I can do this.*

"Unplug the internet," he wrote below Rob's name. *He'll scream. Have to prepare him. What about using the internet for his legitimate schoolwork? Take it slowly? Limit his time? Elizabeth and I will have to talk.*

He looked up at the picture of his family. He kept his pen at Callie's name for quite a while, but couldn't think of anything to write except "Talk with Kristen." *She's got to leave that guy. I'll think of something more—this weekend.*

David put down his pen, rubbed his temple, then looked again at the more familiar pile of USNet problems that needed solving. He put the family pages back in the drawer and picked up the next project at the top of the pile. It was a relief to begin reading the mundane lease summary.

His phone rang. "Mr. Sawyer, hello, this is Phyllis Jordan. Mr. Knox wondered if you would have a few minutes to meet with him."

"Now?"

"Yes, sir."

"Well...sure. I'll be right up."

Five minutes later, coming around his desk, Knox said, "David, glad to see you. Thanks for being available late on Friday afternoon. Here, have a seat at the table. I've just got a couple of quick things to go over with you. Won't take long."

"That's fine. I was just trying to finish some reports before heading for Moscow next week. Our requirement there has actually grown. The country is exploding with internet use."

As they sat down across from each other, Knox frowned, pulled out his pen, and said, "Yes, but that new President Temirov they just elected is copying our President Harper, calling for reforms. As if they can legislate morality! It's actually worse over there. The government has enough power that if they decide to end adult movies or punish those who grease the wheels of commerce with a little cash now and then, they can just do it. Boom! No freedom of speech or checks and balances. It would be *very* bad for our business, so we're watching developments there rather closely. But"—and a smile returned to his face as he offered Sawyer some coffee placed in the center of the table—"I'm sure you'll find just what we need."

"We've got a good broker over there."

"Fine. Well, let me start on the issues I want to discuss with you. First, what's the latest on Mr. Porter and our building purchase?"

"I called him on Wednesday morning and warned him that if Capital Tower closes and he turns out to be part of the purchasing group, then we'll pursue him in court as well as with the Real Estate Commission."

"And what did he say?"

"He said he'd see us in court."

"I was afraid of that. As were you, of course." Knox began to tap the gold pen on the table. "OK, now for a delicate situation. I want you to get rid of that Kristen Holloway woman." Sawyer frowned. Before he could speak, Knox continued. "No matter how invaluable she may appear, we cannot have anyone on our team who will so blatantly contradict our company policies in the national media. She may become a figurehead speaker for those who support Harper's attempts to limit our freedom. We cannot allow it."

"But...she's the most experienced person we've got. She's doing a good job...from Asia to Capital Tower, and a lot in between."

"I would not call Capital Tower a great success."

"That's not her fault. Porter is an unethical thief." The gold on his wedding ring felt smooth between his thumb and fingers.

"Well, it's her project, and it's not going well."

David was silent, the implications of Knox's words sinking in. "But she really is an integral part of our team. We—"

Knox raised the pen. "I'm glad that you've trained her, but you can train others. She has to go, and soon."

"On what grounds? For what reason?"

"I'll leave that up to you. Clearly it can't be linked directly to her television debut the other day. We need some other issues that we can cite as reasons to let her go."

"It might take some time." David hated saying the words, as if he agreed with the order.

"Just do it as quickly and as cleanly as you can." Knox smiled and put the pen on the table between them.

As he walked from the elevator lobby on the thirty-third floor back to his office, David decided not to think about firing Kristen Holloway until Knox brought it up again. *He's got to change his mind.*

That Saturday Todd took his wife Mary to look at new minivans.

"How can we do this?" she asked, as they pulled into the dealership in their five-year-old sedan, their two boys strapped into car seats in the back. "We still owe on both of our cars, plus my student loan."

Todd turned off the ignition and surveyed the gleaming new vehicles in the showroom window in front of them. "I've got some bonuses coming on deals we'll be closing." He opened his door and moved to help her with the toddlers. "We'll put half down and finance the rest. No problem. Wouldn't you like to have a new one? It'll be much safer."

Hoisting one son to her hip, Mary said, "Of course. But I just don't want us to go any further into debt. It worries me, Todd."

"No sweat," he smiled. "Let me worry about our finances. You just choose the one you want."

Closing the door, she responded, "OK. But let's be careful."

Sounding confident, he replied, "We will."

Alex insisted that they have dinner at their favorite neighborhood Chinese restaurant, which Callie knew they could not afford, but he said that he had big news for her. Because they were underage, they each took a pill and had a drink of tequila—Alex had two—before walking to the restaurant.

They arrived early and found a table in the back, away from the families with children near the fountains in the front. After they ordered she turned to him, feeling the effects of their "hors d'oeurves". "So, what's the news? Did you get a job?"

He smiled and faintly shook his head, looking directly at her. "Not exactly. But close. I have a quick and easy way to make two thousand dollars."

"Two thousand dollars! That's a lot of money. What do you have to do? It better be legal!"

"Not just me. Us. That video that we made. It actually won an award for the best amateur couples video last month. You were voted the most beautiful new talent by over a hundred thousand viewers! A producer saw it and sent me an email. We videocalled yesterday, and he has offered us two thousand dollars to make another thirty-minute video. It can be just like the first. Just us. No cameramen or anything." As he watched her face, he talked faster. "They'll give us three cameras to set up at different angles, and then it's just us. A little more light, probably. But just us. It's a paid acting job, which is better than being in a production at school. And two thousand in cash for thirty minutes. Isn't that incredible?"

She stared at him, trying to process all that he was saying.

He took her hand and smiled. "No one will ever know who we really are. We can make up names. There will be no connection to our real lives."

"We'll be making a porn movie." She couldn't help smiling.

"So what? Like, we've already made one. Well, I did, but you're in it. Apparently we're pretty good actors. You certainly are. Porn is strong now—a huge following. Lots of actors and actresses do it. With one already out there, what difference does it make if we do another? No one we know has connected it to us, and this won't be any different. And even if they do, it's actually sort of cool."

"Well my dad and his friend connected the last one to me. And I didn't even know about it."

"I should have told you in advance, but I thought you'd say no. Anyway, this is a *paying* job. And as for your dad"—he shrugged—"he's already disowned you. He doesn't care a thing about you. He told us to make it on our own, and this way we'll be doing exactly what he said. And think what we can do with that money. How long would you have to work at your uncle's office to make two thousand dollars?"

"Would we be, like, again, in our own bedroom?"

"Probably. Or maybe a hotel. I'm not sure. But it will just be us. Very natural." He smiled.

She shook her head a little but continued to smile. "That is a lot of money, and we could really use it. Two thousand?"

"Yes. For thirty minutes."

"Crazy."

The waitress brought their soups and egg rolls.

He picked up a spoon and waited.

"I'll think about it," she finally said.

He nodded, filled his spoon, and took a sip.

David spent much of Saturday in his study, continuing to work through the pile of papers that had to be finished. That night they attended the wedding of the daughter of Elizabeth's college roommate. David could only think about Callie and Alex. Sunday morning they slept late. Over brunch they debated how much of the internet was enough for Rob. Elizabeth wanted to unplug it completely, while David wanted to limit their son's time on the computer. Elizabeth asked how it would be possible to enforce with all the equipment in his room. They debated moving a simplified system, minus the virtual reality gear, to their den, to encourage "legitimate" uses of the web.

After supper on Sunday evening David sat in his study, preparing for the week ahead. His immediate thoughts were about Elizabeth. She was, rightly, pushing to intervene in Rob's life, as he had done in Callie's.

He laid aside the summary report on their Moscow opportunities.

We've given them everything. There must be an answer. Are there counselors who deal with what we're going through? How would I find one we could trust? Not some psycho who blames everything on the parents, or some "born again" Christian who thinks a baptism will fix anything. I've got to help them, and I will.

He picked up the report again and began taking notes.

11

MONDAY, APRIL 25TH

As was his custom, retired General Yevgany Beleborodov was up early that Monday morning in Moscow, finishing his breakfast with his wife, before his driver took him to the offices of NovySvet. He did not expect his cell phone to ring, but was pleased to hear the voice of Simon North, calling from London, where it was even earlier. He stood up and walked into their bedroom.

"My dear General," the Englishman began, "our employers want to know if we would each like to earn an extra million dollars this month."

The Russian smiled. "I'm sure about my vote."

"Yes, well, it's unanimous then. Do you know anyone in Arzamas-23?"

"Of course. Many old friends. The 'closed' city is the center for military research in several fields. And manufacturing of weapons systems."

"There's a slightly complex situation involving three prototypes of the new GoFor cruise missile that they want us to help with. If it becomes necessary, do you have access to any 'muscle'?"

The older man was silent for a moment. "Actually, I still have many friends at all levels in the active military. As you may have guessed from our conversations, I and my friends are not exactly happy with our nation's current weak president, and the direction in which he is taking us. There are many of us who long for the old, powerful Russia, restored to the greatness that we deserve. We meet and we talk. We may even have some organizations of our own. And so, yes, I believe that I can arrange some 'muscle', as you put it. And it will be easy to do so in Arzamas-23, with many military bases nearby."

"Very good. Then I expect to call you again later today."

"We will do whatever we can. I'll await your details."

Kristen was plugging in her laptop when David arrived at her door.

She looked up. "Hi." She inserted the cord and straightened up. "Long time no see. I ought to take a day off more often. After the quick trip to D.C. to look at space on Thursday, sleeping in on Friday morning was just incredible."

He returned her smile, noting how refreshed she looked, and then thought of Trevor's order. His expression quickly changed. "I want to hear all about it, but right now I want you to hear a voicemail that Bill Porter left on my phone last night. He's not a happy camper."

"Why?"

"You'll hear for yourself." She followed him to his office and took a chair. He sat at his desk and accessed his voicemail.

"Listen, David," came the angry voice, "I've been in this business a long time, and no one has ever threatened me like you have! You're mad that I did a great job for my client on Capital Tower. So now you're threatening me, trying to get your way, and I *really* don't like it. Just because you're a giant corporation doesn't give you the right to push around a little guy like me. I got the best price for our client, and that's how America works. You can't threaten me and my family over a business deal. It won't work. So back off, or I'll call my attorney."

There was a long moment of silence. David looked at Kristen. "Welcome back."

Kristen asked, "Who would threaten him over a building?"

"I don't know. We certainly didn't. I've never heard of anything like that. At least not here in the States. Maybe overseas."

"Or the U.S. Congress. Remember what just happened to the Sullivans—and to me."

"I hadn't thought about that. You're right."

Rising, she added, "There *is* a lot of money involved, David. I can see how someone could be really mad at Mr. Porter."

"And the fact that there appears no way for the legal process to intervene. I guess that might anger one of the other bidders."

"But who?" Kristen started for the door.

David shrugged. "Hopefully Bill will sort it out. Kristen, wait a minute. Let's talk. Close the door, please."

She did as he asked and took her chair again.

"Kristen, look, I'm glad you're back, but I hadn't planned on Porter's call to be our first conversation."

She continued to look at him, waiting.

"We've obviously got a lot to go over. I want to hear about the office space in D.C., catch up on the Far East, and brief you before I leave for Moscow. But right now I just want to ask you to cool it when it comes to remarks about Knox, or the Media Bill, or any of that stuff."

She looked both surprised and relieved, then asked, "Why? Can't I have opinions?"

"Sure. Of course. I mean in public. Like the interview you did with that reporter. You know that Knox doesn't like it when employees contradict him."

She gave an expression of disbelief. "But I'm only a lowly real estate exec. I think I said so. *Way* down the USNet food chain. The reporter asked my opinion, and I gave it. David, do *you* think we ought to be making porn films at USNet? Does that give you a sense of pride in our company?"

He looked away and paused.

"Kristen," he spoke slowly, "have all the opinions you want. Tell them to your friends. Tell me. But please don't talk to any more reporters about them. OK?"

She continued to look at him. "Is this message from Knox?"

"*This* message is from *me*."

More silence. Finally, she said, "Well, for the moment I'll agree. But I may want to talk with you about it once I think a bit. I doubt I'll have too many reporters calling me again, anyway." She smiled.

He returned her smile. "Thank you." He rose. "Now, we both have a lot to do."

She stood. As they moved to the door and he opened it for her, she asked, "Is there anything we ought to do about Porter?"

"I can't think of anything."

"Me either. Maybe call Terrell Myers and tell him?"

"Sure. See you at our meeting after lunch. I hope you're able to dig out."

Elizabeth Sawyer finished her sandwich. She had nibbled on it for an hour while sitting in their family room making calls for the upcoming tenth grade spring dance. The thought of a high school dance seemed soothingly "normal," compared to the daily reality that caused her stomach to churn whenever she thought about their children, which was several times every hour.

She had asked David to take some action on Rob. But so far, other than to talk briefly with her, he had done nothing. *If he isn't going to do anything about Rob, I'm not going to ostracize Callie.* Elizabeth put down the student directory, picked up her personal phone book and dialed.

"Hello."

"Callie? Were you asleep?"

"Huh? Oh...Hi, Mom...Yeah...uh...try-outs this week. I studied late."

"I'm sorry, honey. It's just good to hear you. How are you?"

"Um, I'm fine. Fine. How are you?"

"We're OK. Just calling around to the parents about Rob's spring dance in early May. How are your classes?"

"They're good. Like I said, auditions are coming up."

"Callie, Dad told me about Alex and that you're living together."

Silence. Then, "Yes, we are. We love each other."

"Enough to get married?"

"Mom, we're not ready for that yet. People today don't have to get married to live together. Dad acts like it's something awful. Everyone does it."

Silence. Then, "Your father is still pretty traditional, and I guess I am, too. We just want the best for you, Callie, and besides the obvious issue of having a baby, Dad says that Alex has no job and no money. How are you going to support yourselves?"

"You mean now that Dad has cut us off?"

"I think he would say that he never intended to support 'us'. Only you."

"Whatever. We'll do it somehow."

"He didn't want me to call you for a while, but I'm not going to stop talking to you over any issue."

"Thanks, Mom."

"And I'll try to send some money."

"No, don't cross Dad like that. We'll figure it out. We're already talking about some ways to make extra money. In fact, Uncle Rezza is going to let me work part time at his office, and Yusef is going to teach me about selling homes."

"OK. Good. I may not mention that quite yet to your father. Now, tell me more about Alex."

Victor Mustafin was on duty that afternoon, and he had never seen his employer so angry. Following his prayers, Knox had been exercising in the private gym in his office when Mustafin paged him from his duty station. Knox had immediately called from the gym's video panel, and Mustafin had told him about the House vote an hour earlier to approve President Harper's media bill Turning red, Knox yelled into the screen on the wall of his gym, "Find Akbar and get us all on a videoconference together."

Thirty minutes later the two RTI specialists were on split screens on the videoconference set in Knox's conference room; he still wore his gym clothes and carried a towel around his neck.

"You said that our unique assets could stop this pseudo-Christian morality crap," he said quietly, looking from one to the other. "And that we could then use the same approach on future votes."

Akbar Kamali finally replied. "We applied pressure wherever we could, plus the usual media spins through our people. In many cases it worked. In a few it didn't. It was a close vote, Mr. Knox."

"And in some cases it backfired completely, like that Congresswoman Sullivan."

The two lieutenants nodded and waited. Knox leaned forward toward them.

"Can we stop them in the Senate?"

Mustafin took his turn. "Probably not. We can hope for some amendments from our friends to water it down, but in general the Senate is pretty conservative on social issues."

Knox stood and walked over to the window, then returned to stand next to the table, glaring at his subordinates on the screen. "I will not let these self-proclaimed saviors stop what we've spent years building. Americans *want* this stuff. It all comes from allowing their women to live with no modesty, and to mix with men every day. They *want* to experience sex and violence and everything else we give them. Their teenagers love it. We've had free access to them for years—right in their homes—pushing all this. And it's working. Of course it ruins families! That's exactly what we want to happen. It's also very profitable. Only now President Harper wants to take it away. We cannot let her!"

He paused, then continued, his right index finger tapping on the table as he spoke. "They think they're God's Christian Crusaders for America. Today it's movies and television. Next they'll push their agenda back into education. Then even politics and government. Soon they'll be trying to export their ideas to other countries, like this new President Temirov in Russia. Those two are talking about having a summit this summer, and the first item on the agenda is supposed to be how to improve morality in both countries. Can you believe that?" Again he paused. "We *cannot* let this happen!" They waited.

Finally he sat down, looked at each man, and then asked, almost in a whisper, "I was going to ask this at our next meeting, but instead I'll say it today—is there any way to get rid of President Harper?"

Kamali and Mustafin were silent, absorbing the full meaning of Knox's question.

"She's a throwback Crusader, an infidel, and a *woman*. Think how much more effective our work will be if she is gone and the country is confused and on edge. The vice president is weak, and if we can somehow get rid of him, too, imagine the Speaker as President! There will be political chaos—fertile ground for more attacks. I'm asking you again, is there any way to get rid of President Harper—and soon?"

"There must be, of course." Mustafin answered vaguely. "She is so well guarded, though."

"I know. But isn't the Secret Service mostly looking for a gunman or a sniper or a car bomb?"

"Yes," Kamali replied.

"And with all of our technology, isn't there some way—or ways—to go around what they're looking for and take her out? I mean poisons, or lasers, or robots, or missiles?"

Warming to the question, Kamali responded, "Yes, I'm sure there is. We've just never thought about it."

"Well, start," Knox snapped, leaning back in his chair. "What about one of Salim's Stinger missile martyrs from the Army, firing at Air Force One when it takes off?"

"Unlike commercial airliners, Air Force One has flares that may throw off a heat seeking missile."

"How would NovySvet's new technology work on Air Force One?"

"In a year or two. It's not yet perfected against fast moving targets."

"We can't wait that long. Take the time you need to get it right. Figure out a plan or plans. If you have to involve anyone else, obviously mask the real objective. Get back to me. And it should not only be foolproof, but untraceable, of course."

Mustafin and Kamali said nothing. Knox continued. "We must get rid of this meddling President before she does serious damage to our plans for America."

Knox stood up, and Kamali said, "Mr. Knox, I'm sure we can do it. But it will be quite a challenge."

"That's why I have the two of you. We've got our usual quarterly review coming up in about ten days. I want to be able to brainstorm some specific solutions then."

Knox sat down again and raised his hand. "Oh, and that real estate guy who's trying to steal fifty million from us. What's his name? Porter. If there's no response to your message by next week, go ahead and get rid of him. Allah abhors thieves."

When Kristen returned from a quick sandwich, she noted a strange look on Trish's face. As she neared her assistant's desk, Trish said, "I almost just put your phone on voice mail and went to lunch myself, but instead I have these." She held up a stack of message slips. She smiled. "And I think there are at least ten more who asked to leave voice mails. What have you been doing since I saw you an hour ago?"

"I guess you missed the news," Kristen said, taking the stack of message slips.

"I guess so."

"Well, the President and the Sullivans are back in the news."

"So we are, too?"

"Apparently."

"Maybe you could record a special greeting, giving your latest views and news."

Kristen actually laughed. "I don't think so."

She turned and went into her office. As she sat in her chair, the phone rang. After two rings, she answered.

"Kristen?" The voice sounded familiar.

"Yes."

"Hello, Kristen. This is Claudia Coleman from the *Journal*. How are you?"

"Fine. Just fine. How are you?"

"Good, thanks. Listen, I was wondering if you had any comment on the news today about passage of the President's media bill in the House."

"Well, no, I don't."

"But didn't you support it?"

"Yes, of course, as I told you."

"Well, I watched Janet Sullivan a little while ago, and she mentioned the attempted blackmail again, and you. Do you have any comment that we can use in our article?"

Kristen paused. "No, I don't. I'm not a politician or policy person. I'm in real estate. I certainly have my personal views, but I don't think they're relevant to a story on the President's legislation."

"Can't you give me some additional insights into your relationship with the Sullivans, now that you helped the President's victory in the House?"

"Let me ask you a question. Did you follow up on Mrs. Sullivan's assertion that she and others were blackmailed with threats to change their vote?"

"No, not really."

"Why not?"

"Well, you know, time is always a problem, and there are so many stories. We probably should have. But it seemed far-fetched."

"OK, well, I just don't have anything more to say. But if you ever do track down what Mrs. Sullivan was talking about, I bet you'd have a pretty interesting story."

"Perhaps. But right now can't you help us with your thoughts on this bill's chances, from inside USNet?"

"I told you, I don't speak for USNet—unless you want to talk about office lease terms. So, please, call folks in Washington or in the entertainment business, but not me. OK?"

"Yes, certainly. Well, good-bye, Ms. Holloway."

"Good-bye." *I hope that's the end of it.*

Simon North received an email from his anonymous employers including a packet of what appeared to be intercepted telephone calls with several young Russian men in the city of Arzamus-23. And on several calls what appeared to be a potential buyer for their unique product. But the sender indicated that the buyer was actually a member of the Russian police.

Also included were the outlines of a plan for intercepting the purchase.

Which was why North was on the afternoon British Air flight to Moscow.

That evening the Sawyers were seated at their mahogany dining room table, a thick Persian rug underfoot. David would be leaving for Moscow on Friday, and Elizabeth had been organizing extra clothes for him.

"What will the weather be like?" she asked, as she passed the salad bowl to Rob, who was attacking his plate as if he hadn't eaten in a week.

"I got an email today from our broker, saying that it will actually be pretty warm, now that it's almost May. Though there could still be a stray snow storm."

"Hard to imagine," Elizabeth said, shaking her head.

"Yes, so please just include a few sweaters with my regular stuff."

"Don't you need to take drinking water and toilet paper?" Rob asked, in one of his rare voluntary utterances.

Sawyer smiled. "Maybe years ago. But not today. Certainly not to Moscow. I haven't been there since our first exploratory mission in '93, but I'm told that there are all the comforts of home. How was the tenth grade today?"

Without looking up, their son replied, "OK."

"Anything good or bad happen?"

"Nope."

"How did you do on the chemistry test?"

Still not taking his eyes off the food in front of him, Rob responded, "I think it was a seventy-eight."

"Rob, you did much better in physics last year."

"Mm."

David looked at Elizabeth and then said, "Rob, your mother and I have been talking about moving the computer down here, to the family room."

Now he looked up, first at his mother, then his father. "No way! Why?"

"Because you've become attached to it—from games to chat rooms to email. Think about how little time you have left for anything else, including homework. So if you use it down here, it won't take up as much of your life."

"But what about those awesome internet games?"

"You'll have to stop, or play them less."

"No way."

"Rob..."

"No. I like the games and I'm not flunking any courses. And I like the chat rooms with my friends, too. We talk every day about strategy. I can't move it down here!"

He got up, his plate virtually licked clean. He walked into the kitchen, rinsed his plate and put it in the sink. As he was about to leave for his room, he said to his parents, who were still eating, "The computer is a big part of my life. I have real friends because of it. Please don't take it away." And he bounded up the stairs.

"I guess we showed him," Elizabeth said.

David picked up a forkful of lentils and raisins, but kept it near his plate. "I didn't want to start a war one day before I leave."

"Well, we've got to do it sometime! And soon. David, he's a different person than a year ago."

"He's fifteen. It happens to everyone."

"Not like this. We're losing him."

"OK. OK. Just let me get back from this trip and I'll tackle it."

"I called Callie today."

"What?" He put down his fork.

"I wanted to talk with her." She met his look.

He glanced down and said nothing, his anger obvious.

Elizabeth pushed on. "I told you that I wouldn't cut off our daughter for long. She probably needs us now more than ever."

He filled the fork again and chewed slowly. After swallowing, he said, "She cut us off."

"No. She made a bad choice, and you—we—cut her off because of it."

"It's the same thing. Choices have consequences, and I gave her the choice."

"What about love? What about our relationship with her?"

He was silent again, digesting her words. "I think they call it 'tough love.'"

It was her turn to be silent, staring at him. After a few moments, she took a deep breath and said, "David, I've been to this Bible study group twice." He started to speak, but she raised her hand. "I'm not going to give you a sermon—I couldn't possibly. I'm just saying that we read the Bible and talk. Some of these ladies are amazing. They have such wisdom. Anyway, we've been talking about relationships, not religion, at least not as I've ever heard anyone talk about religion. They talk about a relationship with God—as if that's His desire for us. And our earthly relationships being more important than things, or schools, or anything."

She leaned forward. "They actually mentioned tough love the other day, and they said that you have to hate the sin, but love the sinner. Now I've heard that before and always just nodded my head. But here is Callie, and that's just what this is. We've got to love her—keep the relationship—while telling her how much we disagree with what she's doing, and why."

He shook his head. "I never heard about all that God and relationship stuff. In my family there was nothing about that. Only making Allah happy by doing what is right. Making the right choices. It's simple. In our family, God is not our friend. He is Allah, and his will is for us to do right."

"Not our friend? But he made us. What happens when we don't do right?"

"Then he punishes us."

"How can we always do right?"

"We can't. Like Callie."

"And you and me. These women would say that Callie needs her parents, and that all of us need a savior."

"The savior. Jesus. Always back to him. Islam says that God has no son."

"David, I don't want to argue about religion. I'm just pointing out that I think God thinks relationships are important, and that none of us is perfect."

"But as parents, we're to set the right example."

"Exactly! Look at the father in the Prodigal Son story. He loved his wayward son and celebrated his return."

"And I'll celebrate when Callie returns."

"What if Callie thinks she can't return? What if she thinks we've closed her out?"

David thought for several moments. Finally he shrugged. "OK. Talk with her now and then. Keep the door open. But let her know how much we disagree with what she's doing."

Elizabeth smiled. "I will. Who knows what may happen."

12

SATURDAY, APRIL 30TH

David arrived in Moscow on Saturday morning at 10:30. He felt unexpectedly refreshed because he was able to sleep for five hours on the long flight.

Sheremetevo Airport's gleaming new terminals were nothing like what he remembered from 1993—a chrome and glass Soviet-style structure that seemed far too small to be the portal to Europe's largest city. Unlike his previous visit, there were now bright lights, advertisements, and a high speed train to downtown.

Andrei Selivanov had volunteered to meet David at the airport and emailed a picture of himself—tall with dark hair. And today he also held a small sign with Sawyer's name on it. They shook hands, and Andrei took one of his bags. "Welcome to Moscow.".

"Thank you. I'm glad to be back after so many years."

"I think you will see many changes since your last visit," Andrei expressed in nearly perfect English, as they turned and began walking toward the glass doors leading to the parking lot.

"I'm sure I will." Motioning toward all the panel displays and advertisements, he said, "Back then there weren't many choices in anything."

Andrei nodded. "But now there are as many choices as you have in the States. Even in office buildings."

The sun was shining brightly in the cool air. "Yes, you've lined up quite a number of possibilities for our software group. But will we have time to see them all?"

"You've come on a holiday weekend—May Day is Monday. We'll drive past the list tomorrow afternoon, when the traffic won't be bad, and review them on my laptop as we go. You can decide which ones you want to see in person. Peter Goncharov, your local manager, is in Helsinki on business today, but he'll join us tomorrow."

David smiled. "That'll be great. And I can go to a museum or something—I can always use more culture."

Andrei placed David's bags in the trunk of his ten-year-old Audi, and the two men began the thirty-five km journey into Moscow along the ribbon of six-lane thoroughfare that was more than a boulevard but less than a highway. The route led southeast from Sheremetevo Airport; once they passed inside the Ring Road, the traffic increased dramatically, even on Saturday, and their pace slowed. More than ten million people lived inside the Ring Road. As in many continental cities, the driving seemed to be a frenzied free-for-all, and David was glad that Andrei was behind the wheel.

They talked about their businesses, the world markets for real estate, and their families. Andrei was nearly forty with a wife and three children, an almost unheard of family size by Russian norms.

"How did you get into the business?"

"Out of university I was an engineer. Back in '92 when people could start to buy and sell apartments, I made a little money helping friends find what they wanted. I liked it. Then in '95, just as real estate was starting to be a real business, and office buildings and new apartments were going up everywhere, a friend from school introduced me to an American and a Brit with a small commercial firm here. They taught me the basics, from market analysis to ethics. They were great teachers, and now we're partners. Every year we add more Russian staff, and I do most of the training."

"Sounds pretty normal, actually."

Andrei looked over from the driver's seat. "Yes. Just normal, really. But it's amazing that it has happened in this country after seventy years of the communists trying to deny everything from free markets to God. I guess they found out that God and markets are much more permanent than they were!"

David nodded and smiled. They continued along Tverskaya Street, a combination of Fifth Avenue and Madison Avenue, lined by diverse five-to eight-story buildings, all with bright shops on their ground floors. Sawyer's hotel, a modern remake within a handsome nineteenth-century façade, was near Red Square, right in the heart of the city. They pulled up to the door, and a smartly dressed bellman helped with the bags.

"I'll park the car and make some calls in the hotel lobby," Andrei suggested. "You unpack, then we'll have lunch and head over to the History Museum on Red Square."

"So far so good," David acknowledged. "Thanks for the ride in, and I'll see you in the lobby in thirty minutes."

In his room, David splashed water on his face and took two aspirin for the dull ache in the front of his head. With a fresh shirt he felt ready to tackle the rest of the day, and he joined Andrei in the lobby restaurant for lunch.

After they ordered, Andrei took a sip of water and asked his guest, "What brought you here back in '93?"

"Back then I came here with a team of five division heads from USNet, hoping to pick up an operating company, or a cheap building, or new technology, or something that we could use—and help the new Russian economy as well."

"How long did you spend here?"

"Almost two weeks. Our one success was finding the software company to invest in. I think we were one of the first joint ventures, and we're still going strong today. Now we need more space. By the way, can we start our tour in the morning?"

Andrei buttered a piece of bread. "Well, we could, but my family goes to church on Sunday morning, so I'd like to pick you up about one, which will give us plenty of time. We'd love for you to join us at church, by the way, or you can walk to many interesting places from here."

"That's OK," David said, as their soup arrived. "My family came from Iran, where they were Muslims, though I don't practice any religion myself. My wife grew up in a Christian family, but she doesn't attend, either. So please go to church with your family, and I'll walk around Red Square and meet you here at one."

"What about your two children?"

"What do you mean?"

"Religion. Faith. Do you teach them any beliefs?"

"Well, we teach them to be good people, of course. But we think all religions are about the same. Different ways to the same place—or to no place." David smiled.

"How do they know what's right from what's wrong?"

"We've taught them to respect other people, and to help others. I think people generally just know, and we've tried to emphasize examples of good and bad behavior. "

"I see." Andrei returned his smile, and they dug into their food.

Several hours of walking through the museum later, David was ready for an early night. He said good-bye to Andrei at six, had a solo meal in the hotel restaurant, checked in with Elizabeth, and then walked up to Red Square. The sun was setting and couples were walking arm-in-arm through the square that had witnessed almost a millennium of sometimes violent history, and yet that night it was nearly silent, and peaceful.

While her father was sleeping in Moscow, Callie Sawyer, after two glasses of wine, agreed with her boyfriend that two thousand dollars was too much to pass up, and they made plans to cash in that night.

David and Andrei were joined on Sunday afternoon by Peter Goncharov, USNet's local manager. Fifty, tall, and a former engineer in the army, Peter had transitioned well to private enterprise; USNet trusted his judgment on all operational issues.

As they drove around Moscow looking at the properties that might fit USNet's needs, David was impressed with how precisely the city's road system matched a hub with spokes. The Kremlin was at the center, with spokes radiating out to the Outer Ring, an average distance of twenty kilometers. In between there were two other full rings: the Garden Ring and the Third Ring, recently completed by the city government atop the right-of-way of an old railroad line.

By the time they finished and headed to a local Georgian restaurant for dinner, they agreed to focus on three key properties to negotiate the best space and terms for their use.

They were seated at a table in a small room with high ceilings and ancient wooden beams. After they ordered, Peter asked, "Andrei, are the owners of these three properties all honest and reliable?"

"For the most part, yes. Two are joint ventures between local Russians and Western partners. We've put tenants in all of them with good success."

"What about bribes? Obviously we can't be involved with any bribes."

Andrei smiled. "Despite what you hear, they're rare, at least at this level." He noticed the skeptical look on David's face. "Oh, I'm sure that to get the building built, utilities connected, permits issued, that sort of thing, some special considerations were asked and given. The Russian partner usually takes care of that, but these days it's pretty small stuff."

"You'd think from the press that nothing gets done here without a bribe."

"And you'd think from the press that every child in an American school is in danger of being shot by a sniper or schoolmate."

David nodded. "Yes, I guess the media does tend to pigeon-hole all of us with ten-second summaries."

Peter spoke up. "The reality is that some things certainly are done or expedited here with bribes, which sadly is true in most of the world, not just in Russia. But it's more like an old boy network, where people over time develop relationships by doing favors for each other. It came right out of the

Soviet system. Since there were no prices back then for anything, the only way anything ever got done was through personal relationships, keeping score of who owed you and whom you owed."

"I hadn't realized that."

Andrei added, "But now the market has encroached, and decisions are made by a combination of price and relationships."

David reflected for a moment. "A little like the States, really."

"I couldn't be sure, since I've only worked here. But probably you're right."

When David returned to his room that night there were two messages from Elizabeth on the hotel voicemail, urging him to call home. He fixed a drink at the mini-bar, sat on the bed, dialed their home number, and listened to his wife talk almost without interruption for three minutes. As she spoke about their son, he closed his eyes and grimaced several times, then made notes on the pad by his bed.

They spoke for a few more minutes, and he asked her to put Rob on the line. She put the phone down, and he could hear her walk upstairs, with music playing in the background. Then it stopped, and a minute later he heard noise near the receiver.

"Hello."

"Rob. Hey, how are you?"

"Uh. Fine."

"I'd like to bring you over here someday. It's a lot different than most people think."

"Mm."

"Rob, Mom tells me that you were up 'til three this morning—or even later. On the internet, playing those games."

"Mm."

"Son, listen. We told you that we're going to have to make changes if you don't get off that stuff—have a more regular life. And I'm asking you to stop doing those games. There's more to life than—."

"Dad, I know that. But I *like* these games. I've got *friends* out there. Better friends than at school. I can't just cut them off. It's not right."

"But, Rob, you need balance. And real friends. Not just friends on the internet."

"These *are* real friends. Real people. They're just not here. But they *are* real."

"Rob, you only play internet games with them, wherever they are and whoever they are. You don't talk, do homework, go to movies, listen to music."

"So what? We're close. Like in combat, I guess."

David could feel his anger rising, but he tried to hold it down. "Rob, you're fifteen. I'm your father. I'm telling you that there's more to life than internet games, no matter how real they are. You've got to break away from this—this—addiction. It's wrong. And get your head back into school, friends, girls."

"Hey, Dad, I could be 'addicted' to a lot worse things than the internet."

David was silent for a moment and took a deep breath. "I know. And I'm thankful, Rob, that you're not. But *any* addiction is not good. It limits you... changes you."

"Well, I think you're wrong about these games."

They talked for five minutes, and finally Rob agreed to only an hour of games a day until David came home. Then Elizabeth came back on the line.

"He's gone upstairs."

"He agreed to one hour until I get home and we can all talk together."

"He needs to do *none*, David."

"Elizabeth, I know. But for now, this is OK. Please watch him and be sure that he does as we've agreed."

A long pause. "David, I'll try, but sometimes I'm not home..."

"Do the best you can. He promised, so we'll have to trust him."

"We'll see."

"Elizabeth, I love you, and I'm sorry that this is happening while I'm away."

"I love you, too, but I'm just very worried about our son. And the daughter that we've cut off."

"She chose to cut herself off."

"Let's not talk about that again until you get home. Sleep well and travel safe, dear."

"Thanks. I love you."

David hung up the phone, stood up, and walked again to the mini-bar, where he poured himself another drink. Swallowing half of it in one gulp, he thought, *What's happened to Rob? And to Callie, for God's sake? They were just kids a couple of years ago. Rob still is. We've done everything for them.*

He refilled his glass and sat in a gold armchair in the corner of his hotel room. *What was it Andrei asked? "How do they know what's right from what's wrong?" How can they not know? We haven't pushed the Qur'an or the Bible on them. But we've tried to be good people ourselves, and we've taught them to be tolerant and to respect others. Surely they can figure out right and wrong. Callie and Rob are bright. They should know.*

Only a few kilometers from David's hotel, Simon North and Yevgany Beleborodov were finishing their late night planning at the dinner table in the general's apartment. His wife was visiting their son and his family in Novgorod.

"So I think all of the pieces are in place to move this week," North summarized, looking at the papers in front of him. "I like the sound of your Captain Rusnak."

"Yes, he's a good man. A true patriot. Not afraid to do whatever needs to be done for the motherland. And, quite happily, stationed only twenty kilometers from Arzamus-23."

"It appears that it is time to call Mr. Sivyakov."

"Agreed. He will either be in his apartment, or in the warehouse with his friends." Beleborodov dialed the cell phone number which North had brought with him in the packet from London. After a few rings the phone answered with what sounded like an annoyed response to a wrong number.

The general spoke in Russian. "Mr. Sivyakov, good evening. No, this is not a wrong number. I want to talk with you for a moment. Do you have time? Are you in your apartment, or at the warehouse?"

"Who is this?"

"Never mind. That's not important. The point is that we know about your special product, and we would like to buy it. How much will you sell it for?"

"I don't know what you're talking about."

"Of course you do. And I can hear the work going on now in the background, perfecting the exterior of the carrier."

There was silence, and a moment later the noises stopped. "Why should I stay on the line with you?"

"Because I'm going to save you from a terrible fate. The people to whom you think you are selling your product are actually with the police, and when you meet in ten days, as you have planned, they will either arrest you or kill you."

More silence.

"But the good news is that we are not the police, and we will match their offer in cash and take the product off your hands in a few days, giving you the means and the time for you and your friends to leave the country. With your families."

More silence.

"I tell you what. You and your team talk about it for ten minutes, and I'll call you back. We hope that you will take us up on the lifeline that we are offering you. The alternative for you is bleak. I will call you back." Then Beleborodov hung up.

13

That Monday morning, while David was in Moscow, Kristen stopped by Todd's office. The door was open, and she took a step inside. He had a spreadsheet open on his computer, which sat at the far corner of the credenza behind his desk. He swiveled around on his chair when she entered.

She smiled and spoke. "Hey. I guess you heard the voicemail from David at the airport on Friday asking me to review the analysis of Brookglen versus Overlook."

Todd opened both hands towards her and returned her smile. "A great idea, I guess, but I accepted Brookglen's proposal that afternoon."

Kristen frowned. "David was here early Friday morning. Did you run it past him?"

"No, actually I didn't. He put me in charge of the project, so I assumed that meant I could make the decision."

"Well, yes, one of us is always the leader, but we usually check our work with each other, and certainly with David, before making a big commitment."

Todd looked down at the papers spread in front of him and clenched his fists on the desktop. "Brookglen was the clear choice. It's the better project. End of discussion." He looked up at her.

In a calm voice Kristen said, "I recall you saying two weeks ago that the Brookglen rent started out at only thirty-two dollars per square foot but increased fairly quickly in the third through seventh years. Did the present value come out better than Overlook's almost flat rent of thirty-four dollars over the entire term?"

Todd pursed his lips and said, "Yes, of course."

"What discount rate did you use?"

He stood. "I don't remember exactly. And it doesn't matter. Brookglen is better: the floor plates are larger and there's more parking."

"But Overlook's parking is in an enclosed deck, isn't it? That will be important in Minneapolis, I would think."

"Look—I told you, I've already made the decision and accepted Brookglen's proposal. I'm sorry that I'm not perfect, remembering always to check with everyone and praying for the best rental rates. I did what I thought was best."

She shook her head, and her auburn hair moved just a bit. "Todd, there's no reason to say that. Do you think that I think I'm perfect?"

He took a deep breath. "No, Kristen, I don't. I'm sorry. But I don't like being second-guessed when I've been put in charge of a project."

"Call it teamwork, not second guessing." She smiled. "It sounds better and works better."

"OK. Well, next time. But this time, it's Brookglen."

She turned and walked to his door. "All right. But you'd better send David an email and let him know. And let me know if I can help on anything, and maybe after lunch you can check over my assumptions and conclusions on Singapore."

He sat down. "Glad to." Then he turned back to his spreadsheet.

Bill Porter was at his desk when the phone rang. "Mr. Porter?"

"Yes."

"Hi. My name is Taylor Martin. You've been involved in some land developments in the north part of the state, haven't you?"

"Yes. River Mill is the most recent. Almost two hundred homes around a lake."

"It's a wonderful development. Very environmentally sound. I'm calling because my family owns several hundred acres right at the edge of the national forest about sixty miles north, not far from the river."

"Really?"

"Yes. It's beautiful property. Old forest. Rolling topo. And we've just learned that the county is going to run a sewer line right through our property early next year. We think it's time to involve someone like you to help us figure out what to do, and so we thought we'd call."

"Well, I'd be glad to meet with you and take a look."

"Really?"

"Yes, of course. When would you like to get together?"

"Hmm...What about later this week? We could, say, meet you at the River Inn, show you the property, then have lunch. We've got plats and a letter from the county about the sewer."

"Sounds good. What day works for you? I'm free on Wednesday and Thursday."

"How about Wednesday? We can meet in the parking lot. Say about eleven-thirty?"

"That'll be fine. I'll dress for walking the property."

"Yes. By all means. And we'll bring the plats. We'll meet in the parking lot, go look at the property, and then come back for lunch. My brother, cousin and I will meet you on Wednesday."

"Good. I'm looking forward to it."

"Oh, and Mr. Porter. We don't want anyone else to know what's going on with this property. So we'd appreciate if you didn't mention it to anyone else, And can we meet just with you?"

"Of course. I'll come alone."

"Great. We'll see you then. Thank you."

At four-thirty that same Monday afternoon in Moscow, David, Andrei and Peter Goncharov were about to visit the third of the properties that their initial analysis had indicated could be suitable for the USNet software group. As they drove up to a decorative wrought-iron gate at the entrance to a red brick, two story structure, Andrei pointed out the property's distinguishing features.

"This is the Polyanka complex. The Metro station is just over there. We're a little south of the Kremlin, across the river."

"So it's a good central location?"

"Our employees would certainly like it," Peter said.

"Exactly," added Andrei. "This was an old Soviet factory site. The developer first built underground parking and then these office buildings. The one we're going to look at over on the left has both a new two-story office portion and an adjoining old factory building. It should be ideal for the light assembly work you envision as the Russian versions of your software go into production."

A security guard opened the gate, and they drove into a courtyard that had been freshly paved with asphalt. Workers were painting the wood trim around what appeared to be new windows on the office portion.

They left Andrei's car and were greeted by a heavyset man in his forties and a slightly taller woman who seemed a bit younger. Andrei introduced David and Peter to the Russian developer and his female American partner who represented the U.S. investors in the enterprise.

David was immediately impressed with the quality of the workmanship and with the thought that had gone into the design.

Andrei had prepared a good summary of the project, and the tour went well. As they were walking back to Andrei's car, David said to their hosts,

"Thank you again for seeing us on the holiday. We appreciate it. If we were interested in this section, how soon could it be ready?"

The Russian replied, with his partner interpreting," As you can see, we're nearly finished with the base building and the first tenant's office space. If you give us your interior specifications quickly, we can be finished in two months."

"Good. Well, Andrei, Peter and I will talk, and we'll get back to you. If we decide to go forward, will you be available tomorrow?"

"Certainly. Despite the May holidays, we're all here this week. Andrei knows our lease terms. We look forward to hearing from you."

David and Andrei were shortly back on the avenue, heading north to David's hotel near the Kremlin.

"I like that space," David said, looking down at the floor plans in his lap. "At dinner let's review what we've seen today."

Ten minutes later David checked with the hotel reception desk; he had no messages. He called home and said a brief hello to Elizabeth. It was too early there to have any news on Rob's behavior. And it was too early to call the office. So he checked his email and made a chart on his laptop with the major positive and negative attributes of the properties they had seen.

A little after seven Andrei and David walked up to an unmarked door near the Bolshoi Theater and knocked. A tall young woman welcomed them into what, a hundred years earlier, had been the living room of a merchant's elegant townhouse. The décor reflected that earlier era; some of the furniture was ordinary, but a few of the pieces were magnificent. There were only six tables, four already filled, and their hostess directed them to the far corner.

As they were seated, Andrei said, "This is a wonderful restaurant. One family runs it and prepares all the dishes. This is the daughter. The son and mother do the cooking. I think you'll like it."

David smiled. "I'm sure I will."

Andrei suggested that he order, and David readily agreed.

Andrei reached for some bread. "David, I have to tell you what happened this afternoon. When I got back to the office, there was a message to call the Polyanka developer. I did, and he wanted me to know that he would pay me a fee if we could do a deal at his project."

"You mean a bribe to push us there?"

"In a way, yes. This is one of those cultural things. He knows that you are paying our firm a fee and that we are representing you. He suggested that he also pay our firm a fee on a successful transaction."

"Without telling us?"

Andrei smiled. "I'm sure in his mind that would be the case—a little extra undisclosed 'incentive' for the broker to steer the client toward his project."

"Well, that would be a bribe in my book."

Andrei raised his hand. "David, don't worry. The guys who taught me this business—now my partners—explained early on that you can't serve two masters. We accept fees only from the party for whom we're working. So I told him 'No thanks'. I actually think he was surprised--pleasantly surprised, by the way."

"Well, maybe he's all right then. I'll trust your judgment. But it's bad when people start taking bribes. Decisions get made for the wrong reasons and pretty soon everyone in the company is stealing or cheating. We have none of it at USNet."

"So let's talk about next steps. If Polyanka is our first choice, let's try to make a deal."

After the waitress took their order, Andrei said, "Actually, I've already drafted a proposal for your approval. Here's the hard copy, and I also emailed it to you. You can make any changes you want in your room tonight, and I'll deliver it to them before nine in the morning."

David smiled. "Great, Andrei. Great. Let's eat now, but we'll keep talking about the details."

"Fine. Na Zdorovy."

Late that afternoon Kristen was in her office reworking some of the figures for their final office negotiations in Singapore, after she and Todd talked through them. Her phone rang.

"Ms. Holloway, this is Phyllis Jordan, Mr. Knox's assistant. How are you?"

"Fine, thank you."

"Good. Mr. Knox and Mr. Burke are doing some capital items budgeting for the next thirty-six months. With Mr. Sawyer overseas, Mr. Knox asked me to check with you to see if there had been any developments on the Capital Tower acquisition."

"No, unfortunately, there haven't. As Mr. Sawyer probably explained when this first came up, we can't do much about Bill Porter's actions and ethics until he actually closes on the purchase. Then we'll have been 'wronged', and we can sue. But of course at that point he will own the property, and we'd be tied up in the courts for years."

"Yes, I see."

"It's terrible when you can't trust people to behave honestly."

"Yes. Well, thank you, and I'll relay your comments to Mr. Knox and Mr. Burke."

"Let me know if I can do anything else."

"Yes, we will. Thank you again."

Callie Sawyer's desk at her uncle's single story real estate office in the Westwood area of Los Angeles was near the receptionist. She had just finished proofing a flyer for a new home listing when her cousin, Yusef, came out of his office. Tall and a few years older than Callie, Yusef had a neat beard and was wearing a conservative blue suit. Unlike Callie's mother, Yusef's mother was of Persian descent, and so Yusef could easily pass for a local on the streets of Tehran, half the world away.

Callie had of course known him all her life, but only as a distant relative at family gatherings. When she originally moved to L.A. to attend a fine arts college, he had been in the Army; and so she was doing her best to get to know him. So far, despite the family connection, he had been pleasant but "professional".

He came to her desk with keys in his hand. "Time to pick up the Ansaris for their home tour. Do you have the information on each property?"

Callie stood and smiled. "Yes. Copies for each of them, and a map showing the homes, the schools, and the shopping areas, as you asked for."

He nodded and walked toward the front door to the parking area. She picked up her purse and the handouts and followed him.

Several minutes later they were driving east in silence to the hotel where their clients were staying.

Callie finally said, "I enjoyed looking up this information and putting it on the map."

"Hmm."

"Which house do you think they will like?"

"Probably the second or third, because they are closest to the best Islamic school for their children."

"Oh. "

They stopped at a red light. Callie asked, "Are a lot of your clients Muslims?"

He turned to look at her. "Not all, of course, but most. Even though I came home from the Army only six months ago, I'm already getting a lot of referrals." The light turned and he drove on.

"Is that why you changed your name from Joseph?"

He shook his head. "No, I changed my name back to its real name to honor Allah—God."

"Oh."

"But it does help identify me as an Iranian Muslim, which so far has been good for business."

"I see. Great."

"Yes, that's what America is all about, isn't it?"

"I guess so."

He paused, then glanced over at her. "In the future, on a day that we are going out, please wear something a little less revealing. My clients are generally conservative, and a dress like that is inappropriate. When I have a chance, I will privately apologize to the husband."

Callie looked down at the dress which she had picked out that morning because she thought it was so business-like. "Uh, OK. I'm sorry. I'll be more careful in the future."

"Good. Now, here we are, and I think that's them waiting by the entrance."

14

Two mornings later, Bill Porter drove north in his expensive European sedan, talking on his cell phone most of the way. Dressed in khaki pants and a cotton shirt, this was the role he relished: a successful real estate mogul able to escape the city on a weekday to evaluate a tract of mountain land, prime for development. Hopefully it would eventually be his development. His only regret was that there would not be enough time for golf at one of several nearby clubs. He had to be back for a late afternoon board meeting. *Oh well, at least when I arrive at the meeting in khakis, they'll know that I had a better day than most of them, cooped up in offices...*

The River Inn was located in a valley surrounded on all but the south side by foothills. Porter parked at one end of the lot, far from the rustic wooden main building—enough people ate lunch early to fill the front spaces. As he got out, the driver's door of a white SUV parked further to the side opened, and a medium-sized man dressed in khaki pants, blue shirt, and a light brown jacket stepped out and raised his right hand.

"Mr. Porter? Hey. I'm Taylor Martin."

Porter locked his door and walked over to the SUV. Martin offered his hand and said, "My brother and cousin are in the truck." Porter saw a man in the front passenger seat and another directly behind him. They smiled and said hello.

"Glad to meet you," Porter responded. Turning to Martin he said, "I'm glad we could get together."

"We appreciate you taking the time," Martin replied. "Here, please sit behind me." He opened the door. "Next to Tom. Stan has the plats. We can talk on the way out to the property."

"Sounds good," Porter replied, climbing in the back seat. "Let's go see it."

Taylor Martin started the SUV, and they headed east out of town. Two blocks off the highway the houses began to thin out, and soon they were on a wooded country road, heading toward the nearby mountains. They talked about rising land values in the surrounding area and the success of high quality mountain developments.

I've got to figure out how to get a piece of this, if it looks good. A great excuse to spend Fridays and maybe even Mondays up here...

As they started to climb, Porter said, "I thought you said the town is putting a sewer near the property. Aren't we getting pretty far out?"

Martin responded from the front seat, "The county's doing it. They're putting in a plant where Sand Creek meets the river, and the line will follow the creek down to it. Our land's right on the creek."

"Oh. OK. Stan, can I see the plat?"

The man in the passenger's seat turned, handed him a paper, and said, "Sure."

Porter unfolded it and saw what appeared to be a three-hundred-acre parcel, split by Sand Creek; but it also appeared to be in the national forest.

"It looks good, particularly if it will have sewer. But is this your land or national forest?"

Martin replied. "Oh, sorry. The boundary on that map is drawn wrong. Our family has owned that piece for years. No sweat. We'll show you all the deeds and records at lunch. The government just goofed when they drew the darned thing."

"Oh." *The topo looks pretty good for single family development, and we might be able to get a small lake out of that bowl-shaped area near the southeast corner. Could be really interesting. But a sewer way out here?*

They drove upward for five more minutes, seeing no other cars on this weekday. They passed a sign announcing the national forest wilderness area. As if he were reading his guest's thoughts, Martin said, "We pass through this piece of the forest and then hit our land."

Martin slowed and turned left up a hill on what was little more than an unmarked logging road through thick woods, recently green again with the coming of spring. In a few moments they were deep into the forest. "We're almost there," Martin announced.

But they drove on and on, fording two shallow streams, bouncing with the rough road.

"Are you sure this is going to come out near Sand Creek?" Porter finally asked. "I thought it was farther to the north."

"Not the tributary we're on. It's up here on our property. Just a few minutes more."

They turned again up an even less traveled trail, with tall grass growing between the wheel ruts. *Where are we going?* Porter wondered. As if in answer, Martin turned the vehicle into a small clearing, not much larger than the area needed to turn around, and stopped, shutting off the engine. He then opened his door and smiled. "Here we are. Let's get out!"

Once they were out and had stretched, Martin said, "We'll spread the plat out on the hood, and I'll get you oriented."

Porter looked around. The dense forest was impressive. You could not see far through it. *People will love this. But we're going to have to improve the access road.*

They gathered around the hood. Martin spread the plat out, and the men leaned over. Stan and Tom were on either side of Porter. Martin pointed and said, "OK, now this is where we are."

As Porter followed Martin's finger, the other two men grabbed him. "Hey! What are you doing?" Before he could react, each wrist was in a cuff, and the cuffs attached by chain to a metal belt Martin pulled around Porter's waist.

As Porter turned, Martin grabbed him roughly around the neck from the back, bending his head down to the SUV's hood, and the other two quickly cuffed his ankles and ran chains up to the belt. Then they felt his pockets, took his cell phone and keys, and backed off a few paces.

Bending over his captured guest, Martin continued his hammerlock and whispered into Porter's right ear, "Enjoying your trip to the mountains, Mr. Porter?"

The real estate agent couldn't speak. He shuddered.

Slowly Martin rose, bringing Porter with him. He released his grip and turned Porter around toward him. Martin said to Stan, "Get the shovel and pick." The cousin nodded and moved to the rear of the SUV. To Porter he said, "We don't actually own any land. At least not around here. You're pretty good. You almost figured out that something was dead wrong. And I guess in a little while you'll be right!" The three of them laughed.

Porter felt a chill, and pain from the cuffs, which were cinched too tightly around his wrists. "What...what do you mean?"

"We mean, Mr. Porter," Martin spoke calmly, "that we got you up here for your last property visit. In a little while we're going to kill you."

It was the matter-of-fact tone of Martin's voice. *Kill me!?!*

"What?"

Stan returned with the tools, and Martin locked the SUV. "How hard is that to understand? I said we're going to kill you. And the reason is because we're being paid well to do it. Come on, let's go." He pointed past the hood of the vehicle into the woods and turned Porter in that direction. Tom led the way.

Stan pushed, and Porter started to walk but could not take a full step. He followed slowly, looking down at the ground and balancing with his hands out in front.

"Why? What did I do?"

Martin, following behind and watching his captive closely, said, "We don't know. None of our business. We just get paid to do a job, and we do it."

Again he shuddered as they moved in single file under the trees, not on any path. *That's it!* He raised his voice. "The building. Capital Tower. That stupid building! You're threatening to murder me over that stupid building! Is that it?"

"We're not threatening to murder you. We're *going* to murder you."

"Look—I'll—I'll do whatever you want. You can have the building. Give me my cell phone. I'll call right now and cancel the contract. You can have it!"

"Sorry. We don't want it. In fact, we don't know what you're talking about. Well, here we are."

They had reached a small area that was almost flat with plenty of tree cover. Martin came around to face Porter. "Now here's the deal." From inside his coat Martin pulled out an automatic pistol fitted with a silencer. "We've got these tools here. Either you can dig your own grave, which means you'll live a little longer. You can think, pray, whatever—while you dig. Or you can not dig, in which case I'll shoot you now, and we'll have to dig. Which will it be?"

I can't believe this! It's got to be a bluff. They won't really do it. They're just pushing me to see what I'll do because they want the building. When I get back I'll get these people.

"I told you. You can have Capital Tower. People don't kill over buildings, for God's sake! Do you have a paper you want me to sign?"

"And I told *you*. We don't know nothin' about any building—or anything else. I've given you a choice. Dig and live a little longer, or don't dig and die now." He raised the automatic. "Which will it be?"

"I—I guess I'll dig."

Martin smiled. "Good. Stan, unlock his hands from the cuff. Just remember that I've got my gun on you. Here, Mr. Porter, dig over on this side, about where you're standing. We did somebody else about a year ago over there."

Bill Porter looked down and was horrified to see that in fact the earth where Martin was pointing had been disturbed, although it was now covered with pine straw and would never be noticed unless someone pointed it out.

"Thing about this place is, no one will *ever* find you! You'll be missing for days. Then weeks. Years. Just gone. Picked a good place, didn't we?"

Porter felt his stomach turn, and his knees became weak.

"Hey, Mr. Martin...seriously. What do you want? I've got a wife and three kids under ten years old. Please. I'll double whatever you're being paid. Triple it. I'll give them the building. Just please don't kill me."

"Hey, I understand. And I'm sorry. This is just business. If we renege on this deal, we'll all be dead. So, we just have to go through with it. Now I suggest you start with the pickax. Don't dig too slow. And I've got a round in the chamber, so don't try anything funny." Martin backed away and tossed the pickax at Porter's feet.

He bent down and picked it up. *This can't be real.* His mind was running in overdrive, but his motions were in a dream, like he was watching someone else. The pickax came up and made a first cut into the soft dirt. The other men watched. He moved the dirt to the side, and as if on its own, the ax took another swing.

What will Linda do? And the kids? Never see them again! This is insane. I have so much I want to do! All those projects. As he swung the ax again, his view of it was suddenly clouded by tears. They ran down his cheeks and onto his hands.

In the silence of the digging, Porter heard birds and other sounds in the forest. *Should I pray? I haven't prayed in years. God...please, help me! Please get me out of this. I promise that if I get through this, I'll give them back the building—no argument. I'll just give it to them...and ...and I'll give ten percent of everything I own to the church...no, twenty percent. Please, God!*

Porter continued to dig—not too quickly—with both the ax and the shovel.

"Needs to be a little longer, I think," Martin said at one point, when the trench was about two feet deep. Don't want you to be crowded!" The three men chuckled again. Porter shivered uncontrollably, then began to chip away at the end to make it longer.

Should I pray for forgiveness? To 'accept Jesus' like they say on TV? I don't know. What does that mean? God, I'm sorry I've done some things that weren't maybe too good. Please forgive me. But please just get me out of this, and I won't do anything wrong again.

He continued to watch the ax swing...on and on...

He had no idea when they'd say it was enough. He slowed down his pace. His lungs tightened, and he had difficulty breathing. From in the trench, he looked up at Martin. "Please. Look. One more time. People don't kill each other over business deals. OK? I admit that I didn't do exactly right. If you're wearing a wire and you want to get that on tape. OK. I admit it. I'm sorry. I'll give the building back. Let's just stop this charade, and I'll pay you five times whatever they're paying you. Five times! In cash, this afternoon."

"Just keep digging, Mr. Porter," Martin said, and took a few steps closer to look at the work.

Porter bent down to plant the shovel. Unseen by him, Martin raised the pistol toward his head. *People just don't kill people over busin—*

The spit of the silenced automatic disturbed the birds in the trees overhead, but for only an instant.

Earlier that day David and Andrei had finished intense negotiations in which they secured the Polyanka building for USNet's expansion in Moscow. At an attorney's office the two principals signed a simple but thorough dual language letter of intent.

David, Andrei and Andrei's wife had just enjoyed a celebratory dinner.

"Thanks again for a great night, and for a great job," David said, as he opened the door to Andrei's car after their dinner.

"Well, thank you, David, but we still have a long way to go to finish the space, starting with the lease."

"I know. But I'm sure if they even halfway stick to their word, we can work it out." Turning to Andrei's wife in the back seat, he said, "Thanks to you both. I'll check with you next week, Andrei, once we see their proposed lease." He got out and opened the back door, then helped Andrei's wife to the front seat.

The two men shook hands through the window. "OK. Have a good flight."

David turned and walked into his hotel, looking at his watch and realizing that he only had a few hours to sleep before the early taxi ride to the airport. In his room he checked his email, downloading Kristen's final Singapore report, several complex questions from Paul Burke about two of the California properties he had visited, and requests from Todd, Chris and Cheryl for his input on their current projects, all of which he planned to read on the plane. He packed the last items except what he would wear on the flight. He sat on the edge of the bed and called Elizabeth. She confirmed that on Tuesday Rob had only spent a little more than an hour online after school, at least as far as she could tell, and David gave her his flight arrival time for Thursday afternoon.

"So I'll see you tomorrow about supper time," he concluded.

"OK. I love you, David. Have a safe trip."

"I love you, too."

David hung up and decided that he might sleep better if he took a shower. But an hour later he lay in bed in the dark, wide awake. He was already focusing on what had to be done back in the office, after thinking only about Moscow for the last six days.

He glanced over at the illuminated clock on the bedside table: 2:05. He decided to check his email. Five minutes later he saw, among others, a familiar name on his laptop and clicked to open it.

Wednesday 16:47

To: David Sawyer

From: TonyB

Subj: Amateur Mid-East Bombshell Does It All--AGAIN

David,

If this is your daughter, she's something else. Must make your Iranian blood boil!

Or maybe because she's on a USNet site, it makes you proud.

Your friend,

Tony

The link was at the bottom of the email. He hesitated, circling his cursor around the icon, then clicked. A moment later he was whisked to a movie site and into the bedroom of ...his daughter. And there was Alex. He watched for a few moments, fast forwarded, watched again, and then closed it. He stared at his home page for quite a while, not moving. *What is she doing?*

He went back to bed, but for the next two hours, he checked the clock about every fifteen minutes, thinking of Callie and his family. *I can't tell Elizabeth about this. It would kill her. But maybe now she'll understand why we have to be tough with Callie. What if a family member in L.A. saw it?*

His racing mind tripped over the fact that L.A. was eleven hours behind Moscow, so it would be afternoon there. He sat up in bed and turned on the bedside lamp. After thinking for another moment, he got up, washed his face and picked up his handheld. Shortly he was dialing Callie's cell phone from his bed.

He was never optimistic with her mobile phone, but on the third ring she answered.

"Hello," said his daughter's voice, somewhat questioningly. David was not sure whether her digital readout would register a call from Russia.

"Hey, Callie. It's Dad."

"Oh. Where are you?"

"Actually I'm in Moscow—though I'll be leaving for home in a few hours. How are you?"

"Uh, I'm fine. Yeah, Mom told me that you would be going there. How is it?"

"Not at all like I expected. It's really almost a 'normal' place. More like the U.S. than you'd think from watching the news."

"Um. Good. I'm sure that you've been very successful."

The slight sarcasm baiting her voice almost had the desired effect, but he fought back his reaction and plowed ahead, trying to sound normal.

"Yes. Well, I hadn't planned to call you because I assume that you're still with Alex, but then I do really love and care about you, so I thought that I'd check in and see how you're doing."

A pause. "Really good. We're fine. I'm finishing up papers in two classes. Exams will be in two weeks. Just the usual."

"And Alex?"

"He interviewed for two jobs and may go to summer school."

"Well, uh, good. Good. But, Callie, I got a link to another video that you've done, or at least I think it's you—and Alex."

Silence.

"Callie, did you do another one? You don't need to do that. It's terrible."

"You used to help me. But you told us that we're on our own. So it was a quick way to make some good money. And we may make some more because now your company has a program where we can upload a video, and as people pay to watch, we get half. How about that for entrepreneurship? We have a way to make it on our own. No one can really tell it's me."

"I think you're wrong there. I got an email from the same man—he likes to rub my face in it."

"So it's a problem for *you*. Is that the real issue? That someone in the company or in our extended Iranian family might recognize me and call you?"

Silence.

"Is that the real problem, Dad? Well, if they call, you can just tell them that you've cut me off."

"Callie, why are you doing this?"

"Why am *I* doing this? I was just minding my own business and doing what I'm sure most young people do, when my father humiliated my boyfriend and disowned me a few weeks ago. Now I have to fend for myself—with Alex. And we are."

"Callie, making a porn movie is wrong."

"We're acting and just having fun, and most people will never know who it is. And if it's wrong to make one, is it right to make money by hosting them on the internet? If Alex and I are wrong, what about USNet? They've made it so that if we sponsor someone else, we make twenty-five percent of what they bring in. So we've asked Jane and her boyfriend to try it. Then if they sponsor someone, we get ten percent. Your company knows how to motivate entrepreneurs."

"I...I can't argue with you about that. I'm not proud that we do it. But that's business. This is our family. Your personal choices."

"And yours. To disown me and to stay at USNet."

"I can't leave USNet over a tiny piece of what we do. That would be crazy. And I can't countenance you living with a man when you're not married—especially one who treats you like Alex treats you."

"Dad, we're about to get into the same argument that we had three weeks ago. We're getting nowhere. For the record, I'm safe and I'm fine. Let's just stop here before we repeat everything all over again."

Is there nothing more to say to my daughter? "Callie. I love you, and I hope that you'll think again about all that you're doing."

"Goodbye, Dad. Have a good flight."

He put down the phone, switched off the light, and lay back in bed. He was angry with Callie and Rob, and upset with Knox and Kristen.

How can I stop my children from doing destructive things? Can't they see the consequences?

At least for the moment my own part of the business is going well. I'll focus on that, but I've got to come up with solutions for Rob and Callie .

In what seemed like only a few moments, the alarm went off.

I hope I can sleep on the plane.

That afternoon, a few hours after David's plane took off, Pavel Sivyakov was driving out to the warehouse to meet his friends. The last few days had been ones of great worry and tension, but in the end they had decided to take the offer from the second group. So they had purchased plane and train tickets, and he had instructed his wife to begin packing for a short trip—he did not want her to become hysterical about leaving Russia, probably forever.

In four hours, after it was dark, they were to meet with three men who were coming to inspect the missiles, and they were bringing the money. He could not help feeling both excited and relieved. It was almost done.

He had just pulled up to the parking lot which surrounded the former auto repair facility when his phone rang. His friends' cars were not yet there, so he assumed that it was one of them calling. He stopped the engine and answered his phone.

"Turn on your camera," a male voice said.

He turned on the two-way connection, and there, in front of him, were his wife and daughter, with tape across their mouths and their hands bound. Their wild, wet eyes told him all he needed to know.

The voice behind the other phone said, "We mean them no harm. This is just extra insurance that our transaction tonight goes smoothly, and that you do not have any plans to change the terms, or the product. Do you understand?"

He could barely muster the breath to say, "Yes."

When his friends arrived he told them about his wife and daughter. They encouraged him that all would go well, and that they would be living their new lives within just two days. They set about making the launcher and the missiles it contained ready for careful inspection.

Precisely at nine o'clock they heard two cars pull up outside the warehouse, and Pavel went outside through the personnel door next to the large roll-up door which had been closed since their special product arrived. He was confronted by six, not three, large men in blue fatigues. They were armed with rifles and pistols, and two of them immediately began walking down the sides of the building. The one closest to him, from the lead car, said, "Are you Mr. Sivyakov?"

Pavel nodded, looking warily at the men and their arms.

"I am Boris Rusnak, and we are here to do business with you. We would like to see inside."

Pavel stepped out of the way. Rusnak and two others went inside, and he followed.

After nodding to the others standing together inside the door, the two with Rusnak fanned out and looked all around the facility, ignoring the missile launcher in the middle of the floor. When they both nodded, Rusnak used a walkie-talkie clipped to his shirt, and a moment later a third car drove up outside.

The two men who now entered the space were not like the first six; clearly these were men whose expertise would advance the transaction. Without saying anything to anyone, except to ask for the code to operate the launcher mechanisms, the two looked and took readings and examined every part of the missiles and their carrier. Pavel and his friends stood and watched, shifting from foot to foot, and making small talk. Finally the two experts walked to Rusnak, conversed with him for a moment, and left. Pavel heard their car depart.

Rusnak walked over and extended his hand with a smile. "Congratulations. We have confirmed that the product is as you said. Would you like your money now?"

Pavel felt a wave of relief, smiled, shook Rusnak's hand and looked at his friends. "Yes, of course."

Rusnak spoke into the phone again, and a moment later there was the sound of another vehicle outside. Two men came into the warehouse with five satchels over their shoulders, and dropped them on the floor by Rusnak.

"Five satchels with $1 million in $100 bills. Please check them."

Pavel and each of his friends picked up a bag, opened it, and looked inside. Pavel pulled out one of the many wrapped bundles, and was delighted to see so many faces of Benjamin Franklin. He looked around, and the friends nodded to each other.

"Then, please," Rusnak said, "the keys to the launcher. And, by the way, I congratulate you on your craftsmanship and welding skills. It really does look like any other large truck. If you will open the door, we will depart."

Pavel reached in his pocket to hand over the keys, and motioned to his colleague to roll up the door. One of the men who had brought the money satchels took the keys, climbed into the cab, and started the engine.

Rusnak turned to Pavel. "So far all has gone as planned. We do not wish to be followed. For the sake of the insurance that you saw on your phone, stay inside this facility for five minutes after you hear the last of our engines. Then you will be free to go."

Pavel nodded. "Understood. They will be unharmed?"

"You have my word." Rusnak extended his hand, and they shook again. "It has been a pleasure." He looked at his compatriots as the lorry went into gear. "Let's go."

Rusnak waited outside until the lorry and the other car were down the road. Then he took out a small gun-like device and pointed it toward the warehouse for a moment. It beeped. He got into the car and said to his colleague behind the wheel, "Pull up to that rise." The car departed.

They stopped a short distance away. Rusnak looked at his watch. Thirty seconds later he saw the contrail of the incoming missile. A moment later there was a huge explosion and the warehouse was engulfed in flames.

Rusnak smiled. "It's a pity how dangerous welding can be. They should have been more careful."

The driver asked, "What about all that money?"

Rusnak made a motion with his hand as he watched the conflagration. "Counterfeit, except for the first few bills in each bundle. A small price. Let's go."

As they pulled out into the road again, he said, almost to himself, "The bastards. They stole from the motherland. What did they expect?"

15

Friday at the office was a blur. David had not scheduled any important meetings, using the time while his body and brain adjusted to read his mail, catch up with each member of his team, and return phone calls. Saturday afternoon he took Elizabeth to a baseball game; Rob said he was too busy to go. Then they slept late that Sunday morning.

The Sawyers were sipping coffee in bed, about to read the Sunday paper, when the phone rang.

"Hey, David. It's Kristen. Are you awake?" He was surprised. Members of his team knew that they could call him at any time, but, still, Sunday morning was unusual.

"Yes, we're up. How are you?"

"Have you seen the article in this morning's paper about Bill Porter?"

"No. I was just about to start reading the paper. What wonderful thing has he done now?"

"Actually, he's missing. Since Wednesday night. There was a piece on last night's news about it, but the article this morning—it's in the Metro section—has more information."

He put his coffee on the bedside table. "Since Wednesday? I'm turning to it." There was silence as David read the article. "They found his car outside an inn north of here? Wonder what he was doing there."

"Well, it'll be hard to involve us. That's one place where USNet has no assets."

"Why do you say 'involve us'?"

Kristen paused. "Well, I was just thinking about his voicemail—when he said he'd been threatened. And he accused us."

Elizabeth turned the paper slightly in his hand so that she could read it.

"Kristen, why would anyone pull us into something like this? I mean, I hope they find him—wandering in the woods, or on one of his romantic safaris in the mountains with a broker or attorney of the female persuasion. But it would be quite a stretch to implicate us. We didn't do anything."

"I know, I know. But it was so recent—his call. Anyway, I just thought we should talk about it, and that's why I called."

"That's fine. I'll read the article, and we'll talk tomorrow if he hasn't turned up. But, please, Kristen, *don't* call the police and tell them that he said we threatened him ten days ago."

He could picture her smile in the tone of her voice. "Oh, I know not to do that. But I *will* pray for him and his family."

"Good. Please *do* pray for them. And have a great Sunday. I'll be working on all the stuff you guys left for me while I was gone. Now I remember why I hate leaving on these assignments."

"I guess that's why you're the boss. All your real estate children are glad you're back. See you tomorrow."

He hung up and told Elizabeth, who had listened quietly to his side of the conversation, the rest of the story.

"That's terrible. A wife and three young children. You know, you people in real estate *are* too trusting. Meeting people you don't know all over everywhere based on a phone call."

"He'll turn up. Probably doing something he shouldn't. But I hope he's all right. Anyway, when is Rob likely to be up?"

An hour later, over a late morning brunch of waffles and bacon, David, Elizabeth and Rob talked about his internet games. Parents and son recited their previous positions on the subject. In the end they reached a compromise that after a week Rob could resume playing the games one hour a night during the week, and four hours total on weekends. They further agreed that with an A average in all subjects, the restrictions would be off; but if his grades did not improve to at least B's, the games would be cut out all together.

David asked, "Is that OK with you, Rob?"

"Well, I guess it's better than no games at all."

"Our plan makes the result totally up to you."

Rob looked down. "Yeah. I know."

Sounding positive, his father asked, "OK, then, is that our agreement?"

Rob glanced up. "Sure. I guess."

"Good. Now, can I help you with any of your homework?"

"No. I don't have much."

"Well, let me know."

Knox's meeting with Kamali and Mustafin would be at his lake home. He had arranged for his current love interest to visit her mother in Cincinnati for the weekend. Knox had asked his two chief lieutenants to drive out to discuss special projects that could only involve the three of them.

Wearing shorts, knit shirts, and boat shoes, they sat in wooden chairs on the dock adjoining Knox's boathouse, sipping coffee.

"I read in the paper," Knox said, putting down his mug, "that a fairly well-known commercial real estate agent has been missing for several days."

Mustafin nodded, a trace of a smile on his lips. "Yes, I heard the same thing. A pity."

They were silent. The breeze coming across the lake rippled the water.

"Before we begin, Mr. Knox," Kamali said, "let me tell you that I heard from Cleve Danforth yesterday. He reached a definitive agreement to buy a controlling interest in Ezon Communications. Of course the public agreement doesn't mention how we're quietly covering the trading losses rung up by their CFO. The price we're paying is a steal for the technology they control."

Knox nodded and sipped his coffee. "Good. Good. Our RTI capabilities used at their best. Now, what about our Bible-thumping President Harper?"

Kamali looked over at Mustafin, who nodded. "Mr. Knox, thanks in part to the timely acquisition in Russia on Thursday, we think we have a foolproof plan to get rid of her."

Knox cradled his cup in his lap. "How long will it take?"

"Two, at most three months."

Knox leaned back and took a sip. "Good. Let me hear it."

The next morning David was in his office early. *There's so much going on—so much we've got to get done. I need more experienced people, not one less.* He planned to meet with his key personnel, even if the process ran into Tuesday, to be sure that every requirement was on track.

At about ten, as he was finishing his meeting with Cheryl Miller, Kristen stopped by his office door. "Hi. I'm going to the health club for lunch. Want to join me?"

"Uh...yeah. Sure." He smiled. "What time?"

"I'll come by about eleven forty-five. OK?"

One of their employee perks was a fitness center and health bar that took up half of the fourth floor. On the rare days that he had time, Sawyer enjoyed a run to break up the day. The jogging clothes in his locker allowed for spur of the moment decisions, like today's.

After running three miles on a treadmill next to Kristen, he took a shower and joined her in the health bar, decorated with light blue walls and nutrition posters, where she was standing in a short line for a shake. The tables and stools were crowded, and the place was noisy.

He joined her, his tie in hand, and smiled, "Thanks. I needed that."

She turned as the person in front of her ordered a shake. "Yes. Much better. Glad you could come. But you men have it so easy." She ran her fingers through her hair, which was still damp. "I'll blow it dry after our shakes."

"Yep. No question. Listen, tell me what you want and go grab that spot." He nodded to an empty table that was slightly apart from the rest.

"OK. A Caribbean, please. And I'll get some water for us."

A couple of minutes later they were seated together, Kristen to his right. David took a long drink of ice water. Putting down the glass, he asked, "Has there been any word on Bill Porter?"

Kristen shook her head. "Not when I last checked online."

"I sure hope he turns up."

"Me, too."

They spoke for a few minutes about David's trip to Moscow and her projects, and then David leaned forward over his shake and said, "I hadn't planned this, but I'd like to talk with you about something."

"Yes." She took a sip through her straw and looked at him.

"Well, this is not particularly easy. But, well, you know our daughter Callie of course, and that she's been in school in California."

"Yes, sure."

"Well, look. You obviously have values and morals. I mean, never mind about what happened several years ago with that Congresswoman's husband. You're just sort of different from a lot of people."

She put her shake down and smiled. "Is that a compliment?"

"Yes, very much. Anyway, I need help, and maybe you're the right person. It—it turns out that Callie has been living with a guy who I think is a jerk-- Alex. He has no job and no future, and I refused to continue to support her so that they can live together. He even secretly recorded a session of them in bed and put it on the internet! When I found out about him, about a month ago, I told her to choose between him and our family. She chose him, so I cut off her money. What else could I do? Now they've made an actual adult movie. Callie must have agreed. Apparently to make money." He could see the surprised reaction on her face. "It's terrible. Our daughter! And, Kristen, this awful stuff is being hosted by a USNet share site!"

While he spoke he slightly rocked. Kristen sighed. "I'm so sorry."

"You're the only one who knows, besides Elizabeth, and I haven't told her about the videos. Callie thinks no one will know it's her, but someone who used to work here has already sent me the links!"

"You talked with her about all of this, from Alex to money to the movie?"

He nodded and took a deep breath. "Yes, when I was out there, and since then on the phone."

"What does she say?"

"That I've cut her off and they have to live somehow. Apparently these movies pay well."

"Ugh. Bad choices. David, how can I help?"

"I...I don't know, Kristen. But I thought that, well, you're a woman. And you've been through some tough times. Yet you always seem to be OK. Like you know you'll get through it, somehow. Some sort of confidence, even peace." He looked up. "I was wondering if you could help Elizabeth and me figure out what to do. How to get her to stop—all of it. Go back to being a fine arts student, without Alex or these movies. I'm out of suggestions. And I *really* need help."

"Of course, David, I'll do whatever I can. I don't know a lot about pornography, or why someone would do it, but I'll try to find out. And then what? Maybe I should call her? Do you think she would remember me?"

Again he paused. "Kristen, at this point I'm at my wit's end. Elizabeth just wants to talk with her, like everything is OK. That's fine, I guess, but Callie may soon be pregnant or dying of AIDS. She's mad at me, and I alternate between being mad at her and wanting to kidnap her. So *anything* you can think of will be most appreciated. Here's her number. It's a cell phone. Usually it takes a while to get her."

"OK, let me think. And pray. And check with a few people, and then I'll see."

He nodded. "Thank you, Kristen. I don't know who else to turn to."

"I'll try to help. And what about XXXtra Cinema? Isn't it absurd that our own company is doing this to young women—and men?"

"Yes. I tried once to ask Knox about it, but he says that there's too much profit to stop. And 'no victims.'"

Kristen shook her head. "Oh—right. No victims."

"Yes, I know. Well, at this point I'm just focused on one victim: Callie. Maybe I can address the larger issue when I know that she's all right."

"Don't bet on any change."

"I know. I know. Well, thank you. I hope you don't mind me telling you about all of this." He took her empty cup and started to rise.

She pushed back and stood up. "No. I'll do all I can. In fact, since I'm going to Singapore again on Thursday, maybe I can call and stay over in L.A.—going or coming—and see her. Sort of 'girl talk' about all this with her."

He smiled. "That would be great. I'll give you her address. Now I guess we better get back to the salt mines. Phyllis Jordan called, and Knox wants to see me about something at three."

She started to head back to the locker room but turned. "That reminds me," Kristen said. "Phyllis called last week while you were away to ask about any progress on Capital Tower. She said that Knox and Burke were doing capital budgeting and wanted to know if we would be buying it."

He frowned. "I briefed them right before I left on the Porter situation. Odd that they'd call again. Hey, maybe if Porter stays missing we *will* buy Capital Tower."

"David, don't be gross. He has a wife and kids."

"And how many girlfriends?"

"Come on. He's missing, and none of us is perfect."

"You're right. I'm sorry. And on perfection, I guess maybe I'm learning."

Monday 14:30
To: Blue Nine
From: Street War 2100
Subj: New Unlimited Status
Blue Nine:
Your teammates have missed you the last few days. And the world has missed your help in resisting the Aggressor Force.

If you're unhappy with the game for any reason, please let us know. If you've just been away, or busy, we want to welcome you back with a special offer. Because you've been such a valued participant, we're upgrading you to Unlimited status, meaning that you can play any time, day or night, 24/7, for the same monthly fee you've been paying for only 50 hours.

We hope that your new Unlimited status means that you'll be enjoying Street War 2100 even more. Your team welcomes you back. Log on soon. We need you!

Commander Blue One

That night Todd Phelps was leaving a sports bar where he and his Fantasy Football friends spent occasional Monday nights in the off-season watching other sports, in this case Monday Night Baseball. His car was in a lot on the unlit side of the building, parked between two vans.

As he stood by the car door, fumbling in his pocket from the effects of the last three hours, the van door behind him suddenly opened and four strong hands grabbed him. Before he could yell, he was on his knees on the cargo floor, and the door was shut. He struggled, but the two men held him tight, one hand around his mouth. He looked up and saw a third man sitting on a chair behind the driver's seat, facing him, his face dimly visible from the glow of some electronic equipment set up next to him.

The seated man said, "Mr. Phelps, please don't struggle. We're not going to hurt you. May I call you Todd? My name is Taylor Martin." He smiled.

Todd stopped pushing against the hands.

"Good. Now, we want to give you some news, and an opportunity. But we have to be able to talk. If you calm down, we won't harm you, and you'll be on your way home in ten minutes. Do you understand?"

Todd slowly nodded.

"Good. Then Stan is going to take his hand away from your mouth, and we'll talk. But if you try to yell or get free before we're done, then we *will* hurt you. Feel the point of that knife in your back? It would be a great shame to cut you, but we will. Do you understand?"

Todd nodded again. Martin nodded, and Stan slowly withdrew his hand. But the others stayed in place.

Martin smiled again. "Now, here's the first thing we want to talk about." He turned slightly to his left and pushed a button on an MP3 player. Immediately Todd's conversation with Mr. Blevin on the Isle of Man was playing through small speakers. Todd's eyes widened.

When the conversation ended, Martin looked at him and his smile became a grin. "And we've got lots of conversations between you and your good friend Mike Campbell. We'll be glad to play them for you. Plus copies of some bank deposits. Pretty interesting stuff, wouldn't you say?"

Todd just looked at him. Finally he asked, "How?"

"Oh, that doesn't matter. But I suspect a lot of folks would be interested in these, huh? Maybe David Sawyer. Your wife. Even the district attorney. You know, he's been on a crusade lately trying to find illegal business practices, wantin' to get re-elected. He'd have a field day with all of this, wouldn't he? I bet he'd ask for at least ten years without parole. Long time not to see your boys."

Todd stared ahead, trying to understand what was happening.

After a pause, Martin said, "Now, I also said we want to talk with you about an opportunity to think about, along with what we just told you. There's a group that gathers intelligence on companies and on some people, and they need smart, quick people like you to help. It's all done with computers. Probably a little bit of it's not technically within the confines of the legal rules and regulations, but no one gets hurt. It just helps the business make money. In fact, it helps so much that the folks involved can make an extra half million or more a year by being a part of the process. From what the leadership has seen of you, they think you may be good for this work."

"You mean another job?"

"Well, sort of. You'd stay where you are at USNet, and no one would ever know about what we've just been showing you. And several hours a week you'd do this other thing."

"Several hours a week can make half a million a year?"

"Yes, in addition to your USNet salary. By the way, I think you'd have to stop taking Mike Campbell's bribes—someone else might find out about them, which would be bad for you. And they might not have an alternative to prosecution, like we do."

"So you're offering to 'forget' about the situation with Mike—I can keep that money—and you'll give me a way to earn a lot more?"

Martin nodded. "Yep. That's it. That's your choice. If you'd prefer, we can send all this stuff out in the morning to the people we mentioned."

"Who's behind the intelligence work?"

Martin shook his head. "You'll learn more later. No need to know everything at once. Just some smart folks who know how to make a lot of money."

"I see. I guess I don't have a choice."

"Sure you do. In fact, why don't you sleep on it, and call us tomorrow with your answer. Here's a phone that will only call one number once, so be somewhere that you can talk. If we don't hear from you tomorrow, we'll let this information out on Wednesday. Understood?"

Todd nodded. "Yes."

Martin extended his hand, and Todd's right arm was released. "Well, it's been a real pleasure meetin' you. Sorry for the way we started, but I guess you can see that we couldn't just call you on the phone about this."

They shook hands, and Stan opened the side door.

Todd got out slowly, his knees sore from the floor. He unlocked his car's door, got in, and drove off.

Taylor Martin took out a phone and pressed a button. The voice at the other end answered with a slight accent. "Yes?"

"I think your boy will be all right. He's going to let you know tomorrow."

"Good. I hope that the others are as cooperative."

16

TUESDAY, MAY 10TH

The elevator door was about to close when Kristen saw Todd approaching, so she held the door, and they began the ride up to the thirty-third floor.

"Thanks," he said, shifting his briefcase.

"Hey, wasn't that a new version of your old ride I saw you in yesterday afternoon?"

He smiled. "Yeah. I guess so. Really nice."

"I bet. Looks great."

"Thanks." The door opened. They walked through the reception area and down the hall to their offices. Kristen booted her laptop into the network, quickly checked her email and voicemails, and then headed to get a cup of coffee. Ten minutes later, her cup half finished as she emailed final instructions to their brokers in the Far East, her phone rang.

"Hello, Kristen, it's Claudia Coleman. How are you this morning?"

"Uh, fine. But, actually, pretty busy. I'm getting ready for a trip to Singapore and Japan in two days. How can I help you?"

"I won't be long." She repeated the story she'd heard about XXXtra Cinema's major expansion around Los Angeles. "And since it's primarily a real estate matter, I thought that you might be able to help me."

"How?"

"By either confirming or denying it, for starters."

"Well, our boss spent some time out there about a month ago, and I believe our goal is to expand those facilities, but I'm not directly involved myself, so I couldn't say."

"How do you feel about it?"

"About what?"

"As a woman, and one with traditional values, as you have portrayed to me. What do you think about your employer, USNet, taking over a large portion of the adult movie business?"

Kristen turned from her desk and looked out the window. She took a deep breath and leaned back slightly in her chair, trying to pull her thoughts away from the Far East.

"Ms. Coleman, we could talk about that for a long time. But it would have to be totally off the record. I don't make policies here. I love my work, which is basically evaluating and executing real estate transactions. But I don't usually decide which markets, or which product types. You'll have to ask the people who make those decisions."

"But you support President Harper's initiative, which is trying to rein in the adult entertainment industry, and you're in the real estate department of a large company that is expanding in this same industry. Doesn't that seem a little strange?"

"Do you believe that pornography is good?" Kristen asked.

"What?"

"I asked whether you think pornography is a good thing. Should we as a nation encourage it?"

"Well, I would never indulge in it myself, of course, but it's a free country, so I guess if we start censoring stuff, where does it stop? Next thing they'll be censoring the *Journal*."

"I didn't say censor. I just asked whether our nation as a general rule should support and encourage pornography, so that it's literally available on every TV and computer, and at every newsstand and movie theater in the land? Or should it be put back in the sleaze bag that it used to travel in?"

"What I think isn't important. I'd like *your* opinion, since it's USNet that's expanding in this area."

"What about the women—and men—who work in porn? Should it be legal for eighteen year olds to act in these movies? Do you think anything else goes along with that kind of job? As a woman, are women's rights in general advanced by holding up an absurd proposition to men—and to boys—that sex is just free entertainment? Just a commodity. No consequences. And that women instantly consent to every imaginable sex act with occasional men, with beaming smiles on our faces?"

There was a pause. "I guess I can't say that I'm pleased about those aspects of it."

"Well, when was the last time the *Journal* or any other mainstream news organization—print or TV—did any sort of balanced piece on pornography?"

"I couldn't say."

"I've never seen one. Never. That's *your* industry. But it's the sort of thing I grapple with in *my* industry, Ms. Coleman. I'm doing my job, and trying to do it well. But my company may be doing some things I don't like. What do I do? Quit? Try to change it? Forget it? I don't know. And I guess my point is that I'll think about giving you an on the record answer about my personal beliefs when you tell me that you're writing a stand-up piece on the true ramifications and victims of pornography. And even then they will only be my personal thoughts. I don't make USNet policy, and I won't comment on it as long as I'm here."

Another pause. "Well, I appreciate your insight—and even your questions."

Kristen turned back to her desk. "It's not easy, having values and beliefs. Knowing where to draw the line. To say 'enough is enough.'"

"I understand. And I'll think about that piece on pornography you suggested."

"You'd better check first to see if the *Journal* will publish it."

"Of course they will."

"I've talked to a couple of our own reporters about it. And trust me, you'd better check."

"OK. Well, I'm sorry you wouldn't comment, but thanks for confirming that your boss has been working on it. At least I know to keep digging."

"Sure, any time. But my comments were totally off the record, and now I've got a lot to do."

"Understood. Thanks. Have a great trip."

"Thanks."

She hoped she had said the right things this time—nothing--and that the Coleman woman would never call again.

Todd Phelps closed the door to his office and stared out the window.

Half a million dollars a year or more. Think what Mary and I can do with that. Out of debt—forever. Almost anything Mary wants, I can get it for her. Remodel the house. Trips. Our boys can go to college anywhere they want.

I guess I'll have the other thing hanging over me, but maybe there'll be a way to get out of it, once I understand who these people are.

Seems like a no-brainer. Disaster and jail, or lots of money.

He picked up the phone that the man with the country accent had given him and pushed the Call button. Someone with a foreign accent answered and asked if he had made his decision. After Todd accepted the offer, he was given an early morning appointment a week later to begin his training.

A few hours later, Victor Mustafin was in his office at the Real Time Intercepts command center, housed in the back half of an old bank clearing house. The main RTI operations center was half a world away in Pakistan. There, in one large room that resembled a computerized trading floor, twenty-five people at a time monitored the flow of information and passed interesting intercepts to two on-site decision makers. These men, all of whom had business experience in the West, usually decided how to use the stolen data.

But years earlier Knox had realized that this was not enough—to get the most from what they harvested every day from emails and calls, they needed oversight by trusted business people in the U.S., who could make the right decisions based on history, current news, subtleties of language—nuances that only native-speaking business people would understand.

So RTI had a small group of trusted duty officers who stood duty on a rotating basis in the U.S., Europe and Asia 24/7, to make decisions when an issue could not be resolved in Pakistan.

After extensive individual training by Victor Mustafin, each duty officer was on call, monitoring RTI activity from one of the three control centers, making decisions and occasionally referring issues to the unspecified "Council", which was actually Mustafin, Kamali and Knox. With this isolated security structure, the duty officers did not know most of their counterparts, except by code names. These men were paid extremely well—a share of the monthly profits. But they were also the most difficult to select—many came from USNet's ranks, simply because so much could be known about them. Still, they were monitored for loyalty; and the consequences for divulging any part of the operation was clear.

The small US command center consisted of an office, a conference room, and the former massive bank vault, now converted to the control room, complete with two walls full of monitors. Here each duty officer served his hours when on watch.

Kamali and Mustafin administered the operation, though Kamali never visited the office in person—only by remote access. In fact, the two lieutenants made a point never to be seen together in public. There were therefore no visible connections to USNet, and only Kamali and Mustafin knew that the ultimate decision maker was Knox.

The operation was complex, but it had been successful for years. The problem was how to evaluate the ever increasing amount of information which was supplied to them daily by unsuspecting USNet subscribers.

Mustafin had just approved a profitable sell order for their holdings in a German pharmaceutical company that was about to be the target of a lawsuit—they were reading the emails between the attorneys and several unhappy witnesses—when a special phone rang next to his console. He pushed a button to answer on his headset and immediately recognized his boss's voice;

a moment later Knox's image flashed on one of the nearby monitors. He was in their West Coast office, and the two men spoke for several minutes about that afternoon's RTI intelligence.

When finished with that list, the lieutenant said, "I've got some good news, Mr. Knox. Todd Phelps called and said that he wants to join us."

"Excellent. From what you've told me, he should make a good addition. He seems to like making money more than worrying about technicalities. When will you start his training?"

"In a few weeks. Two others just started, and I don't want to overextend."

"Now that he knows about the potential money, he'll be impatient."

"That's good. It'll keep him focused. We have to walk all these new guys in, one layer at a time. We can't tell them everything in the first month."

"I know. Now, what about our special program for the President?"

"Everything we discussed appears to be doable. We're making plans, though of course we haven't told anyone the target. This operation is obviously way too restricted for anyone to know why we want to have a grand opening for our new office in Moscow."

Once again Kristen called Callie, but got her voicemail. "I'm not in now. Please leave your message and I'll call you back."

"Callie, hey. This is Kristen Holloway. You may remember me from a couple of real estate group get-togethers at your parents' home. And a service project we did at the overnight women's shelter before you left for school. Anyway, I'll be coming back from the Far East through L.A. in about a week. I need some R&R, and I really like southern California. Your dad told me you're living out there now, so I thought I'd call you when I know my exact schedule. I'd love to get together—take you to dinner. Or maybe we could go shopping— or whatever suits. Anyway, I'll call you from Singapore when I know what I'm doing, and I hope we can get together. See ya."

Callie did not answer her apartment phone because she was at her desk that morning at her uncle's office. He called her on the internal intercom.

"I'm on the phone working on a listing, and I need the address of that comparable property that Yusef is working on. Do you know where he is?"

"He went outside to use his cell phone." Callie had noticed that her cousin spent considerable time several days a week, walking and talking in their parking lot.

"Well, we were just talking about it. I think it's up on his computer. Please go look at his laptop. It should be on the screen. Third Avenue."

"In his office?"

"Yes. Quickly. I need it now."

"All right." She got up and walked across the hall into Yusef's paneled but sparsely decorated office. His laptop was closed on the desk, so she moved around behind his desk and carefully raised the screen. Instead of a real estate page, she saw a picture taken on a street somewhere of total devastation, apparently after a bomb detonated. There were caved in storefronts, bodies, and burned out cars. Blood was everywhere. The banner over the picture read "Sacred Victory!" The writing was in English, Arabic and Farsi, but before she could look at any of the words in the text she heard an angry voice.

"What are you doing?" It was Yusef, his hand on the door and his face crimson.

"I...your father asked me to get an address from your laptop. You were outside."

His shoulders lowered slightly and he came across to the side of the desk. "The one on Third Avenue?"

She stepped back, the screen still open to the carnage. "Yes. That's what he said."

"I'll get it for him." He looked at the computer for a moment in silence. "Isn't that awful?"

She glanced down. "Yes. Terrible. I can't imagine it."

"Me, either. I was searching under Iranian names for cold-calling leads, and this screen came up. It happens all the time. Either something like this, or porn." He smiled, but his eyes were locked on hers.

"Oh. I can see how that would happen. Well, please just tell your dad, and I'll go back to my work." She moved around the other side of the desk towards the door.

"I will. Thank you." He paused, closing the laptop. "But, Callie,"—she turned—"don't ever come into my office again, unless I invite you."

"Sure. No problem." And she hurried back to her seat.

17

WEDNESDAY, MAY 18TH

Todd Phelps was up early that morning. He brought Mary her first cup of coffee at the door to their bedroom, as she headed to their youngest son's room in her nightgown.

"You're perky this morning." Mary smiled, as she accepted the mug.

"I guess I'm just fired up today. I've fed the dog and emptied the dishwasher."

"Why today?" She took a sip as their son began to bounce in his crib and call for her.

"I don't know. I guess maybe I just got some sleep for a change." He gave her a peck on the cheek. "I gotta go. Early meeting, dear. In fact, I may have a series of these early meetings—and night meetings—in the coming weeks. We're starting some new training, and I'm part of it. So. my schedule may be a bit crazy over the next weeks."

"When is it not? Call me when you know what time you'll be home." She raised her mug, then turned to their son's room.

"I will. Have a great day. I love you."

"I love you, too."

"You're up early this morning," Elizabeth said, as she refilled her coffee cup at the kitchen counter.

David was sitting at their breakfast table reading the morning paper. "I couldn't sleep."

"Why not?" She reached into the refrigerator for the milk.

"I don't know. I guess maybe all the projects at work, and the changes. And then there's Callie and Rob."

She took a seat at the table. "I'm sorry. I guess there is a lot to think about, but you need your sleep."

Rob walked through the door on the way to the dryer for some socks, his hair a mess and his eyes looking like he had hardly slept. Elizabeth asked, "What happened to you last night? Didn't you sleep either?"

He shook his head and replied in a raspy voice, "Not much. Don't feel too good. Studying for exams late."

Elizabeth smiled, "Well, hopefully it'll be worth it."

"Uh-huh."

David stood, folded the paper, and took a sip of coffee. "I've got to go. Might as well beat the traffic and make use of the time." He kissed her on the cheek.

"OK. Well, call me when you know when you might be home. You'll need a nap!"

He gave her another look, and she smiled and winked.

He shook his head but smiled. "How I wish. I'll call. Rob, have a good day at school."

"Sure, Dad."

Twenty minutes later Todd pulled up to a two-story office building west of the city. There was a bank branch facing the street, but Todd had been told to drive to the back, where a separate "Employees Only" parking area was fenced off. The guard let him drive through the gate after he repeated the daily codeword he had been given. Todd parked next to the windowless rear half of the structure and was processed by another guard before being allowed through the one visible door.

Inside he found a small but pleasant vestibule with a few chairs and a sofa. There was a door on the other side, and behind a single, thick glass window sat an attractive young woman. He introduced himself and said that he had an appointment. Todd heard her voice through a small amplifier on the wall.

"Good morning, Mr. Phelps. Someone will be with you in just a moment. Please have a seat."

He elected to stand. There was a buzz, the interior door opened, and a tall man with dark hair and olive skin motioned for him to come in They were in an open area with light gray walls, earth tone abstract paintings, thick carpet, and several doors. The man extended his hand. "Good morning, Todd. I'm Victor Mustafin, I'll be training you."

Todd nodded and shook hands. "I'm looking forward to it. I imagine that I have a lot to learn."

"We look forward to having you. I think you'll find our work both interesting and profitable." For a man clearly cut from military cloth, his voice was calming. "First, we need to give you an overview of what we do. Please follow me."

They turned and walked into a conference room. The same light gray walls, a modern black table for ten, and accompanying furniture.

"Please, have a seat. Would you like some coffee?"

"No, thanks. I'm pretty energized as it is."

Mustafin nodded. "First, I know all the circumstances for you being here—that you took a bribe to place a project for your company, which is illegal and could result in jail time if anyone at your employer, USNet, finds out. So you understandably think that ours is a better alternative. It probably is, but despite all that, if at any point as we're talking today you decide that you *don't* want to join us, please stop me immediately. The nature of our work is extremely confidential, and we can't share the details with anyone who is not part of our group. In fact, we will soon come to a point where there's really no turning back."

Todd nodded.

"Several years ago we perfected a method for intercepting communications from firms and individuals that allows us to know certain events before the rest of the world is privy to them. This capability often gives us an edge—sometimes a few hours, sometimes a day, sometimes longer—to make our own decisions. Or to contact others, though we never reveal our source. This information is available to us real time, twenty-four hours a day. Do you want me to go on?"

"Yes."

"There is a lot of information. It grows monthly. We have computers and staff personnel who read it, look for key words, etc. But at the end of that process there must be a person—a person with knowledge and judgment to decide whether a particular piece of information is worthy of immediate action, can wait, or should be tossed. That person must have special qualities, must be totally trustworthy. And must be a team player."

He paused. "If you want to choose the other path, say so now. From here on, you're in."

"I'm in."

"We rotate that key position every four hours using several locations around the world. So we need a small team of dedicated people who are not afraid to take action when necessary. We believe that you have those qualities. Basically, with the information we get, if we can't make a lot of money, or at least save money that would otherwise be lost, we aren't doing our jobs. And it's that pool of profits that we share. And of course to be effective, it must all remain absolutely secret."

"Who is actually behind the all of this? Is it a government agency? A company? Is it legal?"

Mustafin smiled. "It's a private group, Todd, but for now you don't need to know. And it's not illegal. But, frankly, even if it were, we wouldn't stop. The information is too valuable. And we never hurt anyone with how we use it. We just do our best to make ourselves profitable."

"That's how you found out about me."

"Yes. Exactly. And you see, we gave you a choice, and a great opportunity."

"Hmm. What about stock moves? Financial reports? Marketing plans? Do you have all of that, too?"

"We never know if we have 'all' of it. That's part of our challenge. But we think that we see a lot of it, and we act on it accordingly. Actually, it can be pretty exciting at times."

"How do you do it?"

"You'll find out everything in your training. In a minute we'll go over your schedule. The entire process should take about three months. After that, if all goes well, you'll be standing duty alone here in the command center as the senior watch officer."

"Sounds good. But why does it take so long to train?"

"There's a lot to learn. You need time at the lower levels that filter the information so that you know all the details. Plus you have your regular job, so we'll have to work around our schedules to find time. We don't want anyone at USNet to have any idea that you're working here after hours."

Todd nodded. "Understood."

"One other thing," Mustafin added, motioning with his hand, "everything we do is absolutely secret. You may not discuss it with anyone. Not your wife. Not colleagues. No one. Not indirectly or tangentially. That would result in dire consequences for us, and for you, if anyone knew about this operation. Is that understood?"

"Yes. But that sounds pretty threatening. What exactly do you mean?"

"We don't think of it that way, but there are hundreds of millions of dollars at stake, including your share. So at a minimum, when I mention personal consequences, I mean the loss of that income. Beyond that, it would depend on what you said or did. The best thing is just not to say, do, or imply anything about these capabilities. Conduct your real estate work as if RTI—that's what we call this capability—did not exist. You'll have to be careful to keep whatever you learn from RTI out of any regular business considerations and discussions. One other thing: Taking any personal advantage will not be tolerated. If you learn something on your watch about, say, a particular company, you can't buy or sell its stock based on that information. We're all in this together, and we don't want anyone's personal activities attracting any special attention. Understood?"

"Yes."

"There's a manual loaded on the computer over there." He nodded toward a desk and terminal in one corner. "You'll have to study it here. When you finish, either today or tomorrow, we'll show you the command center and a separate cubicle that mimics the first level data gathering operation in our facilities around the world. You'll start by sifting through the emails and cell phone conversations that our computers queue up for us to evaluate."

"I'm ready when you are."

"Good. No notes, by the way. There's a self-administered test that helps you focus on the important points. And let the receptionist know when you've finished. Right now you have access only to this area of the building. I'll answer any questions during the first tour of the facility."

"OK."

Mustafin left Todd alone in the conference room. He walked over and touched the keyboard. A document of fifty pages appeared. Todd scrolled down and noticed technical writing, diagrams and pictures. He sat down and started reading.

This is awesome.

On David Sawyer's desk that morning were the usual piles of real estate projects and issues; he checked voicemail and email. Twenty-six messages. One was from Andrei in Moscow. After handling a few other quick questions with Julie, he picked up his phone and dialed their Moscow broker.

"Hello, David, how are you?" Andrei asked.

"Great, Andrei. Sounds like you're next door. How's the family?"

"We're fine, thank you. I was calling to let you know that we've worked through all the lease issues. I think you'll be pleased. We'll email an English version of the lease for your review."

"Good news, Andrei. How soon can we be in our space?"

"That's the even better news. Remember the space that was almost finished for the first tenant? Well, there's apparently been a merger, and that space is not going to be taken. So the developer has offered it to us. It's almost exactly the same size. The planner likes most of what is already there. So if you approve the switch and we turn her loose to begin ordering materials, I think you can be up and running in six weeks."

"That does sound good. Let me have a look at the lease and think about the floor plan, and I'll give you an answer."

"OK."

"Thanks, Andrei."

David hung up, but his phone buzzed again instantly. "Yes, Julie."

"Mr. Sawyer, Barbara says there are two police detectives here to see you."

"Uh, OK. I'll be out in a minute."

He walked out of his office, gave a small shrug to Julie, and continued to the real estate group reception area in the middle of the floor. Two men in suits were standing by the receptionist's desk. The shorter and slightly older one stepped forward.

"Mr. Sawyer? I'm Lieutenant Don Akers. This is Lieutenant Kirk Hoover."

The three men shook hands. "How can I help you, gentlemen?"

"Is there somewhere we can talk?"

"Sure. The small conference room should be available. Can we get you some coffee?"

A few moments later they were seated around the conference table with the door closed. Akers began. "Mr. Sawyer, Lieutenant Hoover and I are investigating the disappearance of Mr. William Porter. You know him, I assume."

"Yes, of course. I've known him professionally for years. Not well, but we've done some deals together. He runs a good shop."

"Yes. Well, as you probably know, he hasn't been seen or heard from since May 4th—two weeks ago."

"It's a real mystery. I thought at first that he'd turn up in some love nest, or on a cruise." David smiled, but the two policemen remained serious.

Hoover spoke. "Mr. Sawyer, do you have any first-hand experience with Mr. Porter to substantiate that kind of inference?"

David stopped smiling. "No, I don't. I'm sorry. I hadn't realized that it's been two weeks. I'm sure that his family is very upset."

Hoover continued. "Yes. We're going back through Mr. Porter's diary and are contacting everyone with whom he met in the month preceding his disappearance."

"That will be quite a task."

"Yes, but hopefully worth it in the end. We noticed that a week before he vanished he made a note to call you and, uh, Ms. Holloway. Did you talk with him?"

"He left a voicemail for us."

"Is Ms. Holloway here now?"

"No, she's in the Far East. She leaves there tomorrow and will be back in our office on Monday."

"What did he say?"

"He was upset. He said that someone had threatened him over the sale of Capital Tower. Well, I think he said that he *felt* as if someone had threatened him, and he implied that it could be us."

The two policemen looked at each other. Lieutenant Akers leaned forward. "Why didn't you come forward and tell us earlier, Mr. Sawyer?"

"Well, I guess I should have thought of it, but, frankly, it was so absurd that. I mean, you don't really think Bill is dead do you? I've thought he would turn up any day now and never connected the two. Killed over a business deal? Not likely."

Hoover spoke. "Why did he say he felt he was being threatened?"

"At the time, we and several others were trying to buy Capital Tower, which he was marketing. But Porter apparently decided to buy it himself, which we, and presumably the others, considered to be unethical. Apparently someone called and told him to back off his own purchase of the building, or something bad would happen to him. It was so crazy that we didn't even call him back."

"Capital Tower. What's happened to that deal since Mr. Porter disappeared?"

"It's only been two weeks. In real estate that's not much time. I guess it's in limbo, waiting for him to come back."

The policemen looked at their pads and continued to ask questions for several more minutes about Porter's past transactions with USNet, his contact numbers, Kristen's schedule, etc. Finally, Akers said, "Well, if that's it, I guess we're finished. Here are our cards, Mr. Sawyer. If you think of anything else that could help in our search, we'd appreciate it."

As they rose, David said, "Of course. We all hope he turns up soon. If I think of anything, I'll call you."

"Thank you. We'll check back with you."

"Hey, Callie, it's Kristen Holloway. Sorry I got your machine again. Anyway, I'm leaving Singapore in a few hours, and I'll be staying in L.A. over the weekend. I'll be at the Crown Royal Hotel downtown. Please call and leave a message at the hotel if we can get together. Any time is fine with me. See ya soon. Bye."

Callie was not at home to answer her phone because she and Alex were at their favorite restaurant, celebrating the success of their latest upload. It had quickly gone viral in the world of amateur pornography, and every day their account was credited with additional funds by the USNet website.

Before their first courses arrived, Alex slipped her a pill under the table, and then checked their account from his handheld. "Another twelve hundred dollars today! And a quote from one of the reviewers: 'Samantha is the best new actress in the industry.'" He smiled, took a pill, and toasted her with a glass of water.

She joined him, raised her glass, and drank. "I get it. Lots of money. Not bad."

"They sent us an email today, asking whether we would like to break out from our amateur venue, to become professionals."

She frowned. "You mean with cameramen and a director and all that?"

"I guess." He nodded.

Callie was quiet while she picked up some spinach dip with a chip. "Alex, I like the money a lot—it's freed us from my parents, and we can do what we want. But I'm not sure I'm ready for that kind of public notoriety. Or for taking my clothes off in front of strangers. Besides, I think the slightly obscure way that you put the videos together adds to their appeal. So, no, I don't mind doing a few more of these, until we have a lot saved, but this is not the career that I had in mind when I started acting."

"Others have transitioned."

"Alex, let's just keep doing what works."

"But our fans will want more. And there will be even more money. Much more."

She thought for a moment and then said, "We'll see."

He took a sip. "OK. I guess 'Samantha' calls the shots."

As their main courses arrived, Callie smiled. "It's crazy isn't it? All that money and no hassles."

18

FRIDAY, MAY 20TH

Early the next morning Todd was back at the Real Time Intercepts control center. Victor Mustafin gave him a new ID badge, complete with his picture and thumbprint.

"This gets you into the entire building, except the control room itself. For now, I'll take you there, and we'll talk about the schedule. Your training will begin in about a week. OK?"

Todd clipped the badge on and followed him along a short central corridor. At the end, Mustafin inserted his badge into a slot and placed his right hand over a pad at shoulder height on the wall. There was a click, a door opened, and they entered a dimly lit rectangular area only about the size of a conference room, with a center computer console wrapping around two padded chairs. It looked to Todd like the flight deck of a modern jet, except that above the console walls were screens with maps, stock trading tickers, commodity prices and an array of other information. As his eyes adjusted, Todd watched the back of the single man at the console, who was focused on one of the several screens in front of him and involved in an intense conversation over his headset.

Mustafin spoke softly to Todd. "The goal of our training is to have you in that chair, able to make decisions quickly, and pass along critical information to whoever needs it."

For the first time Todd realized the gravity of what he had agreed to do. It was not just going to be learning what companies were secretly thinking about a particular issue. It was making split-second decisions on what to do with a constant flow of information on an unlimited range of subjects.

Mustafin noted his expression. "Don't worry. We'll train you well. None of us gets everything. It's too much. We'll teach you to judge what's important and to catch most of it. You'll quickly find ways for all of us to make a lot of money."

"I've been excited the last few days—but what a lot to learn."

"You'll be ready. Let me show you the rest."

Five minutes later they were seated at the table in the conference room. There were several screens on one wall, but only one was on. There was what appeared to be a live picture of a large area filled with people in cubicles.

Mustafin looked over at Todd and smiled at his surprised expression. "That's our first level of data gathering, on the other side of the globe."

"Man!"

"They think they're working for a private security company to find breaches in corporate security. At the first level we like to recruit computer geeks who will do almost anything if they believe it's improving security or finding others' mistakes. So when you talk with them on the intercom, please keep that in mind."

"Sure. There are so many. Where is it?"

"As I said, it's half the world away. We don't want any of them, or anyone here, to connect what they are doing with our Real Time Intercepts."

"It's so quiet."

"No need to talk much when you're on a console. Most communicating is by computer."

Todd nodded.

"That's it for today. I have to relieve the duty officer in a few minutes. We'll take a look at the schedules and figure out when we can run your first watch."

"Yes. The sooner the better."

"Understood. I'll show you out. Remember, not a word or a hint to anyone, at home or at work. You should open an account at the bank branch in the front of the building so that there is a normal reason for you to be here. We'll meet again next week."

Following Friday prayers Councilman Hassan Farrahi had accepted an invitation to have lunch with two of his original supporters from the Tampa mosque, along with two visitors who would be joining them from Detroit. Farrahi arrived at the restaurant a few minutes after the older men and greeted them warmly. Although he had spoken on the phone with the two visitors, this was the first time he would meet them face to face. The five men took seats at a large round table at the back of the Middle Eastern diner.

"So, how is it going after your first month in office?" the taller visitor, Amir Ali, asked.

"Busy, very busy. There is much to do in our district, and across the city. The schools and hospitals in particular need so much help. People and families are really suffering."

"Yes. You are right," said Rahim Tahymouri , the older of the two, with silver hair and dark eyes.

They were interrupted by the waiter, and then Rahim smiled. "Hopefully we can help. We're here to let you know that our foundation is ready to fund a new, large health clinic—truly it will be a small hospital--only two blocks from here. And we will provide an endowment to insure that health care will be free, or nearly so, for everyone. And we would like you to be the one to announce the details in the coming week."

"Are you kidding?"

"No, no. We are very serious. We already have the contract to purchase the site, and the preliminary design is ready for submission to Planning and Zoning. What do you think?"

"It's incredible. Thank you very much."

Amir Ali leaned forward. "And a month from now you will announce a new community center, which can double as a school once we get the paperwork approved."

"Wow. That's incredible. It will transform the neighborhood."

"Yes. We hope so. We will supply the teachers for the first three years, and they will be firmly grounded in our faith and in the truth. We believe that your young people will enjoy learning from them."

"Is there some hitch? Are there strings?"

The four men laughed. Amir Ali said, "No, of course not. Just let our teachers teach. We believe that we should help all people, and particularly brothers and sisters and their families. And we have money to spend that the government no longer has."

"Again, it's incredible."

"No, it is what Allah has commanded us to do. We may ask you to travel occasionally to some other cities, to tell smaller communities how to organize as you have done. And we may have ideas about higher elected offices for you in the future, but that will play out in Allah's time."

Farrahi simply looked at the four men. Finally he said, "Of course, that would be fine. Whatever you think, I'll be glad to help."

"Good. We hope so. This is why our faith will ultimately win over the world, because it is not just faith, but also a way to live, and a way to govern. All aspects are united as one. Others are splintered into political factions, denominations, 'church and state'. Allah has designed Islam in this way so that one day His truth will rule the world. While everyone in the West argues and debates, we will command."

"Peacefully," Farrahi added.

"Yes, of course. You are part of that. Allah has chosen you to do great things. You are blessed."

"Thank you."

Kristen had decided to splurge and stay at one of the beautifully restored older hotels in downtown Los Angeles. On arrival she had been particularly pleased to hear Callie's voicemail, and now, a day later, after a little sleep, she was sitting in the elegant, noisy lobby, waiting for the younger woman. Kristen wore a stylish but simple dark blue summer dress with a single strand gold necklace.

They had agreed to have a late breakfast and then head off for some shopping. On the phone Callie sounded reluctant to commit to much time, but Kristen was thankful that they could at least spend a few hours together. She saw Callie walking in through the motor lobby entrance, wearing an open collar white top, designer jeans, and sandals. She carried a large, colorful straw bag.

As Callie looked around, her dark glasses perched atop her head, Kristen stood, smiled, and walked toward her. When Callie turned her way, she made a small sign of recognition, and the two women met near the middle of the lobby under a large chandelier.

Kristen, slightly taller, extended her hand and shook Callie's. "I'm so glad you could come."

David's daughter half smiled and brushed back her hair with her left hand. "Yes, me too. How are you?"

"Oh, I'm fine. The usual jetlag. But I'm used to it. How about you?"

"I was up late studying. But it's a beautiful day, and the drive revived me a bit."

"Good. Good." Kristen turned slightly and motioned toward the open dining area off the lobby. "Shall we have some breakfast—or brunch, I guess?"

Callie returned her smile. "Yes. I'm starved, actually. Thanks."

A few moments later they were sitting in a booth on a raised area along the back wall, not far from the buffet tables.

"I guess you want the buffet," Kristen said. Callie nodded expectantly, eyeing the serving tables. Kristen looked at the menu, then put it aside. "Well, at my age I'm usually more the fruit and yogurt type, but, hey, today I'll join you."

"Good, can we start now?"

Kristen nodded to the waitress, who was bringing coffee and juice. "We'll do the buffet."

Five minutes later they returned to their booth. Kristen had tried to use a little restraint, but Callie's plate was filled, including a ham and cheese omelet.

As they began to eat, Kristen remarked, "I guess studying makes you pretty hungry."

Callie nodded. "It sure does. And, like, no time to eat, either."

"Well dig in. Have all you want."

Callie cut a slice of fruit. "Thanks. Do you, like, see Dad much?"

"Sure. All the time." A small frown crossed Callie's face. "I've worked with him for—let's see—three years now. Your dad *really* knows real estate, and I like working with him."

"Why?" She didn't miss a beat with her fork.

Kristen paused. "Uh—good question. I guess because he's always struck me as very knowledgeable, professional, and...honest. And I think he cares about people."

"Really?"

"Yes. You don't agree?"

"Oh, he probably cares about the people he works with." Before Kristen could respond, Callie asked, "Why were you in—uh—Singapore?"

She told Callie the story of Trevor Knox's sudden switch from Hong Kong just before the government there changed its policies—and the resulting scramble for office space. She filled in some of the details on her negotiations, careful not to get too involved in business topics, but Callie seemed to be interested. "So that's how I wound up here in L.A. on this gorgeous day. Hey, where do you suggest we go after you finish off the buffet table?"

Callie smiled and sat back from her plate. "Just resting. Those sticky buns are awesome. I know some great shops in the South Bay area. They're in a small shopping area off the beaten path—like, great clothes. Good restaurants nearby, too. What are you looking for?"

They discussed their problems with the latest fashions for the summer. Kristen added. "I might even try to find a swimsuit while I'm out here. You know, California girls and all."

"Whoa...well, we should, like, be able to find some in these stores. I'm just not sure they'll be your style."

"We'll see. You know, I'm not so old! And I'm still looking for Mr. Right. I gotta look a little enticing, even for a real estate exec."

"OK. Maybe, then."

"And if you'll help me, I'll buy you a new dress, too."

Callie smiled. "Really? That's awfully nice. I'm actually working part-time at my uncle's real estate office, and I could use a new dress that's more business-like. And"—she leaned slightly toward the older woman—"I may have some real estate questions that you can help me with, since my uncle is so busy and you've been in it so long."

"No problem. Ask about anything. I'll be glad to help. Now, how about you? Are you seeing anyone?"

Callie paused and looked down for a moment. "Uh, well, I'm actually dating a guy I met at college. His name is Alex."

Kristen inched forward as she cut a biscuit with her fork, "What's he like?"

Callie looked up and smiled. "Oh, he's really nice. He cares about me a lot. But he doesn't say too much."

"Are you going to do another round?"

"Thanks, but I'm pretty full. It sure was good. Thanks."

"Glad you liked it. I'll get the check, and we'll be off."

A few minutes later they were standing in the motor lobby. The valet brought Callie's ten-year-old red European convertible down from the parking deck. "A classic!" Kristen said with genuine admiration.

As she slid past the door held open by the valet and fastened her seatbelt, Callie looked over at her and smiled. "Southern California. Even if it's old, this is what you drive."

Callie pulled out of the hotel driveway with a quick squeal. After a few minutes of just driving and taking in the beautiful day, she said, still facing forward, "So, what did Dad tell you about me?"

"I think he said that you're about to finish the semester and that you're doing well. He also said you're going to be in a play. He's excited for you. So am I."

"What about movies? Did he, like, mention any movies to you?"

"Are you doing movies?"

"Uh, no, not really. Though I guess it's a dream I've had."

Kristen looked over. "That would be great!"

"You're *really* here just to relax? To shop and have fun?"

"Yes, of course. I'm due some vacation days, I've been working my tail off, I thought it would be good to stop here, and I'm just glad that you're here. I'd love to have a friend in L.A. Especially one with a red convertible who can help me shop."

Callie looked over at Kristen, then back to the road. "Well, OK. Good. That's good. I'll show you some great shops. And this first place we're going has lots of swimsuits."

Kristen looked down the road ahead. "I'm with you, girl."

Friday 18:20
To: David Sawyer
From: Andrei Selivanov
Subj: Lease for Moscow Expansion
Dear David,
The developer has agreed to incorporate your comments in the lease. The space they've already fit out appears to work well for you. Pictures are attached. I met with both attorneys this afternoon, and we should have a final lease to execute on Monday. Congratulations! We'll begin working with the space planners, and you should be in your new office by early to mid July. Call if you have any questions or additional input. Have a great weekend.
Andrei

Late that morning Yusef dropped off his first clients and noted that he was not far from Los Angeles' huge airport, LAX, one of the nation's busiest. He could not pass up the opportunity to drive by it. He did this often, though careful never to stop for long or bring any attention to himself. The terminal was like an island between two long parallel runways. But there were plenty of residential roads and stopping places on the north side of the vast complex. And it was through some of those that he now drove, thinking about how glorious it would be during Ramadan, when he would be a hero and a martyr.

And he thought of Salim, his friend, spiritual mentor, and teacher. Four years ago Yusef had joined the Army, like so many young people, to "see the world". Instead, Salim had helped open the world of his faith, and brought meaning to his life.

After Basic Training, Yusef had been assigned to Fort Bliss, Texas, for missile school. And Salim was one of the instructors on the Stinger Missile, a one-man plane killer. While teaching him everything about the missile, Salim also opened his eyes to the Qur'an and the true power of the faith that his parents acknowledged, but did not practice.

The Army officially encouraged Salim to search out and train the young Muslim enlistees in religious studies, in the name of diversity. Out of the hundreds that Salim had taught in this way, he had singled out only a handful, like Yusef, for special time and extra study.

Yusef pulled into a parking lot at a school near the western, or ocean end of the airport. Without getting out, he rolled down the windows and watched the big jets as they climbed up from the runway, full of fuel and people.

He imagined back to his training at Fort Bliss. The missile launcher on his shoulder, tracking the plane as it climbed, waiting to hear the tone in his earpiece signifying that the heat seeker had acquired the infrared signature from the engines. Then fire the missile. So fast. In only a few seconds it would climb to the target and explode, ripping the plane into pieces, killing everyone onboard. And because it was passive infrared, it never alerted the pilot to its presence until the wings were blown off.

Yusef smiled. Just a few more months until Ramadan. He hoped that when he got the signal to proceed, it would be a sunny California day like today. With the wind off the ocean, so that the planes would be headed west. Then the wreckage and bodies would fall into the sea, making it that much worse. And a great day to die for his faith.

"Oh that looks good on you," Callie said, as Kristen emerged from the dressing room at a small boutique specializing in expensive business attire. It was three hours later, and the two women had shopped up and down the streets in Callie's favorite area of South Bay.

Kristen turned and looked at herself in the mirrors on the wall. "Yeah. It's kind of tough to mix 'feminine' and 'conservative' in one business suit, but I'd say this one pulls it off better than most. I'm just not sure I can afford it."

"It's classic. It'll last for years. And if Mr. Right is ever at a business meeting with you, he'll definitely be interested!"

Kristen smiled. "You're right. Hey, how often do I shop in southern California, anyway?"

"Good."

Ten minutes later they were on the sidewalk, each with several shopping bags. "We've done well, Callie," Kristen said, looking down the street. "Thanks for showing me these shops, and for your advice. And I hope that your new dress works well with your uncle and cousin. Want to do a late lunch—maybe call it a 'tea'?"

"Sure." Callie looked at her watch. "I've got a rehearsal tonight that I need to get ready for. But let's walk down to Dave's. Have you ever had fish tacos?"

"I don't think so."

Dave's had high ceilings and a bright, casual, open look with lots of plants, and an outdoor patio, where they were soon seated at a table for four, their bags piled in the adjoining chairs.

"This has been great," Kristen said, after the waitress took their orders. "Wonderful shops. I can see why you like living here."

"Yeah, it's pretty nice."

"Do you ever miss your family?"

"My friends, yes. But I didn't have a lot, and two are coming out to visit this summer. My family? Well, my brother and I talk on the phone sometimes. Mom and Dad—I don't know. I guess."

"I don't know your brother or your mom very well, except what your dad has mentioned about them. Of course I know that he loves you and is very proud of you."

"How do you know that?"

"Well, because he tells me that he is."

"Have you talked to him recently?"

"Why?"

"Then you'd know that he has cut... Hey, let's, like, talk about something else, OK?"

Kristen noticed the change in Callie's expression and smiled again. "Sure. And look, all families go through some tough times. But they're still families. And if I can ever help you, please call me. I've been through some tough times myself, and I know that being alone is no fun, especially when times are rough."

"You? That seems impossible. What kind of hard times?"

Their lunches arrived. A Caesar salad for Kristen and a beef stir fry for Callie.

"Me? Well, you probably haven't been following it, but the whole country was recently treated to my past, thanks to some overly zealous press people—and my own stupidity."

"What happened?"

"Well, several years ago I did a terrible thing and had an affair with a married man—an attorney—a wonderful man with two children."

"You?"

Kristen nodded and took a bite of salad. A moment later she continued, "Yes, me. We all can do stupid things. I'm not sure why, except that God made us with the ability to choose. The problem is that when we do stupid things, there are always consequences. Sometimes sooner, sometimes later. But they *always* come. And they aren't pretty. We hurt others and ourselves. And so of course that's what happened in my case."

"What happened?"

Kristen told Callie the story of her affair with Richard Sullivan, what had happened then, and what had happened to all of them that spring with the revelations in the national press.

"Wow, that would be awful," Callie said.

"Yep. It was pretty awful. But I have to tell you. The peace that settled on me, on all of us, when Janet Sullivan forgave me—it was like nothing I've ever experienced. It was like a chain had been wrapped around me and was choking me, but it was suddenly broken. A great freeing. Genuine forgiveness is about the most potent force on earth."

"Why?"

"Because I don't believe it's human. There's nothing in human experience that explains forgiveness. Just the opposite. We're all wired to want personal revenge, justice, our way. So forgiveness must come from the one who made us—from outside us. And when it suddenly happens, it just changes everything. Regular human experience stops in its tracks when faced with true grace and forgiveness. I know. I've experienced it."

"Mm."

"Sorry, I didn't mean to get into all of that."

"No, I asked. What a story. I would never have known." Callie smiled. "I just thought you were a boring real estate executive, like my dad."

Kristen returned her smile. "Your dad isn't boring! He's terrific." Kristen held up a hand. "But I'm not here to defend him. I do know that he loves you very much, however he may have expressed it. It may have come across as telling you what to do, but in his mind I suspect that he thinks he's helping you."

Callie frowned and looked at her watch. "We've got to go in a minute. I have to get ready for tonight, and the traffic will be getting rough soon."

"OK, I'm almost finished. Listen, Callie, I've enjoyed today. Thank you for showing me around. We did pretty well."

Callie looked at the packages and brightened. "Yes. I've had a good time, too. I'm really glad you came. If you're ever coming through again, please call me."

"I certainly will. Listen, tomorrow is Saturday. Any chance we could spend a little time at the beach? I ought to try out this new swimsuit."

"I'm not sure. It depends on how late tonight goes. But Santa Monica would be good. How about if I call you around eleven tomorrow?"

"That'll be great. I hope I'll see you."

19

MONDAY, MAY 23RD

David was seated at his desk early the next Monday morning, trying to concentrate on managing their projects but wondering as well what Kristen had found out about Callie.

That morning the news was all about the latest demonstrations and near-riots in Tehran. He was worried about Omid and Goli because there were rumors that the opposition had looted an armory, meaning that the Basiji's violent tactics might be met by equal violence in the coming days.

He took out his cell phone and dialed the number in Estonia; a moment later Omid answered in Tehran, but the loud noise made David move the phone away.

"Hello," Omid yelled.

"Omid, it's your cousin. Are you OK?"

"Cousin? Yes. I thought you were Morad." A siren sounded nearby. "I've been looking for Morad and Ramin all day." There was a loud explosion, and his phone clearly fell to the ground.

"Omid? Omid?"

A scraping noise and heavy breathing. "Yes. I have to get across this square. They're charging us. I'll call you later." And the phone went dead.

David turned and looked out the window. He called Elizabeth and told her what he had just heard.

"That's terrible. I hope they're safe. I'll ask Sally if we can pray for Omid and Goli this morning at Bible study," she volunteered.

"Yes. Thanks. When I hear more, I'll let you know."

He thought for a minute about praying. *Allah, or God, please protect our family in Tehran.* He did not know what else to say, so he was silent, thinking about what Omid must be going through.

Then he turned back to his desk and ran down his master list of the group's work in progress. All of them were in the office that morning except Cheryl, who had flown out to Kansas City to survey additional telecom sites with a local broker. Todd would be flying to Minneapolis that afternoon to deliver their executed lease for office space and to meet with architects to move forward on the design and pricing of their fit-out.

We actually seem to have our major issues fairly well contained for the moment. At least until Capital Tower gets going again, if it does.

Kristen stopped by his door at 8:30, her large purse over her shoulder. "Hey." She smiled.

David stood up. "Hey. Glad you're back. How are you? Sorry I missed your call yesterday."

"No problem. I'm fine. Let me put this stuff down and check my emails. Ten minutes?"

"Sure."

She returned with a coffee mug and a writing pad. They moved to his small table by the window.

"You look good," he commented. "Did you get some sun?"

She smiled. "Yes. Saturday. With Callie at the beach."

"Really?"

"Yep."

"Tell me about it."

"In a minute. First, we're finally all set in Singapore. The space looks great, and we got a decent deal, given that the whole world is moving there from Hong Kong. Here's a short summary. I signed this letter of intent. The attorneys are working on the lease now."

"Kristen, you've done a great job on our new Far Eastern offices. Twice. Thank you for both times."

She leaned back and took a sip of coffee. "Let's just hope Knox doesn't change his mind again."

"I don't think he will this time."

"Hm. Well, now about Callie. We had a great time."

He inched forward. "That's wonderful. What did you do?"

"Just girl stuff. Lunch, shopping, the beach. She's a complex person. Obviously she has some real problems. And she's struggling. A lot of anger towards you right now." She took a long sip and set the mug on her lap in front of her. "But we had a good time. I can't wait to go back. Do we have any assignments out there that don't involve porn movie facilities?"

"No assignments at all right now. But tell me about Callie—the movie stuff. What did she say about that?"

"We didn't talk about it."

"What?"

She shrugged and put the cup on the table. "We never talked about what she does. Outside of her acting in school and working for your brother."

"But that was the reason you went to see her!"

"Well, yes. We did talk about you and your relationship. But the movies just never came up. David, she hardly knows me. If I'm ever really going to understand her and help her, she has to trust me—and for real reasons. It's a guy thing to walk in and 'solve problems.' But women would rather get to know each other. I genuinely hope I can go back and spend time with her. She likes to shop and has a better eye than I do for putting the right stuff together. And I never have time to look for clothes when I'm here. So maybe if we can start there and get along, eventually something will come of it."

"Did you learn *anything*?"

She leaned back again and smiled. "Oh, definitely. She looks fine, though she's eating like a horse. Anyway, she made excuses about being up late to study, and I didn't question her. She mentioned Alex, but I didn't meet him. No details. She knows some great shops and a wonderful stretch of beach."

"But you have no idea when or if she'll ever quit making these movies?"

"No, I don't. But once I earn the right to be let into that part of her life, I'll do my best, as I promised, to help her get out of it. Anyway, isn't the Senate supposed to pass President Harper's reform bill this week, making it illegal for anyone under twenty-one to participate in creating porn?"

"Yes, but there's already a long line of lawsuits ready to challenge the President's entire package of reforms as soon as she signs them into law. And to carve 'homemade' movies out all together."

"We regulate the legal age to drive, to drink, to go to war, to get married—you'd think it would be OK to move the age to work in porn movies."

"I know. But others think it's censorship, or a loss of human rights."

"The right to copulate at eighteen for thousands of guys to watch? I'm sure Jefferson, Washington and the others were thinking just that when they risked everything they had to birth our nation."

"Kristen, don't get started."

"I won't." She took a sip. "But it's *your daughter* who's caught up in it. And I imagine that USNet is funding at least some of those lawsuits."

He looked down. "I don't know."

She put her mug on the table and stood up. "Well, you're right. No need to get wound up this early on a beautiful Monday. God's in charge, not me. I meant what I said about hoping to go back to visit Callie. She's a good girl who needs someone outside her small world whom she can trust. Maybe I'll be that person. I don't know. But we'll see."

"What should I do?"

"Now? I don't think you should do anything about Alex or their movies except call her, and see her if you can. Listen to her without pushing her. She already knows exactly how you feel about Alex. You've made your point. So now just be her father in every other way. And maybe I, or other people, can reinforce what you've told her."

She started to move toward the door, and he stood up. "Kristen, in my background, a father has to enforce what is right, not ignore wrongdoing, especially when it is so gross and so public."

She stopped and nodded, then returned to her chair. He did the same.

Kristen thought for a moment, then spoke. "Yes. I understand. In my background, a father is supposed to somehow both enforce what is right *and* give grace whenever it is needed. We have the story of the prodigal son, but it is really as much about the father. After his son grossly and publicly dishonors him, the father still so longs for their relationship that he runs to meet his returning son, while he is still a far way off. Your family is from the Middle East, mine isn't. But I understand that no older man ever runs for anything, much less to embrace a wayward son. Jesus tells this story to illustrate the truth about our God, that He is both lawgiver and grace giver, requiring right actions but providing love and grace when we fall short."

"The Allah of my parents never heard about love or grace. Instead, he watches what we do, enforces his will, and keeps score on who obeys and who doesn't. That's why I can't act with Callie as if nothing has happened."

"I understand. Left to our own devices we would never imagine the concept of grace. No other religion ever has. All of them are based on keeping score and earning your way by what you do. Win or lose. And that's what is completely unique about Christianity—which is why I believe it must be divinely inspired. If you bring grace into any human situation, it instantly changes everything. It's amazing. People are simply overwhelmed by true grace."

"It seems like weakness to me. I don't think I could or should forgive her, or even talk with her. She's made her own bed."

Kristen smiled. "Actually, true grace and forgiveness are much harder than paying back. That's why it changes everyone. Because it's from God. He let his son pay the price for us, and he forgives all who believe. Unconditionally. And runs towards us, calling our name, even when we are still a far way off. Imagine that."

He paused. "It's impossible for God—Allah—to be like that. He is all powerful and would never care that much for us."

"Maybe not Allah, but God did—two thousand years ago. And He does every day. No more score-keeping. It's amazing. You should check it out."

"Well, I'll think about it. Anyway, thank you. I owe you a lot—both for Callie and for Singapore."

She turned slightly and smiled. "I had a chance to say a little bit to Callie about what a good man her father really is."

"Thank you. We'll see. And I just remembered something: before you get into everything else, you need to know that the police came by last week to talk with us about Bill Porter's disappearance."

"He's still missing?"

"Yes."

Kristen frowned. "That's not good. Not good at all."

"I know. The police were checking with everyone on his appointment calendar for the previous month. I told the police about the voicemail he left us, and I pointed out that other buyers could be just as angry."

"So, what happens next? Do they have any leads on where he may be?"

"No. They definitely think he's dead. I'm still not convinced. Anyway, they might call you, since you weren't here, and I just wanted you to know."

"OK. Thanks. One thing, David."

"Yes?"

"I won't lie over this. We had nothing to do with whatever might have happened. But if they ask me a straight question on any aspect of this, I'll give them a straight answer."

He nodded. "Yes. Of course. That's what I want you to do. Just wanted you to know."

"Thanks. I'll send you an email with the full report on Singapore."

"Good. And I'm glad you're back."

After Kristen left, David dialed Omid's number on his cell phone. Following the connection in Estonia, the phone in Tehran rang and rang.

"I'm sorry that Stan couldn't make it tonight," Mike Campbell said, as he sipped his double Scotch. He and Todd were at a table in the bar at one of Minneapolis's most exclusive clubs. "But he'll see you in the morning when we sign the lease."

Todd smiled and raised his drink to his old friend. "No problem." He lowered his voice. "But I want to talk to you about the balance of the financing fee."

"You'll have earned it as soon as we sign tomorrow, as we agreed."

Todd took a long sip. "Good. No, actually, great! But here's the thing. I may seem paranoid, Mike, but I don't like the paper trail in the islands, or all of our emails and calls. Can you just give me the second half in cash?"

"Sure. It'll take a few days."

"That's fine. We'll be getting together again soon."

"Listen, Todd, along those lines. We're looking at several great development opportunities in Chicago, Denver and Kansas City, but we need a strong prelease in each case to get financing. Do you have any requirements coming up in those cities?"

Todd thought for a moment. "We almost always have a need in Chicago. And I think Cheryl left this morning for a telecom requirement in Kansas City. I'll have to check. But no more calls or emails. Let's just communicate about the leases themselves, and we'll agree now that I'll earn this same percent for new ones in the future, in cash."

"Well, now that we know that our private financing system works so well, that sounds fine to me."

Todd tried not to grin but couldn't help it. He looked at his friend. "You mean, this same sort of arrangement?"

"Perhaps adjusted a bit for project size—a bit smaller or larger. But of course with a minimum to keep it interesting. You know we'll do a great job for USNet. Your folks will like any space we build for them."

"That's what's so good—getting paid a little extra to make the decision I would make anyway, because you guys are so good."

"Exactly!"

"Well, I'll check with Cheryl, and look into Chicago and Denver. But I'm serious about no more phone calls or emails. We'll just talk in person. And you know, I'm really starting to like having gone to business school with you."

Mike drained his glass. "Excellent. Excellent. It's early, so why don't we grab some dinner, and then maybe go back to Cabaret later tonight?"

Another grin. "I thought you'd never ask. I could get used to regular trips to Minneapolis to sign leases."

Callie,
I enjoyed being with you last week. Both the day in town and the day at the beach were wonderful. Thank you for taking time from your busy study and work schedule to show me around.

Enclosed as a small thank you is a gift
certificate to Dave's Restaurant, which I
downloaded. I hope that you enjoy some more
fish tacos. They were delicious.
     I also hope that I'll have a reason to get
back to L.A. again soon. And if you visit
your parents, I'll show you some great new
shops here.
     Good luck with your acting.
     Yours very truly,

Kristen

Late the next evening at the RTI command bunker, Todd Phelps and Victor Mustafin were in an area next to the control room in a special cubicle with two chairs and keyboards.

As directed, Todd took the left seat. Mustafin followed, and they put on their headsets.

Mustafin said, "I'll log on with my code, and we'll walk through the process. The goal today is to show you how it all works, and maybe in a while you'll try handling some messages yourself. Remember that this is the lowest level of review. We'll be seeing and hearing raw data that the computers have pulled out because of key words, or in the case of about five thousand names worldwide, because of who is involved."

"You mean there are some people for whom we basically listen to all their conversations?"

"And their emails, of course... OK, now look, the screen is coming up, and you'll see that it's divided into a top third and a lower two-thirds. The top third shows the word or words that interested the computer, plus what is immediately before and after them. It prints a cell phone conversation in the same way."

"So we don't actually listen?"

"We can, which I'll show you in a minute. But since we read faster than we hear, the computer translates to a written format. That brings us to the lower portion of the screen, where you see several options you can select for what to do with the passage. Notice in the lower left is the option Audio, which you can click for intercepted phone calls, in case you want to hear the speakers' tones of voice or inflections to understand what they really mean."

Todd smiled. "Amazing."

"Yes, it is, but you haven't seen half of it yet. You can send the same passage to several people. So, for example"—he moved the mouse as he spoke—"if we have an email that is discussing government plans to allow drilling for oil in a new part of Alaska, you could send it to this address, which is preset for the oil industry, and to this one, which says 'State', but then lets you scroll through a list of all fifty, and to this one, which says 'Federal'. At the other end are individuals who specialize in these areas and will be in a better position to know whether this is truly new information, and what, if any, action to take."

Todd just nodded.

"It's your decision what to do. You wind up tossing the majority. But in general at this first level you want to err on the side of passing them along. You're like a gatekeeper, routing the passages to others. For brief periods it can be boring, but there are usually quite a few gems on every watch. I love the emails from the free wireless airport and coffee house systems that we offer. Remember, these people have no idea that we're reading and listening, so they say incredible things to each other. We'll connect to the flow. See this icon? Just click here."

Immediately a message appeared in the upper third of the screen.

"The highlighted envelope in the upper left corner signifies an email; if the handset were lit in the upper right corner, it would be a cell phone call. Notice the key word highlighted in the middle is 'earnings.' That's one of about twenty key business words that the computer always searches for. What does it look like to you?"

"Well, looking at the lines just before and after, it appears to be a father inquiring about how much money his son has made since moving to a new city."

"I agree. So we'll toss it. Hit the trashcan there on the right, twice. And it's gone. But we keep a rolling seventy-two hour back-up in case you suddenly have a different take on something you've read and want to check again."

"That's good."

"The next time you see the word 'earnings' it could be a CFO giving his boss an internal heads-up that their earnings are about to be significantly higher or lower than was expected. *That's* the kind of earnings information we're interested in. In that case, you can send it to one of these pre-designated areas—" he pointed to the screen—"like oil, airlines, telecom; or else type in an industry name, and the computer will find the right expert."

"Impressive," Todd said, smiling.

"Yes, it is. Imagine all the screens overseas, continually snagging all of this information. Let's do the next one."

Todd nodded and turned again to the screen, reading the next highlighted message intercepted by the computer. *This is going to be incredible.*

It was late the next afternoon, and David was about to switch off his computer and leave the office.

He, Elizabeth and Rob were to attend a graduation party that evening for the daughter of a noted architect whom David had employed on several projects. The young woman attended Rob's school, and David was looking forward to the mix of family and professional friends who would likely be there.

His phone rang, and he could see that it was Paul Burke.

"Hey, Paul. Working late on Wednesday afternoon. Are you going to make it to Pat's party tonight?"

"I think so, but that's not why I'm calling."

David could hear the turmoil in his friend's voice.

"I've just emailed an article to you that someone in News downloaded and sent to Trevor. You'd better read it and then call me back immediately. The article will be out this weekend in the print version of *Journal.* He's going crazy."

"Give me a minute and I'll call you back."

He clicked to his email and opened the attachment to Burke's message.

USNet expands in Adult Entertainment
Internet Giant will soon be the "King of Porn"

By Claudia Coleman
Los Angeles
On the same day that President Harper signed her landmark Media and Entertainment Reform bill, at least one company is moving to take advantage of the recent uncertainty in the adult entertainment industry.

Through a series of quiet acquisitions, internet and communications giant USNet is set to become the world's largest producer and distributor of "adult movies" and related goods and services.

USNet is widely known for its large market shares in internet hosting, email, cellular telephones, broadcasting, and other industries, most associated with high tech applications.

It is not so generally known that through its wholly owned subsidiary, XXXtra Cinema, USNet is also already a major factor in the adult entertainment industry. But industry sources, most wishing to remain anonymous, report that over the last sixty days USNet and its flamboyant chairman, Trevor Knox, have quietly penned deals to purchase almost all of the remaining independent production houses in the San Fernando Valley.

Neither Knox nor USNet would respond to inquiries about these acquisitions, but it is believed that the company's goal is to reduce costs and increase prices by virtually controlling every aspect of the industry, including the actors, production, distribution and even showings through its internet, DVD and dedicated satellite systems.

Since XXXtra Cinema and its parent USNet are private companies, exact figures are not published, but it is widely believed that if this type of vertical integration could be achieved in the adult entertainment industry, the profits would be enormous.

While the acquisitions are being made through dummy companies to avoid notoriety, a USNet real estate executive confirmed that a senior member of the company's real estate group has recently spent significant time in the San Fernando Valley, evaluating the targeted assets.

Although content censorship seems an unlikely possibility today, even with President Harper pushing for reform, one industry watcher quipped that these acquisitions may spur the government to consider anti-trust investigations into the mostly secret world of legal pornography.

Several attorneys familiar with the purchases report that they are set to close over the next thirty days.

David was used to press speculation about USNet's operations and future moves in its various markets. Such reports were usually only moderately accurate and never involved quotes or inferences from his real estate group. This article, on the other hand, was highly accurate and apparently leaked from someone on his team. And the only logical person was Kristen Holloway. His heart sank as he finished it.

What has Kristen done?

He called Paul Burke. The COO answered. "You read it? OK. I'll conference in Trevor, who's in L.A." Instantly the three of them were on the phone together.

"David's on the phone with us, Trevor."

"David, it has to be that Holloway woman!" His anger was apparent. "We can't have these kinds of leaks and rumors. A female reporter getting information from a female employee to help a female President's absurd policies on adult movies. This is unacceptable. I told you to get rid of her weeks ago."

David responded calmly, almost quietly. "We said that we'd talk about it. She's the most experienced person I've got, with a full slate of projects. I talked to her, Trevor, and told her not to make any more public statements about her work or company policies. She agreed and said—"

"Obviously it didn't work."

"David," Burke said, "this time she really has gone too far. No company can have this kind of confidential information spread around by people on the inside."

"I know. But I'd like to talk with her about it. Maybe the reporter put words in her mouth, or maybe she didn't realize that—"

"David." It was Knox. "Fire her."

He closed his eyes and grimaced.

"Did you hear me, David? Are we agreed?"

"Can we at least try probation? Then if there is one—"

"David, you warned her after her last public criticism of our business. If she gets away with this, what's to prevent others from doing the same? Actions have consequences. Paul and I have agreed. She has to go."

He paused then said, "All right."

"Good. As quickly as you can. Have a good evening."

Knox and Burke hung up. David put the handset in his lap and rubbed his temples.

This is impossible.

20

Victor Mustafin had a special room in the middle of the RTI control center to which only he had access. He and Akbar Kamali, via a remote link, used it for communicating on their most confidential operations—ones that even their own team of duty officers had no need to know--operations that clearly broke laws or risked lives.

Mustafin was alone in the darkened room at one that Thursday morning, with Kamali on a secure link, to observe a test being conducted east of Moscow, ten time zones away. Facing them on the large screen, standing on the bluff overlooking the firing range, were Simon North and General Yevgany Beleborodov. Kamali and Mustafin used an encrypted feed through transmission cut-outs that made it impossible for those in Russia to determine the location or identity of their new owners. The Russian side could hear Kamali and Mustafin, though they could not see them.

Mustafin spoke. "Congratulations again, gentlemen, on your acquisition three weeks ago."

Their counterparts smiled, and Simon North spoke into the camera, "Yes, the General's team did a great job. A sad accident, indeed, for auto enthusiasts. But their handiwork is now safely stored and guarded in our warehouse, waiting its first use."

"And that should come soon, depending on today's results."

General Beleborodov spoke, his look serious. "Understood. But you're asking us to push our system to the limits of its capability. Hitting a moving target on a battlefield is one thing. But on a city street, even in a suburb, is quite another."

Kamali countered. "The cars may be traveling at high speed, but certainly not too quickly for a GoFor missile."

"It's not the target's speed. This isn't an aircraft," said the Russian. "It's the difficulty of tracking a specific target when it's surrounded by similar targets, and all of them are moving. If a car being illuminated stops at a traffic light, and the car next to it leaves first, it's possible that the satellite will mistakenly shift to the second car. The true target will be lost."

The general received a note from an aide off camera. "The short-range test missiles are inbound," he read, and turned to look out across the valley. As the view shifted on the screen, he spoke. "The targets are the two red cars being driven by remote control. They were illuminated and tagged twenty minutes ago. The eight blue and green cars are simulating conditions on an urban avenue, as you have directed us. They have been running in parallel with the red cars since they were illuminated. We've marked 'intersections' in the valley, and the controllers are stopping the cars at each one as they might in the real world, alternating speeds but staying in the general vicinity of the targets."

Mustafin and Kamali could clearly see the automobiles proceeding along the wide valley, now green with spring grass. North's voice said, "We should have contact any second now. We didn't arm them with explosives because..."

Suddenly, as if from nowhere, one of the red targets was demolished by an incoming missile. A split second later the second missile hit a blue car, two hundred yards ahead of its actual target. The general slapped his hands together and cursed in Russian. "They were together two intersections ago, but number seven pulled away more quickly, and the motion fooled the satellite tracker."

There was silence for a few moments while the camera focused in on the smashed blue car. North quietly asked, "Is there a solution?"

As the camera panned back to take in the two figures on the edge of the bluff, General Beleborodov turned to face his new anonymous owners. "To hit that kind of target it will take more than passive reflection of energy from a satellite. We'll need an active tracking device in or on the car."

"What do you mean?" Mustafin asked.

"I mean some type of GPS repeater. It can be small. Like they use in America to track criminals' locations. Any transponder code that we can feed into the computer to discern the true target in a sea of lookalikes."

"OK. Understood."

"We will work on this end," North responded. "And if our new owners have input, I think that we will quickly find a solution."

"Mr. Knox, it's Victor."

Knox was just strapping into his special seat at the control center in his jet when Mustafin called him on the secure videophone. It was that same afternoon, and the jet was taxiing out to take off for a trip to Los Angeles, where Knox had meetings with two of the last adult entertainment owners holding out against his purchase offers. With the passage of President Harper's reform law, the time was right to make them a new, lower offer. Knox had good reason to expect, given the level of funding from USNet's coffers, that the new laws would be tied up in court for years. So it made sense to pressure other, less informed owners.

As the jet began to roll, Knox answered his lieutenant's call on the monitor built above the custom-paneled control desk.

"Hello, Victor. It may be noisy for a bit."

"That's all right. This should be short. We've seen several messages that imply that President Harper's summer trip to Moscow is definitely on. And it appears that it will be around July 4th."

"The Fourth of July in Moscow?"

Mustafin nodded. "Yes, sir. There's a huge celebration every year at one of the old pre-Revolutionary estates. It centers around the U.S. business community over there, but it includes everyone who wants to come. The weather is usually good, and it stays light until late—it's a big deal."

"So it might be kind of historic for an American President to celebrate the Fourth of July in Moscow, particularly with a Russian President who is so committed to the same throw-back policies."

"Yes, that seems to be what they're planning."

"OK. How are our plans coming together to rid ourselves of this President? Will we be ready by then?"

"We're close. Akbar and I saw a test earlier today. We need to refine the targeting for a moving car, but we think we have a solution. Give us another few days."

"Victor, this *has* to work. And think how great it would be if we could eliminate both the American and Russian Presidents at the same time! Europe's economy is shambles, and China is on the verge of a meltdown. Only the US and Russia—besides the Zionists—can oppose us. To take out both of their leaders at once would be a great stroke. I'll talk with Paul Burke tomorrow about our public plans. As soon as you're confident that it will work, I'll put out the bait."

"Yes, sir. Have a good trip to L.A."

"Thank you. This sounds promising. You know how to reach me."

As the plane leveled off, Knox opened a briefing book on the last competitors left in the adult entertainment industry. He silently thanked President Harper for making his upcoming purchases less expensive.

It was long after midnight in Tehran, and Omid was in his chair looking out at the lights from their sixth-floor apartment. The television was on, but muted. He still had bandages on his head and hands, applied by a friendly doctor. He had been afraid to go to a hospital after the Democracy March on Monday.

But it was not the pain from the wounds that kept him awake. He had not seen Goli since Tuesday afternoon, when she had left their office to buy some printer paper. Nothing. No trace. No cell phone call. No answer to his calls. Nothing.

Their friend Ramin had also disappeared.

Omid, their parents, and his close friends had used every connection they knew to find her. They had cautiously approached the mullahs who earlier had approached them. They made inquiries on the internet. One friend had even gone to the police, who had laughed. There was no trace and no news.

Bastards was the word that repeated in his mind whenever he came to a dead end on how to find her. *I should leave our apartment, but what if she comes back here?* He tried her number again; it just rang.

I should have sent her away. The route through Turkey. David offered to help once she got there. What now? Bastards.

It was two Friday morning, and David couldn't sleep. His mind wouldn't shut off. He was trying to work out what to say to Kristen in a few hours.

He was replaying Kristen's situation yet again, when he heard a muffled thud on the floor above. He lay still and in a few moments there were more sounds. He stood up, feeling tired, and walked to the stairs in his pajamas. A moment later he was quietly listening outside Rob's door. The sounds of Street War 2100 were unmistakable.

He knocked and tried to open the door, but it was locked. He knocked again. The sound stopped. The door finally opened. Rob stood before him in his full VR battle gear, his visor pulled up and his microphone swiveled to the side. Rob had pulled the mattress off his bed and positioned the VR floor plate on top of them; clearly he had hoped to deaden the noise.

"Rob, we agreed to four hours on the weekends. It's Friday morning. What are you doing?"

Rob hung his head, then looked up into his father's face, and a note of defiance crept into his voice. "They need me, and USNet offered me a special deal because I've been playing so long. These hours are free, so I'm playing."

"But it's late and you'll be a wreck tomorrow. And, more importantly, we agreed to four hours until you bring up your grades."

"I know. But this is too good a deal. It's free! I'll sleep late and do my homework in the afternoon. I promise. It's no big deal."

"I...We'll talk about it tomorrow. With your Mom."

"I left my squad in a mess. I gotta get back." He pulled down his virtual reality visor and headed back to the special floor plate. "Blue Three, Blue Nine is back. Did they go down that street?"

David watched for a moment as his son went back to his virtual playground. *We really are losing him.* He pulled the door closed and retreated downstairs to their darkened bedroom. Elizabeth was breathing quietly. He lay down beside her, another issue separating him from rest.

Friday morning David was in his office early. He had not slept at all. The day before he had alerted Human Resources, so the paperwork was ready. He checked his screen and reread the salient points that he was required to go over. *I can't believe this.* As he read through the clinical-sounding end to Kristen's career at USNet, his mood deepened. *At least most of the others are traveling this morning, so she'll be gone before they get back.*

He had asked Julie to let him know when Kristen arrived, and her call came just after eight-twenty. Ten minutes later Kristen appeared at his door. She looked tanned and healthy, her hair a shade lighter. She held a magazine in her left hand, and her face was troubled. He motioned her to come in, but he stayed at his desk.

She walked toward him, and as she spoke she raised the magazine. "David, I got back late last night and only looked through this new copy of *Journal* by chance as I was checking my mail. I know it probably looks like I told this reporter about our studio acquisitions in L.A., but I *promise* I didn't. She already knew about them."

He didn't smile and motioned her to take a chair in front of his desk. "But, Kristen, you must be the 'real estate executive' who confirmed that a 'senior member' of our team had been working there. Isn't that you?"

Her face grew red and more troubled. "I...uh, I *did* talk to the reporter—Ms. Coleman. But I told her that I had *no* comment for the record, that I didn't make policy here *or* comment on it. Just like you asked me to say."

"Well, what *did* you talk with her about?"

She was silent for a moment, looking at him. "I gave her my general views on pornography and the media, but *none* of that is in the article. They were my personal comments, and she knew it."

"But *are* you the 'real estate executive' who gave credence to her whole story by telling her that I was in L.A. working on it?"

"I—I guess I am. Unless she talked to someone else."

"Not likely."

"I know."

He stopped and looked at her. *She's such a good person and great real estate exec. And she's helping me with Callie.* After some silence, as they looked at each other, he said in a low and measured voice, "Kristen, I have to let you go."

She sat back and put the magazine in her lap. "What?"

"You're leaving our real estate group. Leaving USNet. Effective immediately."

"Because of this?" She held up the magazine again.

"And the earlier statements. And the problems on the Capital Tower project."

"What 'problems' on the Capital Tower project?"

For the first time he looked down at his desk. "We had the high bid, but we didn't buy the property." He looked at her again. "It was your project. You were responsible. We should have bought it."

"David, that's ridiculous and you know it!"

"We still haven't bought it."

"Because Bill Porter stole it!"

"It was your project. You should have foreseen it." *This is killing me...*

"Is that in my personnel record?"

He took a deep breath and exhaled slowly. "It will be."

She paused, her anger obvious. "So that you can always say that you fired me because I didn't perform well. And not because of those articles."

"Both, I imagine."

She turned her head and looked out the window. "You're really firing me over those two articles?"

"And Capital Tower."

She turned back to him. "David, who's *really* firing me?"

"What do you mean?"

She paused. Then suddenly her expression changed. "Come with me, David! Let's quit together." She leaned forward, excited. "We'll start our own firm. The corporate types will hire us in a minute to outsource their problems. We'll make good money! You won't have to worry about Knox, or anyone."

If only I ... He stopped, deeply touched by her enthusiasm and excitement for working with him, even as he was firing her for no real reason. Finally he said, "Kristen, I can't. I have too much invested here. And too many bills to pay to take the chance."

She slumped back. "Fired. Not because of what I did, but because of what I said. Or what you think I said."

"Kristen, I'm genuinely sorry."

She stood up. "I bet you are. Who's going to do all that I've been doing? You don't have enough people here now."

David rose to meet her. "No, I mean about you."

"I hope that's true, David. But I'm not sure. This is such a scam. How can you put up with it and not quit yourself? Don't you have principles any more? All of this just because I spoke out once as being personally opposed to pornography? David, you of all people, ought to support me, not fire me!"

"I understand. I'm going to try to get us to scale back our adult movies, working from the inside."

"Good luck. Look at me. This is absurd and you know it!" She quickly brushed her eye.

They were silent.

"How long do I have?"

"You have to go now."

"Now?"

"Yes, it's corporate policy. You're due one month's severance and you have ten days of vacation coming. If you'll quietly resign, I've prepared a memo to HR to pay you for three months, which is the maximum I can do under corporate policy. I hope you can find a job in that time."

"Me, too. What sort of a rec will you write?"

"It will be very positive."

He could tell that she was not encouraged. "So that's it? After all this time? After all you taught me? After all we've done?"

He looked down again, then walked to the side of the desk. "Yes, I'm afraid so. There's a security guard outside and boxes in your office. You'll have thirty minutes to empty your desk. Please don't call anyone or have any long conversations. We'll issue a press release this afternoon saying that you've resigned to pursue other interests."

Almost to herself, she said, "I always wondered what that meant." She moved toward him. "What about Callie?"

"I...I'm glad you saw her. I wish this had worked out differently. I don't know what I'll do now."

"She's a very angry and confused young woman, David. Angry at you."

"I know."

"You should go see her. Anyway, I've started something with her, and I'll see her again if I go to L.A. while job hunting. Not for you, but for her."

He tried to smile and took a half a step toward her. "That would be appreciated." He held out his hand. She didn't take it.

Instead, she turned. "We'll see. I've got a lot to think about and a lot to do. Obviously none of this was on my USNet To-Do-List this morning." She began walking toward his door.

"I know."

She stopped and turned. "David, you were a great mentor and, I thought, a good man. But I don't think a lot of you now. You can call the reporter who interviewed me and confirm I told her that my personal comments were off the record. And if Knox is pushing you, you should have the guts to quit. You've apparently sold out."

"Kristen, I hate it. I just can't leave. I'm sorry."

"Sure. Have a nice day." She opened the door and was met by a uniformed security person. As they turned to walk to her office, she looked at her boss.

Any words he might speak had been drained from him. He just watched her walk away. After Kristen left, Julie put her head through the door. "I've got all the papers for her to sign."

"Fine. Please take them down to her office. Thanks."

He turned and stared out the window. *I just fired Kristen, one of the best people I've ever known or worked with. Can it get any worse?*

21

Late the same afternoon David was on the phone at his desk when Todd appeared at his door. He motioned him in. Todd walked over by the conference table but did not sit down. When he hung up, David said, "How does our space in Orlando look? Can we sublet some of it?"

"Sure. It's fine. Look, I just got back, and I wanted to ask you about Kristen. She left?" His tone and facial expression indicated disbelief.

David put his hands on the desk. "Yes. She resigned this morning. Said she had other things to do."

Todd stared at his boss for several heartbeats. "When I called in from the airport, I heard that she was gone. I couldn't believe it, so I called her at home. She said the same thing, but I still can't believe it."

David leaned forward again. "Yes, well, it's a dynamic market. Lots of opportunities. I just hope that *you* won't quit! In fact, you're now my senior exec, and I hope you can help take up the slack on some of Kristen's projects. And, oh, there's a raise and increased bonus that go along with the promotion to vice president."

Todd smiled. "I do like the sound of that."

"Starting with Capital Tower. It's your project again. Julie has pulled together all of Kristen's files. Whatever has happened to Bill Porter, whether he's missing or whatever, I want you to follow up with the owners and find out what we have to do to buy it."

Todd's smile broadened. "Good. I'll read the file and get back to you after I call them."

"Move quickly. I imagine that they're struggling with a decision, and I want to be there with the highest offer when they're ready to move."

"What else?"

"Here are the other properties I need you to take over. You and I are going to be working closely together, and hopefully we can add some more people shortly."

There was a loud knock on the door that awakened both Omid and Morad from their chairs in the living room. Neither had shaved or showered for days, and the kitchen was full of trash.

As he pulled himself up, Omid heard boots running down the stairs.

The two men looked at each other, knowing that their arrest or a bomb might be next. Morad nodded.

Omid, his heart racing, moved to the door, unlocked and opened it.

No one was there. No policemen. No bomb. He looked over to the side, where there was a pile of clothes. A hand in the middle of the pile made him realize that he was looking at his wife.

"Morad!" He knelt quickly and rolled the pile over. Goli was dressed in a full burka, her face and hands bruised and scarred, her lips swollen. One eye was closed from a bruise, but the other tried to open.

Omid lifted her and carried her into the living room. Morad tossed his coat and some books off the sofa, and Omid lay her there. She groaned.

Kneeling beside her, he started to pull off the burka, then realized that she was naked.

He turned to Morad. "I will take her into the bedroom. Call her parents, and find out if a doctor is available to come now."

Morad went into the bedroom and switched on a light by the bed, then withdrew, pulling out his cell phone.

Tenderly Omid lifted his wife and took her to their bed. As gently as possible he lowered her, but still she moaned as her left leg stretched out on the cover, its angle not natural.

He knelt again and whispered as he stroked her matted hair, "Goli, sweet Goli. You're home. It's going to be all right."

She opened one eye partway, but both were filled with tears. She imperceptibly shook her head.

His own tears came, but he wiped them with his sleeve and kept stroking her hair. "What did they do to you?"

She continued to move her head slightly from side to side, her eye closed. Finally, her lips
parted.

"Everything. They beat me. Omid...Omid." She grimaced and she raised her hand to touch him. "They raped me. Many, many times. I..."

"Shh," he whispered and lowered his head next to hers.

"They said. They said that unless you stop, they will kill you. And...and if you try to leave, they will kill both of us."

"Shh. It's going to be all right, my sweet Goli."

She began to sob.

Todd had gone back to his office after meeting with David. He sat at his desk, but his mind was racing. *New responsibilities here, as well as with RTI. But I really don't want RTI to be listening to all that we're doing.* He frowned. *What if I can get our team to cut down on cell phones and email, while I can listen to our competitors? Seems like that would give us a huge advantage in the market—and not bad for my career.*

But how can I get us to cut down in some way that will never be traceable to me? Victor would not be happy if he knew I was mixing RTI with work.

Victor Mustafin was at the special room in the RTI center early the next morning, and Akbar Kamali joined him by video. The two were anonymously watching events in central Russia on their large screen.

"This time it will work." General Beleborodov was standing next to Simon North on the observation post at the edge of the same broad valley. There were sounds of engines and heavy equipment moving in the distance. "With the added edge you've given us, there's no reason to run a test. Of course the missile will find its target."

North nodded in agreement. "This time we're running one red car and five blue decoys very near and parallel to it as it stops and starts. We've put the USNet ID card in the back seat of the red car and dialed the mock employee's ID number into the satellite guidance system over in the control room." He motioned to his left, off camera. "The 4 C was launched a little while ago. Let's take a look."

The screen view was magnified as the camera zoomed down on the red target car moving along a broad open area, similar to a large square in a European city. The other cars were right around it. They heard Beleborodov start to say, "Here it—" when the red car was suddenly torn apart by the missile splitting its windshield.

After a moment of surveying the shredded car, the camera panned back to take in the two men, now smiling on the platform. "I think we can say that your suggestion worked," said the general, beaming. "I just wish our enemies in the old days had worn GPS locators!"

Mustafin switched off the feed from the valley and looked at Kamali on the split screen. He smiled. "That should work really well on the broad avenues of Moscow."

Kamali nodded. "Or, better yet, coming through a window of the Kremlin to take out all the key people in both governments at the same time."

"Hi, Callie. It's Kristen. Sorry I missed you. I've unexpectedly got some time on my hands, and I'm going to visit my dad in Texas, and then some friends. I don't want to be an imposition, but I'm planning to visit L.A. again after Memorial Day, on my way to San Francisco, and I'd love to see you. By the way, everyone says the clothes look great, especially the purplish dress I worried about. You were right! Anyway, let me know your schedule, so we can get together. I won't be on the expense account, so please give me some recommendations on places to stay. Talk with you soon. Thanks. Bye."

Bradley Fuller was President Harper's domestic policy advisor, his office in the White House. Because Monday would be a holiday, early that Saturday afternoon he was sitting at his desk reviewing a synopsis of the latest legal maneuvers filed in several jurisdictions to thwart the administration's Entertainment and Media Reform law. He was growing more frustrated with the unending legal logjam when his phone rang.

"Yes?"

"It's Senator Bulloch, sir."

Senator Joe Bulloch was from the other party, but was known in the capital as a thoughtful and honorable man. On many occasions he had sided with the President on social and moral issues, including the Entertainment Reform legislation, although he still tended to want to spend more than the Chief Executive. Fuller would certainly take his call.

"Hello, Senator. How are you today?"

"Fine, Bradley. Except for all the flack I catch in the backside for supporting the President on so many issues," he quipped.

Fuller knew how important that support was, and how much the two elected officials thought of each other. With genuine sincerity, the advisor said, "Your support on those issues is very much appreciated, not only by the President, but also by the American people."

"Maybe. I hope so. I'm just doing what I think is right. Anyway, I'm calling about a fellow from our state who hasn't always seen eye to eye with the President but who wants to make amends."

Fuller knew that there was always a reason for a call like this. "Really? Who is that, and how can I help?"

"Trevor Knox."

Fuller almost interjected an immediate note of skepticism, but Senator Bulloch continued, "Trevor and I go way back, since before his uncle died. He called a little while ago and asked me to put forward an invitation to President Harper on his behalf."

Fuller shifted in his chair and took out a pen. "We'll be glad to listen, Senator, and to respond, of course."

"Good. Trevor has heard rumors that the President is considering a trip to Moscow to visit President Temirov this summer, probably around the Fourth of July."

"I'm not sure of the dates, but there are discussions going on about a trip."

"Yes. Well, Trevor's company, USNet, has the longest running joint venture in Russia—a software company—dating from the early days of Perestroika. It's actually quite profitable and moving to new headquarters not far from the Kremlin. Mr. Knox would like to extend an invitation to the President to visit the new facility. Sort of a grand opening to promote Russian-American business and good will."

"I'm taking notes, Senator. Foreign policy is not my strong suit."

"I know, Bradley, but domestic policy is. And I think you'll like the next part. Trevor asked me to tell you that he's considering dropping his opposition to the President's initiatives in media reform, and to announce that change before the President's visit in Moscow. He's willing to embrace the reforms as good for both countries. Now he's not going to get out of the adult movie business, but he'll agree to the President's ideas on how to operate, and he'll also stop funding legal challenges to the new laws. Trevor would like to have a sort of 'bury the hatchet' ceremony with the President in Russia."

Fuller sat back. "Senator, that *is* a lot to think about. It seems like quite a change for Mr. Knox."

"I know. And that's why I called you today. I believe he's sincere, and I'd like to set the wheels in motion so that the President can respond back to him pretty quickly. What do you think?"

"Again, I'm not up on the foreign policy issues as they relate to that visit. But I'll certainly check today with my counterparts and then ask the President. As for domestic policy, it sounds like it would be a great step."

"Yes. That's what I thought. So I can tell Trevor that you are cautiously positive and will get back to me in a few days?"

"Yes. I think you can say that. I'll call you back. And thank you, Senator Bulloch."

"Don't mention it. I just hope it turns out to help both of them."

That afternoon Todd Phelps worked alone in his home office. Using the internet to check names and addresses, but pulling from his recent experience at RTI to create the content, he wrote to David Sawyer what looked like a well-crafted marketing piece from a company specializing in communications security. In great detail it described how cell phones and email were being intercepted by government agencies and private groups, and the information then used to the detriment of those communicating. The letter encouraged alternate connectivity, like landlines, and made a plug for encryption software.

Todd hoped that he would get David's attention by listing at the start of the letter the names of several people whom Todd knew David corresponded with regularly. He dropped them in a list to look like they came from a spreadsheet of intercepted calls.

When he finished, he looked all over the house for a large envelope and stamps—items that he no longer used regularly. Late that afternoon, he deposited the piece in a snail-mail box outside their local grocery store.

"Hi Kristen, it's Callie."

"Oh, hi! How are you?"

"Fine. I got your call."

"Good. Listen, I don't mean to intrude on your life, but I'm planning to be out there again, and I'd love to see you. You've done wonders for my wardrobe, so I'd like to at least buy you another dinner. Maybe meet Alex."

"Yeah, sure. Thanks. When do you think you'll be coming?"

"Sometime next week, after Memorial Day. I'm going to visit some other people, and maybe my dad in Texas, then head to the coast. I'm just chillin' a little."

"Sounds good. I'll be here. Let me know. You said you needed ideas on a place to stay?"

"Yeah. I'm not on the USNet ticket any more."

"How come?"

"Well, actually, I'm not working there any more."

"Why not?"

"Well, I'll tell you more about it, but basically your dad let me go."

"I can't believe it! Why?"

"It's a bit of a story. I'll tell you when I'm there."

"Wow! Well, look, I think Jane, my roommate, will be away for a week. She's, like, in movies, and she and Alex have gone down to Mexico to try out for small parts. Alex is supposed to come back, but she's staying a week, so there's a spare bedroom. Anyway, I'd love to hear that story, so if you're not working, why don't you just stay with me to save some money?"

"Really? Are you sure it would be all right?"

"Yes. It won't be a problem."

"Well, that would be great. I promise not to get in your way. Thanks a lot."

"Sure. Call me when you know you're coming."

"OK. See you then."

The Sawyers had just finished dinner, and Rob was headed upstairs to play some parent-sanctioned weekend Street War 2100 when the home phone rang.

"David, it sounds like Omid," Elizabeth said from the kitchen, handing him the walk-around phone.

David took the phone but stood so that Elizabeth could hear the conversation. "Hello."

"Cousin, how are you?"

"We're fine, but how are you?"

"Not so good tonight. My uncle is very angry and took it out on my wife. A doctor has seen her." Elizabeth gasped.

David spoke. "What can we do?"

"I will let you know soon."

"Next week will not be soon enough."

"I know. We'll see. David. It is not easy. There is one other thing."

"Tell me."

"Our friend, Ramin. He was missing for a week. Now he can't walk. We don't know if there has been any breech, but we have destroyed the first cards you gave us and have moved to the second set. I'm using one now."

"That sounds like a good idea. Shall I send some more?"

"Yes. Please deliver them to the same address in Turkey. Our friend will be there in a week."

"Of course. I'll send fifty new ones."

"That will be expensive."

"Don't be ridiculous."

"You are kind, cousin. I will let you know if we can work out a plan."

"I'll visit you in Turkey and work to get you to the States."

"As Allah wills. I hope to call again soon."

"Please be careful."

Omid hung up, and David looked at Elizabeth. "The thugs are clearly in control."

Elizabeth stepped back and gently shrugged. "Poor Goli. I can't imagine. They just want to have some freedom." She paused and then said, "Is that so dangerous?"

"I guess it is to those in power."

Two hours later.

Blue Six: That was awesome!

Blue Nine: You made a great shot from behind those rocks.

Blue Six: Thanks for nailing that guy sneaking up behind the cars.

Blue Nine: What's a partner for?

Blue Six: Hey, I see from your website that you live close to me.

Blue Nine: Yeah? Cool. Where do you live?

Blue Six: In Vinton. Listen, I'm having some other guys over—Sunday night—Memorial Day. They do StreetWar, too. We're going to talk about strategy, do some stuff, maybe a little pot. It'll be cool. Want to come?

Blue Nine: Sure. But I don't have a car.

Blue Six: No sweat. I'll pick you up. Where do you live?

Blue Nine: Broughton. Let me figure out a place to meet. I'm still living at home. I have a friend, Justin, who plays. Can he come, too?

Blue Six: Sure. How old are you?

Blue Nine: Fifteen.

Blue Six: No problem. You'll really like these guys. I'll give you my phone number, and we'll figure it out. OK?

Blue Nine: Sure. That'll be great. Sounds like fun.

As the sun set Master Sergeant Salim Moradi drove his new SUV out the main gate of Fort Bliss and headed for downtown El Paso. He had two important calls to make, and he wanted them to be lost in the clutter of the urban cell phone towers.

MSG Moradi had been stationed at Fort Bliss for almost ten years, teaching soldiers, Marines and sailors how to use the FIM-92 Stinger missile to bring down aircraft. He was the senior enlisted member of his team and enjoyed wide respect among his peers as a hard working professional who was dedicated to the Army and to their base's training mission.

Salim had never married and was known to his closest acquaintances as a quiet professional. But they never ventured with him to Las Vegas, where he went alone three or four times a year. On those trips he indulged every passion he could imagine, confident that Allah would overlook his transgressions because the rest of the year he was on the front line of Jihad. In the US Army, the very belly of the Great Satan.

Born in Jordan, Salim had become a true believer in his early teenage years at their local mosque, where an Egyptian imam taught the Muslim faith interlaced with hate for America and all things Western. When his parents immigrated to Detroit, Salim of course followed. There, after an email exchange between his old imam and the youth leader at their Detroit mosque, Salim continued his radical studies. One evening when he was about to graduate from high school, three older men met him at the mosque and talked to him about joining the US Army. That had been fifteen years ago.

During his years at Fort Bliss, Salim had trained thousands of young soldiers how to use the Stinger missile. And during that time he had kept his eyes open for a particular kind of student, one who might share his fundamental beliefs. Over those years he had grown relationships with fourteen young men, but only two had actually committed. For now, they were enough. It was to them that he would place his calls.

Ten minutes later Yusef Sawyer was driving alone along the interstate in Los Angeles, coming back from a showing. Before he had finished the Army's Air Defense Artillery School at Fort Bliss, his instructor and mentor had given him ten prepaid cell phones, each with a number marked on its case. There had been two previous calls, and Yusef had been faithfully charging and carrying phone #3 for almost six months. Just as he turned onto the exit ramp, that phone rang in his coat pocket.

His heart raced. Because he was not with anyone, or at a location that could be connected with him by GPS, he knew that he could answer. Steering with one hand, he pulled the phone from his pocket and hit the green button. The familiar voice said, "There is no god but Allah. Muhammad is the messenger of Allah." Yusef nodded and repeated the two sentences back into the phone.

"Good news, my brother. The day for celebration may now be the Fourth of July. Prepare yourself in every way, and I will confirm all details soon."

"Understood."

"May Allah go with you." The phone went dead.

Yusef pulled into the parking lot of a large retail center. He sat for a moment, taking it in. *Six weeks!* His body shuddered. Then he got out and put the phone just ahead of his left front tire. As he drove off, crushing the phone, he made a note to remember to charge number #4.

Meanwhile, at a similar retail center parking lot in El Paso, Salim had just completed the same call to Perviz, a Pakistani-American Army graduate of the same school who lived in Manhattan.

22

TUESDAY, MAY 31ST

Normally it would have been tough for Todd to be up so early on the first workday after the Memorial Day weekend, but on this Tuesday, six am was just fine. He would spend his first three hours alone in the RTI training cubicle. During the past week he had logged three additional training sessions with a senior person. He told Mary that he and David Sawyer had an early meeting with an executive search firm to evaluate the resumes of possible additions to the real estate group, before his flight that afternoon to Kansas City. So finally he was alone in a cubicle—and about to go online for his first traffic.

Feeling a rush of excitement, he clicked the mouse and immediately was fed a cell phone call from inside a publishing house in New York. It appeared to be an attorney discussing the final pricing for an Initial Public Offering of stock that morning, explaining why she thought the price was too low. Todd quickly noted the industry involved and routed the message to the appropriate desk. *OK, I did one.*

He continued for more than an hour, gaining confidence with each message he routed or deleted. He felt a tap on his shoulder and turned to see Victor Mustafin. "How are you doing?" he asked.

Todd logged off and removed his headset. Smiling, he answered, "Great. I think I'm getting the hang of it."

"Good. A few more of these sessions and we'll move you up to the next level. There's more to learn, of course. Then to the control room, probably in about two weeks. If we stay on schedule, in about two months you should be ready to stand watch as the duty officer."

"That's hard to believe," Todd said.

"You'll get there. And, by the way, here's a little incentive to help." Mustafin handed him an envelope.

Todd opened it to find a check for $25,000 made out to him from International Specialists in Geneva. He looked up at Mustafin, a question on his face.

"The first of many installments, Todd. We like what you're doing, and we want to give you a glimpse of what this work can mean for you. It's drawn on a legitimate company, and the income will be reported to the IRS. It's a real estate consulting firm. When the money really starts flowing, we'll create some more of these situations, so the income will be on the up and up."

"Thanks." Todd smiled, slipping the check into his coat on the back of the chair.

Mustafin put his hand on Todd's shoulder. "Just keep doing a good job, and you can expect one of those every few weeks. Have a good one."

Todd returned to his monitor, smiling. *This is good.*

Before logging online again, he decided to try something that he'd been curious about but had not wanted to try with a mentor. He clicked on the People icon at the bottom of his screen. The computer asked for his password, and he typed in the new one that Victor had given him when he graduated to solo duty. Up came a form for a name and address. He typed in his own name. When he clicked it, his USNet file appeared, complete with picture, address and many choices for further information, including Family, Income, Expenditures, Hobbies, Medical, Phone Messages, Emails, even Location. He couldn't help frowning. *Who else in here has access to all of this USNet data on me and my family?* He clicked through the information in several of the areas, and it appeared to be accurate. Finally he clicked on Location, and a map came up pinpointing him within the unlabeled RTI HQ. He wondered whether his cell phone or the USNet ID card in his wallet identified his whereabouts to the computer.

Todd sat back in his chair, realizing that the RTI system had captured virtually every fact about his life. And tens of thousands of other lives. *I need to be more cautious about what I say on the phone. But the government probably has the same stuff. And who else does? Are we really the only ones doing it? I've just got to focus on getting all the money I can from this, so my family will have what we need. And then retire as soon as possible.*

To check the system, he backed out and typed in David Sawyer's name. Todd was impressed that David had so much information on file, and he took a minute to scan it. When he clicked on Location, a map came up with the crosshair on their office. *Impressive. Very impressive. I'm glad I'm on the inside.*

Later that morning David and Todd finished meeting with representatives from an executive search firm and were reasonably positive about two of the candidates they proposed. David asked them to set up interviews, but also to keep looking. He believed he needed at least three experienced real estate professionals, and he needed them quickly.

After seeing his guests to the elevator lobby, he was back in his office, looking at the view toward downtown and Capital Tower. Todd had told him that the building's owners were meeting in early June to decide how to proceed after Porter's disappearance. David instructed Todd to ask for a meeting, and they were waiting word. But as David looked out at the building from his office, he couldn't help thinking about Kristen and wondering where she might be. He had not heard from her since she walked out of his office ten days earlier.

His phone rang and it was Paul Burke.

"How goes it?" his colleague asked.

"Fine. Just looking at Capital Tower."

"How's the family?"

"We had a quiet Memorial Day. Sorry we couldn't join you at the lake. Rob spent most of the weekend at the movies. And Elizabeth and I just did our usual thing. How about you?"

"We're fine. Amanda is going out to do the waitress thing in Aspen with some friends. I thought she might try to visit Callie, or vice-versa."

"Good."

"Yes. Listen, David, I'm calling on a sensitive matter that isn't set in stone yet, but I want to give you a heads up so you can be thinking about it."

"OK."

"Trevor wants to invite President Harper to the grand opening of our new Moscow office when she's over there for the Fourth of July—we think she's going then. We already have feelers out to key members in the administration to issue the invitation. Do you still think our space will be ready?"

"Yes. We're scheduled to sign the lease on Thursday, and the space, at least the office portion, is virtually finished. But President Harper? Why would Trevor invite her, and why would she accept?"

"I know it's hard to believe. Trevor told me last week that he wants to 'bury the hatchet.' Not actually get out of all the stuff we're doing—casinos online and adult movies. But try to conform more with what the President is trying to do with her reform laws."

"You're kidding. Why?"

"I'm not sure. He said that he's just tired of fighting the issue and wants to move on."

"Now that we're about to own almost all the production assets in the country, I guess it won't hurt to be on better terms with the government."

"I guess that might be part of it. But I think he's also ready for a change. He's directed us to stop funding the legal challenges to the President's reform law, as a measure of good faith. Anyway, we want you to be an early part of the planning, since you know the new office and a little about Moscow. The President hasn't accepted yet, but we'd like to begin some contingency plans with our media and PR people right away, from how to conduct the ribbon cutting to the guest lists. So we'll need your input."

"I'm glad to help. Will this mean I'll be going over there again?"

"I would think so. Maybe a few days before."

"I'm game. When will we know?"

"The ball is in the President's court. But we're having a first meeting in my office tomorrow at two. Can you make it?"

"Uh—sure. I'll put down some thoughts beforehand."

"Good. See you then."

"Great." David hung up and looked at the pictures of his kids on the desk. *If the reforms go through, Callie will be out of these terrible movies. God—or Allah—I hope so!*

Then he picked up the receiver again and dialed an internal number. "Abigail, hi. It's David. Can you get me fifty more SIM cards, as soon as possible? And five or ten of those pre-paid 'throw away' cell phones?"

That afternoon at Callie's apartment in Long Beach, Kristen was sitting on one of two sofas arranged in an L around a coffee table in the living room, reading a book. She was dressed in khaki shorts and a light blue short-sleeved blouse. An hour earlier she had been sunning on Callie's back terrace, but now the air conditioning felt good. She glanced up as Callie opened the front door.

"Hi," Callie said, as she came through the door wearing short shorts and a purple tank top, and carrying a bag of groceries.

Kristen stood and smiled. "Let me help you."

"I've got it," Callie said, walking through and putting the bag on the table. Free of the bag, she turned and accepted a hug from Kristen.

"It's so nice of you to have me back again so soon, and to let me stay here."

"No problem. Did you find the key OK?"

"Right where you said. I put my stuff in the bedroom on the left upstairs, and then I sunned for a while."

"Not bad for being unemployed, huh?"

"Nope. What about you?"

"Oh, the usual. Classes and then rehearsal for the play. Kinda wears you out."

"I bet. We can get dressed and go out to dinner whenever you say."

Picking up the grocery bag and walking a few steps to the kitchen counter, Callie said, "We don't have to go out. I got some salad stuff, a frozen pasta thing, and some bread. Alex will be here in a little while. Let's just stay in and chill." Reaching in the bag, she pulled out a bottle. "I even got some wine. The fake ID works every time at the grocery store."

"Fine. I look forward to meeting Alex. All we need now is my own Mr. Right."

Callie smiled. "He's out there. I think I found mine." She handed the bottle of wine to Kristen. "Before he comes, I want to hear about your plans, and we'll talk about going to Fashion Island in Orange County. I haven't been in a while, and I think you'll like it."

"That works for me. Where's the corkscrew?"

"It'll be a heck of a development," Mike Campbell remarked, as he cut into a steak. "Your people will love being in a mixed-use facility, with restaurants and retail."

Todd Phelps looked around the rustic restaurant, made to resemble a Kansas City saloon in its cowboy heyday, and sipped his drink. "You're right, Mike. The converted brewery can be a great mixed use development for us and for you."

"Man, this is a great steak. Listen, I've penciled out the numbers, and we'll need to net at least nine dollars and fifty cents a square foot for your space in the old warehouse."

Todd put down his drink and frowned. "But we just need fiber-connected warehouse space for our computer servers. Cheryl says that we can lease that kind of space all day long in Kansas City for about five bucks."

Mike paused, holding his knife and fork next to his plate. He looked directly at Todd. "That may be. I don't know. But to make the brewery work for us, given the renovation cost, we'll need to get nine-fifty. And, by the way, that also makes it work for you."

Todd looked down at his plate, then picked up his knife and fork. "OK. Well, we'll need to package it so that overall it comes out in the ballpark of the others."

"I understand. We'll sharpen our pencils. Your lease is the key," Mike said, emphasizing the point with his knife, "and we'll certainly consider that as we build in our 'financing fees.'"

Todd paused, then looked at his friend. "Just be sure that we talk like we're doing now—no more emails or cell phone calls—and make those deposits quietly."

Mike smiled. "I got it."

Todd nodded. "Give me some specifics as soon as you can, and I'll do my best to get it approved."

Mike smiled. "Early next week. I'll put the lease proposal in writing, and I'll call you. Now, please, enjoy your steak."

Kristen and Callie were each half-reclining on opposite ends of the sofa, the bottle of wine and a plate with cheese and crackers on the coffee table. Five CDs were loaded, and Paul McCartney was into "And I Love Her." Callie took a sip from her glass. "So, I don't have classes tomorrow until the afternoon, if you want to try Fashion Island. What are you looking for?"

"Another business outfit like the last one. At home I just don't see any like we bought here two weeks ago. Hopefully I'll have some job interviews soon, and I want to look good. Another one or two of those, and then some casual stuff. Maybe pants. Let's just look."

"Sure. No sweat. So, tell me what Dad did to *you*."

Kristen leaned forward, poured herself a little more wine, and picked up a piece of cheese. Then she sat back. "Well, in the simplest terms, he fired me." She noticed a small smile and a nod from Callie.

"Why?"

"Not because of anything I did directly relating to real estate. But really for other reasons. I made the mistake of letting my personal views become a little too public, and that wasn't appreciated by USNet's top management. Although your dad didn't say so, I'm sure that Trevor Knox and maybe Paul Burke put pressure on him to get rid of me."

Callie brought her knees up and took a sip from her glass. "Wow. So you, like, got fired for what you thought? That sounds pretty much like what he did to me."

"What do you mean?"

"Don't you know that he disowned me because Alex lives here with me?"

"Disowned you?"

"Yes, cut me off. No more support. Almost no contact."

"That must be tough on both of you. And your mom."

"Not sure about them. I guess it's that conservative Iranian thing with him. Can't stand the thought of me sleeping with the man I love. And I'm almost twenty!"

"I see."

"And now he's cut you off, so to speak. Fired you."

"Well, I was disappointed. I was angry and disappointed in him and USNet a week ago, and that's why I'm doing this traveling. I called and talked with the Sullivans. She's the Congresswoman—the one I told you about—with her husband, Richard. By the way, their son Tommy is about your age. You might want to check him out. "

Callie shrugged. "I love Alex. She's the one who knew you'd had an affair with her husband?"

"Yes. That's why I wanted to talk more with her. You see, she and I—and her husband—share the same faith. I thought I knew what to do about my anger with your dad, but sometimes it's still hard to put faith into practice. So I prayed and decided to talk with her, since she's older and since I had made *her* so angry."

"I guess that could make sense," Callie said more slowly.

"So the three of us talked. Janet reminded me that everyone is capable of letting everyone else down. It's just being human. And my anger about it would only hurt *me*. Your dad wouldn't wake up every morning feeling worse because I was disappointed in him. Only I would. And eventually that anger would eat at me so much that it would hurt my other relationships—like us."

"Hm." Callie reached for a piece of cheese and a cracker.

"So we prayed for guidance and strength, and then I forgave your dad."

"But he didn't ask you to forgive him. He didn't even say he was sorry."

Kristen smiled. "That's the whole point, isn't it? You see, me forgiving him is about me, not about him. I do hope that someday he realizes what he's done, and that we can talk about it. But forgiving is what *I* have to do, not him. And," she added, smiling, "I'm happy to tell you that I've done it. I'm free from all that anger and hate—free to talk with him, and to move on, without all that baggage. It's a great feeling, much better than anger."

"Wow. That would be hard. I think I'm still, like, pretty angry with him for not accepting Alex."

"I've noticed."

Callie shrugged. "Well, maybe someday I'll be able to do what you said."

"I hope so, but it won't come easily or naturally. Like I think we talked about before, forgiveness is not a particularly human trait. I suspect that we are only capable of it if we acknowledge that it's from God, and if we're seeking him."

"You're pretty deep into religion, aren't you?"

Kristen laughed and sat up. "Not religion—but faith, yes. Unfortunately many of us have to fail first to appreciate it. When we run out of our own alternatives and we hit rock bottom, like I did with that affair. The main thing I learned through that awful experience years ago with Richard and Janet is that God made me, loves me, and wants a relationship with me—like with my human father, only deeper. That's where the capacity for forgiveness comes from, Callie. I realize that he has forgiven me—and for a lot worse. Then comes a time of healing and restoration of hope. With all that, how can I hold a grudge against your dad, or anyone else?"

"That's how you really feel? That you have a *relationship* with God?"

"Yes. Absolutely."

"How?"

"It's simple—and powerful. In the midst of that mess, after I'd seen what God did so powerfully in Richard's life, I gave up. I stopped trying to be in charge and instead gave my life to God's son—the one who sacrificed his life so that God *could* forgive me. I asked Christ to forgive me and to take over."

She frowned. "And—what happened?"

"He did. Now my heart tries to do what God wants, not what Kristen wants. I'm obviously not perfect. You know that. I try to find out what he wants—that relationship I talked about, by praying and by reading his Word."

"You mean the Bible? *You* read the Bible?"

Kristen smiled again. "Yes, almost every day."

"Really? That's so random. I can't believe that a cool person like you is into the Bible—and 'faith.'"

"I'm not sure how cool I am, but why do you say that?"

"I thought religion was, like, for weak people and losers."

"No, faith like I've described is for *all* people. And it's actually pretty powerful, like I said. It's what's let me get past all the anger that would otherwise be eating me up right now."

"Yeah, well, I see that, I guess. I just never thought about it. I've, like, never been around anyone who said she had a strong faith. It's kinda weird."

Kristen laughed and ate a cracker.

Callie took a sip. "Like you have something that others don't have. You're not even mad with Dad, and I certainly am. Sort of spooky, I guess."

"Well, the power comes only from the relationship, and that's not spooky at all—and it's open to anyone and everyone."

"Everyone? Even to someone like me?"

"Yes, of course. I'll be glad to help you start that relationship, any time."

They heard a car door close outside.

Callie stood up. "Well, I don't think I'm ready for a relationship with God just yet. If there *is* a God, he'd be pretty upset with me right now." She looked out the window and smiled. "Alex's here. And I'd have to change a lot of what I'm doing. So, for now, I'm pretty starved. How about we just fix dinner?"

"That's fine." Kristen rose as a key opened the door.

Callie greeted Alex with a hug and a kiss. Turning, she motioned toward Kristen. "Alex, this is Kristen Holloway, who I told you about. She works with dad—well, used to. She's cool. Kristen, this is Alex Spalding."

"Great to meet you," Kristen said, offering her hand.

"Yeah, me too," Alex replied, giving her hand a half-hearted squeeze.

Turning to the kitchen, Callie said, "We were just finishing a discussion on everything from jobs to God—I guess that there's even a Job in the Bible." She smiled.

"Ugh," Kristen replied.

Alex looked confused.

The two women went into the kitchen.

"But I do appreciate you sharing all of that with me. It seems pretty far out. Here, check the directions on the pasta while I get some water boiling."

"I know it can seem far out," Kristen said, taking the package. "It did to me, too. But once you experience a real relationship with the God who made you, it goes from being far out to being deep inside. I know. It's the only thing that's given me the ability to experience true peace."

Callie turned to put water in a large pot. "It's just that I'm still young and not ready for all that yet."

Kristen smiled. "You sound like I sounded."

Callie shrugged. Alex came up behind her and gave her a hug.

It was early morning in the Intelligence Office at the Russian Army Base not far from Arzamas-23. Captain Boris Rusnak was leaning over a table filled with aerial photographs and speaking to Lieutenant Mikhail Andryushin.

"Your task is to find a large, isolated field which is near a suitable road, but also hidden from view to houses, passing cars, etc., in this general area." He pointed with his finger to the large scale map on top of the others. "We must be able to secure it, set up the launcher, test all systems, fire and depart, with as little chance of interference as possible."

"A total of about eight hours," the younger officer stated.

"Yes. That should do it."

"I'll take Mishkin and Polyakov."

"Good. You have one week."

Rather than salute, Andryushin gave the hand sign of the secret group into which he had been inducted by Rusnak two years earlier. He then nodded, picked up the photographs, and left for his car.

An hour later Callie, Alex and Kristen were seated at the table, finishing their dinner and the wine. They had planned the next day's outing.

"Hey, after dinner let's go out and have some fun," Callie said. "We know some great bars with guys who you might find interesting. You can experience all the stuff that I don't want to give up to have a relationship with God!"

Alex smiled and took Callie's hand. "I'm in. I don't need God—you're all the relationship I need."

Kristen shrugged. "Well, it's not my usual thing. But, hey, when in Rome. Just so long as there are a few older ones, and you get me home in one piece before too late."

"Oh, there will be plenty of older ones. But listen"—she took a last sip of wine—"you never told me what you said that got you in trouble with Dad's company."

Kristen took a deep breath and moved her plate to the side. Picking up her glass, she said, "Well, actually, I made some comments to a reporter on two occasions that I'm opposed to pornography being on every corner and on every TV. And since USNet owns a lot of adult movie production assets and is buying more, that didn't go down too well with Mr. Knox."

Callie frowned. "You got fired over adult movies? Why don't you like adult movies?"

Kristen sighed and leaned forward. "I could give you lots of reasons— from obsession and addiction to trashing women to impossible expectations to broken marriages to rampant premarital sex to pregnancy to the degradation of our expectations and values in general. A lot of pain and problems for a lot of people, all caused because we're not doing what's right."

"You really think that adult entertainment causes all of those problems?" Alex asked.

"Not by itself, but the men I work with now feel it's 'normal' to spend the evening looking at naked women dancing on tables as part of business. And that's just a tiny sliver of it. Anything you read on the subject will tell you that, like alcohol and tobacco and drugs, for many people it's easy to become addicted. And it used to be that, like alcohol and drugs, it was difficult to find, particularly for a kid. But now we've sort of become numb, and it's everywhere...in our homes, on the internet, in the movies. Another powerful lie that derails lives and causes pain."

Alex sat back, looked at Callie, then said, "You really *do* have an opinion! You believe that all of that is caused by some movies?"

"I'm not naive, Alex, to think that all our problems are caused by adult movies, or any other one thing—of course not. But I'm sure that all of that sex being pushed at us, and at our kids, creates the kind of environment in which I felt that it was 'OK' to have an affair with a married man, because he wasn't 'understood' at home, or didn't have a great sex life, or some other excuse. It was reinforced by all the supposedly free and wonderful sex with no consequences that's portrayed in every porn movie and on every adult TV show. But what we did caused *real* pain. I got hurt. But also Janet, his wife, and their kids got hurt. We almost created a divorce, maybe even a child. Of course affairs happened long before there were adult movies. But they're just part of the pattern that makes people think it's OK, when, believe me, it isn't."

Callie stood up and headed for the kitchen. "I think I need something else. Would you like some tequila? I don't even have to ask Alex."

Kristen smiled. "Sure. A little. Listen, when was the last time an adult movie or TV show ended with the partners being diseased, the woman unable to have children, the kids left with one parent and suffering on less income, or at an abortion clinic? I mean, is that what the adult movie industry portrays for us?"

Callie put a bottle and three glasses in front of them. "No, I guess not."

"Well, that's what *really* happens, among other painful things, when people have sex like in those movies. So..." She smiled again and raised her water glass. "That's why I had a thing or two to say—though I didn't quite say all of that, nor did I mean for it to be publicized in the way it was."

Alex poured for each of them. Callie took a long sip and put down her glass. "I see. Yeah, I can imagine that those views would not sit well with the big guns at USNet. But, listen, since we're on this, I think I ought to tell you that... well, Alex and I have actually made some of those adult movies. And we might make more. The pay is pretty good."

Kristen nodded. "I know."

"You do? How long have you known it?"

"Well, I guess since before I met you a few weeks ago."

"Wait. All this time you've *known* we did those movies?"

"Yes. Your dad told me."

Callie glanced at Alex, her face turning red. "So all of your coming here and pretending to like me and coming back has all just been my father's idea? To send in a religious nut to make me think I like her and then brainwash me into 'doing good' and dumping Alex? I can't believe you!" Her arms were folded, tears were forming in her eyes.

Kristen shook her head. "Callie, you're wrong. Your father did ask me to come to see you the first time. But the friendship I have for you, and the fun we've had is real—it's not fake. I like you for you, no matter what you do."

"Wait a minute. Let me get this straight. You've just lectured me on how bad adult movies are, and yet you like me, even though I've made two of them? Come on!" She reached forward and took another long sip.

"Yes. Of course. You're a wonderful, talented young woman. You won't always make these movies. You have talents far beyond them. One day you'll understand how destructive they are, see the pain they're causing. But that's not a condition for our friendship, any more than my supposed perfection ought to be."

Callie stood, and Alex followed her. "Whoa...this is like really heavy! You hate the movies we made, but you like me?"

"Yes. On both counts."

"I...look, I gotta, like, figure this out. I'm sorry. I think you could be trying to trick me or something. Why don't you chill out here and—read the Bible or something—and Alex and I will go hang out at the bar with some friends? I doubt you'd like them anyway. And I gotta think. OK?" She, picked up her drink, turned and walked to her bedroom.

Kristen spoke to her back. "Yes, whatever you say. But I don't want you to go out upset with me. I just told you the truth when you asked."

Alex waited a moment then said in a low, angry voice to Kristen, "Don't push your religious ideas on her. We don't need them." Then he followed Callie upstairs to their bedroom.

Kristen took her dishes to the sink and rinsed off the plates and glasses. Callie came out wearing a low-cut, tight-fitting dress with slits up both sides, and moved to pick up her purse. "I know, I heard. But...well, I'll see you in the morning. We'll probably still go shopping, but I really gotta get out and think and talk with my friends. This has been a *really* heavy night."

Kristen walked to the center of the room as Callie ran a brush through her hair and renewed her lipstick in a mirror by the door. "Callie, listen. You can question why I came the first time. But ever since then I've just wanted to be your friend, and I've truly appreciated your advice on clothes. Your father *fired* me, but I still wanted to come back and see *you*. So I hope that tells you something. I'll stay here and read and go to bed, but I hope you'll realize that my opinion on adult movies, or any other issue, is not the same as my opinion about you. The two of us will never solve the issues. But the two of us can be friends."

As Alex came down from the bedroom, Callie said, "Yeah. That sounds good, but I just want to talk with Alex and check it out in my head tonight. So I'll see you in the morning. Lock the door, but don't click this latch, so we can get in. See 'ya." She turned and walked out into the southern California night. Alex turned to leave with her, looked back at Kristen, shook his head, and followed Callie out, closing the door.

23

Early the next morning Todd was in his hotel room, utilizing the special encrypted laptop with headphones that Mustafin had loaned him during training to handle the calls and emails that the RTI system intercepted. It was fascinating to see and hear what so many people thought they were writing and saying in private. It gave him a rush every time he clicked online and thought about how they were using this information to get ahead of everyone else.

Hopefully at the next level I'll be able to move from raw messages to decisions. It'll be interesting to see what our competitors are planning and to check out other people's deals. But at USNet we really shouldn't be putting sensitive information in emails or cell phone calls—this group, whoever they are, will instantly know all our plans, and alert our competitors. We should go back to land lines and conversations. What if I started writing business letters, like people used to do? I hope David reads the letter I sent him.

Near the end of his first hour he clicked for a new message and up came a cell phone call that appeared to be between a husband and wife, or boyfriend and girlfriend. The only reason he imagined it was captured was because at one point the woman used the word "earn" in berating the man's poor performance. But at the end of the call the man threatened to harm her and was heading to her home.

Todd couldn't remember anything from his training about this situation, and he couldn't find an icon on the screen for an emergency. So he forwarded the message up to the next level, the role he would play next week, with an email message asking whom they should call.

A minute later, as he was handling another message, the email reply came back: "We don't call anyone. Not our business, and it could compromise us. But we save the message in case he really does something and we can use it later. Thanks."

Todd was momentarily stunned. *We do nothing to help this woman?*

He was a little less enthusiastic for his last hour.

Kristen awoke early that morning in California. Making as little noise as possible, she brewed a pot of coffee and fixed a bowl of yogurt. She was afraid to turn on the television. So she read and then turned on her cell phone to retrieve messages from her home voice mail.

Ten minutes later her cell phone rang, and in the quiet of Callie's home, it startled her. She quickly answered it, talking low.

"Hello."

"Hello, Kristen. It's Janet Sullivan."

"Oh, hi. It's great to hear your voice. I'm talking low because Callie is still asleep. How are you?"

"Fine. Has any of what we talked about been useful to you with her?"

"I thought so last night, 'til I blew it. I came on too strongly about the consequences of adult movies, and I guess I offended her—and her boyfriend."

"I understand. For now it'll be hard for her to accept that she's hurting not only herself, but others."

"Yes, well, anyway, I'll just be me and hope that it makes a difference."

"You will. And I may have some good news. Or at least I want to ask you a question, and it's about this same subject."

"What?"

"Bradley Fuller, the President's domestic policy advisor, called me yesterday. He knew from the press conference that you and I had a connection at USNet, but he didn't know that you were no longer there. He was calling to ask your take on a proposal from Trevor Knox to accept the President's media reform package. To try that out on you and to see if it sounds plausible or not."

"Boy, that would be a change—a big change. Nothing I saw or heard would indicate that. But, trust me, Knox can change his policies and actions on a dime. Why would he do it?"

"Bradley's contact indicated that Knox is just tired of fighting. And he wants President Harper to attend the grand opening of USNet's new office in Moscow when the President visits President Temirov this summer."

"Oh. Well I *can* confirm that we're moving our Russian operation to new offices in Moscow. I keep using 'our'! David was over there a month ago looking at space. So that much sounds right."

"Good."

"But I'll have to check on the other. It's been a week since I was there, and Knox can change policies in a lot less time than that."

"How could you check?"

"I'll just call David. We haven't spoken since he fired me. He's probably got at least a couple of deal questions he needs help on. And he should know if something is going on."

"Well, if you could, Bradley would really appreciate it. They're apparently inclined to accept the offer—to recognize successful business and trade between the countries—but they know Knox's reputation on this subject, and they'd like a little comfort that what he's saying is real."

"Sure. I'll call David in a little while. Should I just call you back?"

"That'll be fine. Let us know what you find out."

"I will. And, again, Janet, thank you for all that you've done for me. I can't ever thank you enough."

"I'll wait to hear from you."

As Kristen flipped her phone closed, she was startled by a shadow behind her at the window, and then there was a key in the front door. A moment later Callie came in, her hair a mess, still wearing the same low-cut dress from the night before.

"Oh, hi," Callie said, smiling with bloodshot eyes. "You're up early."

Instantly the apartment smelled of last night's hops and sweat.

"Hey. Not really. I thought you were in your room, and I've been trying to be quiet."

Callie laughed. "Sorry." Then she grabbed her head. "Whoa!" She bent over for a moment. Straightening up, she looked at Kristen. "Let me get some aspirin and a couple of hours sleep, and we'll go out shopping. Probably not all the way to Orange County. Maybe The Beverly Center."

"Callie, I don't think..."

"Oh sure. It's not a problem. We do it all the time. Well, Alex does. He's still at our friend's house—on the floor." She started walking upstairs to her bedroom. "See you in two hours. We'll make it to the stores in plenty of time." And she closed her door.

Kristen turned and sat again on the sofa. *I've certainly done a great job with Callie. Maybe I ought to just leave now.* After a few minutes she slipped to her knees and prayed.

When Todd arrived at USNet that afternoon, he knocked at David's open door and asked, "Want to grab some coffee in a few minutes?"

"Yeah. Sure. I'd like to hear about Kansas City."

"There's a great opportunity for telecom space in an old brewery that's going to be a mixed-use development."

"Good. Whatever you and Cheryl think. Maybe she can join us. Let me return a couple of calls, and we'll go."

Todd turned to go, but David spoke again. "Hey, look at this report I got in the mail. It says that we should assume that all of our emails and all of our cell phone calls are being intercepted and read."

David held out the report, and Todd took it. After flipping through the pages, he said, "Seems plausible to me. I've wondered for years whether someone was doing this, and the report seems to verify it."

"Yes. I'm glad you said that, because I've also wondered, but I didn't want to appear to be crazy or paranoid."

Todd smiled. "We may never know, but it can't hurt to act like it's true. I guess we could use land lines as much as possible. Emails are tougher, but presumably there is encryption that we could get, at least between each other. And then be more careful with what we put in emails to others."

"I think I'll mention it at our next group meeting. And I also wonder about overseas. I'm trying to help my family members still living in Tehran, and I wonder what their government does to gain information."

"I would think that they're doing some kind of interception for sure. And maybe they have the capability to listen to our calls here."

David frowned. "Well, thanks. I'll ask Akbar Kamali, who runs our IT security, to look into this whole area for us."

Todd smiled and handed the report back to David. "Great. I really think you should." He turned. "Let me know when you're ready for coffee."

David turned to his computer and wrote a few emails. *Maybe there is something to that report. How would we know? Could that be what has happened to Omid?* He found himself adjusting the words he used, and asked two vendors to call him at the office, rather than spelling out his plans. When he stood to head for Todd's office, his phone rang.

"Hello."

"David, hi. It's Kristen."

He smiled. "Kristen! How are you?"

"I'm fine, David. How are you?"

"Uh, OK. We're OK. Where are you?"

"I'm in California. Actually, I'm calling you from Callie's apartment."

"Sounds like you're on a cell phone."

"Yes. Mine."

"Listen, can I call you right back?"

"Sure."

"OK. Just stay there, and I'll give you a call."

David walked over and closed his door, then called Callie's apartment from his office phone. "It's me."

"Oh, hi. I was expecting you on my cell."

"How are you? And why are you at Callie's?"

"I'm fine. I just came to visit her on my way to San Francisco." He paused. "How is she?"

"She's...well, she's asleep right now. We talked some last night."

"And is there any change?"

"I'm afraid not. We actually talked about their movies. She's proud of her acting in that area, or at least she seems to be."

David was silent, the visions of his daughter replaying in his head.

"David, isn't it a little bizarre that you fired me for opposing what you hate your daughter doing?"

After a pause, he said, "Yes. And I can't tell you how much I appreciate that you are still trying to help Callie—and us—after what happened. Thank you. But one is business and one is personal."

"Really?"

"Look, Kristen, we've been through this. I'm sorry for both things—you and Callie. But I had to let you go if I'm going to stay at USNet."

She paused. "Listen, David, I thought I ought to call and find out if you need my help on any of my old projects? Anything I can clarify?"

"Yes, actually. It would be good if you could call Todd. He's handling Capital Tower, and we're waiting to meet with the owners, maybe this week."

"Still no word on Porter?"

"No."

"I'll call Todd later. And, listen, David, I've got one for you. I've heard that Trevor Knox has invited President Harper to the grand opening in Moscow and has offered to stop fighting the entertainment reforms if the President will join him."

"Where did you hear that?"

"The proverbial little bird told me. Is it true?"

"Well, I just heard about it yesterday—from Paul Burke—and we have a meeting this afternoon to plan for it, in case the President accepts Trevor's offer. I asked Paul the same question, and he says it's real."

"If the new law were really implemented, Callie would have to quit, 'til she's twenty-one."

"Yes, I know. That's a great encouragement to me now, and I hope it's true."

"So you think the invitation and offer are real?"

"From what I know at this point, yes. But why are you asking?"

"Actually, Janet Sullivan—the Congresswoman—called because someone in the White House called her, looking for insight. They didn't know that I'd 'resigned to pursue other interests.'"

"Hm."

"I told Janet that I'd call you and ask. So I appreciate it, and I'll let her know that it seems legit."

"It does."

"David, could you call me if you get wind of anything different? Our input might help the meeting go forward, and I don't want to cause Janet or the President any embarrassment."

"Uh, sure, I guess so. I'll know more later today."

"OK...well, let's just keep this conversation between us, and I'll report that it seems fine. Will you go over there again if the meeting happens?"

"Probably."

"It should be interesting to meet the President."

"Yes, I'm looking forward to it. And please do what you can for Callie."

"I am, David. When she wakes up, we're supposed to go shopping. I've been praying for her."

For the first time David reacted positively to Kristen's statement about prayer for his daughter. "Thank you. We need all the help we can get."

"David, when someone is this hooked on something—like these movies, or drugs, or alcohol—prayer is about the *only* thing that offers real hope. Breaking this kind of addiction is not like making a New Year's resolution to avoid cookies after dinner. This is very serious, and very powerful."

"I know, I know, Kristen. Or I guess I'm beginning to realize it."

"Well, I'll pray and do what I can. I feel like until she has an experience that brings her up short, like I did with Richard, she'll just keep living all the lies that society and our company—I mean your company—tell her. That everything is wonderful and there are no victims or consequences."

"I wish. Kristen...thank you. I don't know where you get your strength or your insights, but I appreciate them."

"Anytime you want to know, David, I'll be glad to tell you."

"I think I know what you'll say, but not now. Thanks. And I'm really glad you called."

A moment later he headed for Todd's office and the break room for that cup of coffee.

Two hours later David was in Paul Burke's office, gathered around his conference table with five other key USNet managers, brainstorming the possible visit by President Harper to their new Moscow headquarters in little more than a month. Included was a security consultant with former ties to the Secret Service and experience in working with them on public events.

He was concluding, "I've worked some in Russia, starting with the Goodwill Games, and I can say that their security forces are generally very good and very professional. Since you've invited both Presidents, our Secret Service will work hand in glove with the Russians. They'll have the final say on everything, but I can give you a good sense of what to expect and what not to propose. What does the facility look like?"

All eyes turned to David, who produced some pictures of the grounds and the interior. "There are several two-to five-story buildings in the walled-in complex, which spans the entire width of one large block, overlooked by these taller apartment buildings across the adjoining streets. In this first building inside the gate we have our new office space—one open floor on each of the ground and second floors—backing up to this old factory shop, where we expect to do assembly of the software packages once we go into full production."

He passed copies of the photos to his colleagues around the table. "Since the second floor has a higher ceiling, I thought we might set up a small raised platform there to act as a stage and let the ribbon cutting and speeches go on against this back wall adjoining the assembly area, so guests and reporters can easily tour that space as well."

The consultant looked at the photos and listened to David. "That all sounds pretty reasonable. There's no real rocket science to this, just thoroughness. The Secret Service will want to run background checks on everyone invited, so you should put together your list pretty quickly. They'll have to rely on the Russians to check their invitees, but," he added and smiled, "with their old KGB files, they're really pretty quick, and very good.

"They'll have a sniper posted on these tall apartment building roofs. They'll check the sewers for bombs, and an hour or so before the Presidents are due to arrive, they'll send dogs around the complex and inside the building, sniffing for explosives. I see that there are two gates giving access, so at the last minute they might reroute the limousine carrying the Presidents to avoid too much predictability, but that will be up to them. At this point I think you should begin working on your guest list, including who will cater the event, and get a set of building plans for the Secret Service to review. Otherwise, it looks like they ought to be pretty pleased with what you've planned."

David asked Paul Burke, "What time of day are we talking about?"

"We've left the time, and even the exact day, up to the White House. We presume that it will be on Monday, the Fourth, which of course is not a holiday there, and maybe in the afternoon. We've pointed out that the site is just a mile or two south of the Kremlin, so they could even make the visit as a sort of 'break' from other discussions or negotiations. We'll wait and see."

It was almost noon when Callie emerged from her bedroom in a long T-shirt that stretched to her knees. Her hair was a mess and her face puffy; she needed a shower. She smiled at Kristen, who was reading on the sofa. As she walked to the refrigerator she rubbed her head and said, a little sheepishly, "Well, the good thing is that I got an email that we don't have class this afternoon. So we have time to grab some lunch and go downtown."

Kristen closed the book but stayed on the sofa. "That would be good, Callie. I really appreciate your help."

Pouring herself some orange juice at the counter, Callie said, "Sure. No problem." She turned toward Kristen. "Listen, I'm sorry about last night—and this morning. I didn't mean to say all that. I...I'm sorry."

Kristen smiled and put her book on the coffee table. "That's OK. Really. We all say things sometimes that we later wish we hadn't." She stood up and walked toward the kitchen. "That OJ looks good. Can I have some, too?"

"Sure." Callie turned and reached for another glass.

"And I'm sorry that I came on so strong about your movies. Maybe I've just seen a little more of the end result than you have."

"Maybe. But it actually seems pretty cool to me."

"Things like that often do, at first." She smiled and put her hand up as Callie started to speak. "Hey—let's not go down that road again. I agree that we have differences. I heard you, and I think you heard me. Is that OK? Truce?"

Callie thought for a second and smiled, nodding her head. "Yes. Truce. Here, we'll drink some orange juice to it."

They clinked their glasses and took a long sip. Callie spoke. "Now I've got to get ready so we can hit the stores."

"Callie, listen, I think I'm imposing on you, so I changed my reservation and I'm leaving for San Francisco at six tonight."

Callie seemed genuinely agitated. "Oh, please don't. I'm sorry that I got upset last night. I *did* think about it, and I believe you about coming here for real and not for my father." She looked down at the glass in her hands. "I wish you would stay a few more days."

"Well, thank you, but I don't do wild parties too well any more. Really. It's fine. I like you a lot, I'm glad we talked, and I'll come back again some day if you'll have me. But for now, it's probably better that I go. So let's have a great lunch, and you can drop me at the airport, or a taxi, and get back to your studying."

Callie put her glass in the sink and nodded. "OK. But I hope you'll come back. I liked talking with you, even though I sort of freaked out. I never had a sister, and I guess this is kind of how it would be to have one."

Kristen smiled. "I never had a sister either. So, get dressed, and I'll pack my suitcase. We have some serious shopping to do."

24

SUNDAY, JUNE 5TH

Early on the following Sunday evening, David and Elizabeth were sitting in shorts and casual shirts on their patio, salmon cooking on the grill.

"It's nice tonight," Elizabeth remarked, taking a sip from her glass. "Not too hot or muggy."

"A good start to summer."

"Yes. I'll be glad when Rob begins working over at Mail Express. I don't like him just sitting around the house all day now that school is out."

"Well, it's only for this week." David looked at his watch, stood and walked over to turn the fish.

"I just wish Callie were here, too—even just a visit." Elizabeth looked over at her husband. When he nodded but said nothing, she continued. "I miss us all being together. Oh, hi!" Elizabeth smiled as Rob joined them on the patio.

"When'll supper be ready?" Rob asked, eyeing the grill.

"Couple more minutes. Mom's got everything else ready."

Turning to his mother, Rob said, "Justin called, and I'm going to spend the night over at his house. OK?"

"I guess so. More computer games?"

"Maybe. Or maybe a movie. Dad, can you take me over to Justin's after supper?"

"Sure. I've got to go into the office tonight."

Standing, Elizabeth said, "Well, I'll get the salad and rolls. Rob, can you help me with the food and the iced tea?"

"Sure, Mom."

Thirty minutes later Rob and his father were in a hurry to leave. "Don't you want some ice cream?" Elizabeth asked, as they pushed back their chairs.

"Tomorrow," Rob said.

Looking across the table at her husband, she asked, "And you have to leave, too?"

"I know it's crazy, dear, but I've got an important presentation for Trevor tomorrow, and the plans and plats were just too big to bring home. So I'll be in the office getting ready."

Elizabeth frowned. "You guys are no fun. Eat and run. Well, I'll have a blast cleaning up and then I'll watch TV."

"Don't do too much of that addictive TV," Rob chided, smiling as he rose with his empty plate.

"Don't worry. This will be the only TV I'll see all week."

"OK, but don't get hooked!" He disappeared inside.

"I'm sorry, dear." David rose.

Elizabeth shook her head good naturedly from her chair at the end of the table. "Just no one be out too late, please."

An hour later Todd Phelps was seated in the special tandem training cubicle at the USNet RTI headquarters. Victor Mustafin was seated beside him, and they were using their headsets to communicate.

"All right, Todd, we're going to log you in now as a middle manager. Here's your new password. After today I won't sit with you. But a senior person will review all your decisions for the first few sessions, and you'll get a critique with suggestions when you next log on."

Todd smiled. "I'm looking forward to it."

"Good. At this level you'll be receiving general pass-ups from the entry level monitors. Your role is the same as before: designate the intercept to a specialist, copy it to several specialists, pass it up to the control room, or send it to the dustbin. To help you there are these new menus of policies and history, so you can quickly research how we've handled a similar keyword or situation in the past, and also what our current policy on it may be. At this level we hope you'll take time to think and associate, rather than just pass on."

Todd scrolled through the two new menus. He was impressed with how comprehensive they were.

"Finally, as we get started, we have one more role for you. With this new password, we're designating you as a specialist in real estate, which means that you will also receive pass-ups from any entry level analyst in the entire system who believes the intercept requires a real estate expert. Now this is fundamentally different, because with this designation, you can *act*, not just review and pass. So, for example, if you see a message you think requires us to buy, sell, change a policy—anything—you can initiate it."

Todd nodded.

Mustafin continued. "Everyone at this level functions as both a general reviewer and a specialist. If you stayed here, you'd be expected to be conversant in at least five specialties. They could be energy, autos, environment, banking—

all those same categories that you've been sending to. We think real estate is an easy place for you to start, and in the control room you will have to be a bit of a generalist, ready to take on most things. I suggest that whenever you have any free time you scroll back through the History archive on the Real Estate menu. It will show you our current issues and how we handled earlier opportunities."

Todd shook his head. "Are you sure I'm going to be able to do this?"

Mustafin smiled. "Of course. Here, let's log on and see what we get."

When Rob and Justin were let off at the movie by Justin's older sister, they walked inside but never bought tickets. They had been sure to tell each set of parents that the other would probably pick them up after the movie and a few video games, so they figured that they had at least three hours. A few minutes later, at the appointed time, the familiar silver BMW pulled up outside the theater, and they walked over to it.

Rob opened the passenger door, Justin the back. The driver greeted them. He was in his mid-twenties, well built, with black hair and a small tattoo on each arm. He was wearing a gray T-shirt and black pants over black boots. A ring in each earlobe completed the look. "Hi, guys. Whatzup?" he asked, as they slid into their seats.

"Nothing much," Rob said, smiling at their new friend.

"We're going to have a great meeting and a blow-out tonight! You'll love this guy's house."

"How come?" Rob asked, as they pulled out into the traffic.

"It's *wired*!" Rob knew from Blue Six's voice that it must be really something. "He's got a T-One line to his *house*, if you can believe that." The driver looked back and forth from the road to his guests as he spoke. "There's an HDTV flat screen in *every* room and two special game rooms with *ten* virtual floor plates in each one. Three bedrooms with surround sound and flat screens everywhere. When you're on the bed, it's like you can imagine you're anywhere you want. He even closed in the garage and made it mostly a Street War 2100 game room. It's awesome."

"Sounds incredible," Justin said from the backseat.

"We'll be there in a minute."

They could tell the home from the cars parked in the drive and on the street. They parked, got out, and walked up to the front door. Blue Six opened it without knocking. He motioned the boys to follow. "The meeting's probably about to start. All these guys are in Street War 2100 with us. Here, get a beer."

They walked through the deserted dining room where pizza boxes were open on the table and stood in the kitchen by a keg. They looked out into what had been a family room but was now a large open space outfitted with folding chairs. There was a huge flat-screen TV above the mantel, and speakers on both sides. Their host was wearing a headset and pointing to the screen, while about twenty young men and half as many women watched.

Blue Six whispered as they took their beers and sat at the back of the assembly, "We're plugged in with about a thousand other Blue players for our usual Sunday night critique. Randy is handling it for our group."

As the boys watched, Randy and several other group leaders carried on a conversation that the rest could hear over the speakers. Many of that week's better engagements were replayed on the screen, and the action was stopped at several points for a brief discussion of the tactic employed or the opportunity missed.

The meeting lasted for almost an hour, and Rob learned a lot. He was impressed by the commitment of all these adults to the game he loved so much. He and Justin sipped their beers, occasionally looked at each other, and smiled.

When the tactical session was over, the participants broke into smaller groups, and some went toward other parts of the house. Blue Six took his new friends over to their host, Randy, who was still standing by the mantel.

"Hey, Randy, meet Blue Nine and Blue Ten."

Randy, tall and thin, was dressed in tight jeans and a shirt that was almost molded to his body. He extended his hand. "Great to have you. We've seen your work. You're good. Blue Nine, we noted your great move in Wednesday's game just a few minutes ago. Did you see it?"

Rob beamed and nodded. "Yes, thanks."

Randy smiled. "Good. Make yourselves at home. We shift to party mode after the recap, to finish off the weekend. Lots will be going on." He looked down at their empty beer cups. "If you want something stronger, we got plenty. In fact, try these." He handed each of them a pill. "They'll make you feel really good while you're here."

The two boys exchanged glances, then Rob took a pill and swallowed it. "I'm in."

"OK...Excuse me for a minute. I've gotta shift the mood."

Randy went over to what would have normally been a built-in bookcase, but in his house it was the control panel for his media/recreation center. He began pushing buttons.

Rob, Justin and Blue Six were on the way to the kitchen when the lights dimmed down, rock music began playing from every speaker in sight, and the flat screens offered two girls and two guys rapidly peeling in a large bedroom for what promised to be a round of adult entertainment video. The two boys tried to act nonchalant; watching both the screen and Blue Six as he expertly pumped the keg and refilled their cups.

Six glanced up and had a look at the screens. "Not bad tonight. You know, that's happening just down the hall."

Justin couldn't take his eyes off the screen. "What? That's not a video?"

Six laughed and moved closer to Rob. "No. That's four members of our Blue Team. We're a close group."

Justin stuttered. "You mean those—they're here? At our meeting?"

"Sure. Randy has cameras everywhere. He can throw any room up on the monitors. Here, have some more beer."

"And they know?"

Six laughed harder and put his arm loosely around Rob. "Of course! We're not inhibited. In fact, it's kinda cool. We'll go in there in a while."

"We will?" Rob asked.

"Why not? We came to party, didn't we?"

Twelve hours later, on Monday morning, Senator Joe Bulloch received a phone call in his Georgetown townhouse. Standing by a small desk in their second-story bedroom, his wife put her hand over the mouthpiece and said, "It's Bradley Fuller from the White House. Sounds like he's on a cell phone in his car."

Senator Bulloch slipped on his white shirt and walked from the closet. Taking the phone, he said, "Hello, Bradley. How are you on this beautiful morning?"

"I'm fine, Senator. Sorry to call so early, but I wanted to catch you."

"That's fine. What can I do for you?"

"I wanted to get back to you on your proposal for Moscow. We discussed it at Camp David over the weekend, and we're inclined to accept. But we need to know pretty quickly exactly what Knox is prepared to say and do to endorse the Media and Entertainment Reform Bill."

Bulloch nodded. "Of course. Of course. Good. I'll call and let Trevor know. Is there someone they can call in your office?"

"Yes. JoAnne Brooks. If we can get comfortable with the draft of the written communiqué, I'd like to meet with a senior USNet person myself—

probably later this week, given the short time. And then, if we're on the same page, we'll go public, after confirming with President Temirov, of course."

"Yes, of course. Well, I'll suggest to Trevor that one of his senior people contact Ms. Brooks, and then hopefully they can work out the right language and schedule a meeting with you right away."

"That'll be good, Senator."

"Fine. Good. Thanks for arranging it."

"It's not done yet, but we certainly appreciate your help. We won't forget."

"Just trying to help, Bradley. Just trying to help."

Within four minutes Trevor Knox was reading a word-by-word transcript of their conversation on the monitor at his desk. He smiled.

At ten that morning the real estate group assembled in the large conference room on the thirty-third floor. Bagels, doughnuts and coffee were on the credenza.

David began. "I'm sure you'll all be interested to know that I'm talking with a few candidates to add to our group. Nothing definite yet. For now, let's do the usual review of our projects. Todd, you want to start?"

"Sure. Perhaps of most immediate interest, David and I met on Friday with the lawyers representing Capital Tower. Since Bill Porter has been missing for six weeks, they're finally ready to consider another offer. We told them that since we were the next highest bid, they ought to work with us, and we offered to match Porter's price. We think they appreciated our willingness to help them make up for lost time, and hopefully we'll hear this week."

Phelps paused in case there were any questions, then continued. "On Brookglen, the project is well under construction and appears to be on schedule. In Kansas City, the same guys have an interesting redevelopment deal, and Cheryl and I are trying to make the numbers work for our telecom facility." He glanced at Cheryl, who nodded.

Sawyer's group continued in this way for the next hour, and then their boss wrapped up the meeting. "If all goes well, I may go back to Moscow at the end of the month to help orchestrate the grand opening of our new facility there, and sometime in between I may have to visit L.A. for a few days to oversee our recent acquisitions and planned dispositions. Any other questions?

"Finally—there will be more on this later—please try to use your cell phone and email as little as possible for really sensitive information...OK? We've got landlines for important calls, and I'll be looking into encryption for our emails. It may take a little longer to communicate, but it may also be more secure.

Even the small chance of being read by others concerns me. So, for now, please humor me, as you always do."

Late that morning Trevor Knox had Paul Burke in his office; Bud Purcell, who ran their XXXtra Cinema operation in Los Angeles, was on the video conference screen. It was still early on Monday in Los Angeles, and Bud looked like he needed another cup of coffee. But he had done as Knox requested and emailed a draft of their proposed corporate statement on the President's Media and Entertainment Reform bill.

"Thanks, Bud," Knox said. "We're under a little pressure to get this to the White House, and I want the three of us to agree on the language."

"No problem," Purcell said, and sipped his coffee.

Paul Burke reread the draft he had received an hour before:

> USNet has always been a champion of individual adult choice in a free society, and for that reason we applaud President Harper's work to make choice the hallmark of the new Media and Entertainment Reform legislation.
>
> Within the next three months we will, therefore, ensure that all of the programming on our cable networks' Basic Packages will be G rated, and that other programs will be available only to those who choose them.
>
> Second, we will adopt recently developed log-in software to positively ID each user on the internet and ensure that no inappropriate material is made available to a user who is under twenty-one.
>
> Finally, we will voluntarily make certain that everyone associated with our Adult Entertainment subsidiaries in America, including actors, crews and distributors, is a minimum of twenty-one years of age, so that each may make a responsible choice.
>
> Once all of these changes are implemented, we believe that we will be in full compliance with the new law, and we urge others in our industry to comply with these same legislative guidelines.

"Those are some pretty big changes," Burke said. "How will they affect our business units?"

"I'm not crazy about them," Purcell offered.

Knox nodded. "I know, but we need to move on. And it won't be a total lay-down. We'll change our basic cable package so that it's pretty limited. Subscribers will call us for more variety, and that's when we'll encourage them to OK the other program ratings. And we'll try this new internet log-in software. If it doesn't work, no one will be able to blame us for ditching it a few months later. But, all in all, let's try to comply, at least to the letter of the law. Don't forget, we own most of the U.S. adult entertainment industry now, and we want to be on reasonably good terms with the government. This seems like a highly visible way to do it."

"You're right about that," Burke agreed. "President Harper ought to love hearing you speak these words about her legislation."

"Agreed," Purcell added. "So long as we can keep our options open."

"We will, we will," Knox assured them. "But for now, let's comply."

"You're the boss," Purcell said.

Burke turned to Knox. "I'm OK with the language if that's our plan."

"Good. Paul, please contact Ms. Brooks in Bradley Fuller's office in the White House at this number, and send her our draft. Hopefully they'll like it, and we can begin making plans in earnest to have both Presidents open our new office in Moscow. "

That evening Kristen was in the living room of her apartment, watching a baseball game on television, when her home phone rang. It was David.

"David. How are you? And what's that noise?" She picked up the remote and turned down the volume on the game.

"Oh, sorry. Just people talking. I'm calling from a pay phone in a restaurant. How are you?"

"Fine. Glad to be back from my travels. A pay phone? I didn't know there were any left. I'm interviewing tomorrow with a commercial brokerage firm, and on Thursday I'm flying to Ohio to meet with a pension fund that wants to open an office here to invest in real estate."

"Sounds good. I hope one of them works out."

"Me, too. I can't wait to find out what other interests I quit USNet to pursue."

"OK, OK. At least you're being paid well while you look. And I'll give you a good reference."

"You're right about the income. So, how are you?"

"Fine. I want to pass on the news I heard late today from Paul, because I thought your friend in Congress would want to know. He and Trevor went over a position paper about USNet changing its position to conform with the new law, and Paul told me that Trevor is really behind it."

"Great!"

"Yes. So maybe he and President Harper will have their meeting in Moscow, and Callie will have to get out of the business. Wouldn't that be great? It would be such a load off me."

"Yes. That would be wonderful. I hope it happens soon. And how are you? Still busy?"

"As ever."

"Oh. Wait a minute. It's my other line." She depressed the button on her phone. "Hello."

"Kristen? Hi. It's Callie."

"Callie! It's so good to hear you. Let me clear the other line. Just a minute." She pushed the button again. "David? It's Callie. What timing. Let me talk with her. Can I call you back?"

"Uh, no. Let me call you tomorrow."

"OK. Thanks for the heads up. I'll pass it along to Janet Sullivan."

"Good. And let me know how Callie's doing."

"Will do." She clicked to switch to the second line again. "Callie? Hey, how are you?"

"Oh, I'm good. How are you? Did you enjoy San Francisco?"

"Yes. It was great." Kristen shifted on the couch to get more comfortable and muted the television. "I actually stayed a little longer than I planned. I love that place."

"I went there earlier this year. Really nice. But, like, I called to find out about your trip. And what you're doing now. I don't know—sort of like what we talked about. Keeping in touch."

"Thanks. Thanks, Callie. I'm glad. I'll always be really happy to hear from you. My hotel was right downtown, and so I was able to walk almost everywhere. You wouldn't believe this red dress I saw. It looked *just* like the one we..."

And the two women discussed Kristen's trip, her job search, and other subjects for almost forty minutes.

As David drove home from his business dinner, he was more at peace than he had been for months.

Finally it's all coming together. Rob has the summer to work, without pressure from school. Callie won't be able to make any more of those videos, at least for a year. With my bonus we can offer her a college in the Northeast, away from Alex, or whatever she wants.

And hopefully we'll bring in some good new people this month. If Todd and Cheryl will just stay, maybe we can have a functioning department again. It would be nice if I could actually enjoy the trip to Moscow to meet with the President.

Now I've got to focus on Omid and Goli—to get them away from those fundamentalist Muslim thugs who've taken over my parents' country. What a tragedy. How can anyone believe what they believe?

If I prayed like Kristen, I guess I'd thank God for our family here, and ask His help for our family there. He paused. *And I guess for that I'd have to pray to God, not Allah.*

25

WEDNESDAY, JUNE 8TH

Two mornings later David and his son were sitting at their breakfast room table having cereal and fruit. Each wore a white shirt and gray slacks.

"How's the shipping business?" David asked.

"It's OK."

"What have you learned so far?"

"Oh, that rich people with jets going on vacation send their suitcases ahead by express delivery."

"Really? I had no idea."

"They want giant bags delivered the next day. Crazy expensive. And crazy people."

"Dealing with crazy people is great training for whatever you eventually do." David smiled.

"Yeah. I know. But it's sort of boring, too."

"Yes. A lot of business is. But sometimes the most boring is the most necessary."

"I guess." He nodded his head and took another spoonful.

"You came in kind of late last night, didn't you?"

"I don't know. About eleven thirty."

"I thought I heard the door close after midnight."

"Maybe." His son stood and took his empty bowl to the sink. "I gotta put on a tie."

"All right. I'm flying up to Washington with Paul Burke. We have a meeting tomorrow in the White House."

Rob turned. "The White House?" It was the first words he'd spoken that morning that indicated any interest.

Finishing his cereal, his father said, "Yes. Paul's meeting with Bradley Fuller, the domestic policy guy, and I'm meeting with Sandra Van Huyck, the President's foreign policy advisor."

"*You're* meeting with Sandra Van Huyck?"

Rising, he smiled. "Sure. What's so odd about that?"

"I mean, she advises the President every day."

"Yep. I didn't know that you'd know about her. Tomorrow we're talking about the President's trip to Moscow. We hope to host her at our new USNet headquarters there, and I'm sort of in charge of the details."

"Really? Whoa!"

"My thoughts exactly." He smiled again as he put his bowl in the sink. "Can I tell anyone?"

"Not yet. It's not public. But probably by the end of the week."

With a carefully measured portion of near-respect, Rob surveyed his father again and said, "That's cool."

Late that morning David was beginning a review of the acceptance documents for the space in New York that Kristen had negotiated two months earlier, when Todd came through the doorway, beaming.

The senior executive walked over to stand in front of his boss's desk and said in an excited voice, "David, I just heard from the attorney for Capital Tower. They've agreed to accept our offer to match Porter's price, and they want to close as soon as possible. Isn't that great?"

David clenched his fists in front of his shoulders. "Yes!" He stood up and shook Todd's hand. "Great news! Great job, Todd."

"Thanks. They've asked us to come over this afternoon. Can you make it?"

"If we don't meet too late. Paul Burke and I are scheduled to leave for D.C. at five, but I could probably make it later if no one else needs the jet."

"I'll check with you right after lunch. OK?"

"Great. Knox and Burke will be really pleased."

"I'll start reviewing our due diligence file. And, David, can I ask you one other thing?"

"Sure."

"On Kansas City—if the two deals are close, let's go with the brewery. It'll be a great project, and we'll have office space to grow into. The guys who are doing Brookglen will do a great job for us."

"We'll see. It sounds good. But they need to get right on their rent, too. Anyway, let's get Capital Tower in the barn, and then I'll owe you one. How's that?"

"Fine. But we've got to make a decision soon, and I think Cheryl is leaning toward the cheaper space. But it's not necessarily the best, if you ever think we'll expand in that market."

"How about you and Cheryl work out a priority of recommendations, and we'll take a look? But for now, go nail down that appointment and let's make a deal with those folks on Capital Tower before they change their minds."

Todd turned and walked toward the door. "You got it."

Later that night, delayed by two hours, Burke and Sawyer left for Washington in USNet's smaller corporate jet. David couldn't contain his pleasure after the meeting that afternoon with the Capital Tower attorneys, who agreed to let USNet buy the property for the same amount offered by Bill Porter. The two executives spent much of the flight seated on opposite sides of a small table, going over the plans and forming preliminary ideas on how to combine Capital Tower with their own West Capital Grand to create a new, striking corporate headquarters.

"This will be a real showplace." Paul nodded as they concluded.

David smiled. "Yes, but very functional, and actually less expensive."

"Yes. It was a great idea, David."

Genuine compliments were few and far between in the corporate world, even among friends, and David appreciated the words. "Thanks." He smiled. "Let's just hope that there are no surprises. We can celebrate when we move in."

The next morning the two men were picked up at their hotel and driven to the White House gate designated for guests. The driver showed his badge to the guard, who looked quickly into the backseat and made notes on a clipboard. The gate opened, and they were deposited at one of the private entrances. A pleasant young woman greeted them, gave them badges, and led them upstairs.

As they entered a small waiting room, their guide offered them seats and said, "Mr. Burke, Mr. Fuller's assistant should be here in a few minutes. Mr. Sawyer, Ms. Van Huyck's office is just across this hall; someone will come for you in a bit. Can I get you gentlemen some coffee while you're waiting?"

The two men shook their heads and thanked her. Then she left.

"Have you ever been here before?" David asked in a low voice.

Burke smiled. "No. You?"

David shook his head. "It's kinda neat, isn't it?"

They heard steps and voices outside. A moment later President Susan Harper came into the room, accompanied by Bradley Fuller. Several other men and women waited just outside the door.

The two visitors stood up. President Harper, wearing a dark blue suit with red trim, greeted them. Smiling warmly, she shook their hands. "Thanks for coming. Brad was just telling me about your meetings, and I thought I'd stop by for a minute and let you know how much we appreciate what you're doing."

Burke and Sawyer nodded, and Paul said, "Thank *you*, Madame President. We appreciate the opportunity to do this together."

"Yes." She was about their same age, and she looked briefly from one to the other. The President continued. "It means a lot to us to have USNet onboard to cut down on the prevalence of 'adult' entertainment, if not eliminate it. It's pushed right into our homes, schools, libraries. Anyway, you already know that, and I really appreciate your willingness to help us contain it."

Burke spoke again. "Yes. And Trevor Knox asked me to tell Mr. Fuller that we're one hundred percent committed to the pledge we made to you earlier this week."

"Good. We have to make the changes. This stuff tears down kids and families. Devastating. So, thanks again. And, Mr. Sawyer, we're glad you're here, too. As Sandy will tell you in a few minutes, we've been looking for the right place and time to announce some major new initiatives with the Russian government, and your reception may be just the right spot."

David smiled and said, "It's an honor, Madame President."

"Yes. Good. Well, I'm sorry I have to go, but Brad and Sandy will take good care of you. If all goes well I'll see you in Moscow—in less than a month." She extended her hand to each man.

"Thank you," David said. "We'll do our best to make you feel welcome."

"I'm looking forward to it. Should be exciting. Thanks again." President Harper turned and left. Bradley Fuller, who had been standing a little behind the President during their conversation, said, "Paul, let's walk around to my office. David, I think Sandy will be ready for you in a minute. I'm glad you had a chance to meet the President."

The two USNet executives looked at each other briefly. "Yes. We are, too," Burke replied for both of them.

As soon as the two men left, David looked out the window at the White House lawn and thought, *'Tears down kids and families.' She's so right. Why on earth do we produce the stuff?*

His thoughts were interrupted by a young woman. "Mr. Sawyer? Ms. Van Huyck is ready to meet you. Please come with me."

For the next twenty minutes, Sawyer met with the President's fiftyish foreign policy advisor about the opportunity the reception would give to emphasize US-Russian cooperation in many business and government areas.

As they finished discussing the combined invitation list of business and government leaders, there was a knock on the door. A woman in her early thirties came in.

"Here's Tanya. Ms. Prescott, please meet Mr. David Sawyer of USNet. You two will be working together for the next few weeks."

Tanya Prescott was of medium height with short dark hair. Her face reflected the high cheek bones of her Slavic mother and the piercing blue eyes of her American father. She smiled and extended her hand. "A pleasure to meet you."

David took it and was impressed with her grip. "Yes. I'm looking forward to working with you."

"Let's sit for a few minutes and go over our general plan," Van Huyck offered, "and then the two of you are welcome to meet in the adjoining conference room for as long as you need."

"Sounds like quite a party," Tanya commented, when David and Sandra finished. "David, when I get to Moscow I'll need a few days on the purely governmental events and to meet with our Russian counterparts. Then I'll want to meet with the head of your USNet security team and check out the site. Hopefully it will be pretty cut and dried, as you've suggested. But we'll have to be cautious, since this event and the Fourth of July celebration are the only ones that are outside government circles."

She paused. "Why don't we go next door to continue, unless you have anything else for us, Sandra?"

"No. I think you have it well in hand. David, we appreciate your offer to host the reception, and as you can already see, we'll try to take care of the details so that you and your guests can enjoy yourselves."

As they walked to the door, Tanya said, "David, I think you ought to be there by the end of June, if the event will be on the Fourth."

He nodded.

At the door they shook hands with the foreign policy advisor. "Have a safe trip home, David, and to Moscow, Tanya. I'll see you both soon. Thank you for coming."

Once outside, Tanya indicated a small conference room, where they reviewed the plans in detail. When they finished, Tanya walked David back to the reception area. "I imagine that we'll be talking a lot. You have my cell phone number, and I'll check in with you in about a week, once I've been on the ground a few days." She smiled. "It's been a pleasure meeting you. See you again soon."

They shook hands. Ten minutes later he and Paul Burke retraced their steps to the car.

Outside, as the driver opened each door for them, Paul said, "That was an unusual morning. How was your meeting?"

They took their seats and the driver started the engine. David answered, "They want to expand the reception to include more government types and announce some joint programs. Should add about fifty people—and be good for business."

Burke smiled. "Yes. Sounds like it. Our meeting went well, too. We're going to announce our support for the President's program tomorrow. I called Trevor, and he concurred. That way a couple of us can be available for the Sunday morning talk show circuit, if anyone wants to pick up on it."

They drove through the gate. "That's good," David agreed. *And maybe I can get Callie home in a few weeks.*

David looked out the window, and Paul pulled out his cell phone and dialed his wife. "Sarah? Hi. David and I just met the President." He went on to describe to his wife their meetings that morning. "Isn't that something? Yeah. We'll be leaving shortly. See you for dinner tonight. Bye."

As he hung up, David turned back to him from the window and asked, "Do you ever think about whether our cell phone calls are secure?"

Burke looked puzzled and a little taken aback. He dialed the number for his voicemail messages. "No. They're pretty secure, aren't they? I mean, who could listen to all these phone calls? That would be impossible." He clicked the buttons for his mailbox and pass code, then began listening to his confidential messages.

David looked out the window again. "Yeah. I hope you're right."

It was too warm that evening to eat outside, so the Sawyers gathered in the breakfast room. Elizabeth had prepared tacos. David had changed into shorts and a knit shirt. Rob was in baggy shorts and a blue T-shirt. The main topic of interest was, of course, David's visit to the White House.

"So you actually met the President?" Rob asked a little incredulously. "Like, President Harper of these United States?"

His father smiled as he passed the taco sauce. "Yes. The actual one."

"What's she like?"

"Very friendly. She seemed genuine. Interested in what we're doing. She said she was glad that USNet is now supporting her initiatives." David went on to describe their meetings in some detail.

When he finished, Elizabeth said, "It sounds like the reception in Moscow has turned into a major event. Do you think the press will be there?"

"I would think so."

"Will they broadcast it live here?"

"Maybe. It'll be the Fourth of July, so they might. At least on the cable news channels. With the time difference, our afternoon reception will be early morning here."

"So maybe we'll see you," Rob said. "With the President."

"Yes. Maybe."

"Extreme."

"When do you have to go?" Elizabeth asked.

"I'm not sure. Sometime at the end of the month. We'll start working on the ticket and visa tomorrow. And, oh"—he looked across the table at Elizabeth—"before Moscow, I may have to go to Los Angeles again."

She brightened. "Really? Can I go, too, and visit Callie?"

"Uh, I'm not sure. Maybe. Let me see how many days I have to be there."

"Try to combine a weekend, dear. It would be great to see Callie."

"Yes. I'll check."

Rob was finishing his last taco. "I bet that Tanya woman can do karate."

David paused for a moment. "Uh? Oh, yes. I bet she can. She had quite a grip."

"I wonder if she's ever tried Street War 2100?"

"I don't know. I'll be talking to her. Would you like me to ask her?"

"Really? Could you? That would be awesome. If she's on a team, I could tell our Blue team to look out for her."

"Yes. Speaking of which, I noticed you haven't been online as much lately, but haven't you been staying out late? Or at Justin's? What time did you come in last night?"

"Uh, I'm not sure. About midnight."

Elizabeth frowned. "No it wasn't. I'm sure you locked the door after one."

He looked down at his plate. "Uh, maybe."

"What are you doing out so late?" his father asked.

"Just hangin' with Justin and some friends. Usually at Justin's house. No big deal."

"And who brings you home?"

"Most of our other friends are sixteen, and they drive me home."

The parents exchanged glances. "Rob, we don't want you out after midnight, being driven home by sixteen year olds. Either be home on time—

without speeding—or call home, and one of us will come get you. And don't
do anything crazy."

Rob kept his head down. "I won't."

Late that night David went outside on their patio and dialed the number
in Estonia with one of the new cell phones that his colleague in IT had secured
for him. He had not heard from Omid since their conversation about Goli,
which worried him.

"Omid, how are you?" he asked, when the second connection was made.

"Cousin David. We are here. Goli is just starting to be better, thanks to our
doctor friends, but she says almost nothing. She just sits at our window and
looks out at the city. I cry a thousand tears inside, but I'm trying to be strong
for her."

"Omid, what can I do?"

"I may be close to a plan. If we can visit family in Turkey, can you help
her?"

"I'll do my best. But you must come together."

Omid paused. "I must stay and try to change this madness. These crazy
people are not Iran. They are thugs, clinging to personal power in the name of
Islam. We must change our country, and if people like me leave, who will do
it?"

"Tell me how I can help."

"Just be there when we need you. It may be soon. A plane ticket and some
money for Goli"

"For both of you. I will, but don't call on my old phone. At least not your
phone. Have a friend call me, and I'll call you back on another one."

"OK, cousin. I'll be back to you soon."

"Elizabeth and I will be waiting to help"

"Thank you."

Knox was alone, seated at his desk in his top floor office early the next
morning when he received a video call from Mustafin and Kamali.

"Is everything ready to go?" Knox immediately asked, laying aside the
report he had been reading on their operations in Brazil.

Mustafin spoke. "Yes. The Russians at NovySvet are able to track the
micro-GPS repeaters virtually anywhere on the globe."

"And what about the missile?"

"We went over that in detail this morning," Kamali answered. "The team is ready, and they've found a suitable site in the area we designated."

"And these men can do the launch?"

"Certainly. Actually, once the physical cover is removed from the transport, which resembles a large lorry, and the missile is prepared, we can give the command to launch it from here, or even from your plane, for that matter. We just need them to get it ready."

"Yes. So you think anyone who later traces the flight path will think Chechnya?"

"In Russia, the Chechnyans are an easy way to explain anything unpleasant. The missile will launch from inside Russia and fly well below the floor of their domestic air surveillance radar. But in case anyone on the ground happens to notice the missile and remembers it the next day, the launch will be on a line from Chechnya to Moscow, so the implication will be clear."

Knox thought for a few moments. "It sounds plausible. Keep working on the details, and let's review them next week at our regular meeting. And signal Salim to prepare for the Stinger martyrs in Los Angeles and New York, right after we take out the leadership of the two countries that persecute us the most. Besides the political chaos, the U.S. will have to shut down all air travel—maybe for months or years. Imagine the economic impact. We'll have to think well about what to buy and sell in anticipation. What a great day for the faith it will be! We're about to set the events in motion by making our announcement in support of President Harper."

"When?" Mustafin asked.

"Burke and I are holding a press conference in our auditorium at ten this morning. And David Sawyer will be there as well—since he's an integral part of the public part, we want him to be very enthusiastic. Watch us on TV if you can. We're great supporters of the President now."

The two men chuckled. Kamali said, "I can't wait to see the transformation."

"It'll be good," Knox assured them. "Academy Award material."

After the press conference and lunch, David welcomed Akbar Kamali to his office. Over the years the two had never been close, but they had worked on several cross-department projects together. And they had talked occasionally about events in Iran, Kamali's home, though usually just to regret the demonstrations and violence.

"Thanks for coming by," David said, as he rose and motioned the Persian to a chair at his small conference table.

"Sure. Any time. How may I help?"

David took the seat across. "Of course I know that we have extensive special security on our servers and our databases, but I was wondering whether you think that our USNet emails and cell phone calls are secure. Could someone, somehow, be listening or gathering information, without us knowing?"

Kamali did not answer immediately, but looked intently at David. Finally he said, "Why do you ask?"

David took his smartphone out of the holster on his belt and put it on the table in front of him. He glanced down at it. "I don't know. I'm not a technical guy. But I've read stories over the years about the possibility—even that the government is doing it—and now that we depend so much on these for so much of our communication, I wonder whether some supercomputer couldn't be monitoring and stealing information from what we say and write."

Kamali paused again. "Do you have any indication that your calls or emails have been compromised?"

David leaned slightly forward. "No. But I would think that anyone doing it would be careful to keep it secret. But I did get this report." He held up Todd's letter, ostensibly from a Midwestern security company.

"May I see it?"

"Sure." David handed the document to Kamali, who quickly scanned it. "May I have a copy?"

"Of course," David said, as he reached to get it back. "I'll ask Julie to scan a copy and send it to you."

"Thanks. I'll look into it. Right now I'm not sure, but I'll get back to you."

"Good. I appreciate it. You, know, I've been trying to help two family members in Tehran, and I worry that maybe their government is monitoring every call."

Kamali shifted slightly in his chair. "In Tehran? How have you been helping?"

"Mostly with encouragement, I'm afraid. But I've also sent my cousin Omid and his wife phones and SIM cards. They have a group that is trying to expose the excesses of the thugs who are running the country."

"Really? Good for you. How do you get the phones there?"

"Through another cousin who makes business trips to Turkey. We're also hoping to get Omid and Goli out of Iran soon. She was beaten and raped by the police."

"Terrible. It sounds like your cousins are very brave. I hope that you continue your help."

"We plan to. It's just very difficult."

"Yes, of course. I have family there as well, of course, so I know."

"Well"—David glanced at his watch—"thank you again, Akbar. I've got another meeting now, but I look forward to hearing what you find out."

The two men rose. "Hopefully it will not take long, and, if necessary, we'll think about some extra measures."

David nodded. "Good. I'm just trying to help." As Kamali walked through the door, David put the security report on his desk.

RobSaw: Whatzup?

Calliente: Studying.

RobSaw: It's summer

Calliente: Doing summer school to get thru

RobSaw: Acting?

Calliente: And history. U?

RobSaw: MailDrop job.

Calliente: Is it good?

RobSaw: It's OK.　Did u know Dad met the President?

Calliente: When?

RobSaw: Yesterday in Wash.

Calliente: Why?

RobSaw: Big meeting in Moscow soon.

Calliente: Pretty cool.

RobSaw: Yeah.

Late that Friday afternoon David was finishing up the final invitee list for the Moscow reception. With Julie's help he had applied for his Russian visa and had reservations on several flights to Moscow, waiting word from Tanya Prescott on how early he should arrive. The phone rang, and he could see on the readout that it was Kristen's cell phone.

David picked it up and then returned it to its cradle, cutting the connection. The phone rang again. Same number. David frowned and repeated the hang up. Ninety minutes later he was driving home and dialed Kristen's apartment with one of his new phones.

"Hello."

"Hi, Kristen. It's David. How are you?"

"Fine. Hey, is something wrong with your phones? I tried twice today to get you, and each time it was like the phone answered and then hung up."

"Actually it was me."

"Why?"

"It's complicated. I want to talk with you, but I prefer to use this new cell phone."

"Why? It sounds like a spy movie."

"Yeah. It's not that. I just think that it's too easy for people to listen, and our conversations now are not strictly business."

"David, are you serious? That sounds paranoid."

He nodded to himself. "Maybe. My cousins in Iran have taught me to be much more cautious. The same with emails. Please just humor me, OK? Call me like you did; I'll see the readout and call you back, just like I'm doing."

"Where are you?"

"Driving home."

"David, are you in some sort of trouble?"

"No, actually, just the opposite. Things are getting better."

"But I can't call you or use email? That doesn't sound better."

"Hey, why did you call?"

"A couple of reasons." Her tone brightened. "First, I think I got the job with the Ohio pension fund to open their office here."

"That's great!"

"Yes. They're doing background checks, and assuming I pass those, they want me to start July 5th."

"I'm really pleased for you."

"There's still time for you to quit USNet and for us to open our own corporate service firm."

He smiled. "I wish. Maybe, some day."

"If it's the money, David, I know we'll make a *lot*."

"We've been through this, Kristen. There are too many reasons why I can't leave."

"Is one of them why you can't talk to me on an office phone?"

"You said there were a couple of reasons why you called me today."

She paused. "Yes. Did you see Knox's news conference this morning about the Media and Entertainment Reform Law?"

"I was there."

"Do you think he's real?"

"Yes. Of course. Why?"

"I don't know. I just had a bad feeling watching him. I couldn't match what he was saying to what I was seeing."

"Burke says that he means it."

"I know. I hope so. I just..." She was silent.

"I'm counting on it being right, because I think I'm going to L.A. before Moscow, and I want to tell Callie that this means she and her wonderful boyfriend can't do any more of their videos until she's twenty-one, in a year. Hopefully by then she'll have seen the light and moved on."

"That would be great."

"I know. That's one of the reasons I said that things are actually looking up. Maybe she'll dump Alex and focus on finishing school."

"I hope. She and I talk several times a week, now."

"Really? About what?"

Kristen laughed. "Just stuff. She calls me or I call her. She's actually very good with fashions. She's helped me a lot."

"What about the movies?"

"She knows how I feel. But I don't push her and I don't lecture her. I'm just there."

"I hope you can make a difference. By the way, Elizabeth may go to L.A. with me, and I hope she won't find out about all of that."

"Can I tell Callie you're coming?"

"No, not yet. I have to set it up. But I'll let you know. Maybe you can help reinforce not hurting her mother."

"Sure. I think she actually understands that. I think she just wants to get back at you when she can."

"For what?"

"Well, the trigger of course is your disapproval of Alex, and cutting her off. But she told me once that you always criticized her and never congratulated her, even as a little girl. That if she made B's, you'd ask her why not A's. And why wasn't she the fastest, or the best. And then you were usually not at home. David, I'm not trying to be a dime-store psychologist, but you asked me, and I don't know what really happened. But she has a precocious personality, and I think she's been trying to get your attention and your approval all her life, but now you've disowned her. So with Alex and these movies, she's finally got your attention."

"She certainly has," he added softly.

"Well, but now all of that should change, thanks to President Harper's new law."

"And Knox dropping the lawsuits."

"Yes. I'm glad you think he's genuine. I feel better."

"Kristen, he has to be. There's way too much riding on it."

"All right. I just felt like he wasn't for real."

"Congratulations again on your new job."

"It's not quite official yet. So keep it quiet 'til I tell you."

"OK, but they're getting the best."

"Only because you trained me. Say hello to Elizabeth for me, and call me sometime on a pair of tin cans."

He laughed. "Will do. Talk to you soon."

Knox was finally able to respond to an earlier encrypted email from Akbar Kamali, asking for a videoconference with him and Victor Mustafin. With his office door locked and the late afternoon sun flooding his penthouse office, he dialed both of his lieutenants on their secure video network.

After their initial greetings, Kamali related his conversation earlier that day with David Sawyer, including the security report David had given him to read.

Knox listened attentively, then sat back for a few moments before speaking. "First things first. Do you think there is any connection between David's sudden concern for security, and that Phelps man who works for David joining us in RTI?"

From the right half of the split screen, Kamali replied, "It's hard to say. When I can get into the report, we should know whether it's an issue, but I doubt it. People have been speculating for years. And I think all of it may have been some sort of cover for his real concern: his cousins, whom he's helping to work against Allah and the Revolution."

"Yes. That's the second thing: his help for Allah's enemies. Why didn't we know about this sooner?"

Mustafin said, "Because our system is focused to find business intelligence, not Iranian security issues. David has been calling his family for years, so it didn't rise to an intercept."

"Well, then Allah be praised that he confided in Akbar." Knox again paused, looking out at the setting sun. "David is another tragic loss, like my cousin. Sold out to the lie of America." He sighed. "Praise Allah that there are other, better men—believers—coming along to take his place."

Both men on the video screens nodded.

"But David is very good at real estate for USNet, and we need him right now with the President in Moscow. So we'll leave him there—doing his American job, and we'll also let him keep calling his cousins in Tehran. We'll flag all his calls and use him to take us straight to his cousins and their entire organization. He will help us silence more voices that are opposed to Allah's truth." Trevor smiled.

26

FRIDAY, JUNE 17TH

Todd had a lot on his mind as he pulled into the RTI Control Center at seven on Friday morning a week later. *First time in the control room itself. And we're signing the contract on Capital Tower at eleven.*

He parked and went inside. He was greeted by Victor Mustafin. They shook hands, and Mustafin held up a new ID card. "Here's your new, and final, card. It gives you access to the control room itself. Let me have your old one."

Todd still had it in his hand from swiping the entrance and gave it to his mentor, taking the new one in return.

They used Todd's card and his handprint to go through the airlock and into the control room. As their eyes adjusted to the dimmed lighting, Todd put the new card in his wallet. He looked around and couldn't help a small smile. *This is it. Seemed like I'd never learn enough, but I actually feel pretty well prepared. So much opportunity. So much money.*

Mustafin said, "I'll be taking over as duty officer in a few minutes, and you will sit next to me."

"Fine." In a few minutes both he and Mustafin were online.

With no active message in front of them, Todd heard Mustafin through his earphones. "Just like at the lower level, there are archives here that you should review, catalogued by day and by subject. It's always a good idea to arrive twenty minutes early and scroll through the chronological file for the days since you were last on. At least you'll be aware of how the issues were handled, in case more of the same comes up on your watch. Here are the icons. And these can only be read from consoles in this room."

"Thanks. I'll look through them when we have a break."

"Good. OK, here's one. Looks like an email that's been correlated with one from last night. It appears that the opposition in Malaysia is planning demonstrations to disrupt the government. Attached is a summary of our interests there. It's prepared automatically when one of the evaluators highlights a word in the message or types one in, then pushes the Summary button. Luckily we don't have many, but Malaysia is the world's leading producer of tin, so we can expect supplies to be interrupted. I'm typing a note to our traders to buy as much of the current supply as they can, and to sell short the shares of the mining interests. There. That should produce a tidy sum before the rest of the world even has a clue."

"Nice."

"Yes. Notice that we don't intervene in anyone's politics or influence a government to change an outcome. Whether Malaysia, China, Iran—anywhere there are arguments or upheavals going on. If we did, it could give us away. And it would be almost impossible to manage. We just use the information we get before others have it to make money."

"Makes sense."

"Yes. Here's another one."

Three hours later, Mustafin was relieved as duty officer, and he and Todd walked the corridor back to the main entrance.

"What do you think?" Mustafin asked.

"It's certainly more interesting than the first level. By the time issues reach here, they're pretty significant. It's incredible to think, having been at the other levels, how much other stuff—potential profit for us—is handled at those levels. You must get a daily or weekly summary, right?"

"Yes. Both." Mustafin nodded.

"And in a way it's calmer. The decisions are pretty clear, really. We only passed one on to the Council during our watch."

"Yes. But there's no pattern. Next time we might handle ten genuine crises ourselves *and* pass ten to the Council. There's just no way to predict. That's why we always need a competent duty officer on watch." They stopped at the exit to the reception area. Are you on again this weekend?"

"No. I'm due here again on Wednesday."

"Good. There's still a lot to learn, but it's basically just time in the chair now. You learn by doing."

"And keep cashing those checks."

Mustafin smiled. "Yes. Of course. We should have another one for you next week. And, oh, Todd, by the way, please remember that nothing that we do here can slip into anything outside. Nothing in your personal or business life. Not even a hint, This all has to stay here, with us."

"Yes, of course."

As he walked to his car, Todd wondered what he might be able to learn about the inner workings of their competitors, and even of USNet, through RTI—but he'd have to be very careful.

Given his senior position in the Stinger Missile training command at Fort Bliss, and the trust that he had built up with those in the program over the years, Salim had been able to steal six of the missiles through a combination of falsifying destruction reports and forging signatures on two-man control documents.

Each missile was now housed in its own climate controlled mini-warehouse bay in the El Paso area, surrounded by attic-quality furniture, in case anyone took a cursory look.

Late that afternoon Salim began a week of much-deserved leave. After driving out of the base, he parked his truck at his home. He went inside and came out with a small travel bag, then walked the four blocks to the truck rental facility whose location had helped him determine where he wanted to rent his home.

An hour later, after a stop by one of the mini-warehouses, he turned east on I-10, for the start of his drive to New York.

David paced the floor of their hotel room in L.A. that evening, while Elizabeth finished getting ready.

"Don't worry; she'll be here in a minute," Elizabeth said from the bathroom. "Probably the traffic."

"I guess," David said, moving gold curtains and looking out their tenth floor window as the cars inched along the Los Angeles freeway below.

"I'm glad she could bring Jane. It'll be great to meet her."

The phone rang.

"We're downstairs."

"Good. We'll be right there."

Five minutes later the Sawyers met their daughter and her tall, blond roommate in the lobby, near the elevator bank. David was wearing a dark gray suit and striped tie. Elizabeth was in a blue dress with pearls. The two younger women were in much more casual attire: Callie had on dark blue pants with a multicolored shirt, and Jane was in a low cut light-green sundress. Both of the younger women were deeply tanned and chewing gum.

Elizabeth held out her arms, beaming, and mother and daughter exchanged hugs and pecks. Callie gave a cursory hug to her father, looking the other way, and then introduced Jane.

"This is Jane, my roommate. She's also a theater major." Everyone smiled. "Jane just got back from Mexico this afternoon, and I thought she could join us for dinner."

"Yes, yes. We're delighted," said Elizabeth. Jane nodded. Elizabeth turned to her daughter. "Where do you want to go?"

David interrupted. "I already set that up with the concierge. How does Torini's sound?"

"That's kind of expensive, isn't it, Dad?"

He smiled. "How often am I out with three beautiful women in Los Angeles?"

"David, it's fine with me if it's OK with the girls."

They nodded. "If that's what you'd like, then fine," said Callie.

"Let's get a cab."

While riding in the minivan taxi they exchanged stories about the day's travels, the weather, and David's upcoming trip to Moscow to greet the President.

"That's way cool." Jane responded. David retold the White House trip story, and the cab pulled up to the restaurant. Callie said nothing.

Ten minutes later they were seated at a candlelit table in a quiet alcove of the northern Italian restaurant. Each table was lit by a large red candle. David and Elizabeth sat across from each other, with one girl on each side. After they ordered drinks, Elizabeth turned to their guest. "Jane, where are you from?"

"Dallas. At least that's where I was raised. Actually I lived with my grandparents. I never knew my father, and my mother has been in and out of rehab most of my life."

"I'm sorry to hear that," Elizabeth said, the concern obviously genuine.

Jane smiled. "Oh, it's nothing. It's really all I've ever known. I got a scholarship and a loan for school, and now with some money from a job on the side, I'm OK."

"Are you in the same classes with Callie?"

"One this semester."

"And what kind of job do you have?" David asked.

Jane and Callie exchanged glances. "I pick up a little extra money modeling."

"I see. That must be fascinating," Elizabeth said.

Jane nodded and smiled. "Yes, it certainly is."

"Were you on vacation in Mexico?" David asked.

"Sort of, I guess, but I was also doing some, uh, modeling."

"Do you like Mexico?" Elizabeth asked.

"I love going down there. It's beautiful where we go."

"Oh, I see," Elizabeth smiled. "I'm sorry to say that I've never been."

Their drinks arrived, and they ordered dinner.

At that same hour, Callie's brother and his friend Justin were finishing a late Friday night session with Street War 2100 at Justin's home, where Rob was spending the weekend while his parents were in California.

Justin took off his helmet and stretched on the VR plate. "You nailed that guy coming at me after I dropped my gun. I was starting to sweat big time."

Rob opened his visor and smiled. "He was certainly surprised to see me."

"A good night's work."

"Should we sign off?"

"I guess so. It's late. But while we're here, let's use our WorldPoints. We should have about fifteen minutes of free time for all that we've played this week." He smiled. "Let's go to their XXXtra Cinema site."

Rob nodded. "I logged off, and here come my points. They're giving me a code to use."

" Have you seen the XXXtra Cinema amateur site?"

"No. Is it good?"

"Is it good?" He motioned for Rob to come over beside his chair in front of the monitor, then put in the code he had just been given. "We're in. Have you seen this Arab chick, Samantha?"

"No."

"Where've you been? She's awesome!"

"I guess I've been saving the world while you've been ogling."

"Here, look. This is her newest, 'Samantha Calls the Shots.'"

Justin turned to catch Rob's reaction and found him staring, his mouth open.

Rob looked at his friend and then back at the screen. "That...that's my sister, Callie!"

Justin turned back to the screen. "Hey, I haven't really seen her in a couple of years, but, no way, man."

The camera pulled back to reveal her body. Rob said nervously, "Yes, the face, the voice. It's her. I promise. It's Callie. Or her perfect twin."

Samantha looked at her partner, smiled, and said, "I'm here for you..."

Justin asked again, incredulously, pointing at the screen, "That woman is your sister? Samantha?"

Rob almost whispered, "Not Samantha. Callie. It's gross."

"Wow! No one will believe this."

Rob dropped down to face him at the console. "And you won't tell them." She started to remove her panties.

"Stop! Turn that off!" Rob almost yelled, and reached for the on/off switch.

"You crashed the computer."

"I don't care. Listen. Don't tell anyone about this. Just chill this weekend. OK? I am *grossed out!*"

"Well, OK. But you gotta tell me what you find out."

"Sure. Now, let's fold up for tonight."

They stood and placed their SW 2100 guns in their charging stands. Rob said, "I can't believe this."

At the Sawyers' table at Torini's, Jane asked, "Mr. Sawyer, what exactly do you do?"

He took a sip from his drink and replied, "I'm in charge of all the real estate for USNet, a large communications company. We have facilities in almost every country, so we stay pretty busy."

"Wow. Is that why you're here?"

"Yes. I've got to do final inspections on some properties we're acquiring in this area."

"What kind of properties?"

David looked at his daughter, who smiled. "Oh, some office buildings, and, actually, some film studio assets."

Callie turned to her friend and said, "Dad's company is in the *adult* movie business."

David could feel himself turning red. "A subsidiary. I don't really do much with it."

Elizabeth asked her husband, "I never think about that. Why is USNet in that business, anyway, David? Is that why you had to come out this time?"

He took a long sip. "I'm just the real estate guy. I don't choose our product lines." He and Callie exchanged glances, and then he looked back at Elizabeth. "There are some new laws, like preventing anyone under twenty-one from working in the industry, including acting in these kinds of movies." He glanced again at Callie. "So I'm not sure the future is so bright." He saw Callie's eyes widen just a bit.

"Well, good," Elizabeth said.

"But to answer your question, dear, there are a lot of assets in several acquisitions that Trevor put together that I have to walk through. I warned you that I might be really busy. Bud Purcell is picking me up at ten in the morning. We figure there will be less traffic over the weekend for driving to the properties."

"So, what shall we do, girls? Shop?"

Jane smiled. "I think we should be able to do that."

Callie put her napkin down. "Before our dinners arrive, I need to go to the restroom."

David stood up and pulled her chair back. "Me, too."

"David, please call and be sure that Rob is OK. You know I didn't feel good about leaving him at Justin's, and they ought to be there."

"OK." Father and daughter left Elizabeth and Jane in deep conversation about the next day's itinerary.

The restrooms were located off an alcove, not in view of their table. Callie was leading the way, but when they entered the quiet space, David asked, "Did you hear what I said about that new law?"

She stopped and turned. "Yes. But I don't believe it."

He smiled. "Callie, it's true. It's now the law, and the legal challenges are finished. No one under twenty-one can participate in porn any more."

"Well, then how am I going to pay my way? Uncle Reza doesn't pay enough for us to live on."

"You should have thought of that before you decided to live with Alex."

She stood up straighter and clenched her fist. "Why are you making this so hard? Just pay for your daughter's college like everyone else does!"

"My daughter has chosen to live with a man she's not married to."

"Me and a couple of million others!"

"That doesn't make it right."

"Forget it. We'll survive somehow."

"Just leave him. You can concentrate on legitimate theater. I've got some bonuses coming, so after graduation we could send you to New York, or wherever you want."

"It looks like I'm going to Mexico. How about Mexico? It seems to be pretty popular."

"Mexico?"

"It's, like, what Jane was talking about. She and Alex went down and started some paperwork that registers them in the Mexican Actors Guild. I had a test so I couldn't go. But I'll go next week.'

"What?"

"Yeah. The XXX upload site now requires us to be registered in Mexico or Denmark as actors. Something about how the movies will now be registered abroad and we have to have to provide some number. I think we'll now be working for a Mexican company."

David's mouth opened as he listened to his daughter.

She was smiling up at him. "So, like, I'm not sure about all the details. Jane says it was easy to do. She has to go back once the papers are ready, and I have to start mine so that I'll be official in Mexico. And the site is going to pay ten percent *more* because there are so few legally registered actors for the movies. Not bad, huh?"

He couldn't breathe. He didn't speak.

Finally Callie asked, "Hey, I really do have to use the bathroom. Are you all right?"

"Uh..." He shook his head. "Callie, look, I've got some extra money. You don't need to do this. I'll put you through any acting school, anywhere you want. Just away from here."

As she turned to go, she said, "The money's part of it, but actually I *like* what I'm doing."

You couldn't. Not really.

He watched her until she went through the door. He didn't move for a full minute.

Callie's not coming home. Trevor's statement about supporting the President is a lie, and I've told everyone, including the President's foreign policy advisor, to believe him.

As if waking from a trance he thought of their son and called him on his new cell phone.

"Rob, it's Dad. Are you and Justin at his house?"

"Yes."

"Good. Just checking."

"Uh, Dad. Is Callie there?"

"Yes. We're at a restaurant with a friend of hers."

"She's in school out there, right?" Rob asked.

"Yes. Why?"

"I don't know. Somebody told me he thought he'd seen her in, uh, a movie, or on the internet, or something."

David closed his eyes. "I doubt it. But maybe. I'll, uh, tell her you asked about her. OK?"

"Yeah. I haven't talked with her in a while, anyway. Maybe I'll call her tomorrow."

"The girls will be out shopping tomorrow. Maybe try on Sunday or next week."

"Sounds good. Say hello to Callie, and tell her I'll call her soon."

"Thanks. Good night, son."

David closed his phone and leaned against the wall for support.

Todd had come into the office that Saturday about noon to pick up some files that he needed to work on at home. An hour later he headed for the parking deck. There were not that many cars in the deck, and he noticed Akbar Kamali, the head of their IT Security, getting into his black Mercedes two rows over.

I'd like to talk with him about email and cell phone encryption in a way that doesn't seem like I'm pushing it. Maybe I can get David to create a small working group to look into it—give me a reason to meet with him.

Todd went through the parking gate right after Kamali, and both cars turned right on the side street next to their office, Then right again on the main street. Through two traffic lights, Todd remained directly behind Kamali.

Todd was changing tunes on his MP3 when Kamali stopped in the middle of the next block. Traffic kept Todd from going around him. A moment later the door opened at a computer store and Victor Mustafin walked quickly across the sidewalk to the curb. He waved and smiled at Kamali, then got into the car, and the two sped off.

Todd did not move. *Kamali and Mustafin know each other?*

27

WEDNESDAY, JUNE 22ND

David was in the aisle seat, looking across Elizabeth's sleeping form as the sunrise rapidly turned the sky from black to dark blue and pink. He had not slept at all on the "red eye" from L.A. As the pilot reduced the throttle and began the first stage of their descent, scratchy eyes and the first thuds of a headache welcomed David home.

He had not been able to sleep because his mind would not stop racing. After Friday night's dinner he had immersed himself in checking out their new properties and formulating the final hold/sell/lease plan with Bud Purcell. He instinctively knew that hard work was the best way to dull the pain caused by Callie's "registration" in Mexico and all that it implied. And so he had thrown himself into it, even arriving late for Monday evening's dinner alone with Elizabeth, while Callie and Jane studied. But Elizabeth did not seem to mind any of the inconveniences. She had a wonderful time shopping and talking with their daughter and her friend. David was thankful that their relationship seemed to be OK and that Elizabeth apparently never found out that Callie had done videos with Alex.

But even as he had worked hard on the assignment, given his daughter's behavior, he could not help being repulsed by what USNet was doing. With the project completed and the report ready to be typed, David found himself thinking more about Trevor Knox, the company, the President, and their upcoming trip to Moscow. His mind replayed for the hundredth time the events of the last few weeks and the possible consequences. *Maybe there's just a misunderstanding,* he thought, as he rubbed his forehead. *Moving the eighteen to twenty year olds to a Mexican company is so obvious. What will happen when someone finds out and calls us on it? But who's looking? Maybe that's what Trevor is counting on. Or maybe he expects the law to change again, so he's just parking them temporarily. I don't know, but I hope it's a misunderstanding and Callie will have to quit. I guess I can ask at today's meeting with Trevor and Paul. I wonder what Paul knows.*

And what if it's not a misunderstanding? What if Trevor is doing this for real? What do I do? Make a big deal out of it? And lose my job? That would be real *smart. What should I tell Kristen and that congresswoman? And Sandra Van Huyck? The President? Something? Nothing?*

He gently nudged Elizabeth. "Good morning, dear. We're descending. Did you have a good sleep?"

She nodded groggily and cracked her eyes. "I guess, but a short night. I don't see how you do this so often."

"You get used to it, though usually I grab a few hours sleep. Tonight I was just thinking too much."

"Well, come home early. We'll have dinner and go to bed." She smiled and nuzzled her head on his shoulder.

"Yes." He wished that he could return her feelings, but his mind continued to race.

Todd told Mary that he had an early breakfast meeting, but the day before he had organized some extra time at the RTI console when the load would normally be light. The Mustafin connection to Kamali had him deeply troubled. Mustafin had recruited him onto the RTI team with the threat of letting USNet know about his illegal "finance fee." But if he and Kamali were friends? What did Kamali already know? Did they somehow work together?

After logging into the system and handling a couple of routine intercepts, he switched his console to Busy within the network and went looking in the extensive data banks. He typed in his own name. A large file came up, with intercepts of his conversations with Mike Campbell. David Sawyer: the file he had seen earlier. Akbar Kamali. No information. He tried different spellings. Nothing. Victor Mustafin. Nothing. Trevor Knox. Blank. The CEOs of USNet's main competitors. A short paragraph on each. Paul Burke. A full file.

Then he shifted to companies. For E-News, which USNet had just acquired, there was a huge file. As he drilled into it, he found intercepts implying that its CFO had published false financial figures and that the CEO had agreed to help cover it up. All that a few weeks before the acquisition was first announced.

He typed in USNet. Almost nothing—just short stories from various newspapers.

So as not to attract any attention, he clicked off the Busy and handled several intercepts. Then he returned to his investigation. He could not print and take anything out of the building, but he made notes on a few small slips of paper.

Callie was still high as she, Alex and Jane opened the latch to their apartment and collapsed on the sofa at three that morning. After a final dinner with her parents and seeing them off to the airport in a taxi, Callie, Alex and Jane had partied with friends. Tequila and energy drinks. And now Callie was looking forward to a long morning's sleep; Alex had already headed for their bedroom.

From the sofa she reached for the answering machine by the phone and pressed the Play button. First there was a message from Kristen, hoping to "just talk and catch up." Callie smiled at Kristen's voice and decided to keep the current messages as a reminder to call her unusual friend.

There was one more. "Hi, Callie. It's Rob. What's happening? I'm busy this summer at MailDrop. Pretty boring, but OK money. And my computer stuff. Listen, I just wanted to call and let you know that a friend saw a movie— an 'adult' movie—and swears that you're the star. Can you believe that? Weird. Anyway, I just wanted to say hello and find out how you're doing. I guess mom and dad have just been out there to see you, so I'll talk to them. But I'd really like to talk, too. OK? Call me when you can. See 'ya."

Callie curled up on the sofa. Jane stood up to go to bed. She had heard both messages.

"What will you tell your brother?" she asked, heading for the bathroom.

From her near fetal position on the sofa, Callie said, "I don't know. But I can't think now."

All during the morning David handled the routine business that always piled up when his work week in the office began on a Wednesday. A call to Tanya Prescott's private line confirmed that the plans for Moscow were proceeding as they had anticipated, though she admitted to being more concerned at this point about the state functions than the USNet reception. He hastily put together written notes for his afternoon meeting with Knox. By lunch the thud in his head had become a pounding.

David had a sandwich at his desk and felt his stomach tightening and his heart racing as his mind moved ahead and tried to imagine how he would broach the subject of Mexico when face to face with Knox.

A little before three he gathered his notes and walked slowly up the stairs. He stopped by Paul Burke's office, and the two men went together to the top floor. In five minutes they were seated at Knox's conference table, and David went deliberately through the items on his agenda, from the Capital Tower contract to his trip to California to fulfilling their latest needs for web hosting space in the Midwest, including Kansas City.

Throughout the briefing the other men listened and took a few notes, saying little. David finished with Moscow, repeating what Tanya had said that morning, that the plans were on track.

"They've decided to have our reception at five, which will allow them a full day of work, plus a short dinner afterward at the Kremlin before leaving for the Fourth of July party. Also, that's nine a.m. on the East Coast, so there can be some legitimate live press coverage, too.

"I plan to fly over on the first. I'll get in on Saturday about noon and have the weekend to help handle the last-minute details. "

"Good. I'll be coming in on the third," Knox said. "When I arrive we should meet to review how the plans are coming along. And of course you can videophone me anytime."

"Sounds good. I think it will go smoothly. Paul, that's about all I had on my agenda, except that there was one thing I wanted to ask you, Trevor."

"Yes?" Knox put down his notes.

David could hear his heart pounding in his ears. "When I was in California touring our new properties with Bud Purcell, he mentioned that some of our actors are going to visit Mexico so that they can work for our new Mexican subsidiary." As he watched the frown grow on Knox's face, his stomach rose into his mouth. He took a deep breath and continued. "I was wondering how that will work, and will it conflict with what we've told the President about complying with the new laws?"

Knox stared at him. Finally he said, "Why do you ask, David?"

He breathed heavily again, and noticed out of the corner of his eye that Burke had not moved. "I was wondering if it would change the allocations for the spaces we've just acquired."

Knox seemed to relax a little. "No. No, I don't expect this situation to last very long. It's a temporary change, which is why you shouldn't worry about it."

"Oh. And...our pledge to the President?"

Knox's eyes narrowed. Again a long pause. "David, we're keeping our word. We said that no U.S.-produced movies would use anyone under twenty-one. We'll abide by that 'pledge', as you call it. Why are you asking this?"

David had been watching Knox intently. He smiled. "I just wanted your assurance that I could say exactly that if anyone I'm working with at the White House questions me on it."

Knox continued to search him. "David, there is almost no way it could be found out or come up before our Moscow visit. So I don't think you have to worry."

"I know, but I just wanted to be clear, to know what I can say, so that I wouldn't be blind- sided."

Knox paused for a moment. "Yes, well, it's probably good that you and Paul do know about it, in case it should come up in Moscow."

"And what about after Moscow?" Burke asked, finally participating in the conversation.

Knox smiled a little. "We're focused now on the boost the President's visit will give to our Russian business. We'll worry about that after we get back."

"All right," David said, collecting his papers. "Thanks. That's all I had."

Knox nodded as Sawyer rose. "Thanks, David. Paul and I have a couple of budget items to go over. Congratulations again on Capital Tower."

"It's not done yet."

"I know, but you're in charge, so I'm not worried. And, oh, David—please worry about our real estate, which you do so well, and leave these issues to others."

David smiled broadly. "Yes. Sure. I just wanted to know what to say."

"Good. Now you do. See you over there, if not before."

"Thanks." David turned and walked to the door, opened it, and walked out past Phyllis Jordan. He went down to the thirty-third floor and directly into the empty men's room. Looking at himself in the mirror he confirmed that he was drenched in sweat. He wet some paper towels and wiped his face.

I guess I told him about living up to one's word, was all he could think. He looked again and wiped his hands with the cool towels. *If there is a God, what would he think? Or even what would Elizabeth and Rob think? Rob was so proud of me. Hey, just keep your head down and take the money. Say what Knox says to say and let him take the flack if it's not right.*

But I'm the one who told Van Huyck and Kristen to believe him. I believed he was telling the truth. It's not my fault that he changed, is it? What about Callie?

At that moment Callie was sitting at the conference table in her Cousin Yusef's office, several files and property listings spread out before them. Callie was looking through the properties. "Here," she offered a flyer to Yusef, "this home might be perfect for the Payamis. It's right next to the school, and it has enough bedrooms."

Her cousin took the flyer, glanced at it, and threw it in the trashcan under the table. "No, that will not work."

"Why not?" Callie ventured.

Yusef sat up straight in his chair and looked sternly at his cousin. "Because it is the listing of Jim Forrester. And it is owned by Adam Lawrence."

Callie was silent, a questioning look on her face.

"Five years ago Mr. Lawrence agreed to give the listing on their previous home to my father. But the next day Forrester called him and told him that it was worth more than my father had estimated, and so Mr. Lawrence reneged on his word and gave the listing to the other agent. Since then we have never sold any listing of Forrester's, and we certainly would not do so with the Lawrence home."

"But that was five years ago. And what if it is the perfect house for the Payamis?"

"It cannot be. And it doesn't matter. We will never forget what Forrester did. And as for Lawrence, he must be taught a lesson. We will not help them."

"Even if it also helped your own client? Isn't that idea of revenge a little misplaced?" She smiled.

Yusef leaned toward her. "Revenge is important. Allah directs it."

"OK. I get it. But I've got a friend, a woman I met in commercial real estate, and she's been telling me about forgiveness—and grace. She says that they are the only way to heal a wound and go on. What do you think?"

Her cousin was silent for a moment, his anger clearly building. "These concepts ingrain weakness and defeat." He picked up the papers. "They are foreign to our faith and to our family. We follow Allah's will as revealed in the Qur'an. And Allah wills that we exact revenge from those who wrong us. Don't ever forget it. Now, do another search."

He handed the papers to Callie, and stood to end the meeting.

"All right. I'm sorry. I won't ever bring up a Forrester listing again."

As she turned to leave, he said, "You are right."

Once Sawyer and Burke left his office, Knox sat at his console and read through the RTI messages forwarded or originated by the duty officer. He thought about their earlier conversation, made two notes and called Akbar Kamali, who answered on his encrypted video phone.

"Yes, sir? How are you?"

"Fine. But I have some good and bad news concerning David Sawyer. He just asked about the younger actors being registered in Mexico—says that Bud Purcell told him. I can't believe that Purcell would tell anyone about that—even David—but how else would he find out? Check it out for us.

"The good news is that the Moscow reception has been set for five p.m. Allowing for some slippage, I think our target should be seven. What do you think?"

"That sounds about right, given the short distance to the Kremlin from USNet's office."

"OK. Let them know. Does it have a camera in the nose?"

"Yes. North says it'll be a great show. The Kremlin, up close and personal."

Knox nodded and smiled. "And after it's flown four hundred kilometers, only we will have the ability to abort the mission, right?"

"Yes, at that point control will automatically pass to us, and then only we can abort it with a code known to you, Victor and me."

"Excellent. So the Stingers should strike about two hours later. Let the media get worked up and the emergencies declared, and then we'll paralyze commercial air traffic for the foreseeable future. Tell Salim to launch at 1pm in New York, which will be 10 am in Los Angeles. Imagine America with no leadership and no air travel. It's less than two weeks. Stay on schedule."

"Yes, sir. And I'll check with Purcell about what he may have told Sawyer. Not smart."

"Have you checked out that security report that David mentioned about cell phones and emails?'

"No. I haven't received the copy that David promised."

"Akbar, David has been with me for twenty years and has done a great job for us in real estate. But now he's trying to help the traitors in Tehran, concerned about cell phones, and tells Paul Burke about our moves in Mexico. That could cause real problems after Moscow, given our public initiative with the President.

"I don't need to tell you that the next two weeks will change the world. With one stroke we have the opportunity to cut the heads off of two great serpents. America will be leaderless, on her knees in confusion and finger pointing. The Zionists will be easy to pick off. Islam will advance more than in the last two hundred years. All because of our plan.

"I don't know what David's up to, but I don't like it. Maybe it's just a coincidence, but we've got to watch him. I want you and Victor to personally review *all* his calls, in case the lower levels don't connect something. And we need to keep him close. We don't want him going anywhere or talking to the wrong people—intentionally or not. We need to figure out what he's doing, and who he's talking to. And why."

"Yes, sir. We'll monitor him closely."

That Friday evening David and Elizabeth left home for an early movie. He wanted to spend time with Elizabeth before departing for Moscow in a week and missing the entire Fourth of July weekend with her.

Rob was upstairs playing Street War 2100; the Blue Team had a big party scheduled for the following Friday night of the long weekend, and Rob and Justin had already concocted a plan of bogus places they would tell their parents they were going in order to join their Blue teammates.

In California, Callie was preparing to go to class. She grabbed her keys from the table by the door.

Her younger brother picked up the phone and dialed her number. He had called several times from his cell phone, but she had never answered. He thought maybe the home phone might be luckier.

She heard the phone ring and checked the caller ID. She had dodged at least three calls from Rob. The ID was her parents' home.

"Hello," she answered.

"Hi, Callie. It's Rob."

"Robbie..." She was the only one who called him that, ever since they were little. "Hey, I'm sorry I've been so busy." She put down her keys. "I got your call, and I planned to call back this weekend."

"No problem. How are you?"

They talked for several minutes about school, his summer job, and their father's upcoming trip.

"Sounds pretty exciting, doesn't it?" he concluded.

"Yeah, I guess. If you're into politics." She moved to sit on the sofa.

"Or government." He paused. "Listen, Callie, did you get my message about the adult movie? Isn't that wild? This guy won't leave me alone until I talk to you. I told him there's no way it's you."

She was silent. Then she took a deep breath and said. "Well, Robbie, like, actually he's right. It *is* me."

"Callie, no...that's *you*?"

"Yes."

He felt his stomach turn as he remembered the vision on the screen. "Gross."

"Why gross? I bet you've watched lots of adult movies."

Now he was silent for a moment. "Well, I guess. But they weren't my sister."

"I'll tell you the same thing I told Dad: 'they' are all somebody's daughter or sister. This one just happens to be me."

"*Dad* knows about this?"

"He does. But not Mom, I don't think."

"What did he say?"

"What do you think? He wants me to quit."

"So do I."

"Rob, Dad cut me off. And do you know how much money I make?"

"I don't care. It's still gross. You'll get some disease."

She heard the pain in her brother's voice. "What if it were Jamie Tatum?" she asked, referring to a girl in his high school class.

"Callie, it's not Jamie. It's you. But it's the same thing. I don't want my sister or a friend doing that gross stuff on camera for thousands of guys to watch."

"But someone you *don't* know *can* do it, right?"

He paused again. "Maybe it doesn't make sense. But I'm not their brother. I'm *your* brother. And I'm asking you, please, stop, no matter how much money you're making."

"Are you still doing those internet games you told me about?"

He closed his eyes. "Yes."

"A lot? Like it keeps you from studying?"

"Sometimes."

"Why don't you stop?"

"Callie, look...it's ...it's not the same."

"It's probably closer than you think."

"Thousands of guys aren't fantasizing about me while I play that game."

"Isn't your game one big fantasy?"

"Maybe, but it's not the same."

"What I do is not all bad."

"Gross!"

"Robbie. *Neither* of us is perfect. What do you want to do now?"

"I'll think about stopping, if you will," he said, not really meaning it, but wanting his sister out of porn movies.

"Fair enough. I'll think about it. We'll talk again."

"Yes."

"OK. But now I gotta go. I'm going to be late for class."

"Please don't do another one."

"I said I'd think about it."

"Gross!"

"You already said that a few times."

He smiled for the first time. "Then you did hear me? I meant it every time. Here, I'll say it again—*Gross!*"

"I get it, I get it. I'll really think about it. But I doubt anything will change."

"Callie, please."

"We'll talk. Bye."

Callie remembered Rob when they were younger. How much she had wanted to teach him to do the right thing. And now she was disappointing him. She lingered for a moment, thinking again of her brother. Then she shook her head, locked the door, and left for class.

Early that Sunday afternoon David was in his study, dressed in shorts, reading through property reports, lease abstracts and tenant fit-out proposals so that he could leave a long to do list with his team when he departed on Friday. Elizabeth was across the street at a neighbor's, learning how to bake healthy whole grain bread. Rob was out. The doorbell rang. *Who can that be?*

When David opened the door, he found Kristen Holloway. She was wearing a light, conservative summer dress, carrying a brown pocketbook, and appeared to be tanned and healthy.

"Hello, David." She smiled.

"Hello!" He opened the screen door and stepped aside. "Come in and get out of the heat."

She stepped in, and he gave her a friendly hug. "How are you? And what brings you here?"

"Well, church just got over, and I haven't seen you or Elizabeth for a while, so I figured if a cell phone call is bad, a personal visit must be all right. So here I am. Can we talk for a minute?"

"Sure. Sure." He motioned for her to walk ahead of him into the den. "Elizabeth's across the street, but she ought to be home soon. Rob is out somewhere. Can I get you some water, or something?" He offered her a seat at the end of the sofa, and he sat in a large cushioned chair nearby.

"No, thank you." She smiled as they sat down.

"It's great to see you."

"Yes. Me, too. I figured that you would be leaving for Moscow soon, and I just wanted to see you and hear about your trip to see Callie. And tell you how proud I am that you've helped move Knox just a little closer to reducing the company's porn business. Or at least making it less accessible to families and teenagers."

He tried to smile and nod, but couldn't find words.

"Are you all right?"

"Yeah. It's just that I haven't done much."

"Knox *is* still going to do what he said, isn't he? So that Callie can't continue. Right?"

David paused. "Uh. Yes, Callie will be making some changes."

Kristen sat back and smiled. "Good! I'll ask her about how she feels about them the next time we talk."

David frowned. "She and I talked a little when we were out there. Elizabeth doesn't know about any of this, of course, so I didn't push it."

"I see. Well, good. I believe if she can get out of that awful environment, away from the other people caught up in it, before something worse happens, she'll be fine. We'll all look back on this in a few years like a bad dream."

David closed his eyes for a moment, his stomach turning over. "I hope so Kristen. I really do, with all my heart."

"I know. I talk to Callie pretty regularly. Not about her business, but just about 'stuff'. We've adopted each other as the sisters we never had. She really is a wonderful person, but she drinks too much, and she's so deceived that what she's doing is just all fun and money, with no consequences."

David lowered his eyes and almost whispered. "I know. Thank you for being her friend."

"It's not a problem. Oh, that sounds like Elizabeth."

Elizabeth entered the den, and Kristen stood and greeted her with a hug.

"How long have you been here?" Elizabeth asked, sitting in another chair.

"Just a few minutes. I dropped by after church to see you and to wish David a safe trip to Moscow."

"That's nice. Do you need anything to drink? No? Well, tell us about your new job, and what you've been doing."

"I start a week from Tuesday, on July fifth. And I'm really looking forward to working on the investment side with this pension fund."

They talked for almost thirty minutes, catching up on the Sawyer children, Kristen's new job, and the details of the Moscow visit, at least as David knew them.

Finally Kristen stood and smiled. "Well, I know from personal experience that David must have a *lot* to do before a trip like this, so I'll be on my way. David, if there's anything I can do to help, just let me know. And we'll all be watching on TV next Monday morning. It should be really exciting for USNet."

As they walked to the door, David said, "Thanks, Kristen. You've already done a lot. Hopefully everything in Moscow will go smoothly—and also with your new job."

Callie and Alex returned to their apartment that afternoon after spending several hours at the beach. Alex went to the refrigerator to get some cold water, and Callie clicked on the phone for a voicemail.

"Callie, this is Yusef. My father and I have decided that your internship has ended. We don't need your assistance any longer. We will mail you a check for the time that you've spent during the final two weeks. Please do not come by the office, or call. We appreciate your help and hope that you have learned something. Thank you."

After the sun set Yusef parked in a dark area of a large retail outlet that was open 24/7. A few minutes later a rental van with Texas plates pulled up next to him, and he transferred to the van's passenger seat. He smiled and shook hands with Salim, who then started the engine, and they drove out of the lot.

They took a circuitous route in the event that someone might be following them. An hour later, satisfied that they were alone, Yusef directed his friend to the large mini-storage complex near LAX airport where he had rented a climate-controlled space for a year.

Knowing that they would definitely be on cameras, they took their time unloading furniture, crates and boxes into the large space. When finished, they locked the van, went inside the space, closed and bolted the roll-up door, then turned on the lights.

Salim directed his student first to the crates that contained the pieces of the Stinger Missile. Yusef smiled as the two men took their time sitting on boxes and assembling the high-tech weapon. Then they turned to the crates containing the high explosives and detonator for the bomb that would be waiting in the van after the plane went down. When it was all done, Yusef ran his hand over the length of the missile launch tube and pronounced himself ready. "In ten days I will be in Paradise." He laughed.

"Yes, my brother. After killing many infidels and throwing these blasphemers into panic."

Yusef nodded.

His mentor continued. "There will be other events that morning that you will hear about as they happen. You are to listen to the airport tower frequency, and take out the first plane that departs after ten. It will be closely timed with another action that will double the panic."

"I am ready. It's time to make the video that you will play that night."

"Yes. I brought the equipment." Salim stood and walked over to a smaller crate. "Here is the background curtain, the head scarf, and your script. I'll set up the camera, and we'll begin."

"Allah be praised."

28

THURSDAY, JUNE 30TH

A few mornings later Todd Phelps was at his desk in Kristen's old office, rationalizing the advantages of a lease for a portion of the brewery in Kansas City, wishing that he had never taken that first financing fee, now that he had the extra income from RTI. But of course that's how he came to RTI, he reminded himself. And all the extra money. *I don't need both. Now that I know that RTI pays well, after the next finance fee from Mike, I'll stop taking them. And then hopefully build some distance from him.*

The question he next waited to focus on with more time at the console was: Who was behind RTI?

The phone rang, and it was Mike Campbell, calling from what sounded like his cell phone.

"Hey," Todd said. "I was just finishing our response to your proposal on Kansas City."

"Good. Are we going to make the deal?"

"Yes, I think so. On all the key points, including the rate and term, we're very close to your proposal. I think you'll like it."

"Great. Way to go, Mister Finance Minister!"

Todd frowned. "Please."

"Fine, but I wanted to give you a head's up on a little problem that's come up."

"What is it?"

"It turns out that the land for Brookglen was originally zoned for retail use, and now there's some question about whether the sewer is sized large enough for offices. The previous developer was supposed to pay for an upgrade, but now we're not sure that he did. The county is trying to sort it out, but they haven't done it yet."

"What? You're kidding."

"No. There was a misunderstanding."

"But you warranted it in our lease, and I didn't check behind you because I trusted you."

"Hey. It happens. They say it'll be done sometime in the next two years for sure."

"*Two years?* But we're supposed to be in our space in, what, fourteen months? Mike, David will go crazy!"

"Well, don't tell him, at least not yet. Let us see what we can do at this end to fix it sooner."

"But we might have to shift to another development."

There was silence on the other end for a few moments. "Don't *ever* say that, and don't even consider it. We made a small mistake. But your fee was no mistake, and I'm sure you wouldn't want anyone to know about it. So don't let anyone talk about moving anywhere else."

"But obviously we have to have sewer, and you said it was there. I should have checked."

"So for many reasons you better just ride along with us. We're checking up here on what to do. But even if the sewer is delayed, we can't let you break your lease. We've got a deal, the financing depends on it, and you've got your fee, so we just need to figure out a solution."

"And what about Kansas City?"

"What about it?"

"What should I be checking on there before we send the response to you?"

"Nothing. Everything's good in Kansas City. I know it myself. But even if it wasn't quite perfect, you need to keep pushing it, assuming you want to maintain a positive and quiet relationship with us."

Todd was silent, rubbing his forehead with his right hand. Finally he said, "I see."

"Good. So just keep that Kansas City response coming, and we'll work on the sewer issue here in Minneapolis."

"I gotta give David some version of this, and soon. The longer I wait, the more difficult it will be to explain if it does blow."

"Well, we should know something soon, so I'd wait a couple of days, at least. Maybe there'll be a quick solution."

"Yeah, maybe. I hope so."

Late that afternoon Kristen opened the door to her condo and dropped several shopping bags on the living room sofa. A friend had set up a double date to the baseball game for Saturday, and she had been shopping for a summer hat she could wear in case it was sweltering in the sun. And while shopping she'd found a few things to take home on trial, which might work for the following week, once she found out how dressy the corporate culture was at her new job.

She put the boxes in her bedroom and fixed a glass of iced tea. The phone rang. She looked at the readout and saw that it was Callie's apartment number, so she picked up.

"Hi, Callie. How are you?"

"Kristen, I'm not good."

"Why?"

"Jane's dead."

"*What?*"

"I, like, don't know the details. She and Alex went to Mexico to pick up their papers. She..." Callie started to cry.

"Callie, I'm so sorry. What happened to Jane?"

"I'm not sure. They called me from Mexico a little while ago to tell me that she died—of an overdose. Kristen, she was just here!"

"I know, Callie. Who called?"

Callie continued to cry, but spoke. "Alex. An overdose. That's what he said, and he has to stay there. She was always so happy. They told me the police have to come search our apartment, and that I shouldn't, like, touch anything in her room."

"Oh, Callie."

"So I have to stay here in L.A. 'til they come and, like, figure this out. I don't know what they're going to do with her—her body. They asked if I have her parents' number. And I...I think I may be pregnant."

Kristen closed her eyes while Callie began to whimper.

"Do you know for sure?"

"I've missed for several weeks, and I got one of those test things, but I'm scared to do it alone. Jane's not here."

"Callie, I'm coming out. Just stay there for now, and I'll call back with my flight information. It may be too late to get a flight tonight, but I'll be out either tonight or early in the morning. And I'll get a taxi to your apartment. Will you be all right 'til I get there?"

"Kristen—I've really messed up. And Jane's dead."

"I know, and I'm sorry. But I'll help. So don't do anything crazy. Just stay there in your apartment. You'll be fine there. And I'm on the way. OK?"

"Yes. Thank you."

Kristen nodded. "We all need friends, Callie. I have some remarkable ones, and you're one of them. So I'll call back as soon as I know my trip details."

"Yes."

"I'm on the way." She hung up and dialed the airline.

Driving home David called Iran via Estonia from one of his cell phones. Omid answered and told him that Goli was a little better, but still depressed. Omid had stopped attending meetings or otherwise participating in the opposition, until he could get Goli to safety.

"I've been working with some people in Tabriz who say that they can move us over the border into Turkey in a few days."

"Both of you?"

"Yes. I think that I must get Goli to Istanbul and safely on a plane to you and Elizabeth. Then I'll return to Tehran for no more than six months to help the revolution and to train others. Then I will come to the U.S.—or bring Goli back."

"I hope you can move quickly. "

"I'll try. Can I put Goli on now, and you can tell her about Callie and Rob? She looks forward to meeting them. Callie must be a beautiful American lady now, and you must be very proud."

"Yes. She is. It's great to see the kids growing up. Please put her on. And when you know about getting out, have a friend call from Europe, and then I'll get back to you."

"OK. Thank you. Thank you for all your help."

"We haven't done anything yet."

"But you're there."

"Yes. We're definitely here, and we'll help."

"Callie, hi, it's Kristen. How are you?"

"Not good. The police called and said they're coming over in the morning to look through Jane's things."

"What time?"

"They weren't sure. About ten."

"That's about when I get in. There were no seats available tonight, but I'm on the first non-stop in the morning. Callie, don't worry about the police. They just have to do it—it's procedure."

"What if they find some 'stuff'?"

"I don't know. Do you have any?"

"I did. Not now."

"OK. Just take one day at a time. I'll be up early and out to help you. And, oh, I'm praying for you, and for Jane's family."

"Thank you."

"Dad?"

"Yes?" It was two hours later, and David was in his bedroom, standing by the bed, a shirt in hand. There were a few items left on the bed to go into his carry-on. His son stood at the door.

"Can I come in?"

David smiled. "Sure."

Rob closed the door. "Mom's in the den reading. I wanted to talk with you before you leave, about Callie."

"Callie? What about her?"

"The movies. The *adult* movies. Dad, Callie and her boyfriend have done some porn movies."

He felt a chill. There was a long silence. Finally he replied, slowly, "Yes, Rob, I know about Callie. I've known for about three months, I guess. I'd just as soon your mother doesn't find out. I'm trying to fix it, to get Callie to stop before something happens to her."

"I talked to Callie, but she doesn't sound like she wants to change, because of the money. I asked her to quit. It's so gross."

"I know. I know." He shook his head. "I don't know why she's doing it. Money isn't everything."

"She said it's because you stopped paying for her school, and so she has to do it."

David paused. "I told her that I would not support her as long as she was living with that Alex guy in the apartment that I was paying for. He's the one who got her started in this kind of 'acting.'"

"Oh. I didn't know that."

"Yes. I love your sister as much as any father can. But I can't pay for her to live with that creep."

"I guess it's pretty tough on you with my games and Callie's movies...."

David continued to shake his head.

"Dad, I really will try to do less, or stop. And I'll work on Callie."

David looked at his son and could see his distress. He made a tentative move toward him, then reached out and hugged him. They stood together for a moment. "When I get back from Moscow maybe we'll try to talk to her together."

Rob pulled back. "That's a good idea. Together, maybe she'll listen to us. I just wanted you to know, and I hope you have a great trip. It's awesome what you're doing."

"Thank you, son."

Rob opened the door and left. David stood staring at his suitcase.

David's flight was scheduled to leave at one the next afternoon, about the time Kristen's flight would land in Los Angeles. She had almost called him on the way to the airport early that morning, but she remembered his aversion to cell phones and had decided to see Callie first before involving him, particularly with the importance of his next few days' work.

For his part, David went into the office early in an effort to finish off USNet real estate business. The offices were empty, and he sent a few final emails to their team in Moscow. Thirty minutes later, he was putting files in his travel bag when Todd came in. He looked pale, and his eyes were red.

David straightened up from behind his desk. "You look like you haven't slept all night."

Todd closed the door. "I haven't." He stood still. "David, I ...I have to talk with you."

David looked at his watch. "Sure. Of course. Sit down." David moved to one of the two chairs in front of his desk, and Todd joined him.

As Todd started, he focused on the desk, then his hands. "David, I know that you're leaving in a little while, and that's why I'm here. I...I've got to tell you about some things that won't be easy, and about what I've found out. I'm afraid, and if anything happens to me, I want you to know this, even though it means the end of my work here." He finally looked up at his boss. "I'm very worried for Mary and our boys, and I've got to get out."

"Todd, what is it? Out of what?" David shifted in his chair.

"I'm not proud of what I'm going to tell you, but I felt like we needed more money for our family. And so I did something very stupid. I accepted a bribe from Mike Campbell to put our operation in their building."

"What?"

"Yes. I know. I let you down. And now there's a question about whether the site even has adequate sewer capacity."

David leaned forward. "What?"

Todd raised his hands. "David, as impossible as it sounds, I wish that was all that I have to tell you. But it's only the beginning." He took a deep breath, rubbed his hands, and then told David about how he had been thrown into a van by some thugs. And then someone named Victor Mustafin had blackmailed him into joining the RTI operation by threatening to expose his illegal income to USNet. But the blackmailer also offered a way to make more money than he had ever dreamed of having.

"I don't understand how this guy found out about Mike Campbell's bribe. Did Mike tell them?"

"That's the really unbelievable part." Todd described in detail his training in RTI, all the information it gathered, and how. David just listened. "And they threatened serious 'negative consequences' if I told anyone about what they do to extract and then use all of this information."

"That's really why you've been so down on email and cell phones. They've been intercepting our calls."

Todd nodded. "And everyone else's. That 'report' that you got in the mail—I wrote it and mailed it to you."

David turned to his desk. "Here it is. Akbar Kamali reminded me a day ago that I forgot to give him a copy. I guess he just got it."

"If I believed more in God, I'd imagine that He had something to do with your forgetfulness."

"What?" Todd was silent. David continued. "So who are they, and why are you telling me now?"

"Because now I'm scared for all of us, and I don't know where else to turn. From what I've just learned, I think USNet is actually behind RTI and uses the information that it gathers to destroy our competitors, and maybe even to destroy people."

David leaned back. "USNet? What makes you think that?"

"Have you ever heard of the guy who approached me, Victor Mustafin?"

"No."

"Well, he and Akbar Kamali are best friends. They spend a lot of time together during the week, away from the office."

David shook his head. "Is that all?"

"No, of course not. When I learned about them, I started drilling down into the information that RTI gets and keeps. David, there is a ton of information about you, me, Paul Burke, and everyone at USNet, except that there's nothing about Kamali or Trevor Knox. Like they don't exist.

"And there is a lot of information about people and strategies at other telecom companies. But almost nothing about the plans and strategies at USNet. Nothing on our company. Just mostly personnel files with key words that trigger reviews by the RTI systems.

"Then I figured out, by looking over a long period, that all of the intercepts of emails and phone calls are only from USNet's servers—there are none from any of our competitors' systems."

David frowned.

"So I started looking into business that we've done. David, there are lots of intercepts about the Hong Kong office market, E-News, those adult movie companies, Ezon and every other company we've ever bought. And about every competitor that has suddenly gone out of business. And all of that information stops once USNet takes an action. It's like something focuses RTI on a company or a person or an issue, and then USNet does something. I think the entire RTI network is somehow run by Kamali and Mustafin, and maybe even Trevor Knox, to take advantage of everyone else."

"It's not possible."

Again Todd was silent. When he spoke again, he almost whispered, and he was clearly distraught. "What I stumbled on late last night were intercepts about Bill Porter."

David straightened. "Bill Porter?"

"There are a lot of intercepts about him, both calls and emails, starting right when we first had problems with him over Capital Tower. All the calls that you and Kristen made to him, the emails with the offers. Everything."

Todd was silent for a moment, looking at his boss.

"But they end after he set up a meeting with some guys to look at some development land in the foothills. There are calls as he is driving up there the day he disappeared, and then they all stop. None of the later articles, emails or calls about him were captured. It's as if someone turned off the search. Like they knew that he was never coming back.

"David, here's why I'm scared. The first contact I had from RTI were three tough guys in a van who threatened to tell USNet about the bribe if I didn't cooperate. I listened to Porter's archived calls—the other voice on several of them sounds exactly like the guy who threatened me that night.

"I think USNet did something to Porter, and he'll never come back. If USNet can do that over an office building, then what will they do to me if I ever slip up? I've got to get out, but I'm afraid to go to the police. And if anything happens to me, I wanted you to know that it might not be an accident. What can I do?"

David said nothing for a long time. "Is there anything in writing that can prove all of this?"

"No. We can't print anything at the center. I have some notes that I made as I tried to piece this together."

"So you took a bribe from Mike Campbell, and you believe that our company may be responsible for illegal taps, extortion, blackmail, and maybe worse, but you can't prove it."

Todd nodded. "That's right. I guess I could take you or the police to the control building. But I imagine that all of what RTI does could disappear with the flick of an electronic switch."

"You've definitely said a lot."

"I know. It's awful. But that's why I'm here. I hope that maybe on your trip you can help me think how to deal with all this. I don't want anything to happen to any of us, like I think happened to Porter. Just don't call me on my cell phone, or send me an email about it. Here, please take this number. It's a cell phone I bought that's not on USNet's system. I think it will be safe for you to call me on it, from a landline, if you have any questions."

"Todd, I don't know. You've obviously said a lot that I've got to digest. It doesn't seem possible."

"I know. But please, David, it's true. It's real. Help me."

"OK. Let me think about it while I'm gone. I'll call you on this number if I need to, and we'll try to figure it out as soon as I'm back. Just hold it together until then."

Todd stood. "I'll try. Thank you, David. Thank you. I'm sorry for what I did. I...It's all my fault." He turned and left, closing the door behind him.

David returned to his desk and ran through in his mind all that Todd had told him, trying to make sense of the possible connections, and the implications. Todd's fear was palpable. Should they all be afraid? And whom could he trust?

At 10:50 Elizabeth called from the street to let David know that his ride to the airport had arrived. She had volunteered that morning to take him, so he could leave his car in USNet's garage. She had enticed Rob to join them by offering to let him drive to the airport on his learner's permit.

When they pulled up to the passenger drop-off area, David hugged Rob again and told him good-bye. Rob actually hugged back. A moment later, out on the sidewalk, Elizabeth gave David a kiss. "You seem worried about something. Are you all right?"

"Yeah, sure." He smiled. "Just thinking about all that I have to do to in the next few days."

"We'll look for you on television."

"Maybe live, the morning of the Fourth. Or on the news later. I sure hope it goes well."

"It will. Have a safe trip. We love you."

"I love you. Everything with the kids will work out. I promise." She didn't answer—just nodded. He turned, picked up his bags, and walked into the terminal.

It was just after eleven when Kristen's taxi arrived outside Callie's townhouse. She paid the driver and walked up the stairs, her travel bag over her shoulder. She knocked and was surprised when Alex opened the door. He was apparently on the way out.

"Uh, hi," he said. "Come in."

Callie was sitting on the sofa but smiled and stood up when she saw Kristen.

Alex stepped aside, then moved toward the door again. "You really didn't have to come all the way out. I drove up last night. Now I've got to go down to the police station to file some papers about getting Jane's body out of Mexico, if they can't find a family member." He frowned, shrugged his shoulders, and left.

Kristen walked over and hugged Callie, who was in khaki shorts and a blue blouse, without make-up. It looked like her hair had not been washed for several days. They embraced for a few moments, and Kristen felt Callie start to cry.

Wiping away tears, Callie said, "Can I get you a Coke or something?"

"Don't worry. If I need anything, I know where to find it. How about you? Want to talk?"

Callie nodded and sat at one end of the sofa. Kristen took the other. Callie was barefoot and swung her feet up on the cushion. Kristen took off her flats and joined her younger friend.

"Thanks so much for coming. I'm not sure what to do."

"Have the police been here already?"

"Yeah. Early. They, like, woke me up. They looked all through Jane's room. They, like, took some of her stuff. They're going to try to find out where her family is."

"Did she ever tell you?"

"Not really. I think she was from Dallas—parents divorced."

"Did they question you?"

"Yeah. When Alex was still in Mexico, he told me just to say that I couldn't remember anything, like about the drugs."

"And that's what you said?"

"Yeah. They seemed OK. They said they'd call me if they needed anything else." She paused and looked at Kristen. "I...I'm so glad you came. Like Jane was just here and now she's—Kristen, it could so easily have been *me*."

She started to cry again. Kristen gently pushed Callie's feet to the floor, then slid over beside her. She took Callie's head and laid it between her breast and shoulder, and hugged her tightly.

David was one hour and two drinks into his Moscow flight that evening. *What have I done? I've driven Callie off. I've let Rob live in another world that he now prefers to real life, though maybe there's hope. I should have listened to Elizabeth about both kids. I'm a great father.*

I fired Kristen, the best real estate person I've ever worked with, to keep my job. I didn't train Todd well enough to turn down a bribe, and a major project is in trouble because of it. And if Todd is telling the truth about the intercepts and the violence, I've got to help him stop it, or else go to the police. If Todd will take money, could he be lying about all this to cover it up? It sounds unbelievable, but he's obviously scared. And if it's true, then the company I've worked so hard for all these years is somehow involved in all the messes I've made, with my family and with my staff. I'm a great father and an even better businessman...

"Let's go for a walk," Kristen said from a chair across from the sofa. Callie had cried and finally fallen asleep in her arms. Kristen let her sleep on the sofa for a couple of hours.

Callie rubbed her face. "People don't walk much in this heat."

"Well, then let's go for a drive. Go somewhere for dinner. Something."

"I'd rather just stay here."

Standing up and walking over to Callie, Kristen smiled and said. "No. We need to get out. Let's get cleaned up and I'll drive your car to somewhere outside the city for dinner. We can find some fish tacos. Come on, sleepy head. Let's go before the traffic is terrible."

Callie swung her feet to the floor. "The traffic is always terrible. But I guess you're right. OK, I'll get up." She stood.

"Good." Kristen looked at Callie. "Listen, I didn't ask you earlier. You said that you might be pregnant. Did you find out?"

Callie looked down. "I didn't want to take the test alone. I put it in my room."

"We'll do it in the morning then."

"I don't really want to know."

"Yes, you do."

"Uh, all right. We'll do it in the morning. But, Kristen, I—"

Kristen raised her hand. "Let's get ready, and we'll talk about it as we drive."

"OK." Callie nodded, gave a small smile, and turned to the bathroom.

When David's flight arrived in Moscow on Saturday morning, Peter Goncharov met him outside Customs, and they drove southeast into the city. The news from Peter was good. Sales were up, their new space was virtually finished, and the move-in had begun the day before. Their internal preparations for the Presidential reception were well on track: caterers, response lists, parking, press releases, display photos from their first days in Russia, decorations, security checks, corporate information, etc.

"Tanya Prescott called yesterday. If you feel up to it, after you check into your hotel and clean up, she wants to meet us at three to drive the route from the Kremlin to our new office and then review our joint security plans."

"Sure," David replied, his head a little fuzzy but the adrenaline flowing. "That's what I'm here for."

They talked more about business and how quickly Moscow's real estate landscape was changing and improving. When they arrived at the hotel, Peter had coffee in the lobby while David unpacked and changed.

David had just unzipped his large bag when his company cellphone rang. Expecting it to be Peter, he answered without looking at the readout.

"Hello."

"Cousin, it's Omid. How are you?" His voice was quiet but filled with excitement. Before David could answer, he continued. "Our plans have changed, and I didn't have time for anyone to call you from Europe. Goli and I are in Tabriz at her sister's house, and we're leaving in an hour for the border, which we'll cross tonight."

"Omid, that's great news, but…"

"So we'll need help with the visas in Istanbul in about a week. Will that be OK?"

"Uh, yes. I'm in Moscow right now, but I should be home in a few days, and Elizabeth can wire money."

"I think we're all right with money. But the visas."

"I believe I know exactly who to call now. But, Omid, please don't call me on this phone. I'll try calling you later today from a different phone."

"Yes, Cousin. Hopefully Goli can be in the U.S. in a month or two, and I will follow right after. Thank you."

"Soon. Yes, very soon. Great news!"

A few hours later David and Peter were standing outside the hotel, as arranged, when a large black SUV with darkened windows pulled up, the front passenger door opened, and Tanya jumped out. She ran around the front, smiling, shook David's hand, was introduced to Peter, and then ushered them into the vehicle. As soon as the doors closed, her driver, a large American, moved the SUV into the traffic.

Tanya turned in the front seat to face her guests. "David, good to see you. How was your trip? Good. Everything on our end is going well. President and

Mr. Harper arrived a little while ago and will spend the weekend with President Temirov and his wife at the Presidential dacha—pretty doggone secure. Then they'll all come into the city late Sunday afternoon for the conferences and state dinner on Monday, the Fourth, at the Kremlin." She pointed over her shoulder toward the Kremlin, as they made their way south, only a few blocks east of Red Square.

"We figure your reception will start at five on Monday afternoon, last 'til about six-thirty, and then they'll return to the Kremlin before heading out for the Fourth of July celebration at Kuskovo Park. Now that's going to be a security nightmare, but both of them are determined to do it."

David shook his head. "I'm glad I don't have to arrange all of that."

"You get used to it. By the way, our people tell me that your people have done a great job, which is why I've waited this late to see the place myself. OK, here's the bridge across the Moscow River just southeast of the Kremlin, at the foot of Red Square. I understand they'll come out of that gate, turn right, and head immediately across the bridge, then straight down Bolshaya Ordinka to the site." She nodded at her driver. "Let's do it."

David looked out the window at the Kremlin towers sparkling in the sunlight, and the ancient spires of St. Basil's Cathedral.

"Of course the presidential motorcade will have escorts, sirens, and blocked side streets, so they should make it pretty quickly," Tanya said. They arrived at the office complex in just three minutes. As they turned in, she saw several new two- and five-story office buildings, surrounded by surface parking. It was the site of an old factory, long since razed. Around them stood older, taller apartment buildings.

"Just like the briefing said it would be." She nodded as they drove up to the building in the back left corner. They got out, and she looked around. "How is there enough parking here for all of these offices?"

"The entire complex is built on top of three levels of underground parking," Peter explained. "Comes in handy in the winter."

"I'll bet. We'll have to seal it off. The tenants won't like that." She continued to look around, surveying the taller surrounding structures, and then they went inside, where they were met by the chief of USNet's Russian security team. He showed them the ground floor entrance and the stairs leading up to the large open area where the reception would be held in two days. A small raised stage was under construction along the back wall.

Tanya nodded. "Looks good. Everyone will need to be up in this room by five twenty-five, which is when we expect the motorcade to arrive. Mr. Knox and the two of you, David and Peter, will greet them at the front door and bring them up the stairs, then around the right side of this room to the stage. Mr. Knox will give an introduction from a podium that we'll provide tomorrow, and then both Presidents will speak with interpreters. Afterwards they'll do the ribbon cutting, and a slow walk out, meeting and greeting the guests—and that's it. Down the stairs, into the motorcade, and back to the Kremlin. That was a one way street coming south. The return is a one way street a block to the east. Yes?"

Peter replied. "Another straight shot back."

Tanya smiled. "Good." She looked around and nodded at David. "Good work. Looks like it'll be a piece of cake."

Early that evening Omid and Goli were having coffee at an outdoor café in Bazargan, in northwest Iran on the border with Turkey. Joining them was Goli's brother-in-law, Hamid, who had driven them from Tabriz. It was warm; Omid had the local newspaper folded on the table to signal, as he had been instructed, that everything was OK. Morad had organized the run across the border, and they were waiting to meet the man who would lead them, known as Jalil. An empty chair awaited him.

Goli was nervous, and Omid held her hand beneath the table.

"You know what they told me," she said, under her breath.

"All the more reason to be here tonight." He smiled, and squeezed her hand.

"What if they find us?"

"They won't. And how good it will be to be free, and together."

She gave him a small smile and nodded.

Hamid looked at his watch. "They should have been here by now," he said, and sipped his coffee. Clearly he was not pleased to be part of this plan.

"Thank you, Hamid, for helping us," Omid said for the fifth time since they left Tabriz. Hamid nodded and looked around.

A large man with a neatly trimmed beard wearing traditional Azerbaijani work clothes approached the table and sat down in the empty chair.

After he made the traditional greetings and ordered a coffee, Jalil said, "Adding you has been done quickly, and now there is a problem." He shrugged.

"What is it?" Omid asked.

The waiter brought a coffee, and Jalil added several packets of sugar.

He took a sip. "A client who has been set up for several months showed up tonight with his grandmother, his only living relative. We were not expecting her."

"And?"

"And we have only eight empty crates in the lorry, and we have paid bribes for eight people. We cannot take nine."

"One more person? How difficult can that be? Can't you just give them more money?"

Jalil shook his head and smiled. "I've been doing this for fifteen years. There are a lot of people involved. We cannot just pay cash at the border, my friend. Everything has to be done correctly, if we are going to maintain this business. Tonight, only eight can cross, and so I can take one of you, but not both. The other can follow, probably in two days."

"Then we should both stay," Goli whispered to Omid, her eyes large.

He thought for a moment. "You must go, Goli. I will come to you in one or two days. You will be fine." He turned to Jalil. "She will be fine, yes? You have people in Turkey who can look after her until I come?"

Jalil smiled again. "Yes, of course. This is not the first time. We have a home where she can stay until you come. She'll be fine."

"When do you leave?"

"Right now," Jalil said, and drained his cup.

"Then we should be going." Omid signaled to the waiter for their check.

Ten minutes later they were standing by an old Volvo station wagon. A man and a woman were in the back seat, but they turned away when the three new people approached with Jalil.

Goli clung to Omid. "I don't want to go alone. I want us to be together," she said, her mouth pressed to his ear.

"Yes, me, too. But it's too dangerous here. You will be safe. You have your cell phone. Call me, or even call Elizabeth if you are worried. I'll see you in two days."

"Omid, I love you." She hugged him tightly.

"And I love you. You are everything to me. That's why I want you to be safe."

They hugged tightly, and Jalil started the car.

Omid walked Goli to the passenger seat, squeezed her hand and closed the door.

"See you in two days," he said, and the car drove off.

Omid and Hamid walked to Hamid's car. As they started back to Tabriz, Omid's phone rang.

"Cousin," he said in a subdued voice. "It's good to hear you again."

Five minutes later Omid had explained the new situation to David, and David promised to begin the process with the State Department for asylum for both of them.

"I'll call you again tomorrow," David said. "Be safe, and we'll see you soon."

While David was heading to bed in Moscow, his daughter emerged from her bathroom in Los Angeles, where it was eleven hours earlier that Saturday morning. She was wearing a light summer robe. Kristen was on the sofa in shorts sipping coffee and reading a book. She looked up. Callie walked over to her and handed her the reader. "I'm pregnant."

Kristen took a deep breath and nodded. Touching the sofa next to her, she said. "Here. Sit down." Alex was still asleep in their bedroom.

She did, her look expressionless. "This is what Alex and I were talking about yesterday when you got here. I told him I might be pregnant. He said, like, not to worry, that he would arrange for the abortion. He said that he knows the best clinic in the area."

"Do you want an abortion?"

Callie looked down, then up at Kristen. "I guess so. I know that Alex doesn't want a baby—and I'm nineteen. What do you think?"

Kristen was slow to answer, choosing her words and looking intently at her friend. "Callie, this is the kind of situation when you want—or at least I want—to base a difficult decision on clear, firm principles, and not on the immediate circumstances. The principles I believe in hold that abortion is wrong, so those principles speak above the circumstances."

Callie frowned. She slowly shook her head.

Kristen touched her hand. "I'm sure those principles came from our Creator, but I appreciate that you probably don't know about them or believe in them."

"You mean God?"

Kristen smiled. "Yes."

Callie looked up. "Well, I sort of believe there's a God, I guess. But I don't connect God with giving answers to questions like this one. It seems like it's up to me."

Kristen nodded. "Yes. You're right that it's up to you. My point is that a value system helps to set the boundaries within which you choose, and describes the consequences of choosing right or choosing wrong."

"You think there are consequences to an abortion?"

Kristen nodded vigorously. "Yes. For the baby, for sure. He or she will be dead. And for you, and your family."

"You think this thing is alive, like, a baby?"

"Yes. Of course. What else is it?"

Callie thought for a moment. "Alex will want me to have the abortion today, or early next week. To get it over with."

"Today?"

"Yes, he said the sooner the better. He's going to call a doctor he knows."

Kristen sat up. "Callie, I know you don't agree with me that abortion is wrong. But if we talk about it some more, you may at least understand what I'm saying, both about that baby and about you. Or you may not. But if you have an abortion today, and tomorrow you change your mind, it'll be too late."

"You really think it's alive?"

Again Kristen nodded and said more gently, "Yes. *Your* baby." Suddenly Kristen felt a chill, and she looked around, then back at Callie. "We've got to go."

"What?"

"Callie, we've got to leave here. This apartment is all about Jane and drugs and your movies and maybe an abortion. We've got to go somewhere else, at least for a few days."

"What?"

"Trust me—please. Have I ever done anything to hurt you? Please pack an overnight bag, and we'll go check into a hotel. We can even go to one at the beach—wherever you like. Maybe up toward Malibu. My treat. I just want to get you away from Alex and from Jane's memories for a day or two. Come on, it won't hurt."

"I...I don't know. The police."

"They came and you answered their questions. It's the Fourth of July weekend. They're not going to call again. We'll come back on Monday or Tuesday. But for now, let's go."

"I guess I could use a break. But should I tell Alex? What about the abortion?"

"Tell him you'll be back, or leave him a note. There's plenty of time, if you want an abortion. Let's just go. I'll throw my things in my bag. You can talk to all of them again on Tuesday."

Callie smiled. "If you say so."

29

SUNDAY, JULY 3RD

David was piloting a jet fighter on a long, dark mission when the constant ringing in the cockpit suddenly demanded his attention, and he woke up. He looked around. A hotel room in Moscow. Light filtering around drawn curtains. A telephone ringing next to his bed. He reached for it, still groggy from the jet lag and the sleeping pill.

"Hel...Hello"

"David?"

"Yes...Elizabeth?"

"David! Thank God. I thought I had the wrong numbers to the hotel."

"What is it?"

"It's Rob. He's been in a car wreck!"

"What?"

"A car wreck. A bad one. The hospital just called me, and I've got to go down there. He has head injuries and a broken leg. Maybe a broken pelvis and internal injuries."

"What time is it there?" He sat up in bed, suddenly very awake.

"Eleven-fifteen. The wreck apparently happened about ten. David, he was in the car with some man I've never heard of, who is really badly hurt. Justin is hurt, too. Rob is full of so many drugs that they don't know whether they can safely operate."

"What man?"

She almost screamed. "I told you that I don't know!"

"All right, all right."

"You're not here. Rob's hurt at the hospital. How do you *expect* me to react when you ask me who Rob's been with when I thought he was at the baseball game? Obviously he's been lying."

"Elizabeth, I'm sorry—call Paul Burke. At the last minute he couldn't come, and he should be home. See if he can take you to the hospital."

"All right." She sounded a little calmer.

"It's Sunday morning here. Call me at the hotel or on my cell phone once you get to the hospital and find something out."

"David, you've got to come home."

"Elizabeth, I will if it's life threatening. Otherwise, I have to stay. Knox arrives in a few hours, and I have to brief him. They need me here."

"We need you at home."

"Elizabeth, please, go check on Rob and then call me. And use the cell phone. It's OK."

"All right. Good-bye."

David hung up and got out of bed. He walked over to the window and opened the curtain. The room was flooded with bright sunlight. He squinted and looked out at an almost deserted Moscow street on a beautiful Sunday morning. He rubbed his forehead. *What's next?*

An hour later Knox's corporate jet began its descent to Vnukovo Airport, on the southwest side of Moscow. Onboard were Knox, Akbar Kamali, and Victor Mustafin. Mustafin had made sure that they would be given landing privileges at Vnukovo, because it was not as busy as the main international airport and closer to USNet's new office south of the Kremlin. In just over twenty-four hours, its closer location would be critical.

The three men sat around the conference table in the middle of the aircraft and ate a continental breakfast put onboard the previous night in Halifax. Forward of the conference table were two plush seats and then Knox's computer console and mini-command center, on the right side, just aft of the cockpit. As they ate and talked they could monitor the computer screens displaying the same information that the RTI duty officer was seeing.

Knox took a sip of coffee and asked his two lieutenants, "Are all our assets in place?"

Kamali nodded. "While you slept we received a video call from North that the missile crew will be in place and confirmed operational this afternoon."

The Kazakh spoke. "I've arranged for our jet to be parked by itself at the far end of the taxiway, over by a stand of trees on the edge of the apron, where no one will bother us. We'll of course have an armed guard outside the plane at all times, plus a car and driver provided by our security people. We've made provision for electrical power, and I will be here until the mission is finished and we're on our way home tomorrow evening."

"Do we have all the codes?"

"Yes, we'll always be able to run the operation from here, if need be, plus keep up with all the rest of the RTI network."

"Well, Victor, I regret that you have to stay in the corporate jet, but it would not be good for you to be seen with us—particularly in these next days. And let's make sure that these are, in every way, 'normal' days. Sawyer is supposed to brief us later today, and I don't want him or anyone else to remember anything unusual about us. So, Akbar, we'll be *very* enthusiastic about meeting the Presidents."

"Oh, we will be," Kamali agreed. "We definitely will be. It'll be Happy Fourth of July— Moscow style. Lots of 'rockets red glare.'" The other two smiled as their aircraft turned to begin its approach.

Goli's sister was preparing breakfast for Hamid, Omid and her two children in suburban Tabriz when there was a knock at the door.

The adults looked at one another. "Who can that be at this hour?" Hamid asked.

He went to the living room and looked out the window. Three black cars were parked in the street. He turned to Omid and shook his head. Then he closed the door to the kitchen.

Hamid unbolted the front door and started to turn the knob when the door flew open, pushing him back. Six men, three in police uniforms and three in plainclothes, burst in.

"Where is he?" the tallest of the men in suits asked.

"Who?"

A policeman hit Hamid in the stomach, and he doubled over.

The kitchen door opened, and Omid walked in. "There is no need..."

"Bring them," the leader said, and turned to leave.

Goli's sister ran from the kitchen and put her arms around Hamid. "No. He did nothing." A young child started to cry.

"Bring them," the leader repeated, and one policeman separated Hamid from his wife while the other two led Omid between them.

A minute later all the men were gone. Goli's sister was sitting on the floor, looking through the open front door, her arms around her two children, who were crying next to her.

David and Peter were at the USNet headquarters in the upstairs room where the speeches would be given, watching the workers move the heavy Presidential podium into place on the temporary stage, when David's phone rang.

He looked around and moved to a window on the far side of the room where it would be relatively quiet. He sat on a box and put a hand over one ear. "Hello. Yes, it's me. How's Rob?"

"Not good. I'm at the hospital. His left leg is broken, his face is bruised, his pelvis is broken, and they're about to do an MRI to check for internal injuries. Not good." He could hear how upset she was—almost whispering.

I ought to be there. But how can I, with all I'm responsible for here?

Before he could speak, she continued. "But that's not the worst thing, David. The man who was driving Justin and Rob is some guy the police have been investigating for a year, Leonard Tanner. David, they think he's one of those guys who finds kids on the internet and lures them into crazy stuff. Justin's fine, though hung over, and he's been telling his parents, the police and me what they've been doing. David, if you can believe it, Rob and Justin have been going to parties with adults who are into all these same group internet games." Her voice grew in volume. "Drinking, sex, and drugs. This is our son, Rob. He's fifteen! David, the police say we're lucky that he and Justin are still alive!"

His stomach was turning. *I ought to go home.* "What else did the doctor say?"

"They're not sure. It's two am here, and they'll be doing the MRI and more tests."

"I'm sorry I'm not there, but I physically couldn't get there any sooner than Monday evening because I could never make a flight today."

"David, did you *hear* me about this Tanner person, and what they've been doing? All because of that *stupid* internet in his room!"

He closed his eyes. He spoke, trying to be calm. "Elizabeth, yes. There's a lot to do. A lot to talk about. But I can't do it from a cell phone in Moscow."

"Then come home."

"I am. I will. If I change my ticket and leave tomorrow evening after the reception, I can spend the night in France or Germany and then be home early Tuesday afternoon."

"Why can't you leave today?"

"Elizabeth, we've been through that. Is Paul still there?"

"Yes. He's been wonderful."

"Good. Then call me back when you know more about Rob."

"Is that all?"

"Yes, for now. If Rob has serious injuries, then we'll need to talk about treatment, and I'll come home as soon as I possibly can."

"Good-bye."

The phone abruptly went dead. He paused, sitting on the box, looking at the room full of people working on a project that may all be a lie. *Rob in the hospital because of an internet creep. Callie still doing internet porn movies. And all that Todd told me.*

It struck him. *I can't do this myself. It's completely beyond me.* Then another realization. *God, if you are there, as Kristen says, you know the answers. It's beyond what I can understand or fix. Please help me!* He felt light headed; he put his head down. *Please take over. Please help my family.*

Peter walked over. "Is everything all right?"

David looked up. "Uh—yes. Fine. Thanks." He thought for a moment. "Mr. Knox ought to be getting to the hotel soon. We should probably head back to meet him."

Kristen drove Callie in her car north out of Los Angeles. They drove and drove, talking some, and enjoying being out of the city. They finally stopped in one of the small villages that dot the California coast between Malibu and Santa Barbara and checked into an old-style motel with small white frame duplex cabins along the hillside. They shared a single room with two double beds and ate a late dinner in a nearby seafood café.

During the drive and dinner, Kristen had done most of the talking. She told Callie about her childhood in Texas, her early residential real estate career, more details about her affair with Richard Sullivan and its consequences, her move to work with Callie's father, and what she knew about her upcoming job with the pension fund. Callie listened and asked questions.

Now it was a little after eleven on Saturday night, and they were in their beds with the light on, reading magazines they'd bought on the road. Callie spoke. "Kristen, thank you so much for coming out here. I really enjoyed today."

"Me, too. That's a great car."

Callie smiled. "Yes. It's fun. Thank you for driving."

"No problem. Now let's get some sleep and maybe we'll drive some more tomorrow. Or just stay here. We'll see."

"Yes. Fine. Good night."

Kristen switched off the lamp. "Good night."

A few hours later David came down the elevator into the hotel lobby and greeted Trevor Knox.

Trevor smiled as they shook hands. "David, you of course know Akbar Kamali. I've asked him to help us on this project, for security."

David shook hands with his colleague, who smiled and said, "Thanks for that security report. Our team is looking at it. We should hear something after the Fourth."

"Uh, good," was all that David could think to say.

Soon the three of them, plus Peter Goncharov were seated in the hotel dining room for Sunday brunch. There was a huge spread of food arranged in a buffet along one wall in the large ornate room with high ceilings, parquet floors and plush red velvet trim on all the furniture.

"This looks wonderful," Knox said.

"Yes, a Moscow tradition. Or at least a new Moscow tradition," Peter said.

After they helped themselves at the buffet tables, Peter and David briefed the other two on every aspect of the preparations for the reception.

"So everyone must be inside our building and up on the second floor by five-twenty, when they'll cordon off the compound," David concluded. "Mr. Knox, you and Peter will greet the two Presidents at the entrance and escort them up. We think it will all go pretty smoothly."

"It sounds like you've thought of everything," Knox said, finishing his eggs. "I'm looking forward to seeing our new space."

"We're going there right after lunch," Peter said. "Now I have to check with the front desk about our Kremlin passes for later this afternoon. President Temirov himself is giving them to you, and they include access to ancient rooms that are usually not open to visitors."

Knox smiled. "I'm indeed honored. I'll thank him tomorrow at the reception."

Peter stood. "So, excuse me. I'll be back in a few minutes."

After he left, David took a sip of water and looked at Knox. He could feel his heart begin to accelerate and sweat on his forehead. He decided to go ahead. "Trevor, I need to talk to you about taking some time off."

Knox frowned. "Now? Here? Today?"

"I understand. But this can't wait, and I don't know when I'll see you alone again. Our son Rob has been in a bad wreck. Elizabeth is still at the hospital. It's connected to the internet. Actually to using our USNet internet games." He could see the frown deepen on Knox's face. Kamali's expression had not changed.

He looked at Knox. "There are two things. First, I need to get home as soon as I can after the reception. I wondered if I could fly with you to the U.S., or at least to Western Europe, when we finish tomorrow night. The second thing is that I think I need some time off. I mean, like a sabbatical, to be home with my family and try to straighten out whatever is causing this to happen."

Knox glanced quickly at Kamali, then back to Sawyer. "I'm sorry to hear about your son. But how long are you talking about?"

David took another sip of water. "At least a month. Maybe two. I'm not sure."

"Two months? David, believe me, *all* kids have problems and you've got a lot of important projects underway, like in L.A., where you are the key to our success. Two months? We need you now. So I wouldn't think about two months. You certainly can ride back with us tomorrow night, visit with your son until the end of the week, and then come back to work next Monday. That should be more than enough time. Won't that work?"

"Uh, maybe."

"And you don't want a sabbatical from your pay, do you?' Knox smiled.

David looked down at the water glass in his hand. "No."

"So it won't do your family any good for you to take off. The best thing you can do for them is keep your job and your income."

David could see Peter returning out of the corner of his eye. "All right. I'll take the end of this week off. And I'll tell Elizabeth that I'm flying home with you. Thank you."

Peter walked up. "The Kremlin tour is set for three. So would you like to see our new offices now, Mr. Knox?"

"Yes, fine." He put down his napkin and they stood up. "Excellent brunch."

As they walked through the hotel lobby on the way to Peter's car, David's cell phone rang again.

"Hello," he said. Turning to his colleagues, he said. "It's Elizabeth. Give me just a minute." They nodded.

"I'll get the car," said Peter.

David walked a few paces away toward the large glass windows at the front of the hotel. He turned there to face back into the lobby and saw Knox and Kamali looking at him and talking.

"How's Rob now?"

Her voice was heavy from exhaustion. "He's stable. They want to observe him for possible internal bleeding. We're in a room now, David. It's almost five in the morning. He's knocked out, and I'm going to try to sleep for a little while in a chair in his room. Paul just left to go home. He's been great. It's been a long night."

"Yes, I'm glad Rob's better, or at least stable. Listen, I'm with Trevor, and he offered to let me ride home with him in the corporate jet, so I might be home very late tomorrow night or Tuesday morning."

"Whatever." He could tell she was too tired to argue.

"All right. Well, call me again when there's news. And I'll call you when I know my schedule."

"Good. I'm so tired. We'll talk later."

"Get some sleep. I love you."

"I love you, too."

David surprised himself with the next thought. *Thank you, God.* He switched off the phone and walked over to Knox and Kamali.

"Is he better?" Trevor asked.

"Yes, Elizabeth said he's stable."

Knox smiled. "Good. See, I told you. All kids go through these things. Nothing to worry about. He'll be fine."

"I hope so."

They walked out of the hotel to Peter's car, then headed for the USNet office.

"We know about Morad. Who do you think told us about your trip to Turkey?"

"Morad would not speak to you."

Omid was seated at a metal table in a windowless room at the police headquarters in Tabriz. The three men in suits were around the table—the tall one directly across, a heavyset man to Omid's right, and a younger man to his left. All three smiled. "It may not have been voluntary," the leader added.

Omid stared at him.

"We know about your websites and about your friends. We know that your wife may be in Turkey, but we have friends there as well. In fact, we know just about everything about you and what you have been doing for the past two years. How you have been trying to overthrow the rightful government leaders whom Allah has chosen to confront and punish all infidels and crusaders with his justice."

"If you know all of that, then why are you interrogating me?"

"Who said that we are interrogating you?"

Again Omid stared.

"We like to give people like you a chance to tell us more, to put some positive weights on the scales of Allah's justice, before you suffer your fate."

"My fate?"

"Yes. We understand that you like democracy. So we've decided to vote. Everyone who believes that this traitorous scum should be punished today for his treason, raise your hand."

The three men smiled and raised their hands.

"Noted. I'm afraid that democracy didn't work for you this time."

Omid looked from one to the other. "Some day it will."

Elizabeth was alone in the hospital room with Rob, who was in bed with a leg cast and bandages on the side of his head. Two drip bags provided nutrients and a pain killer. Elizabeth was resting in a leather chair after the long night.

Rob opened his eyes. He saw his mother and then looked around. He tried to move, but the pain stopped him. "Ow," he exclaimed.

Elizabeth immediately stood and put a hand on his arm. "Hey. You had a tough night."

"What happened to me?"

"Rob, you were in a wreck. You and Justin, dear. Thank God you're both OK." She wiped a tear and held his hand while she recounted what she knew, including his injuries, and the process that the doctors expected to put him through. After she answered his questions, she asked, "Who is Leonard Tanner? He's in critical condition. Rob, who is he?"

Rob looked away. "A guy...we do StreetWar2100 together."

"And what else?"

Rob spoke slowly. "What do you mean?"

"The police say he's one of those guys who lures young people in off the internet, offers them drugs, then, once they're hooked, sells to more kids through them. What have you done with him?"

"Nothing."

"Rob, I'm your mother. What have you done with him?"

"Stuff."

"What?"

"Nothing much. Like some beer and a few pills. He's got whacko friends."

"In what way?"

"In *every* way!"

"Why did you do all that?"

"It was, like, fun."

"You could be dead."

"Looking at all of this I don't think I'm going to be doing much more any time soon."

"And the people. The police say you'll probably be asked to testify against them—at least Tanner—if he lives."

"He's my friend."

"No he's not. He's a creep."

"Mom, you don't know him."

"I know all I need to know."

Callie awoke a few minutes after eight on the California coast She slowly opened her eyes and saw the sun streaming through white curtains around a window on the back side of the cabin. She quietly looked around and was surprised to see Kristen kneeling beside the other bed, facing her, with her eyes closed. Her lips were moving. She was still wearing her long white nightdress. Callie couldn't make out what she was saying, but obviously Kristen was having an intense dialogue.

She watched Kristen for several minutes. Occasionally Kristen would open her eyes and read from a book that lay open on the bed in front of her. Then she would pray some more.

Finally Kristen finished, closed the book, and started to get up. Callie propped up on one elbow and smiled. "Good morning."

"Oh. Hey. Good morning. How are you?"

"Fine. I slept like a log. Say, what were you reading so early?"

Kristen smiled and picked up the book. "Oh, the Bible. I read from it every morning. This morning I was reading Ephesians. The last chapter. It's about spiritual warfare. I figured we needed it."

Callie sat up. "What's spiritual warfare?"

"It's the war that's going on for our souls. God versus Satan. Good against Evil. Satan wants us with him for eternity, and God wants us with him. How we make decisions here decides where we'll be forever. Spiritual warfare is about the angels and demons who are warring all around us, trying to get us to make decisions that will take us to heaven or hell. And the best way we can help fight the battle is through prayer."

"You really believe all that?"

"Yes, I really do. Because I've experienced both the pain of Satan's way and the joy of God's way in my own life, and I know which one I want."

Callie stood up in her oversized pink T-shirt and turned toward the bathroom, continuing as she walked. "That's pretty heavy for before I've even washed my face. But I have to admit that there is something different about you—something my friends don't have." She started to shut the bathroom door. "I thought it was just because you're older, but maybe it *is* God. Wait a minute."

When she returned, she propped up a pillow and returned to bed. Kristen had opened the blinds on the front window of the cabin and was sitting in a chair nearby. "Do you want to go back to that same café for breakfast?" she asked.

"Yes, I'm hungry. But I want to ask you about this God business. Do you *really* believe there's a God and that he really cares about us?"

Kristen pulled her knees up and put her arms around them. "Yes. I know so. Look what he did for me—for Richard, Janet, dozens of others I know. He changed me. I've told you what I was doing, how I was hurting so many people. I had to arrive at the end of myself before he could change me and use me."

"The end of yourself?"

"I had to have tried and failed in every way I could imagine to run from God—I was focused only on me. When all my own attempts at happiness failed, he could finally change me and work in me."

Callie frowned slightly. "Run from him?"

Kristen took a deep breath. "Yes. I think it's what you've been doing for a long time, too."

"Why do you say that?"

"Callie, would you *really* like me to watch one of your movies? Should we go to the internet and see one? How would you feel about that?"

Callie looked down. "I...I don't think I'd like that."

"How about if your parents watched? Or your brother?"

She shook her head.

Kristen spoke slowly. "Then imagine that a totally holy God exists and created you and wants the very best for you. That he wants a relationship with you. That he wants to lift you up and love you as his little girl. Unconditionally, no matter what you've done. Would you like him to come to your taping sessions?"

Callie shook her head harder. "No."

"Then that's why I think you've been running from him. You know, there's a small voice in all of us. It's been talking to you since the first time you ever thought about doing those movies, telling you 'No. It's not right'. That's him. You've been running from him. But he was there. He saw you making the movies. Taking the drugs. It broke his heart. But he let you."

"He saw that? All those times?"

Kristen nodded.

"How could he want me then?"

Kristen smiled. "That's the depth of his love. He was there when I messed up, too. But he loves us so much. Remember, he made each of us in his image. He knows us like no one else—every hair on our heads. He wants us back, no matter what we do."

Callie shook her head. "I can't believe that he'd want someone like me... I've screwed up so badly. Those movies. And I'm pregnant! My own father would kill me, much less God."

"You've been running from him, too. Haven't you?'

"Who?"

"Your father. You've been trying to get his attention, hurt him because you think he hurt you. Haven't you?"

Now Callie pulled her knees up and rested her chin on them. "I...I guess."

"Callie, listen to me. Both God and your father want you back. They love you totally."

She shook her head. "Not my father. Not if he knew I was pregnant. He just wants me to stop embarrassing him with these movies."

"Callie, you just told me that *you're* embarrassed by them. So why can't he be embarrassed, as well? I think you've hurt him pretty badly, actually."

She was silent. Finally she asked, "Who would want me now?"

"I do. Your parents do. God does. But it's up to you."

"I can't imagine. Hey—I'm pretty hungry. Can we, like, get some breakfast?"

Kristen smiled. "Sure. I'm hungry, too. Let's get dressed and we'll drive over to the café. It looks like it's going to be a beautiful day."

"Maybe we can walk on the beach."

At the same moment David was sitting down to dinner in an ornate private room in an elegant Moscow restaurant with Trevor Knox, Akbar Kamali, Peter Goncharev, Andrei Selivanov, Tanya Prescott, and four of Peter's lieutenants in USNet's Russian operation. Trevor had asked David to set up the dinner as a thank you to those who had helped in their recent growth, and they had invited Tanya as a thank you for her hard work on the next day's reception. David was seated at the foot of the table facing his boss.

After their drinks arrived, Knox said, "The new office looks great. In the Russian tradition, I'd like to propose a toast to all of you who have made it possible."

Everyone smiled, touched glasses, and drank.

"And I'd like to thank Ms. Prescott for joining us. Here's a toast to you and your team. May everything go smoothly tomorrow."

More smiles and tinkling of glasses. After raising her glass, Tanya said, "I think it will. We've planned for almost any problem, but we don't think there will be any."

As the toasts and the discussions continued, David found it difficult to participate. His mind was on his children, and Todd, not USNet's continued success in Moscow. He wrestled with what he should do to help Callie and Rob. And Todd. *Maybe tonight in my room I can write out steps for each situation. And maybe even pray about it. If God will listen to someone like me. Figure out what to do and who to call when I get home. What if Todd is right? What has USNet been doing?*

Several times during the meal he looked down the table to see Knox staring at him.

Inside Knox's corporate jet, parked at the far end of the tarmac at Vnukovo Airport, Victor Mustafin manned the control console while an armed guard stood outside on the ramp. The door to the aircraft was closed, and its systems were running on a nearby diesel generator. Mustafin was having an encrypted video conference with General Beleborodov and Simon North, sitting at their own consoles at NovySvet's eastern base. Mustafin could see and hear them; they only heard his slightly altered voice.

"We tracked the micro repeater all the way across the Atlantic," Beleborodov said. "until you switched it off over Helsinki."

Mustafin nodded and smiled. "Well done. And the missile launcher?"

"Its own repeater shows that it's in transit to the launch position." This time it was North. "Once it arrives, we expect a coded signal from the team leader declaring the missile to be operational."

"Good. Less than twenty-four hours."

Kristen and Callie came out of the café and got into the car to drive back to the motel. Callie pulled her cell phone out of her bag, switched it on, and scrolled through five missed calls. She looked over at Kristen, who was driving. "There are four from Alex, but one is from a number I don't recognize. I guess I'd better call it." Kristen nodded.

"Hello. Oh, hi, Mom. Where? The hospital? What? Oh, God. Rob? Listen, we're just pulling up to a place from where I can call you back and it won't be so noisy. Yes, I'll call you in just a minute." Kristen stopped in front of their cabin. "It's my brother Rob. He's been in a bad wreck. They're at the hospital."

"What next?"

"I don't know. I gotta call."

While Callie listened to her mother on the phone, Kristen changed into walking shorts and shoes. When she finished the call, Callie recounted the details to Kristen while she also changed. She included information on the driver, and Rob's uncertain prognosis.

"I'm so sorry," Kristen said, as they headed for the door.

"Those games he plays on the internet."

Locking the door to the cabin, Kristen said, "I bet your mother wishes your father were home right now. I wonder when he's due back?"

Fifteen minutes later they had parked in a public lot near a long stretch of open beach, moderately full for early on a Sunday afternoon, and were beginning their walk. As they strode out, Kristen asked, "In all the confusion of those people on Friday, I never asked you. Why was Jane in Mexico when she died? Was she on vacation?"

As they walked side by side, Callie said, "No, actually many of the newer movie uploaders are going to Mexico to spend a few days and get registered with some company or guild. Jane was there to get registered."

"Move to Mexico? Why would you do that?"

"The instructions on the website told us we had to. The younger actors and actresses. I'm not sure about all the details—something about new taxes or laws or something. Anyway, it's supposed to be a good deal for us. They're going to pay us more."

As Callie finished, Kristen abruptly stopped. "Wait a minute." Callie stopped and looked at her. "You mean the *younger* actors are being registered with a guild in Mexico. Like the ones under twenty-one?"

Callie put her hand over her eyes to shield the sun and nodded. "Yes. I guess so."

"And they're going to keep making these movies?"

"I don't know why else they'd do it."

"So Knox is *not* planning to comply with the new laws on adult movies, like he promised. All this time I thought you knew the new laws meant that you'd have to quit because you're only nineteen. And you've been expecting to be able to keep shooting. What a farce. I wonder if your dad knows. Or if President Harper knows. That man Knox is simply no good."

"What's the big deal?"

"The big deal is that tomorrow in Moscow President Harper is going to share a podium with Knox and the Russian president. She's going to promote Knox's business and joint trade, all because Knox said that he now supports these new laws. I was even asked to check on Knox's intentions through your dad, who told me to believe him. But obviously that's not the case."

"Kristen, I don't understand all that stuff. I just know my roommate is dead and I'm pregnant. And when you leave I don't know what I'm going to do."

Kristen took her hand. "We'll talk about that in a little while. With eleven hours difference, it's probably too late to call your dad in Moscow. And he probably couldn't do anything, anyway. But when we get back to the cabin, let's call your mom and get his hotel number over there. We can call him tonight."

"OK. If you think it's important."

"I do. Believe me, Callie, I do. Now let's get some exercise. It'll do the three of us good!"

Kristen need not have worried about calling her former boss at that hour. It was midnight in Moscow, but David was not asleep. He lay awake in bed, thinking about his family, Todd, USNet, Omid, and the upcoming events of the next day.

After dinner he had returned to his room and tried to write a plan for dealing with each child's problem, and about USNet. But past a few simple ideas, he drew a blank. *How do you make someone want to do the right thing?* His mind raced. *Seems like it would take a lot of time and discussion—talking about consequences. How to start when each child is in a crisis right now? And do Todd and I just go to the police with all that he has told me? That would be the end of my job. Or do I tell Trevor first and ask if he knows anything?*

He tried to stop thinking about his problems. But he couldn't relax. His mind kept going. *I ought to be home. But I need to be here.*

So he got up and checked his email. A high priority message came from an unknown address in Europe. There was a link and a one-word message. Omid.

David clicked on the link, and a video started. There was a brief title page written in Farsi, Arabic and English. The latter said Eynali Mountain and 3 July. Then several men were shown standing outdoors in a rocky area at the bottom of a tall cliff. It appeared to be late afternoon; they had their backs to the camera. They had on suits, and one of them, the tallest, was talking on a cell phone. He looked up and waved.

The camera followed his gaze up toward the top of the cliff, several hundred feet above. Suddenly two men came flying off, their arms and legs flailing. The camera followed them until they smashed into the rocks, twenty yards from the men in the suits.

The three men and the camera walked over to the two bodies. A hand reached down and rolled them over. David clearly recognized, despite the shattered face, the lifeless form of his cousin Omid. The video ended.

David stared at the blank screen for almost a minute; then he felt weak and nauseous. He barely made it to the bathroom before he was sick.

Early that Sunday evening Kristen and Callie were sitting around a wrought-iron table on the patio of their cabin, watching the low sun over the Pacific Ocean and eating Chinese take-out.

It had been an intense afternoon of discussion. Kristen had pointedly encouraged Callie to describe what she did in making movies and was glad that verbalizing the descriptions seemed genuinely to embarrass the younger woman. Then Kristen had described several key choices in her life, and how they had impacted her, for good or for ill. Later, and on into dinner, they'd spoken about their childhood experiences, and Kristen had mentioned several occasions when *her* father had let her down. And, inevitably, they had spoken about babies and abortion.

"I knew someone who was in a situation like yours a few years ago," Kristen said, as she put down a cardboard box of fried rice and sipped her drink. "Her name was Amy. She was the daughter of Richard Sullivan's next door neighbor. It's a long story, but she was in high school and decided to have the baby and let a wonderful couple who couldn't have children adopt him. Then she went back to school and is now doing well after college. And the couple with her baby are very happy. I'll be glad to get Amy's phone number for you."

Callie looked down at her half-eaten container of sweet and sour pork. "Uh, sure. Yes, I guess I'd like to talk to her."

They were both silent for a long time, watching the sun move into the ocean. Finally Callie looked at Kristen and spoke. "Kristen, you've been wonderful. I don't know where I'd be or what I'd be thinking if it weren't for you. I've enjoyed today and all the other days. You've helped me deal with Jane's death. You *have* been like a sister. But the reality is that if tomorrow weren't the Fourth, you'd be gone, and I'd be nineteen, pregnant, and trying to cope with a lot of bad stuff all by myself.

"I've done sex, drugs, booze—a lot. Now I'm knocked up. You say there's a baby alive in me that I shouldn't kill. Alex says it's a 'problem' that we need to take care of. I was embarrassed to tell you about the movies I made. But when I'm, like, doing them, there's a power, a rush—and a lot of money. And then there's my friend Jane... Now she's dead. It could so easily be me." She started shaking her head. "I just don't know what to do."

Kristen reached across and touched her hand. "Callie, first, I'm not leaving until we figure this out. I'll just be a day or two late for my job."

"Your new job? You can't do that."

"Sure I can. Second, and listen to me, people have to make these kinds of decisions *all the time*. You're not alone. Big, tough decisions. Right or wrong. And it's impossible to make those kinds of decisions in a vacuum. You need a framework, a value system that gives you points of reference for why what seems to be the easiest way is not necessarily the best way."

"Where do I get that—that framework?"

"From the one who gave it to me—God. From a relationship with him."

"How? How do I do that? How do I get what you have?"

"By asking him to forgive all that you've done, by believing that his son, Jesus, died as the once-and-for-all payment for all that you've ever done, and by asking his Holy Spirit to fill you and guide you every day."

"How do I prepare? When can I do it?"

Kristen smiled. "You don't have to prepare, other than be honest. When you want to change and start your life over, you can ask him."

"Can I ask now?"

"Yes. Of course."

"Then I want to ask."

"Let's kneel right here and pray. Just talk to God and tell him what you've done, and tell him that you want a real relationship with him."

"Out loud?"

"If you want. Or silently. He'll hear you either way."

Callie knelt with Kristen holding her hand, closed her eyes, and prayed.

Five minutes and a lifetime later, Callie wiped her eyes. Kristen reached over and hugged her.

"It's going to be OK," Kristen whispered, stroking her hair. "Now you're back in God's arms, and he'll never let you go."

They cried and prayed for a while longer. Kristen asked out loud for guidance and wisdom for Callie, her father, and their whole family. Finally Callie smiled, wiped her tears, and regained her chair. Kristen sat again, too, and looked at her friend.

"What do I do now?" Callie asked.

Kristen smiled. "You've taken care of the most important decision you'll ever make. Now you need people. With God's help we'll ask for advice from other believers who will help you—us—figure out all the stuff you're dealing with. And then there are family and friends who really care about you, who know you and love you and will give you good advice. That's how you'll make the right decisions."

"You mean *my* family?"

"Yes, Callie. I'm your friend." She smiled. "Almost your big sister. But your mom and dad—even your brother—have known you a lot longer than I have. You need to talk with them."

"They would never want me back after all I've done. Those movies will be around forever. How could anyone love a nineteen-year-old, doped up, pregnant porn actress?"

Kristen squeezed her hand. "Callie, that's *all* you were thirty minutes ago. You're still those things, but now you're also a child of God. He loves you. I love you. And your parents love you."

"No they don't. They couldn't. I've done too much bad stuff."

"Callie, they raised you. And that's their grandchild you're carrying."

Callie's eyes widened. "I, uh, hadn't thought of that."

"Look, I can tell you what I think God's word says about each of your problems. His is the only permanent value system that really counts. And how to start getting it inside you. But your family is also key. So many people have parents who don't care about them—like Jane. You're blessed with a mom and a dad who love you and want to help you. Don't turn them away."

"My mother doesn't even know. And do you really think my father will want me back? After all I've said to hurt him—and all I've done?"

"Yes, I do. Let's call him and ask him."

"Now?"

"Yes. It's, let's see—she looked at her watch—seven in the morning in Moscow. He's got a big day today. Let's call him and wish him a Happy Fourth of July."

"Now?" Callie was smiling and crying.

"Yes. And then we'll call and get some seats on a flight home in the morning. It will be good for you to be back with your family."

"OK. Whatever you say. Can we call Dad now?"

30

MONDAY, JULY 4TH

After the horrible video of Omid, David had finally fallen asleep about three that July 4th morning. He had asked for a wake-up call at eight, but his phone was ringing, and when he looked at the clock, it was only seven-fifteen.

Sleepy and angry that the hotel operator had called too early, he answered with a gruff "Yes?"

"David?"

"Yes?"

"It's Kristen. Good morning." She sounded up-beat and happy.

He sat up. "Kristen. I, uh...where are you? Why are you calling?"

"I've got someone here who wants to talk to you."

"What did you say?"

"Daddy?"

"Callie?"

"Oh, Daddy—I—I'm...fine. But I'm so sorry for all that I've done. I don't think you'll ever forgive me. Alex. The movies. Trying to hurt you." She cried for a moment. "I...I'm sorry..."

"Callie." He couldn't stop the tears forming in his own eyes. "I'm so glad you called." He was silent for several heartbeats. "I'm the one who has to ask for forgiveness, not you. I've been thinking about you all night. I was so lousy to you. Never enough time to share. Then I forced you to make an impossible choice. And gave you bad advice. Not much of a father. Can you ever forgive me?"

"Can I come home?"

"Come home? Of course!" He stood up by the bed.

"I can? You won't be mad about all that I've done?"

"No! I'll hug you and love you and be so glad to see you! When are you coming?"

"I'm not sure. Kristen and I were just talking. Maybe like tomorrow."

"Great! I can't wait."

"Daddy?"

"Yes?"

"I want you to know something and be thinking about it."

"OK."

"I don't know how else to say this, so I'll just tell you. I'm pregnant."

"Pregnant?" He sat down again. There was a moment of silence. "Are you all right otherwise?"

"Yes, I am. But, Dad. My friend Jane is dead."

"Jane? Oh, no. How?"

"Drugs."

"I'm very sorry. Are you sure that you're all right?"

"Yes, except for being pregnant. Alex wants me to have an abortion, but Kristen doesn't. She wants me to talk about it with you and mom."

"Kristen's right. Callie, we love you and want you home with us. The sooner the better. Even with Alex."

"Really?"

"Yes."

"Well, I'm not sure about him now."

"OK. But we'll talk about everything when you're home again."

"Oh, thank you, Daddy."

He paused, as Kristen's words over many months gave him new thoughts. "Callie, will you forgive me?"

There was another pause. "Yes, I will. If you'll forgive me, and we can start over."

"Yes. I do. I promise. In fact, I'll try to be home when you get there."

"From Moscow?"

"Yes."

"Extreme!"

He laughed, and she laughed in return. "Callie, let me speak to Kristen for a minute."

"Sure."

"David?"

"Kristen. What a wonderful surprise—and gift! Thank you."

"David, she means it. All of it. You can start over with her. God—and I mean God, not Allah or anyone else—has done an amazing thing in Callie these last two days. And Elizabeth told us about Rob and the wreck. Now Callie is coming home with her own joys and challenges. What do you feel about all this?"

David was silent, his eyes closed. Then he spoke. "Kristen, the common denominators in both of their lives are me and USNet. I've been thinking about it a lot."

"You're partly right. David, the *real* common denominator is the lack of any value system. You haven't had one, so your kids don't have one. Do you see that?"

"Yes, I do. And I'm tired of it. I want to change. I even prayed for God's help with Rob."

"He always listens. We've talked about it before, David. And we'll talk again when you get home. I think you'll see a change in Callie. Are you ready for that?"

"I'm at the end of my rope, Kristen. I give up. No more plans by David Sawyer on his own. But I'm afraid it's too late."

"Never. Think about me. Anyway, USNet has been pushing all of that stuff at everyone in our country. Callie tells me that she and Jane—the younger ones—were going to Mexico to register for the movie business. Did you know that?"

He paused. "I'm sorry to say that I did."

"David!" There was real despair in her voice. "You knew and said nothing?"

He spoke more quietly. "I just found out."

"David, they're using Mexico just to get around the laws that Knox promised to support. How can you work for a company that poisons our country, threatens your own children, and then lies to you, me, the President and the whole nation?"

You don't know the half of it.

He felt a chill and shook involuntarily. "I just...I don't know. But now that Callie is coming home and wants to start over, it's like nothing else matters except getting right with Elizabeth and our children. And I guess with God, if you can help me understand what that means." He stood up again.

"Yes."

"Kristen, I'm going to quit. Maybe I'll do it here, away from the office. I think it'll be easier, and I need to get home."

"You mean, today? In Moscow? And come home?"

"Yes. Today. Now. If Knox is going to lie about everything, I want out of his company."

"Great!" He could hear her smile. "And we can talk again about working together. I'm glad we called!"

He laughed. "Glad? I'm ecstatic that you called. I feel like a new man." Then he paused and turned serious. "But there is also some terrible news. I didn't have a chance to tell you when you put Callie on, but the police in Iran just killed my cousin Omid. They—somehow—sent me a link to watch a video of his execution."

"Oh David, I'm so sorry."

"Besides everything else, I've got to find out if his wife Goli is still alive, and help her."

"Yes. I'll pray for her, their family, and you, 'til you're home safely—and beyond. Here's Callie."

"Dad, are you coming home today?"

"I'm not sure, dear. It's still early here, and maybe I can get a flight. I'll try. But I'll definitely be home in a few days. Listen, why don't you call Mom and tell her that we're both coming home? She'll be very happy. I love you. And thank you. Take care of that baby."

"What? Oh, yes. I will. And I love you, too. Come home soon."

David hung up and almost laughed. He went into the bathroom and washed his face. *I'd better think through exactly how and when to tell Trevor. Let's see if I can get a flight.*

He returned and found the phone book, looked under Airlines, and called, not expecting anyone to be there so early in the morning, but was pleasantly surprised.

The lady on the other end was helpful but told him, "I'm sorry Mr. Sawyer. For today to New York there are no business class seats remaining, only coach."

"I'll sit in someone's lap. I don't care where I sit; just put me on the plane. And thanks!"

"Fine. And your connection is set. Please be at Sheremetevo Airport by one to adjust your ticket and check in."

"Great. And thank you. You've already made my day, and it's early!"

So I'll have to tell Knox this morning and then head to the airport. We're supposed to have breakfast with Peter at 8:30. I'll tell him right after that. Gotta pack! But let me try this first... God, I think you're there, and I'm going to try to know you more, so let me start by thanking you now for Callie and for Rob's safety. I want to change, too, and I'll try to do a better job of this from now on. I'm going to need some guidance and help this morning.

Victor Mustafin remained on duty in the corporate jet throughout the short summer night, napping in one of the passenger seats just behind the command console area.

A little after eight, as planned, he received a video call from Simon North. He moved over to the swivel chair in front of the console. "Good morning, Simon."

"Good morning. This is the day we've been waiting for. I'm not sure where you're from, but I guess as a Brit I should wish you a Happy Fourth of July."

"Thanks. This one really will be *our* independence day."

"Well said. We've received word from our team that the missile is fully operational. They're awaiting word from us to prepare for launch."

David's stomach was churning as he came down the lift and walked into the dining room. Knox, Kamali and Goncharov were already seated and having orange juice. Like David, they were dressed in business suits.

David greeted them, sat down, and in a few minutes they were sampling the large buffet. Back at their table the conversation turned to the unusual events of the day ahead of them.

As the waiter poured more coffee, Knox said, "David and Peter, I've got copies here for you of the talk I plan to give at the reception. I'd like you to review it and give me your comments."

Knox handed each of them a page of notes, and David glanced at the paragraphs. He quickly scanned the parts about acting responsibly to restrict adult entertainment to adults and about the great future for family entertainment on the internet. He felt his anger rising and suddenly hoped that he wasn't turning red.

"Thank you," Peter said. "If I have any suggestions I'll make them on the paper and leave it at the front desk. What time is your luncheon at the embassy?"

"Noon," Knox replied. "But we have to be there thirty minutes early."

"The same at our headquarters this afternoon."

They continued their conversation through breakfast, and forty minutes later, as they were standing to leave, David smiled and said, "Trevor, can I see you for a few minutes?"

"Why, of course. But now?"

"Yes, if I could. Up in your room."

Knox frowned slightly but nodded. "Fine." He looked to Kamali. "Can Akbar join us?"

"I guess so."

"Good."

After planning with Peter to meet again at four for the drive to the new offices, the three men rode the elevator up to Knox's floor in silence.

Knox had a suite on the top floor. They entered the living room, which had two sofas, two desks, a television inside an armoire, and several chairs. Knox's laptop was open on one of the desks, and there were several papers next to it. "Have a seat," Knox said, indicating the sofa with two chairs in front of it.

Sawyer looked at the arrangement and took a chair, leaving the other chair for Knox and the sofa for Kamali.

When they were seated, Knox took out his gold pen and began rotating it on the arm of the chair. "What's up, David? Is this about a sabbatical again?"

David felt as if his heart were not beating. *I've got to do this. Please give me strength.* He looked directly at the older man. "No. Actually, it's more than that. I'm quitting, effective immediately."

Knox's eyes dimmed slightly and the pen stopped, but his face remained expressionless. "Quitting?"

David nodded. "Yes. I have to do something else. My family needs me, and frankly I'm not crazy about a lot of what we're doing."

"What do you mean?"

"Communications is one thing. That's what we used to do. Now we're into the internet, gambling, games, even pornography. I guess I'm not proud of what we do any more."

"But we've been together while all of that growth happened, and you've been happy to cash our checks," Knox said, with an edge to his voice. The pen took up its flight again.

David looked down for a minute. *Come on! You've seen him do this before. Don't back down!* "Yes. And that's why I'm quitting. I can't keep taking money, given what we do."

Mustafin shifted in his seat, and Knox smiled slightly. "David, I think you need the money right now, don't you?"

"Yes, I do."

"Then we'll raise your base by ten percent, effective immediately"

David paused. "Thank you, Trevor, but the money is only part of it."

"What do you propose to do?"

"I'm not sure. Real estate is all I know. But I can't stay at USNet."

Knox and Kamali exchanged glances. "David, we've been together almost since the beginning."

"I know. I appreciate that. I just want to get on with another life, closer to my family."

"Is there something else that you're not telling us?"

David looked at both men for a moment, trying to figure out what they might know through the RTI that Todd had told him about. "Well, I just watched a video, sent to me on a link, of the secret police in Iran—he nodded toward Kamali—killing my cousin, because he was pushing back against their fascist mullahs. So now I've also got to try to find his wife, if she's alive. As you can see, I have a lot to do with several family members, and I now know that nothing I'm doing at USNet is that important any more."

Knox shook his head. "I can't believe what happened to your cousin. I'm so sorry."

David lowered his eyes and nodded several times.

Kamali moved forward on the sofa and said, "I am, too. But David, I really think you should reconsider such a move very carefully. Are you aware that a senior member of your department has been taking bribes from a developer, which has cost USNet a lot of money?"

David frowned. "What are you talking about?"

"Todd Phelps. We've just learned that he accepted a quarter of a million dollars to put USNet's office in that new space in Minneapolis. Now he's negotiating on Kansas City, and there will be another big payment for him from the developer when that deal is done."

"How was I supposed to know?"

"How could you *not* know? Or maybe participate? And even if you didn't, what sort of a manager does that make you? How do you think all of that will look in the newspaper and on USNet news programs when you try to start something new? We think you should stay at USNet, forget these issues, and one day retire as a wealthy man."

Son of a... His heart started to work overtime. David thought for a moment and then shook his head. "I'll just have to take the hit and do the best I can."

Knox frowned. "You must be a masochist, to trade a great job for personal ruin."

"I guess so."

Kamali said, "Well, there's one more thing that you might want to consider before you decide to turn us down. We have traces on your movements, of course, from the GPS repeater in your ID card. We know that back in April you visited the apartment of a young woman, Samantha, who is now a rising star in the upload adult movie market. Do you think your wife would like to know what you were doing there?"

Kamali and Knox watched as David turned red. He stood up.

"Actually, she already does. That's our *daughter's* apartment I visited."

Knox's eyes squinted slightly, and he grasped the pen with both hands. "Your daughter?"

Still standing over them, his fists clenched, David said, "Yes. 'Samantha' is our daughter Callie...And it's been eating me alive that our nineteen year old does the grossest things and USNet makes money. And while I'm at it, our son Rob is so consumed by our online games that he's been doing God knows what with adults who have stalked him in our chat rooms. That's why he was in a wreck." He took a deep breath. "And, actually, Todd Phelps came to me right before I left and told me about something called RTI. I didn't really believe him at first. It's still hard to believe, and I'd rather just forget about it. But that high tech threat about me visiting our daughter tends to confirm what Todd told me, and it means that I've got to get out! I won't tell anyone about any of this—I just want out."

Knox stared at David for a few moments, as if considering his words, then looked over at Kamali and back to David.

"It sounds like Todd Phelps told you some stories that are made up, to cover his own issues. Or one of you terribly misunderstood the other. Who else did he tell?"

"I don't know. He was looking for my help when I get back from Moscow. But now I don't want to deal with it. He and I just want out. Please just let us go, and we'll both try to do the best for our families."

Knox returned the pen to his pocket. When he spoke, his voice was calm and resolved. "All right, David. We had no idea. I'm genuinely sorry about your cousin, and of course your son and daughter. Perhaps we can help you find something new."

"I..." *I better not mention Kristen.* He unclenched his hands. "OK, thanks. But first I've got to help our children. I just found out this morning that Callie is pregnant and her roommate is dead. Didn't you say our adult movies have no victims, no negative consequences?"

Knox's face did not change. "Presumably your daughter and her roommate made choices."

"Right. And Jane made her choice while in Mexico. Have you told President Harper about moving the younger actresses to Mexico to get around the new laws you've promised to support?"

Knox paused. "Clearly you're upset, David. You've made your choice. We wish you wouldn't leave USNet. But if you've made up your mind, we hope that it all works out. We'll clear up whatever the misunderstanding is with Todd Phelps, and we won't mention it to anyone. Don't worry about it. We sincerely wish you the best with your family. In fact, we'll give you six months severance next week, so that there are no hard feelings."

David took a step toward the door and nodded. "Thank you."

"Yes. Are you planning to leave today, before the reception?"

"Yes. I changed my ticket to the afternoon flight. I have to leave for the airport in just a little while."

"Well, look. Akbar has to go to the airport in a few minutes. Why don't you ride out with him? It'll save you a lot of time and hassle." He looked at Kamali. "You could give David a ride, couldn't you?"

"Yeah. Sure. Are your bags packed?"

"Yes."

"Then check out and I'll meet you with our driver by the side door in ten minutes. It's the least I can do to help you and your daughter."

"OK. Thank you. Believe me, no one will ever know about RTI. I'll forget all about it."

Knox smiled. "We trust you, David. Have a good flight, and take care of your family."

As he turned and walked to the door, David said, "It will be a change, but I'm going to try."

Ten minutes later David walked out the side door of the hotel with his large travel bag and briefcase. A Russian driver appeared from a black Mercedes double-parked in the street. "Mr. Sawyer?" he asked. When David nodded, he said, "Mr. Kamali is waiting for you inside the car. Please let me have your bags, and we'll leave for the airport."

"Yes, thank you," David said, handing him the bags and walking around to the back right passenger door.

When he opened it, Kamali smiled from the other side of the backseat and motioned to him. "Please, get in."

"Thanks. I really appreciate this."

"We're glad to help."

The driver got in and they pulled away.

At that moment, precisely 10:00 a.m., 800 kilometers to the southeast, one of the Russian launch team members pushed a button on his hand-held radio. From the small, secluded valley in which their transport had stopped earlier that morning, a short burst traveled up to an orbiting satellite and back to earth a moment later.

The signal was read by Simon North at NovySvet and automatically relayed to Victor Mustafin at the command console in the USNet corporate jet. It was their preplanned hourly check confirming that the missile was fully armed and operational.

Mustafin smiled and was about to get up from the console to stretch. But then he received an urgent encrypted email from Trevor Knox.

The car with David and Akbar drove along the south side of the Kremlin, between its high red brick wall and the Moscow River. The two men didn't say much, and David found it a little uncomfortable. Kamali spoke in some language with their driver, who occasionally looked at David in the rearview mirror. *I probably shouldn't have come with Akbar. But I guess I need to keep some sort of decent relationship with him, given what I heard about RTI—assuming that Todd was telling the truth. I just want to disappear from all of this and get back to my family.*

David knew central Moscow reasonably well from his days of searching for office space with Andrei. He expected them to circle around the Kremlin and head northwest up Tverskaya Street toward Sheremetevo Airport. Instead, they went across the bridge and out Bolshaya Yakimaka to the southwest.

David turned to Akbar. "Why are we going this way to the airport?"

"From here it's actually quicker to go out to the Ring Road on Leninsky Prospekt and then around to the north on the Ring."

David knew that the Ring Road was a fast expressway. They drove southwest out of the city center on the broad avenue, past block after block of Soviet area mid- and high-rise apartments, occasionally broken by a park or a cluster of new retail buildings. Twenty minutes later they drove directly under the Ring Road and kept going. David twisted to the right as they went under the bridge. "Hey, wasn't that the Ring Road?" he asked as he turned back to Akbar.

"Yes, it was." Kamali reached inside his coat and pulled out a black automatic pistol, which he leveled at David's chest.

David looked from the barrel of the gun to Akbar's smile. "What are you doing?"

"We're driving out to dispose of USNet's former real estate group leader."

"What?"

"You've elected to leave us. And you even despise us because of stupid choices your children have made. Unfortunately, thanks to Todd Phelps, you know too much to remain alive. So we're going to have to kill you. And Todd."

"Kill me?"

"Yes." He said it in an offhand way. "It's bad for you, and a great waste for USNet. The fact that we missed your daughter's connection is particularly troubling to us. Mr. Knox and I are initiating a more thorough background search on the families of all our people."

"Wait a minute." David turned slightly. "Does Knox know you're doing this?"

"He ordered it."

David's heart began to race, and he felt light-headed. "So you're just going to take me out into the country and kill me?"

Kamali reached into a coat pocket and, still pointing the pistol at Sawyer, screwed on a silencer. He smiled again. "No. That's not the plan, unless you do something stupid. Actually we *are* on the way to the airport. It's just that our corporate jet is at Vnukovo, not Sheremetevo. We want you to see the Presidential reception that you've worked so hard for and the special events that will follow it. Then, while the rest of us are on the way home, we'll let some of our local people take care of you. We *will* tell them to make it quick. No torture. Your body will be found tomorrow, or maybe the next day. It will appear to have been another chapter in the long-running media hype of how bad the Russian mafia has become."

David felt his stomach filling with acid. Kamali continued. "But I imagine that so much will be going on in Moscow after today's events that few people will notice the death of one American businessman. And if they do," he said and smiled, "maybe the extra bad news will help keep out more Western competition."

"Akbar, people don't kill people over business."

"Our RTI intelligence system is more than business! Knox had to eliminate his own brother twenty years ago. And we killed that Porter fellow a couple of months ago because you told Knox he would cost us fifty million dollars. So why wouldn't we kill you? You know much more than either of them ever knew."

"You killed Bill Porter?"

"Of course. What did you think? Now USNet has that building under contract. I'd say it worked out well."

"You killed Porter," he repeated, almost to himself.

In a few minutes they entered the Vnukovo Airport area. Before reaching the terminal they turned to the right down an unmarked road and drove up to a gate where a guard stopped them. The driver partially rolled down his window, leaving up the tinted rear windows, and Kamali held the pistol pushed into David's side while the driver showed a special pass to gain entrance to the corporate aviation ramp. Once inside the gate they drove past several hangars and about a dozen corporate jets, most in Moscow for the afternoon's events. They continued toward a single large jet parked by itself at the end of the ramp. Next to it was a stand of trees that created a wide buffer inside the perimeter security fence.

As they approached the jet David saw a single armed guard standing by the closed door at the back of the fuselage on its left side. Before they reached the plane, the door opened and a portable staircase automatically deployed. As they parked next to the stairs, David could see another man, dressed in a blue jeans and a Western shirt, starting down. When he reached the ground he pulled a pistol, also carrying a silencer, from inside his coat and opened David's door.

"Get out," he said and stepped back slightly.

As David turned to exit, he heard Kamali open his own door, and he knew that he had two guns trained on him. He stood up and looked at the new man, who was expressionless. Kamali came around the car, and said, "David, meet Victor Mustafin. He's going to take very good care of you."

"I got an email from Knox," Mustafin said. Turning to David, he said, "So stupid!"

Kamali led the way. "I'll go in first, and then you follow our guest up the stairs."

Still light-headed, David climbed the stairs and ducked to enter the jet. Aft of the door was a single row of seats, one on each side of the fuselage, as well as a galley and a head. Forward, to the left, were more seats, all plush leather, one on each side. About two-thirds of the way forward the aisle shifted to the left, and there was a conference table on the right, with four seats around it. Then there were two more seats and, finally, the command console with its own chair, work station and computer monitors. Kamali was standing up by the console and waved David forward with his pistol. Behind him he heard Mustafin retract the stairs and close the door. It was eerily quiet inside; the only sound was that of the air conditioning running in the background.

"Here. Take off your coat, then sit down." He motioned to the single seat to David's right, facing forward, between the conference table group and the command console. Kamali nodded to Mustafin.

David slowly removed his coat and sat in the single seat. While Kamali held his pistol near David's face, Mustafin took out a pair of handcuffs. "Give me your cell phone, David." He put the phone in his pants pocket and then locked one cuff around David's left wrist and the other through an opening in the metal frame of the left armrest. He put the key in his other pocket, pulled forcefully on the cuffs, and said to Kamali, "He won't be going anywhere."

Kamali lowered his gun. "David, you're a fool. You had it made. Soon you'll be dead. I hope you have lots of insurance for those kids you suddenly care so much about."

David felt a wave of nausea overtake him. He was weak and lay back in the seat.

Kamali returned his gun inside his coat and smiled, stepping aside to let Mustafin move forward to sit in the chair at the command console. "We called the airline and cancelled his reservation. We even told the lady that some pressing business meetings had come up. Hopefully she'll remember that.

"Victor, it's all yours now for the last act. I'll join Knox after his lunch with the other business leaders and President Harper. We'll go over to the office early. The missile team is reporting in by satellite every hour. North and Beleborodov are ready to monitor the flight for the first thirty minutes, when control passes to you, here. I'll call you when the Presidents leave the reception, in case it's not on the live news. Then Knox and I will drive back here as quickly as we can, and we'll depart—after leaving our former colleague here with your friends. Except for Sawyer's stupid move, everything seems to be going as planned."

Mustafin nodded. "Yes. But he's just a small bump. Do you have the GPS repeater?"

Kamali touched his coat pocket. "Yes. All set."

"Then have a good reception. Say hello to both Presidents for me."

Kamali moved down the aisle, pulled the lever that opened the door and departed the plane. Mustafin followed him and closed the door while Kamali sped off in the same car that had brought them out.

It was late in California, but Kristen and Callie spent over an hour on the phone with Elizabeth, who was still in Rob's hospital room. In between asking about Rob's latest tests, Callie told her mother everything, from the videos with Alex to her call that evening with her father. Kristen passed on to Elizabeth the terrible news from David about Omid, and Elizabeth asked them both many questions. There were tears and smiles on the call, and Kristen finished by telling Elizabeth that they hoped to be home the next afternoon.

While Callie got ready for bed, Kristen called the airline to book two seats out of LAX in the morning.

As Kamali drove off to meet Knox, Mustafin walked past David, who had not moved, and sat at the console. He depressed some buttons, and USNet's live news came up on one of the smaller monitors to the left of the console.

Mustafin swiveled around so that he was facing David. "Can you see that monitor? European version of our news. Looks like they're outside the lunch meeting, which will soon start at the U.S. Embassy. You'll want to watch the news closely later today." He smiled.

David's nausea had subsided, and he'd tried to follow what Kamali and Mustafin had been talking about, but he wasn't sure. He looked at Mustafin, about six feet in front of him. "Missile? What missile were you and Kamali talking about?"

Mustafin smiled. "Good, David. I wasn't sure you were listening. You look a little ill. It's the missile we're going to use to take out both Presidents. You see, that move to Mexico for your daughter probably won't have to take place after all, and the news of your death in Moscow will be small potatoes because this afternoon, after the reception, President Harper will cease to exist. For someone in our businesses, that's great news, don't you think?"

"Are you serious?"

"Absolutely! Why do you think we wanted to get Harper over here, and to our reception?"

"But...she's so well guarded."

"Yes, she is. But not from an enemy you can't see until it's too late. A cruise missile in its final homing stage. Pretty ingenious, don't you think? And, most importantly, we'll rid the world of two crusaders, two enemies of Allah!"

"What are you talking about?"

"What Mr. Knox, Akbar and I do with RTI. Making money is only a small part. It's true that we don't influence outcomes, *unless* they advance Allah's kingdom on earth. Then we are glad to." Mustafin smiled.

"I don't understand."

"Since no one else will ever talk with you and you have a front row seat, I'll tell you. We share our RTI intelligence, when appropriate, with patriots, mullahs and jihadists around the world. With this capability, the West and Christendom will fall, destroyed from within and without. What a glorious moment it will be when the first European government votes to install Sharia Law!"

"You share RTI with Islamic terrorists?"

"Not terrorists, David. Allah's holy warriors."

"Where?"

"Wherever it can be useful, and we can mask the actual source. London, Detroit, Iran, Somalia, Yemen...anywhere, really."

"Iran? Have you been sharing my phone calls to my cousin Omid with the mullahs?"

"Yes, but probably not for too long. Ever since you told Akbar about helping your cousin. Since then we've been using his calls to follow and gain information on his whole group. Thank you for the tip."

"You killed him."

Mustafin shrugged. "A traitor to Iran, Islam and Allah. And, again, thanks for your help."

When David didn't answer, Mustafin continued. "And, by the way, this will not be the only missile today. A couple of hours after the Presidents and their advisors are killed, we have two martyrs, one on each coast, who will bring down two commercial airline flights, also using missiles. At JFK in New York, and in Los Angeles. Lots of fireworks for the Fourth, don't you think? The coverage should be quite good, but I'm afraid that by then we'll be on the way, and you'll be in the hands of our friends. We'll probably have to divert to Canada, but I guess our discomfort will be less than yours."

He smiled and swiveled back to face the console and brought up the main menu, then punched in some numbers and brought up a map of Europe, which he slowly focused until it showed only Moscow inside the Ring Road. With the push of another button, the box that tracked their USNet ID card repeaters appeared in the top right corner of the screen. It had six blank boxes, and Mustafin scrolled in 654321. As David watched from his seat behind Mustafin, a small white blip appeared in the lower left hand corner, moving northeast.

"Kamali is inside the Ring Road, headed toward the center. See? The repeater he's carrying is working perfectly. We decided to use a missile countdown for its code."

He swiveled back to face David. "And now you know that we have to kill you. You've seen too much in the last hour to let you live. You should have left well enough alone." Then he turned back and continued to increase the resolution on the map read-out.

David's initial weakness and nausea were wearing off, and he no longer felt so light-headed. He looked around. *I'm cuffed to a chair with madmen bent on killing our President, and me.*

I'll never see my family again. Never hold Elizabeth. All the things I wanted to do. To make a difference. Now I won't. I wish I could talk to the kids. I wonder what it will be like to die. Will there be a 'boom'? Pain? Where will my soul go? I wish I'd had more time with Kristen so she could explain that. I think I should try to pray.

God, I'm trying to believe in your power because of what I've seen in Kristen's life—and now in Callie's. You must be real, as Kristen says you are. Thank you for Callie forgiving me...and for her willingness to come home. And for Rob. Please, God, I don't want to die like this. I want to know more about you and your son, as Kristen explained to me. I don't know exactly what to say—but I want you in my life—to save my soul. Because of what you've done, I do believe in you. Please forgive me for all the things I've done. To Elizabeth, our children, others. Please change me. Save our President. And those people on the airplanes. Save our family. Save Todd.

Several hours went by. Over Mustafin's shoulder, David watched USNet's European edition, which included occasional live coverage of the historic Moscow Presidential visit. And every hour on the hour there was a short message on the main screen about the operational readiness of the missile.

At one point David convinced Mustafin that he had to go to the bathroom. The Kazakh blanked the monitors, called in the armed guard from outside and stationed him at the back of the plane. Then he handed David the handcuff key and told him to unlock his wrist, all the while holding the gun at his chest. David then walked to the head, both guns on him, and was allowed to relieve himself without privacy. As soon as he was reseated, Mustafin locked the cuff around his now chafed wrist, repocketed the key, and stationed the guard outside again.

After the four o'clock readiness check, Mustafin made a video call to what appeared to be two men in a command center. They talked about the weather, which was clear over Moscow, and the missile team, which David eventually decided were Russians.

While they talked, David again looked around. *I have to get free! I can't just let them kill the Presidents, so many others, and me without trying to do something. But I'm a real estate guy, not a commando. What do I know about escape and fighting? God, please help me. If I die, I want it to count for something—to save others. Are they going to blow up the reception?* But nothing, no plan, formed in his mind, as he pulled again on the handcuff that fixed him to his chair, and the time wound down.

At USNet's new Russian headquarters, preparations were in their final stages for the upcoming visit. Peter Goncharov stood in the middle of the upstairs meeting room, surveying the final checklist with his assistant. Knox was downstairs, greeting their early guests.

As their security head walked by, Peter again asked him to check on whether anyone at the hotel had seen David Sawyer since he left Mr. Knox's room that morning. The man stopped and talked on his special phone. Peter noticed that the answer took some time and that the man nodded several times. When he hung up, he turned back to Peter.

"They say that no one can be sure, but they think he got into a Mercedes shortly after Mr. Knox last saw him. If it was him, the bellman cannot remember anything about his destination. The interesting news is that the airline confirms that Sawyer called early this morning and made a reservation to fly *today*, but then called back a few hours later and cancelled. So they have no further idea."

"That's really strange. Thank you. Please let me know if you hear anything."

Peter finished with his assistant, glanced again at the large photos of their early operation, and decided that it all looked pretty good. He went downstairs, and, after politely waiting for a break in the conversation which Knox was having with a large Russian businessman—through an interpreter—Goncharov said, "Mr. Knox, there's still no word on David, or why he's not here."

Knox looked disturbed. "What could have happened to him?"

"I don't know." Then he recounted the airline information.

"Home today? That doesn't make any sense. We just arranged for him to fly home with us tonight. We talked about his role at the reception, and I asked him to join us in the receiving line. He left us quite happy. You saw him at breakfast. Did he seem like he was about to go home and miss this event?"

"No. You're absolutely right. It's very strange."

"Maybe you should contact the police."

"Yes, if he's not here by the end of the reception, we'll call the police."

"Good. I don't want anything to happen to him."

"I'm sure that nothing will."

David noticed that Mustafin stayed online with the two men at the other control center after their five o'clock check-in. Mustafin said, "We will launch close to six. That will put the missile in the Moscow area about seven, still with thirty minutes of loiter time, if we need it. Have them begin their final launch preparation."

During his ordeal, David had occasionally stretched. He did so again, this time stretching back and then forward, all the way, so that his head was on his knees. Mustafin was engrossed in his video conversation, and David used the moment to look under the seat. There, clamped to the outboard frame of the seat, was a thick clear plastic pouch containing a life vest, small first-aid kit, and a flashlight. He recognized the flashlight's design: it was made of a strong anodized metal and took three "D" batteries.

David sat up again and noticed that on the USNet news a reporter was interviewing Trevor Knox in the foyer of their new Moscow office building. It seemed so incongruous.

The flashlight. Could he get to it and somehow use it as a weapon? A club? Could he reach down to get the pouch with his right hand alone, without Mustafin noticing?

Elizabeth was in the hospital room that morning watching the USNet news magazine when Rob came out of a sedated sleep. "They say they're going to cover the President's speech at USNet headquarters live, and a minute ago they interviewed Mr. Knox. But we haven't seen your father yet. Right now they're doing a background piece on the Russian President."

Eight hundred kilometers southeast of Moscow, in a small deserted valley northeast of Rostov-on-Don, Lieutenant Andryushin's team ramped the launch rails above the cab so that the missile could fly free. Then they backed away. Andryushin signaled a thumb's up to Captain Rusnak, who was standing beside his car, fifty meters away.

Trevor Knox and Peter Goncharov waited in the ground level of their new headquarters. Most of the invited guests—from all over the world—had gathered and were upstairs in the large hall, looking at USNet information and sipping champagne. The room was decorated in the red, white and blue colors of both nations' flags, and there were several banners showing the two flags together, with "Friendship" in English and Russian written underneath.

As they stood together near the open front doors, Peter said, "I still can't imagine where David is. He's just disappeared. I know how much he was looking forward to this event."

"I hope he's all right," Knox replied. "A good man."

"Yes. Very much."

An SUV drove into the compound, and Tanya Prescott emerged from the passenger seat. "Two minutes, max," she said, as she greeted the two men. "They're having a great day. Hey, where's David?"

"We're not sure," Knox replied. "We haven't seen him since just after breakfast. We're beginning to be a little worried."

"Really? Not good. Let me know if he doesn't turn up, and we'll help in the look-see. Well, here they come..."

The approaching sirens grew louder, and the caravan turned into the compound, led by several black SUV's with blue flashing lights. They peeled off to the perimeter, and a single long limousine with flags flying in front pulled up to the doors of the USNet headquarters. Secret Service agents opened the front doors, looked all around, then opened the side doors, and President Harper and President Temirov emerged. The Russian President was not as tall as his American counterpart. They smiled at Knox, whom they had met at lunch, and walked over to their hosts.

"President Temirov, President Harper, allow me to introduce Mr. Peter Goncharov, who has been our Russian operations manager for five years. He's the reason for our success and longevity in Russia."

"A pleasure to meet you," President Harper said, extending her hand to the Russian.

President Temirov, his dark eyes beaming, also shook hands with Goncharov, and they spoke in Russian.

After exchanging pleasantries and pausing for a "photo op" at the doorway, the foursome entered and walked up the staircase, engrossed in a discussion about USNet's history in Russia, while the press from the motorcade filed in behind them.

When Mustafin switched screens to the Moscow regional map, David could see the red blip, corresponding to ID code 654321 dialed into the digit box, slowly pulsing at the location of their headquarters building.

If I get the plastic pouch loose, will I be able to open it with one hand? And if I get the flashlight out, can I hit him with it in a way that will stop him before he shoots me? I've never done anything like that. Lord, I know this sounds trite, coming from me now, but I really am asking for your help. For my family. And for the President.

It was about 5:45 pm in Moscow, and early morning in the U.S., as the USNet News cameras showed the two Presidents making their way around the perimeter of the large room, shaking hands as they went. The phone on the hospital table next to Elizabeth rang.

"Hello."

"Mom?"

"Callie! My goodness, it's early out in California. How are you?"

"Great!"

"I'm glad. Are you watching the TV coverage of the USNet reception in Moscow?"

"Not yet. I'm in my car."

"I haven't seen your father, but I assume that we will."

"Mom, that's why I'm calling. If you don't see him, don't, like, worry. It means he's on the way home."

"Great."

"Yes. And Kristen and I will be at the airport in ten minutes—we should be home this afternoon. Kristen has her car at the airport. We'll drive home, or to the hospital. How's Rob?"

Elizabeth was watching the Presidents mount the small stage in Moscow.

"He's better. His pelvis is broken, but there don't seem to be other internal injuries. He may come home today, too, on crutches. Did you say Dad is on the way home now? Missing the reception?"

"He was going to try to change his ticket and leave Moscow today, but it would have been too early to call and let us know. If he's on the flight, he'll call from New York. And if he missed that one, he's going to try to get a flight to, like, Western Europe. So I think we'll all be home today or tomorrow."

"Callie, this is great news. I love you and can't wait to see you."

"I love you, too, Mom."

Mustafin glanced at the news coverage that showed Trevor Knox approaching the microphone at the podium. He spoke into his headset to the Russian at the other end of the video call. "All right, General, you have permission to launch."

"Understood. We'll send the confirming signal."

Mustafin swiveled around and smiled at David. "What history we're about to make! Not only will we get rid of the self-righteous U.S. President, but we'll create incredible opportunities to move our people inside the Russian government, as they are forced to rebuild. You have a front row seat for history in the making. Too bad you won't be able to share the experience with anyone." He smiled, turned back to his console, and opened up the range on the map display to show most of Eastern Europe north of the Black Sea.

Yusef had hardly slept, even with a pill. His last night on earth. He had been up for hours, showered, said his prayers, read the Qur'an, and now, dressed in only a T-shirt and shorts, he was heading out the door for the mini-storage unit near the airport, driving the rented van. Given the holiday, the traffic would be light, and he expected to make good time. He noticed what a beautiful day Allah had made, and smiled.

Knox stood at the microphone behind the Presidential podium while the applause died down and the USNet cameras broadcast to the world. Behind him in chairs were Presidents Harper and Temirov, the U.S. Secretary of State, Sandra Van Huyck, and several other dignitaries.

"We are delighted to be here today to celebrate our American Fourth of July in a way that no one could have imagined only a few years ago. We at USNet are particularly honored to have with us both President Temirov and President Harper, signifying the bond between our two nations, which has grown closer at all levels as we have learned to work together: in government, in cultural exchanges, and in business.

"As one of the oldest still functioning—and might I say thriving—joint ventures in Russia, we are honored and humbled to have been selected as the site for our leaders' remarks on the future of business between our two nations.

"On this historic anniversary of our nation's founding, I, particularly as an immigrant, am reminded of our country's underlying principles. The foundations for all business discourse have always been civility, law, ethics and accountability. We at USNet have practiced these principles since our earliest days, and we are pleased to endorse the efforts of both governments to restore morality in the workplace. As you have previously heard, we support President Harper's recently enacted Media and Entertainment Reform Law, and we encourage President Temirov to adopt similar legislation here in Russia.

"Beyond these foundations, we pledge that our company will assist both governments and other companies in making recommendations so that ethical business can more easily be transacted between our two great nations.

"But I know that you did not come here today to hear me, so I will be brief. Before introducing these two great leaders of vision, I do want to take the opportunity to give each of them a small token of our appreciation and a recognition of this special day."

Knox held up a small badge, and the camera focused in for a close-up. "We have for each of them a specially cast friendship pin, showing both the U.S.

and Russian flags, with the word 'friendship' in both languages beneath them. Before they speak, I want to pin this special day's memory piece on each lapel."

Applause erupted in the hall, and Knox turned. The two Presidents stood up, smiling, and Knox approached President Temirov first. He pinned the flags on his lapel, they shook hands, and President Temirov said "Thank you" in English.

Then Knox moved to President Harper. As the applause continued, Knox reached up for the lapel of her suit and said to the President, "Thank you for coming. As you probably know, pins like this are a special tradition for Russians. We hope that you'll keep this one on for the rest of the day, particularly at the Fourth of July celebration tonight."

"Thank you, Trevor, for all that you've done. And, yes, I'll keep it on. A great idea."

"Thank you, Madame President."

Knox turned back to the podium, the guests were seated, and he said, "Now I'd like to ask our Russian operations manager, Peter Goncharov, to introduce President Temirov."

Captain Rusnak surveyed his men in the relative safety of a small ravine one hundred meters from the launcher. He could see the expectation on their faces. He glanced down at the mobile firing board and noted the eight green lights. He pushed the Fire button.

There was a thunderous roar as the booster rocket kicked in and the turbojet-powered GoFor cruise missile was propelled up its short track to flying speed. Almost before they could blink, the deadly missile was on its way north.

The men shouted and slapped each other on the back. As they did so, the missile received its initial guidance information from the command center at NovySvet, correcting its path slightly to head straight for Moscow.

Mustafin reacted to the news from General Beleborodov by raising his right fist in the air. "Great! Yes, yes, I see it."

David leaned to the right so that he could see around Mustafin, and he noticed a white light on the map of Europe. This one was moving rapidly to the north. And he noticed red light to the northwest, which looked to be in Moscow, with a number next to it.

That flag pin Knox just pinned on President Harper must contain the micro-repeater for the GPS system. Code 654321.

Salim's other student, Perviz, used his next remaining phone to call his mentor with the pre-arranged message that he was up and moving toward their storage site near Kennedy Airport on Long Island. The weather in New York was mid-level overcast, but Perviz knew from his training that there should be plenty of time to lock onto a climbing jet before it entered the clouds.

President Temirov was at the podium, his remarks simultaneously translated for USNet viewers. He was praising the American business community for remaining in his country despite sometimes difficult conditions, and for teaching their Russian counterparts. He challenged both the Western and Russian business leaders assembled for the reception to move out beyond the country's largest cities and to bring the benefits of free enterprise to all of the regions.

From his seat David watched as President Harper began her remarks on the USNet News feed, while the pulsing white light moved rapidly north on Mustafin's console.

He could hear the President's encouraging words on trade and business development, new program initiatives, and praise for USNet's leader, Trevor Knox, as an example for all to follow.

He's going to kill you! He thought again about the flashlight, and again he stretched and looked beneath the seat. Mustafin did not seem to notice. *I think I can reach the pouch. Surely it's designed to come off easily. But when should I do it? Mustafin's got to be involved in something intense. Start to finish I'll only have a few seconds, and I'll have to be quiet.*

He could feel adrenaline starting to pump through his system. Once again he looked at the distance from his seat to Mustafin, trying to gauge whether, with his left hand cuffed to the armrest, he could stand, step, swing, and hit the man's head. It would be close. A few inches.

If I miss, he'll kill me. But if I don't try, he'll kill me anyway. I'd better swing low, in case he ducks or pulls back. That way I'll at least hit something. His mind knew that he had to try it, but his heart pumped faster and his stomach was in turmoil.

A few minutes later the President finished her speech, and a short question and answer session began on the USNet News feed. Mustafin said, almost to himself, as he watched the screen, "Hurry up. We need you back in the Kremlin before seven."

They're going to take out the Presidents, the Kremlin, the entire Russian leadership—plus our Secretary of State and several senators!

David couldn't focus on the questions being asked. He kept thinking about his uncertain plan. *This will never work. I don't know what I'm doing. I'm a dead man either way. Lord, I...*

At about 6:15 the questions ended, and Knox looked at his watch. As they stood on the podium, he said privately to President Harper, "Thank you again for coming. I know that you and President Temirov have a state dinner at the Kremlin, so we'll try to get you out of here quickly."

"No problem. Thanks for hosting us and for agreeing to back our reforms. I know they'll be good for the country, and I appreciate your support. And thanks for the flags!" She touched the pin on her lapel.

"Our pleasure. Have a Happy Fourth of July celebration."

"You're not coming?"

"No, we have to head back for meetings tomorrow. But all of our people are attending. I'm sure it will be great."

"Yes. Fourth of July fireworks in Moscow. Who would have thought!"

Knox led the way over to the wide door opening into the software assembly area. With smiles and a flourish for the cameras, the Presidents, Knox, and Goncharov cut the ribbon across the doorway. After general applause, Knox turned and led the two leaders around the perimeter of the room. They stopped to shake hands several times with other guests, and Knox continued to check his watch. Finally, just before 6:30, he put his two guests in their special limousine and waved good-bye as they drove off.

As the limousine left the compound, Knox turned to Akbar Kamali, who had been shadowing him. Kamali nodded. Knox moved across to Peter Goncharov, standing with a group of guests.

"Peter, as you know, Akbar and I have to leave. We have to prepare for an early meeting tomorrow back in the States, so we must get airborne soon in order to make it. But I'm really worried about David. When you hear from him, please let me know. You've done a great job. I hope that all continues to go well."

"Thank you, Mr. Knox."

Knox turned just as the black Mercedes pulled up to the door. "Your bags are in the trunk," Kamali said, as he opened the back door for his boss.

As soon as they left the compound, the driver stopped, smiled and produced a blue police light. He reached outside his window and fastened it to the roof. In broken English he said, "From friend with police. We go to airport very quick!"

"Good!" Knox said, as he sat back and they sped off.

Outside the Departures Area at LAX, Kristen exited the bus from the parking lot first, then turned and took Callie's roller case as she stepped down to the sidewalk. It had already been a busy morning. They had awoken early at the hotel, driven to Callie's apartment to pack her bag and leave a note for Alex, then head to the airport. Kristen, who had been shepherding her younger friend, finally breathed easier as they turned to walk inside.

"We'll use the kiosks to check-in, and then I still have a card to the Business Class lounge from my USNet days, so we'll get some coffee and Danish."

Callie smiled. "Sounds great. Lead on."

At that moment, just two miles away, Yusef pulled up to the mini-storage unit, got out, and, thankful that there was no one else on his row that morning, entered the code on the thick lock attached to the door.

Inside the corporate jet back in Moscow, David watched the white light speed closer to Moscow. Mustafin reduced the scale on the map as the missile came closer. At that moment David detected some slight movement in the red light, even though it was in Moscow.

The Russian in the video conference screen said, "All right, control has passed to you. ETA is about twenty-five minutes."

"Yes. Thanks. I've got it. It seems to be tracking the GPS repeater perfectly."

David sat and watched. The USNet reporter was interviewing a young Russian businesswoman who had attended the reception. *When should I do something?* Mustafin was quietly watching the screen, and he knew in the silence that the Kazakh would hear his attempt to pull the pouch from under the seat. Just then Mustafin turned around, looked at David, and smiled. "It won't be long now. Knox and Akbar will be here soon." He turned back to the console.

David edged to the left a few inches, so that when he leaned over, he would have a better angle to grasp the pouch. *Will it just pull out, or is it fastened somehow?*

At that moment the Russian general on the video phone said, "Hey, isn't the GPS repeater getting very close to the Kremlin now?"

"Yes," Mustafin answered.

"But looking at the ETA, that means the missile will hit inside the Kremlin walls!" the general said, clearly agitated. "We've always planned to hit them on the way to Kuskovo Park. You said they would leave the reception and drive there!"

"I guess they changed their plans," came the nonchalant reply.

It must be time. Lord, please help me. And take me to you if I die in the next minute.

"But that was never the plan! You had us prepare to take them out in the car, not inside the Kremlin, for God's sake."

"Like I said, I guess they changed plans or something."

"But we can't destroy the Kremlin! I agreed to help get rid of a pious U.S. President and a weak Russian one—to reestablish strong leadership in our country. Not to destroy eight hundred years of our history."

"I guess it can't be helped," Mustafin replied tersely, as he moved the range scale again, clearly showing the slow-moving red light to be inside the Kremlin, and the faster white one rapidly approaching the city from the southeast.

As David leaned forward and reached down with his right hand, the general on the screen was becoming angrier. "Whoever you are, you must abort that missile! We can't blow up the Kremlin and the entire Russian government!"

David could just reach the pouch. He closed his eyes and slowly started to pull.

Mustafin raised his voice. "General, you'll do whatever you're told!"

Velcro. The pouch was held to the frame with Velcro, and just as Mustafin yelled, David pulled all the way. The pouch came off in his hand, and he sat up again, keeping the pouch low and behind his right leg.

"We're making great time," Kamali noted, as they raced down the last portion of Leninsky Prospekt before the Ring Road, the blue light flashing and the horn sounding every few seconds.

"Yes." Knox smiled. "We might even get there in time to see the missile hit."

"I hope so," Kamali replied.

The case with the Stinger missile fit easily in the rented van. Yusef took time placing and wedging together the several parts of the bomb for the van, as Salim had shown him. First the explosives, then the bags of nails and ball bearings packed around them. Finally the detonator plug, which he would insert at the final destination, and the cell phone, which would be attached to the detonator, and whose ring would be the trigger for the conflagration. When he had finished and checked everything several times, Yusef said a prayer of thanks and drove off. He was headed to a high school located just north of the northern most parallel runway.

Unknown to him, Perviz in New York would soon arrive in his own van at a deserted housing construction site not far from the southeastern end of the longest runway at JFK.

Meanwhile, Kristen showed her card at the entrance to the lounge, and she and Callie went inside for some much needed caffeine.

The white dot was moving rapidly toward the outskirts of Moscow, and Mustafin and the general were now yelling at each other in Russian.

This is it! David pulled the pouch up and moved it to his left, where he grasped it in his cuffed hand. The flap was also held with Velcro. As quietly as he could, looking up, he opened the flap and reached inside for the flashlight. *Full of batteries. It's heavy.*

Switching back to English, Mustafin said, "I don't have time to deal with you, now."

At that moment David stood, his legs unexpectedly weak from sitting, took one step forward with his right foot, and swung the flashlight for Mustafin's right ear. Sensing the motion, or seeing the reflection in the console screen, Mustafin turned quickly to his right. Simultaneously he yelled, ducked, and started to bring his hand up. But because David swung low, the flashlight connected with the Kazakh's right front temple. David heard a crack, and Mustafin fell off the seat and hit the floor. He didn't move. *Should I hit him again?* Mustafin remained still.

Gotta move fast. David dropped to his knees, and with his right hand grabbed Mustafin's leg to pull him closer. Reaching inside the coat, he found the automatic pistol and put it on the seat. Then he fished inside the Kazakh's pants pockets, found the key, and unlocked his handcuff. For good measure he quickly brought Mustafin's hands together and cuffed them.

The fall had ripped the small headset off Mustafin's head, and it was hanging from the console. David quickly put it on and sat in the chair. The missile was eight minutes out.

"Hello," he said.

The Russian general looked surprised and said, "Who is that?"

Focusing on the videophone screen, David said, "I've been here for quite a while, watching. I disabled the other man. Do you know how to stop this missile?"

"Control has passed to your side. We can do nothing. It's going to be terrible."

"I was listening to your argument, and I assure you that the plan has always been to destroy the Kremlin. He told me so a little while ago."

The Russian appeared to curse. Then he turned to his right, and the other man came back into view. "Simon, did you know this?"

The other man shrugged. "What difference does it make?"

"What difference?" the Russian yelled. "You fool. I won't be known as the man who destroyed the Kremlin! Dmitri, Sasha! Come and take Mr. North. We'll settle with him in a few minutes. Now, who are you?"

"I'm David Sawyer. I've been watching what Victor has done, but I don't know how to stop a missile. Can we abort it?"

"The codes are known only to those on your end. We have never seen them. You are only a voice. At any moment the missile will switch to terminal homing mode, the television camera in the nose will come on, and then no one can abort it."

"So how can we stop it?" David asked loudly again, as he watched the flashing light cross into the Moscow suburbs.

"I don't know."

David looked up at the code in the digital window. "What about another GPS reflector code? Will it accept another code to home on?"

"I'm not sure. It would have to be one within its lock-on range. If the position is not acquired within five seconds, it automatically switches back to the previous one."

"How do I give it a new code?"

"Scroll to the box, right click the mouse, type in each number, and then press Enter. But hurry."

David painted all the boxes with the mouse, right clicked and then clicked the Yes box next to "New code?"

As each box came up he typed in 9-2-7-5-1-2, then pressed Enter.

The code in the box changed, and he held his breath. Suddenly the white light coming from the south turned to the left, the ETA box blinked, and a new number appeared: 2:47. Then the seconds began ticking down.

The Russian general said, "It took the new code! What is it?"

"The GPS in my ID. Here."

"My God!"

David ripped off the headset, looked outside and saw the guard still standing watch.

He reached for his coat, pulled out his wallet, checked that his ID card was inside and threw it on the console.

He put on Mustafin's coat, took the pistol, then bent down and struggled to lift the Kazakh's upper body. As he dragged him aft, he noted on the screen that the picture had changed to that of an aerial scene above rooftops. *Terminal homing mode!*

He dropped Mustafin by the door and pulled the handle to activate the stairs. Keeping his back to the opening door, so that it might look to the guard like Mustafin, he picked up the Kazakh again, slid the pistol into his belt, and started backing down the stairs.

The guard saw one figure coming out, dragging another, but he didn't realize until David had one foot on the ground that it was Mustafin being carried. He immediately cocked his automatic rifle, leveled it at David, and started yelling in Russian.

Help me. Please help me.

David turned slowly, his left hand barely supporting Mustafin, his right hand in the air. He was staring down the barrel of an automatic rifle, with an agitated Russian behind it.

He said the only Russian word he knew. *"Nyet! Nyet!"*

With his right hand he pointed to Mustafin. "Mustafin OK. Mustafin OK!" Then, before the Russian could react, he pointed to the airplane, and made the universal hand picture and sound for an explosion. "Boom!" Then he pointed at his watch and raised one finger.

While the Russian thought about that, David pointed at him, Mustafin, and himself. "We GO!" pointing toward the woods, and just for effect, he repeated the "Boom!" even louder.

Without waiting for a response, David nodded his head toward the trees and started dragging Mustafin.

The Russian looked at Sawyer, Mustafin and the airplane, and made his decision. He slung the rifle over his shoulder and grabbed Mustafin's feet. "OK," he said to a thankful David, as they picked up speed, almost running toward the tree line.

As they were nearing the drainage ditch separating the tarmac from the trees, David heard loud honking and looked back to see a black Mercedes with a blue light racing toward the aircraft.

The police? How? I need to warn them! "Here, get down in this ditch!" he said to the Russian, as they placed Mustafin in the depression, which was about four feet deep, and the Russian crouched down.

From in the car Knox and Kamali saw the plane's open door, no guard, and two figures running toward the trees, carrying something. "That's Sawyer!" Kamali exclaimed.

"Where's Victor? Stop here by the plane. Let's see what they've done inside!" Knox yelled.

As the car screeched to a halt, Knox leaped out of the left side and bounded up the stairs. Kamali came out the right side and saw Sawyer standing and waving. He pulled out his pistol and fired three shots at him. Sawyer quickly dropped down into the ditch. Then Kamali headed for the stairs.

Inside, it took a second for Knox's eyes to adjust to the lower light. He ran up to the control console. There was a wallet open on it. He picked it up, saw Sawyer's ID, then looked at the screen, which showed the view from the nose of the missile. For a moment he couldn't make it out, since he expected to see downtown Moscow and the Kremlin. Instead there were fields...trees...an airport. A corporate jet parked alone. He turned.

Kamali had followed him into the cabin and had never seen such terror on a man's face. "Get out!" Knox screamed, pushing Kamali aside and running for the open doorway.

From the edge of the ditch David and the Russian looked out. A fast moving object came hurtling out of the east, diving directly for the parked aircraft. David pushed the Russian down and covered his own ears just as a huge explosion ripped the air and shook the earth all around them. The heat from the fireball passed over them and singed the trees on the other side.

Half a minute later they crawled up again and looked. Where the plane had been there was now just a tremendously hot fire. Through the ringing in his ears, David thought he heard sirens. The Russian guard hugged him and gave him the universal thumbs-up sign. Suddenly very tired, David nodded, looked down at Mustafin, who was still unconscious, and lay back against the slope of the ditch, looking skyward.

"Thank you."

But he only rested for a moment. Without looking at the Russian guard, who was now standing and surveying the destruction, David rolled Mustafin over and retrieved his own cell phone. For good measure he took Mustafin's as well, and put it in his pocket.

Please work. As sirens started to blare from the main part of the airport, he clicked Tanya Prescott's number from the Recent list and pushed the green button. It took a few moments, but he got her voicemail. He swore and dialed again. Voicemail again. *Please!* He dialed again. This time she answered.

"David? Is that you? Where are you?"

"Tanya, I'm at some airport. Vnukovo, I think. Knox and his team sent a missile to kill President Harper and President Temirov." The sirens grew louder, and the Russian guard started to yell. David covered his ear. "But the missile exploded into Knox's plane, and he's dead.. A big fireball."

"David, wait a minute. I'm parked outside the Kremlin, and the two Presidents just went inside. I can barely hear you. What did you just say about a missile? And what are those sirens?"

"Tanya," David raised his voice. "You've got to listen carefully. I may be arrested any second. Knox tried to kill the Presidents. Move them to somewhere safe. Then come to Vnukovo Airport, and I'll explain everything. But first call whoever is in charge of commercial flights in America and tell them that terrorists are about to shoot down an airliner at JFK Airport, and another at LAX in Los Angeles. Using missiles. He called the terrorists 'martyrs', so it may also involve suicide bombs. I'm not sure, but I am sure about the two airliners and the missiles. People are in great danger."

"David, how do you know that?"

"One of the men who planned it is lying next to me, and you can ask him. But there's no time. You've got to warn the two airports. It could happen any minute. I..."

Just then a Russian policeman grabbed the phone from David's hand and pushed him face down into the oily ground, a gun to his head.

Kristen and Callie had watched the last part of the President's visit to the USNet factory on the television in the lounge. Now, as they were standing in line to board their plane, they watched a reporter on a live feed from just outside the Kremlin wall reporting that the state dinner was just beginning, and that there had been an explosion and fire at an airport on the outskirts of Moscow, but it was many miles distant and was of no concern to the President's visit. Just as the segment was ending, the reporter turned back toward the red brick walls of the Kremlin as a massive gate opened and the President's limousine could clearly be seen to be leaving, several hours ahead of schedule. The reporter look flustered.

As Callie handed her boarding pass to the attendant for swiping, she said to Kristen, "I wonder what that's all about."

Yusef pulled in and parked in the middle of the large, deserted parking lot at the high school. He had picked this location for several reasons, the main ones being its proximity to the ocean end of the runway, and the tall hedges around the parking lot which would hide his actions from the street, until the missile was fired. From this location it would be easy to pick up an airliner when it was at maximum thrust and climbing quickly, as one was doing at just that moment. The angle would allow for a perfect shot at the engines, as the plane headed out over the ocean. He just had to track the plane, listen for the lock-on tone, and then pull the trigger.

He worked quickly, even though he had about thirty minutes. He had to prepare and arm the missile, which he could do inside the van. Then he would insert the detonator into the explosives in the bomb, and carefully turn on and put one of the cell phone pairs in his pocket.

Callie had a window seat on the right side of the plane, and Kristen was seated next to her. Given the holiday, the plane was carrying a lot of passengers, but was not full. They were reading magazines when the captain made an announcement.

"Ladies and gentlemen this is your captain, Kathryn Morgan. I'm assisted this morning by First Officer Drew Roberts. Along with our Los Angeles based flight crew, we hope to make this Fourth of July flight as uneventful as possible. The baggage is almost loaded and the paperwork is on the way. We may be a few minutes late for departure, but we should make that up in route and arrive on schedule. We'll be taking off to the west, over the ocean, so you should have a great view of the coast. Now please settle back and enjoy your flight. Thanks for flying with us on this beautiful holiday morning."

Yusef finished his tasks and tested his three radios. One was the news, one was tuned to the control tower frequency, and one was the police band. They were all working. With fifteen minutes left before the shot, and maybe thirty minutes left to live, he closed his eyes and prayed to Allah.

As the airliner pushed back from the gate, Kristen said to Callie, "What a difference a few weeks can make. It's incredible how God can work in our lives, whether we know it or not. Your Dad fired me six weeks ago, and disowned you. Now we're flying home, probably to big hugs." She smiled.

Callie took Kristen's hand. "You're right. I never could have imagined it. Thank you."

"Thank God, not me."

By the sheer force of her will and the fact that she was at that moment in a high speed motorcade to a confidential U.S. State Department dacha outside Moscow with the President of the United States, Tanya Prescott was finally talking to Adam Oglesby, who was heading up the holiday skeleton crew at the Northeast Air Traffic Control Center.

"Who are you again?" he asked.

Tanya repeated her credentials and her demand that Mr. Oglesby immediately shut down flight operations at all of the airports in the New York and Los Angeles areas.

"And you're telling me this because you got a call from a civilian in Russia who overheard someone talking about a missile shot at both airports? Do you realize what a shut-down like that would do to air traffic in this country?"

"Ladies and gentlemen, it looks like we're number three for take-off. That should put us wheels up at just about ten local time. The weather in route looks very good."

Yusef said a final prayer and got out of the van. He pulled the missile case out and placed it on the ground, then closed the van's rear doors. He put the three portable radios on the ground, and switched on the tower frequency, with the volume loud enough so that he could listen as he stood next to the van. As he had expected, the holiday morning and the hedges meant that he was all alone—at least for now. He smiled as he opened the case and placed the missile launcher on his shoulder. He depressed the Ready button, which made the missile armed and operable.

At the field in New York, Perviz had accomplished the same steps, following his mentor's precise orders.

"Mr. Oglesby, I can't argue with you any more. Do you want me to stop the motorcade and have the President give you a direct order?"

"Los Angeles Tower, PacAir 511," Captain Morgan called on the radio.

"PacAir 511, Los Angeles Tower. Taxi into position and hold, Runway 24 Left."

"24 Left. PacAir 511" She then switched to the cockpit intercom. *"Checklist complete?"*

"Checklist complete," the first officer replied.

"OK. I've got the controls, you call the numbers."

Yusef had listened to the Tower's exchange and could picture the PacAir jet turning onto the east end of the long runway, even though he couldn't see it. *A woman pilot. Even better.*

"PacAir 511, cleared for take-off, 24 Left."
Captain Morgan advanced the throttles and began the take-off roll.

Yusef could hear the sound as the huge airliner picked up speed on the runway. He turned to face south, his finger touching the smooth metal of the trigger.

"V1," the First Officer reported, meaning that they were going too fast to stop in the remaining length of the runway.

"PacAir 511, abort take-off! I say again, abort take-off," came the command from the Tower.
"Past V1. We're going."
"Possible missile threat. All flight operations cancelled."
"Damn." She lifted the nose and the plane pulled off the runway. *"Pull the wheels up."* "What is it?"
"High probability missile threat."
Kathryn Morgan, petite, with a wisp of gray hair and a no-nonsense approach to the cockpit, had flown C-141 Starlifter heavy cargo planes in the Air Force for six years before joining PacAir ten years ago, and she still flew every month with the Air National Guard. She had more take-offs and landings in Afghanistan and Iraq than she could remember. They had always been concerned about missiles, but on her Air Force planes they had flares and counter measures. On PacAir 511 she had only her wits.
She moved the trim tab button forward and pushed the nose over. Immediately a horn went off in the cockpit and a recorded voice said, "Pull up. Pull up." The voice could be heard in the passenger compartment.
"No way," she said almost to herself. *"Hold on"* she told the first officer.
With the warning horns blaring, Kathryn Morgan accelerated a few feet off the ground, just like she had done so many times in her C-141s, hoping that the ocean would come fast.

Yusef heard the command from the tower and cursed. He followed the noise of the jet's engines below the hedges, but the plane never climbed, preventing him from tracking and locking on.
As the airliner neared the end of the runway and the ocean, he caught a glimpse through a break in the hedges, and, knowing that there would be no more planes that day, he led the plane's position and fired the missile, hoping that it would find its target.

When they were almost to the beach separating the airport from the ocean, Morgan climbed a few feet and started a careful turn to the right, the long wing just above the light poles and guy wires.

"Confirmed launch!" came the cry from the tower. "Right quarter."

She increased her turn as much as she dared. Kristen and Callie, along with the other passengers, were pushed back by the G-force, and a child toward the rear screamed.

Then she leveled out, descended, and hugged the deck, flying right up the line where the sand met the water, and where there were no poles and no wires to get in the way.

The Stinger never had a chance to acquire or lock on to the airliner. It flew out over the ocean, and after a pre-programmed time, it self-destructed.

Steve Toller had hit the beach early that morning, hoping to get a good spot before the crowds arrived. He was sitting in his beach chair, facing slightly north so that the sunlight would illuminate the book he was reading, his feet touching the water. Earphones provided soft background music when he felt, more than heard, what seemed like a fast-moving diesel locomotive coming up behind him. He turned his head in time to see the Rolls Royce logo on the starboard engine of a huge jet airliner, just before the noise and the blast hit him full tilt. It was a long minute of cursing before he could hear well enough again to call the police and complain.

Yusef threw the launcher down in disgust and walked around the van, determined to make the infidels pay a high price for this treachery.

"Los Angeles Tower, where do you want us?" Captain Morgan asked. "I imagine we've got some messed up and maybe banged up folks in the back."

"Great flying, mam. We're closed. Suggest John Wayne Airport at Orange County. Fly heading one-five-zero and climb to five thousand."

"Seems an appropriate spot, but we prefer to stay low," Morgan answered. And she finally smiled. Then she turned on the intercom to the passenger cabin. "Ladies and gentlemen, I think we're OK now. Let me tell you what just happened, and why, as we take a short bird's eye flight to the south."

Perviz was waiting next to his own van at the housing site in the Inwood area, across a small bay from the end of runway 13 Right at JFK. Unfortunately for him, when the order came across the Tower frequency to cease operations, no airliner was rolling. He knew that there would be no more take-offs. Frustrated, he looked northwest, to the other end of the runway, and noticed a large airliner descending rapidly on final approach. He immediately turned the launcher in that direction, realizing that the distance was at the far end of the acquisition parameters.

He tracked the plane and thought he heard the lock-on tone. Instantly he fired the missile.

Brannon Ward was standing by the grill in his backyard in Inwood, preparing hamburgers and hot dogs for three families who had joined them to celebrate the Fourth. Like Brannon and his wife, the other couples had young children. All of the men worked with Brannon in the local police department, and so the talk was mostly about bad guys of all types. Without even thinking about it, each one of them wore a pistol on his belt.

"Wow!" Brannon's six year old son exclaimed, when the Stinger went off about two blocks to the west. "Fireworks!"

Before joining the police, Brannon had been a Marine in Afghanistan, and he knew exactly what a Stinger missile sounded like. And, living near JFK, he knew what it could mean.

Handing the spatula to his wife, he motioned to his buddies, whose conversations had also stopped, "Come on." They ran toward their cars at the front of the house.

The Stinger did its best to follow the line of site to the heat from the descending target. But because of the angle, the plane's course took it behind a hangar, just as it was touching down. The Stinger lost the target for a crucial two seconds, and was unable to recover. It hit the edge of the hangar, doing considerable damage, but it did not explode.

Perviz dropped the launch tube and waited by his van in the middle of the field, expecting sirens to start any second, and the police to arrive a few minutes later. Instead, four men in shorts and casual shirts materialized from cars on the street. They fanned out as they yelled, each one pointing a gun at him.

Remember that I tried, he prayed. He held the cell phone open in his right hand, and slowly raised both hands in surrender.

"What the hell are you doing?" Brannon yelled, as he and the other men surrounded him. "Get down on the ground." Sirens could be heard approaching,

Perviz smiled. "Killing you." Then he pressed the Send button on his phone. A huge fireball erupted from the van, laced with nails and metal shards. All five men were instantly torn to shreds.

At Vnukovo Airport, David had been escorted at gun point to a nearby hangar, where he sat by himself in an office, again handcuffed to a chair. Mustafin had started to come around as the police arrived, and now he was in the adjoining office. David could hear him screaming in Russian at the guards outside. He had tried in his best English to explain to the Russians that they could not let Mustafin go. David had asked to use his phone again, but they would not let him.

Yusef had no idea who would come for him in the middle of the parking lot. LAPD? Airport security? FBI? But he knew, especially after missing the aircraft, that he had to kill as many as he could with the bomb in the van. That was why he was dressed so minimally. He wanted no one to have the idea that he was wearing a suicide vest. They should feel safe in approaching him. He stood outside the front door of the van, the empty rocket launcher ten feet away on the asphalt.

His location was, of course, obvious to those in the control tower and around the airport, because of the white contrail left by the missile. The launch had also been seen by Officer Clark Perry, a young African-American who had only been on the force for a year. On this holiday morning he had drawn the "short straw" to patrol both his own area and an adjoining one. Which was why he was driving through the neighborhood north of LAX when the missile went off and, a few seconds later, his police radio erupted.

Perry radioed that he was responding and turned his patrol car in the direction of the contrail's origin, only a few blocks away. Even without his siren, he turned into the high school parking lot in less than a minute.

There he saw the van, a single man standing next to the open driver's door, and what could well be the launch tube near his feet.

Perry stopped just inside the entrance gate, a hundred yards from the van. He was new to the force, but he had seen similar scenes like this before. Six years earlier, before attending college, Perry had been in the Army, stationed in Iraq, training the local police. And he had seen first hand what a single man and a van full of explosives could do to his best friends.

He immediately radioed his position and asked for back-up, including the SWAT and Ordnance Teams.

From the other side of the parking lot two young boys, apparently playing in the area, were attracted by the noise of the rocket and had just seen the police car. They came running across the lot toward the van.

Perry opened his door and pulled out his loudhailer. He yelled to the boys to get back and go home, but they either did not hear him or decided to investigate anyway. They walked up to inspect the launch tube and then went over to the vehicle.

The man next to the van leveled a gun at the pair. A discussion ensued. The smaller of the two boys got in and moved over to the passenger side. Once he was inside, the man shot the other boy in the head at point blank range, his body collapsing on the pavement.

As the killer got in the van and closed the door, Perry heard the smaller boy's scream, along with the wail of multiple sirens rapidly approaching from several directions.

David was not sure of the time. He was still alone, and once Mustafin had stopped yelling, he had decided to pray, particularly for the people on two airliners.

Suddenly there was a commotion outside and a lot of voices. He instantly recognized Tanya Prescott's commands.

The door to the office flew open and a tall Russian in a suit entered, all the time berating the police officer who had taken David prisoner. Tanya was right behind them, smiling broadly. "Where have you been all day?" she asked.

David stood as the officer unlocked his cuffs. Then he hugged her. "I'm so glad to see you. Don't let them give the man next door any leeway. They should watch him every minute. He knows everything about all that has happened, and he might try to kill himself. What about the planes in the States?"

"Two missiles fired, just as you said, but two misses."

"Thank God."

"There were casualties in New York, though, and they've got the guy in LA surrounded. Thank you. Here's all your stuff, by the way." She handed him a bag that she had retrieved from the officer. "My Russian counterpart is telling the other police how you saved the Presidents and the Kremlin, and that the guy next door planned it all."

A moment later, all the Russian police in the building came to shake David's hand.

When the first responding cars arrived, Perry directed them to take up positions around the perimeter, to keep other curious residents from entering the lot. Ten minutes later Captain Eric Dean of the SWAT team arrived. He interviewed Perry, agreed that he had done the right thing not to approach the van, and asked him to stay close. Dean then took command of the scene, as the first SWAT vehicles arrived.

Word was just arriving about a similar incident at JFK Airport only thirty minutes earlier, including the explosion of the van.

Dean, standing behind the SWAT truck just inside the hedges, radioed downtown. "See if they have anybody that I can talk to who saw what happened with that van."

Compounding his problems, the Chief called to tell Dean that Homeland Security and the FBI wanted him to try to capture the perpetrator alive, if at all possible, so that they could interrogate him. "Yes sir, we'll try. He's got a hostage in the van." he replied.

Yusef could not believe how gracious Allah had been in providing the two young boys. Even if the one in the passenger seat would not stop whimpering.

"Shut up!" he yelled, raising the gun to the boy's head.

The boy swallowed and tried to be quiet.

"They should be coming to us," he said out loud. "To rescue you. But if they don't come soon, we'll drive over to them." He smiled.

Another twenty minutes passed. The perimeter was now heavily defended. Two snipers with Barrett M-107 Caliber .50 rifles were positioned at the ends of the parking lot. Dean's phone rang. It was a senior officer with the New York team that was investigating the missile and van explosion at JFK. She was standing near the site and had a witness to the explosion with her.

"Put her on," Dean said.

The nearly hysterical woman described how she had been walking her dog, had seen the smoke and heard the noise, and so she walked one block further west than her usual route. She had seen the two cars pull up to the vacant lot, and the four men get out with guns. She then described what happened, and noted that a piece of the shrapnel had hit her arm.

"So the man was standing outside the van when the men approached him?"

"Yes. He was outside. He had his hands raised, as if he were surrendering. Then, my God..."

"OK. Thank you, mam. You've been a big help. Please put the officer back on the line." Dean then said to her, being sure that his lieutenants and Officer Perry heard. "Probably a cell phone or garage door opener trigger. Let us know if you find any evidence either way. My bet is a cell phone, which an accomplice could also use from a distance in case the perp got cold feet."

Just then the engine of the van cranked up, and it started heading toward the command area by the gate.

Dean spoke into the microphone on his headset. "Sniper One, take out the engine. We want them alive."

Immediately a single loud shot rang out and a .50 caliber round went through the engine block, ending its operation. . The van stopped twenty yards from where it had been parked.

"Perry, who are the cell phone providers in this area?"

"Tri-County, Prime, and USNet."

Yusef cursed as the van stopped and would move no further. Wild-eyed, he looked over at the boy.

Lon Gibson was heading up the morning shift at USNet's LA operations center, ensuring that the voice and data networks functioned properly for their customers. From the center console in a dimly lit command center, he and four other technicians monitored every aspect of their circuits.

Gibson's phone rang. He answered, listened, and frowned. "I can't shut down the entire USNet system in L.A. To do that I'd need approval from our Central Security."

"Where is it?" Officer Perry asked.

"I'm not sure. I just have a phone number."

Perry's voice rose. "Did I give you the proper authentication code for today?"

"Yes."

"Are you in charge?"

"I'm really just an assistant manager, on duty for the holiday. But, uh, yes, I guess so."

"We have an emergency, Mr. Gibson. A police car is on the way there now with the written form, but we don't have time to wait."

"I'm not sure."

Yusef motioned to the boy. "Start screaming."

Everyone around the perimeter of the lot could hear the screams. Then there was a gunshot, and the screams grew even louder.

"What the hell?" Captain Dean asked out loud, trying to see with binoculars into the van through the glare on the windshield. Then he yelled, "Perry, what about those phones?"

Officer Perry turned from talking with two others. "Captain, two are going down. USNet is still talking."

He swore. "We can't wait. We'll have to hope it's a cell phone trigger, and it's not USNet. Send in the TR2. If he gets out, Sniper 1 on his head. Sniper 2 on his knee."

From behind the barricade came a tactical robot, about five feet tall, mounted on a four wheel drive platform, with four arms protruding from a central core, at the top of which was a swiveling video camera and antenna.

Yusef shot into the floorboard again, sending the boy into even louder hysteria. Then he looked up and saw the police robot coming across the lot. He cursed.

He grabbed the boy by the neck and pulled him to him. "We're getting out. Don't run or scream any more, and soon you'll be free. Understand?' The boy nodded.

Yusef opened the driver door and started to back out, one hand holding the boy, the other his gun. When he was standing on the ground, holding the boy around the waist with his left hand, he briefly put the gun on the seat and slipped the open cellphone into the boy's back pocket. He held the boy around the waist with his left arm, hugging him close, both facing in the same direction. Then he picked up the gun again and held it to the boy's head. Protected by the boy's body, he moved two feet farther from the truck.

"Jimmy!" a woman screamed from the crowd by the police command post. The boy squirmed, but Yusef held him tightly. "Don't move," he said. "Or I'll kill you like your friend there."

Lon Gibson's call to Central Security went to Akbar Kamali's phone, but it had been incinerated in the missile explosion. So the call automatically cycled to the next number on its internal list.

David was giving Tanya the most important details when his phone in the bag began to ring. He opened the bag and realized that it was Mustafin's phone. The readout was a number in Los Angeles. Tanya nodded. He answered.

The caller said, "Hello. Is this Central Security?"

David paused momentarily then said, "Yes."

"Oh, good. You don't know me, but this is Lon Gibson and I'm the Duty Officer at the Los Angeles Central Terminal. I hate to bother you, but the Los Angeles Police have ordered us to turn off all of our cell phone connections in the city. And I didn't want to do it without—"

"Do it. Now."

Gibson paused. "Really? You mean it's OK?"

"NOW!"

The TR2 robot stopped twenty feet from Yusef, who was holding the boy in front of him.

Captain Dean's voice came through a speaker on the robot. "Let the boy go."

"No robot!" Yusef yelled angrily. "Come here yourself. We must talk."

"Not going to happen. Let the boy go."

"You stupid people!" Yusef took the gun from the boy's head and shot at the robot.

Sniper 2, following his instructions, saw the gun move away from the boy and instantly fired. Yusef's right knee was blown away by the perfectly placed round.

Yusef dropped the gun as he fell back against the van and reached in the boy's pocket for his phone. He let the boy go for balance, held the cell phone in the air, screamed and pressed Send.

The TR2 moved forward and hit him with a Taser blast as he slumped to the ground.

"Go!" yelled Captain Dean.

Five SWAT Team members and a Medic sprinted forward.

One member grabbed the crying boy and ran toward the perimeter. The rest surrounded Yusef on the ground and used his scream to stuff a rag into his mouth, then turned him and cuffed his hands. Within ten seconds the Medic had a tourniquet on his leg. Then they picked him up and moved quickly away from the van.

Captain Dean had followed right behind the first six and picked up the cell phone on the asphalt. As he moved away with his team, he noted in the display that the phone was on the USNet system, but with no signal.

"Thank God," he said.

When he caught up with the latest American terrorist, who was being transferred to a stretcher, Captain Dean looked around at the mayhem, swallowed hard, and said, "You have the right to remain silent. You have the right to an attorney. You have the right..."

Epilogue

It had been a long four days.

An hour after answering the USNet call and giving a preliminary statement to the police, David was allowed to leave with Tanya Prescott. Mustafin was under house arrest in the nearby regional hospital.

David called Elizabeth, but he had been cautioned by the police not to say much, so all he could tell her was that he was fine and would be home soon.

"David, Callie just called. You wouldn't believe what she's been through."

"Actually, I might."

They talked for thirty minutes while the SUV drove back to the Kremlin. David learned for the first time that Callie and Kristen had been on the plane that was targeted by the terrorist, whose identity was still unknown.

"They're saying that commercial air travel may be out for weeks, even months. No one knows. Callie and Kristen may have to drive, or take the train,"

"But she, Rob and Kristen are OK. That's the main thing."

"Yes, thank God."

"I'll be home as fast as I can. But if airlines are still flying over here, I have to make one stop on the way." David explained to Elizabeth where he was going, and she said that she understood.

There followed an early meeting on Tuesday morning with a very grateful President Harper, Tanya Prescott, and several other advisors. David explained all that he knew, both about the previous day's events, and what he knew about RTI. After answering all their questions and giving them Todd Phelps's number, he asked the President for help on one personal issue. She agreed and instructed Tanya to take care of it.

An hour later they had a second meeting with President Temirov, who expressed his country's gratitude. That afternoon NovySvet surrendered to the Russian police.

On Wednesday morning, when Tanya gave him his travel documents in the hotel lobby, she told him that the FBI had raided the RTI control center, as well as other locations around the world, and they were just beginning to sift through all that they found, with help from Todd.

He gave her a hug. "Let's keep in touch, and thank you for your help on the flights."

She smiled. "I think we may see a bit of each other. As you said, the investigation is just beginning."

Now it was late on Friday afternoon, and the small Air Force corporate-size jet that Tanya had commandeered for David was making a very fast, low level approach into a U.S. Air Force Base.

Thirty minutes later he walked out of the arrival hall with Goli clutched tightly under his left arm. There to greet them were Elizabeth, Callie, and, in a wheelchair, Rob. Kristen was there, too, along with Paul Burke and Todd Phelps. And the press, because much of the story had leaked out, including David's role in stopping a terrorist attack on President Harper.

There were hugs, tears and smiles all around. Rob had been telling his friends what he knew about his father's exploits. Callie and Kristen had found two seats on one of the several passenger trains quickly pressed into service across the country. Since returning home, Callie and her mother had spent hours talking and crying, sometimes with Kristen.

Goli, exhausted, hugged each of them in turn, and nodded sadly at the mention of Omid's name.

David gave Callie a long embrace. "I'm so glad you're home," he whispered in her ear as he held her tightly.

"Me, too, Daddy. And I'm not the same. God has really changed me. Ask Kristen."

David loosened his grip and looked into her eyes. "Maybe me, too. I think so, but I'm not sure. I need to hear more. I know that I never understood forgiveness until this week—when you called me. But someone has certainly been watching over both of us."

"And over Rob," Callie added.

"Yes, yes." He smiled, looking at his son talking with Goli. "And over Rob."

Twenty minutes later the family loaded into a special van. They talked non-stop, their joy tempered by the loss of Omid. Kristen rode with them. Everyone wanted to hear David's story, which he promised to tell them as soon as they got home.

Callie, sitting next to him, asked, "Can Kristen join us?"

Turning to face all of them and nodding to Kristen, David said. "Absolutely. In fact, before I tell my story, Kristen and Callie have someone even more important to talk about, and I want all of us to listen carefully."

Callie smiled and nodded, and David hugged her.

At Trevor Knox's mountain retreat his personal computer, failing to receive Knox's special daily code for five straight days, automatically began transmitting all of the RTI encrypted files of information, contacts, and strategies to Saeed Zeini in Saudi Arabia. Even with the fastest possible transfer speeds, the download took three hours.

"Serious Christians in Germany were at war with something that was unrepentantly evil, that would not listen to reason and would not compromise."

Bonhoeffer
By Eric Metaxas
Page 289

Afterword

The earliest strands of this novel were already woven two years before September 11, 2001. Over the ensuing years I wrote, re-wrote, put the manuscript down, wrote *Ten Lies and Ten Truths*, prayed, sought advice, changed details, and then wrote again.

During that period there occurred the Iraq and Afghan Wars, the Iranian Green Revolution, the rise of the internet as social connector, the Arab Spring and ongoing tumult across every part of the Middle East, worrying about leadership in Russia, longing for leadership in America, the Fort Hood shootings, the Boston Marathon bombing, NSA eavesdropping, the surge of secularism and statism in our post-Christian world, and the general triumph of technology in daily life, for good and for ill.

Through all that I wrote and re-wrote. But, I kept asking myself, with all of this going on, what will the world be like for our children and grandchildren?

On the one hand, I am not encouraged. Our culture is a moral and spiritual vacuum, created by a constant media/government drumbeat against faith in general, and against Christianity in particular, the faith which was foundational to America. It will be much easier for Islam to triumph in Europe and America if there is no strong faith pushing back.

On the other hand, I know that God is in charge, and whatever is coming is His will. My personal decision is to write and to speak, not trying to create a theocracy, but rather to re-weave Christian wisdom back into the basic fabric of our thoughts and ideas. With God's help, and courage on our part, that re-woven fabric will include our families, schools and universities. It will also empower a new group of national leaders with the humility and grace to find ideas and solutions that bind us together. And that fabric will be strong enough to provide the understanding and courage to stand up to those who genuinely want to destroy the very idea of a free America.

Many people participated in helping to write this book, and it is impossible to thank all of them by name. But some made specific contributions at crucial points.

My Iranian-American friend, Iraj Ghanouni of the Christian Center for Islam Awareness, helped with innumerable details, from locations to Islamic doctrines and rituals. Thank you.

Bryant Wright, senior pastor at Johnson Ferry Baptist Church, has been a long-time supporter of my writing and commented on an early version of the manuscript.

The same thanks goes to Pastor Roy Smith and his wife, Carla, at True Lite Christian Fellowship in Midland, Texas. They have a powerful ministry and a church filled with readers.

John Yates, minister and teacher, and his wife, Susan, speaker and teacher, have both authored several books, and their enthusiasm for the story sustained me as I wrote.

Caroline and John Dean gave a great boost at just the right time.

MaryAnne Sirotko-Turner knew where to shop, and Lee Ward is a reader focused on details.

My brother Jim provided important technical advice.

Jessica Lalley was the final sprint Encourager-in-Chief.

It was a joy working again with our son, Marshall, who focused his many talents on the cover design and graphics details.

Thank you, Danelle McCafferty, for helping me focus and prune wisely; you are an amazingly gifted editor and communicator. Of course, any mistakes or oversights are my responsibility alone.

None of these books would have been possible without the love, encouragement and constructive criticism of my wife and best friend, Alida. She is the one who taught me about relationships.

We invite you to visit www.parkerhudson.com, and to sign up to follow our blog and newsletter at www.parkerhudson.com/blog.

Please visit www.goodreads.com or another
online retailer and rate or review
Enemy In The Room.

ALSO BY
PARKER HUDSON

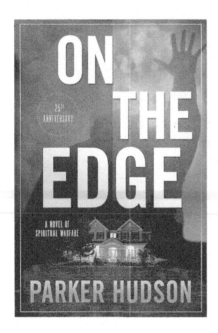

On The Edge
ISBN 978-0-9666614-0-8
Edge Press, LLC

As I read the last chapter of *On The Edge*, I found my heart so full of the Holy Spirit that I thought I would explode. When I closed the book for the last time, I realized that I was crying....I cannot tell you how this book has changed my life and my husband's.

Lori Wells

I finished your book *On The Edge* a few months ago and reflect on its content often. I can honestly say that no novel has ever had as much real and emotional effect on me. I find myself praying more....The final few pages put me in the presence of God...I finished those pages overcome with emotion and sobbing with joy.

Jim Ezell

Available at www.ParkerHudson.com

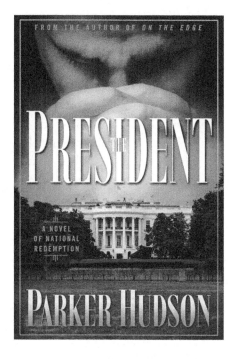

The President
ISBN 978-0-9968665-4-5
Edge Press, LLC

"I just finished *The President* after being unable to put it down for the past six days. It is a great book!"

Phyllis Trail

"*The President* really overwhelmed me. It is possibly the most powerful book I've ever read."

Lee A. Catts

"I just finished reading *The President*. Thank you for such a stirring, challenging work. I just wish it were a work of history and not fiction."

Thomas McElroy

Available at www.ParkerHudson.com

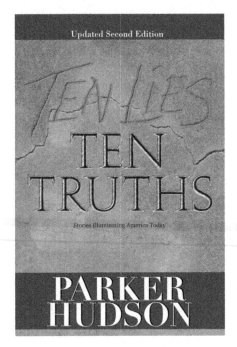

Ten Lies and Ten Truths
ISBN 978-0-9968665-0-7
Edge Press, LLC

"My sense is--most people today don't want to be challenged to think. If that describes you, don't read this book! But if you enjoy being confronted with new perspectives, and truly desire to know the truth--this book is for you."

Jim Reimann

"The book shows the power of fiction to draw the reader into a topic by touching the heart as well as the mind. Hudson's purpose is to break up the concrete around "truths" that people believe without thinking, or without considering the consequences, and he succeeds in a way that keeps the reader turning pages. 'Parable' may be too strong a comparison, but Hudson certainly confirms that fiction can teach truth in a powerful and memorable way."

Dr. Ted Baehr

Available at www.ParkerHudson.com

Made in the USA
Coppell, TX
10 June 2020

27335463R00197